the WEIRD COMPANY

Also by Pete Rawlik:

Reanimators

the WEIRD COMPANY

The Secret History of H. P. Lovecraft's Twentieth Century

Pete Rawlik

Night Shade Books
New York

Night Shade books may be purchased in bulk at special discounts for sales promotion, corporate gifts, fund-raising, or educational purposes. Special editions can also be created to specifications. For details, contact the Special Sales Department, Night Shade Books, 307 West 36th Street, 11th Floor, New York, NY 10018 or info@skyhorsepublishing.com.

Night Shade Books™ is a trademark of Skyhorse Publishing, Inc.®, a Delaware corporation.

Visit our website at www.nightshadebooks.com.

10 9 8 7 6 5 4 3 2 1

Library of Congress Cataloging-in-Publication Data is available on file.

Cover design by Rain Saukas
Cover artwork by David Hueso

Print ISBN: 978-1-59780-545-2
Ebook ISBN: 978-1-59780-559-9

Printed in the United States of America

For

Peter
Elena
Tessa

my own
Weird Company

How fare those who come to the attention of the masses?
It makes monsters of men, and then passes stern judgement.
It makes heroes of monsters, and then celebrates their foul acts.
What acts unseen would redeem or damn one or the other?
What truth lies hidden in what men do not see?

—Robert Harrison Blake

THE ATTACHED DOCUMENT CONTAINS

SECRET

INFORMATION

AND AS SUCH IT MUST BE

RECORDED:
On a Classified Document Register with an assigned JAC-K Identification Number.

STORED:
In a steel filing cabinet equipped with a three-position combination dial padlock.

TRANSMITTED:
In a sealed opaque container, with this cover sheet as the first visible page.

The contents of this document are classified

CAMPBELL
CARPENTER
FOSTER

If you do not have sufficient authorization to possess this document you may be subject to court martial.

Do not
FOLD, MUTILATE <u>or</u> SPINDLE

MEMORANDUM

JAC-K Identification Number: 627-43
TO: Bradford Garnet, Chair, Judicial Advisory Committee-K, Department of
    Justice
RE: Project Gig, Minority Opinion, Supporting Document

As requested, I have collated several disparate documents into this singular report that serves to support my minority opinion on Project Gig. It is my hope that presentation of these documents will serve to inform and educate the senior committee members, and perhaps allow for a reconsideration of the allocation of resources, particularly in light of the ongoing events in Germany. As previously stated, it is my opinion that the continual occupation of Innsmouth, the imprisonment of its citizens, and the ongoing manhunt for those that have escaped previous actions, are a mistake and the policies that sustain such programs should be reconsidered.

The majority of the following report is comprised of a summary of events seemingly prepared by Robert Martin Olmstead, the same person who initially supplied information on the situation in Innsmouth. Supplementary documents concerning the tragic Miskatonic University Expedition to the Antarctic are also included, one of which was actually found amongst the remains of the lost 1936 Secondary Magnetic Expedition. That Olmstead's documentation serves to bridge the gap between the two tragedies, and may supply some further explanation of what happened to the latter, is no coincidence. D. A. Stuart's report on the loss of the 1936 Secondary Magnetic Expedition should be required reading for all members of the Committee.

While I am of the opinion that Project Gig is a mistake, I must also suggest that even if it were not, there are other priorities to which resources should be committed. Recent reports from our agents in Germany suggest that the German Ahnenerbe organization is preparing an expedition to Antarctica. Ostensibly this is to survey locations for a whaling station, but military intelligence opines it is for the purpose of establishing territorial claims and a potential naval station. I once again must dissent from these conclusions and suggest that the real purpose of such an expedition is an attempt to locate and explore the area identified by Pabodie in his account of the Miskatonic Expedition. It is my recommendation that a permanent military presence be established at key locations with the sole purpose of quarantining the continent from those who would seek to exploit its secrets, and to contain the phenomena that originate within.

Signed

Dr. Wingate Peaslee, Senior Scientific Advisor
1 June 1937

PROLOGUE

From the Journal of Thomas Gedney
"Miskatonic University Antarctic Expedition"

January 24, 1931
0720

Six months ago I knew the names of eleven men whose lives had been claimed by the frozen hell that we call Antarctica. George Vince died quickly when he slipped off of an ice precipice on Ross Island in 1903. Ten years later and not more than ten miles away Aeneas Mackintosh and Victor Hayward were lost when the sea ice gave way beneath them near McMurdo Sound. Such a death must have been preferable to that of their colleague in the British Imperial Trans-Antarctic Expedition, Arnold Spencer-Smith, whose death by scurvy must have been horrendously slow, much like that of Xavier Mertz. Mertz avoided the crevasse that swallowed and instantly killed his colleague Belgrave Ninnis, and he cleverly avoided starvation by slaughtering his sled dogs. But Mertz consumed too much of the dog's liver, and died in slow lingering agony from an overdose of vitamin A. Even this must have been preferable to the deaths of Robert Scott and his team of Evans, Oates, Wilson and Bowers. They raced to the South Pole in the winter of 1911–1912 only to learn that Amundsen had beaten them there. On the trek back they succumbed slowly to hunger and the cold. The doctors say Ernest Shackleton died in the South Georgia Islands from heart failure. Those who knew him know that it was the desolate ice and freezing winds that ate at the man that slowly wore him down, before taking him completely. It gives me no pleasure to add eleven more names to that list. Eleven good men, men I knew, men with whom I have worked for the last six months. Lake, Atwood, Mills, Boudreau, Fowler, Orrendorf, Watkins, Moulton, Carroll, Daniels and Lowe, more than half of the Miskatonic University Expedition, lost not to the ice, not to the cold or wind or even to hunger, but to something else, something ancient and forgotten, something that waits in the ice and kills without remorse.

I have no doubts that some of the expedition survived to carry out the majority of our story. Captains Douglas and Thorfinnssen were supposed to have remained in the harbor at Ross Island. We left one of the Dornier airplanes on Ross as well, with young Sherman, who came to study the glacial squid Psychroteuthius, with two of the more astute of the ship's men, Gunnarson and Larsen, acting as his assistants. Of the nineteen men who went into the interior of that windswept continent, we left seven at the base camp including the expedition leaders Pabodie and Dyer, three students Danforth, Ropes and Williamson, and two mechanics McTighe and Van Wall. All good men, I have faith that some survived to tell the world what happened. But none of these men were with us on that strange plateau, none of them saw what we brought up out of the stygian darkness, and none heard the strange keening that shattered the droning silence of the Antarctic and preceded the horrors that would come. They were not there, but I was, and so it falls to me to lay down some record of those events. To hopefully tell the world of the fate of those eleven brave men, and the dangers that await mankind as we delve into the forgotten and unknown past of our own small world.

The seeds for what happened, the rift that developed between Pabodie and Lake, and Lake's near maniacal desire to pursue his own avenues of research; these were planted long before the expedition even arrived at Ross Island. As nominal founders of the expedition, Lake and Pabodie were supposed to come to mutual agreement on staffing issues, but they disagreed on which physicist and geologist to invite along. Lake wanted the more progressive and younger team of McReady and Garry, while Pabodie leaned toward Atwood and Dyer. The impasse was broken when

Pabodie used his influence with the Pickman Foundation to set the team leadership, as he wanted it. Outraged, Lake threatened to resign completely, until a last-minute negotiation mediated by Atwood, putting Lake in charge of selection of the seven graduate students that would join the team as junior partners, defused the issue. Lake's selection of three biologists, two physicists/meteorologists, who were both protégés of McReady, one engineer and only one geologist, only served to strengthen the feud. Thus when those first mid-December borings at Mount Nansen brought up slate fragments containing queer triangular imprints, imprints which Lake claimed were unprecedented in the fossil record, it was inevitable that he would demand further investigation.

Pabodie ignored such requests; as an engineer he was more interested in proving the worth of his newly designed drilling apparatus, and solving the various electro-mechanical problems that arose from the extremes of cold and ice, than in furthering such esoteric research into things long dead. But as the days turned into weeks, and the weeks into a month, Pabodie ran out of problems to solve, and the two student physicists Carroll and Moulton, as well as the geologist Daniels, suddenly joined Lake in pressing for a reconnaissance into the northwestward direction. Sensitive instruments had picked up a fluctuation or variation in the local magnetic field, indicating that in addition to the southern magnetic pole, there was a smaller secondary influence, perhaps a large deposit of iron ore. The discovery of this magnetic source, which they jokingly termed the Little Magnet, would be a significant scientific achievement. That the Little Magnet lay in the same direction as the origin of Lake's interesting slate formation, argued Daniels, may not have been entirely coincidental. The same geological activity that had transformed the shale into slate may also have been responsible for the ore deposit. Or, both could be the result of the impact of an immense pallasite, a meteorite rich in iron and nickel.

Under pressure from multiple sources Pabodie agreed that both he and Lake would carry out a short reconnaissance using minimal resources, and then evaluate the findings. Thus on January 11th the two seasoned researchers accompanied by the students Carroll, Moulton and Daniels, as well as the two mechanics Mills and Watkins, set out on six sledges with forty-two dogs. They returned on the 18th with the physicists confident in the presence and general direction of their magnetic source and Lake displaying a number of slate samples containing more of the unusual triangular impressions. Of Pabodie's sprained ankle, Lake's bruised face and the two missing dogs none would speak, but after ordering that all four planes be made ready under the command of Lake and Atwood, Pabodie retired to his tent and was not seen for most of the next day.

Preparations were completed on January 21st and after a period of rest Lake's team of twelve men and thirty-seven dogs boarded the four aircraft and at 0400 departed in a northwestern direction guided by the sensitive magnetic instruments operated by Carroll. The sky was clear and calm which made flying nearly comfortable for passengers, which were confined in the tight and cheerless compartments of the Dornier Whales with not only the sledges and equipment but the dogs as well. A safety precaution instituted by Mills required that each plane carry at least one sledge and seven dogs so that the loss of any one aircraft would not entirely eliminate this method of transportation. At 0545 we had travelled more than 300 miles from our origin and Lake ordered us to the ground. While the physicists set about recalibrating their equipment and refining their calculations, Mills and Fowler began drilling almost immediately with Lake and I inspecting the samples as they came up out of the bore. Meanwhile Watkins and Orrendorf prepared the materials necessary to widen the boreholes into larger shafts.

At 1100 using a combination of thermite and explosives, Watkins widened the shallow borehole and after clearing away the rubble Daniels descended and began to deliver samples back to the surface. Lake was ecstatic. The slate samples were ripe with those strange large triangular depressions that he was sure were from some unknown and extinct organism. What's more, these samples were found to be mixed with fossils that we easily identified as belonging to the trilobite genus Phacopid that flourished in the Devonian. Lake was so stunned by how the number of triangular marks increased dramatically from between the two samples that it was left to me to point out the more startling implication. Using fossilized species as a guide the original samples had been dated back to the Carboniferous period, approximately three hundred million years, while the new samples dated back to the Devonian, approximately four hundred million years, whole species; whole phyla, had arisen and gone extinct in that time period. The first rooted plants had moved onto land, as had insects and other invertebrates. The first true sharks had appeared, as had amphibians. Yet while all this had happened across the face of the Earth, those marks, those strange triangular marks had not changed in size or shape whatsoever, their source had remained unchanged for more than one hundred million years. Yet as we tried to comprehend the implications of these unprecedented samples, Daniels delivered to us yet another sample that shattered all of our preconceived notions of evolution and geological prehistory. Daniels had sent to the surface yet another piece of slate, this one dotted with the undeniable forms of the Agnostida, trilobites, animals not seen on Earth since the early Cambrian, more than six hundred million years ago. And there amongst the clusters of ancient invertebrates were the unmistakable and undeniable triangular marks of a species that had wandered the Earth apparently unchanged for more than three hundred million years.

At noon, Lake made a cursory report to Pabodie via the wireless and then took Atwood aside out of earshot of the rest of the group. When they returned they revealed that they had set about formulating what I would consider the most devious of plans, one that would require the involvement of the entire group, and guarantee our place in the annals of science. There was no question in either Lake or Atwood's mind that the group would soon have in its possession a find of either geological or biological significance, possibly both. It was also without doubt that as soon as such a find was reported, Pabodie and Dyer would demand that a plane be sent so that they could join the investigation. Once present it was inevitable that Pabodie would assume not only control but also credit as well. Lake and Atwood's notion was to manufacture a storm, to report a gale strong enough to deter any air travel, effectively stranding Pabodie where he was and making sure he got no credit for their work. Not surprisingly every member of the team readily agreed and the plot to deceive was set in motion.

By 1500 we had broken down our drill site, reloaded the planes, and following the course determined by Carroll and Moulton, headed further northwest. Lake made a short and frantic report about crosswinds and a tremendous gale wreaking havoc with the planes. Dyer immediately responded in protest, but Lake chuckled and replied that new specimens were worth any and all risks. As Lake turned off the radio the three of us erupted into riotous laughter, and Orrendorf passed around a flask of bourbon from which we all drank. In that moment of common deceitfulness I knew the true bonds of brotherhood.

After several hours of flight we reached a vast plateau in the shadow of a tremendous mountain range that Daniels suggested would rival the Himalayas. Moulton indicated that his instruments needed to be recalibrated and Carroll indicated agreement, so at approximately 2200 we set down on the plateau and estimated our coordinates as 76° 15' and 113° South and 10' West. From the comfort of the ground Lake reported to Pabodie on the massive mountain range using the most hyperbolic of language. Thirty minutes later Lake made contact with Pabodie once more, telling him this time that Moulton's plane had been forced down and severely damaged. No one had been hurt in the faux crash, but Lake reported that the team was busy transferring equipment in case the Dornier was unsalvageable.

In the meanwhile, Daniels had begun a series of test borings searching for an appropriate spot to drill more deeply, while I and the others set about making camp and catching several hours of sleep. Once Lake was satisfied that Daniels had things well in hand, he and Carroll took one of the planes and went up to deploy the magnetically sensitive instruments over those massive peaks in hopes of pinpointing the exact location of the Small Magnet. The plane returned to our camp at midnight with the required data in hand. The secondary magnetic source was, based on calculations, not far from our camp. We could be there in a matter of hours. After some debate, the team decided that I and Lake would continue work at this location, while after several hours of sleep, Atwood, Daniels, Carroll and Moulton would venture forth in two of the planes in search of their strange magnetic anomaly. Had we only known what was to occur next, we would never have wasted such precious time on redistributing materials amongst the planes.

If Captain Douglas has followed the proper protocols, if Pabodie or Dyer, or any of the expedition has returned to civilization, then the basic facts of what occurred next should be known. However, as our expedition was already committed to a certain level of deception, it should not surprise the reader that certain details reported by our team to the others via the wireless, and then onto the world, were less than accurate. I should also say that the events of that day January 23rd, 1931, are in my mind not entirely clear. The rapid pace of events, my physical and mental exhaustion, coupled with a significant trauma to my head makes recalling the events of the day and their order extremely difficult. It is my full intent that the account I lay down here is as accurate as I can remember it.

Early in the morning Lake reported that our rouse was in jeopardy. A talk with Douglas and Dyer had led to the conclusion that Pabodie, Danforth and the rest of the staff would be joining us at our new camp as soon as possible, and that any future transportation to and from Ross Island would be over Lake's newly discovered mountain range. Sensing that his ability to direct his own research was about to cease, he, Atwood and Carroll quickly prepared one of the aircraft and took off in a desperate search for another, perhaps more productive, site and the strange magnetic anomaly. In doing so Lake made it clear to me that if the next three hours of test borings did not produce I should be prepared to move to another site.

Given such a short timeframe I quickly reset the drill team to an area about a quarter of a mile away from the camp in an outcropping of soft sandstone. The drilling was easy, and much progress was made with little supplemental blasting. Approximately one hour after we had begun, the rock being brought up suddenly changed. We had apparently run into a vein of Comanchian limestone and almost instantly we were rewarded with the most magnificent of specimens including minute fossils of cephalopods, corals, and other marine invertebrates as well as the occasional suggestion of bones which I recognized as being from sharks, teliosts and ganoid fish. As I marveled at such finds, for these were the first vertebrate fossils we had found during the entire expedition, my attention wavered from the drill and was only brought back when Mills and Orrendorf suddenly began yelling. The drill mechanism had begun oscillating wildly back and forth, kicking up large chunks of rock which were being launched at terrific speeds in all directions. A rock the size of a golf ball flew past and imbedded itself in the ice beside me. Other pieces ricocheted off the drill itself leaving dents and gashes in the casing. Orrendorf had taken refuge behind a case of drill bits, while Mills had taken to cowering behind the spoil mound. Knowing that I was responsible for not only the drill but what also appeared to be an extraordinary fossil bed, I foolishly ran headlong for the motor engine all the time being pelted by a torrent of rock and ice. I flinched once as something hard caught me in the fleshy part of my cheek, but carried through with my resolve, reached the gas engine and quickly turned it off.

Without power, the drill slowed down and there arose the most horrendous of sounds. It was a cracking noise, a great cacophony of something ancient shattering, fragmenting into shards and dust as we stood beside it unable to act. A great cloud arose and the drill, suddenly denied of support, tilted forward, swung wildly and then settled slowly onto its side. When the dust and ice had cleared we emerged from our various shelters and beheld the most spectacular of sights. A portion of the limestone vein had caved in, creating an opening about five feet across that opened into a shallow hollow. Fearing another cave-in, the three of us cautiously crawled across the ice to the edge of the newly opened cavern and peered down into what had until recently been a stygian darkness. The hollow was no more than eight feet deep but extended off in all directions. The roof and floor were abundant with stalactites and stalagmites, some of which met to form the most spectacular of crystalline columns. But most importantly, what set me rushing back to greet Lake's plane was the vast wash of shells and bones that seemed to cover the entire floor of the cavern.

It was just after 1400 when we finished securing the winch and our team carefully lowered down into the cavern. Within minutes all of us had realized that we had discovered what was possibly the greatest cache of paleontological samples ever discovered. We quickly identified the most amazing diversity of samples I had ever seen including mollusks, crustaceans, primitive sharks, placoderms, thecodonts, mosasaur skulls, pterodactyls, archeopteryx, primitive horses, and titanotheres. There were however no Pleistocene samples, no mastodons, camels or deer, and thus we concluded that the cavern had not received any new materials for at least thirty million years. There was however a curious abundance of primitive life generally found in the Silurian and the Ordovician, which seemed a tremendous contradiction to the latter more evolved species and the rock in which they were imbedded which was without a doubt Oligocene in origin. The fantastical conclusion that we drew from such information was that in some manner the life of more than three hundred million years ago had continued unabated and uninterrupted, mixing with the species that we knew had come into existence only about fifty million years ago.

It was at this point that Lake scribbled a hasty note and handed it to Moulton for dispatch over the wireless. The young engineering student had not been gone for more than five minutes before Fowler began calling for Lake and I to come and examine a large section of sandstone. For there in the relatively young sedimentary rock were several distinct triangular striated prints nearly identical to those we had found in the slate samples at other sites. There were some minor differences, the new samples were smaller and the markings bore a slight curvature at the end, Lake postulated that these markings indicated that the species might be undergoing a reversion, returning to a more primitive or decadent form, although I disagreed on drawing such conclusions based on limited data. Regardless I concurred with the note he quickly jotted and handed to Mills suggesting that our discoveries would be as important to biology as Einstein was to physics, as they would seem to indicate a remnant species surviving from a previous cycle of life prior to that currently in dominance perhaps a billion years old.

Lake had barely finished dispatching another radio message when Atwood brought our attention to several of the large vertebrate fossils, which showed strange wounds. These injuries seemed to fall into two categories, first there were the skulls of which we found more than a dozen, all showing a straight strangely smooth penetrating bore into the brain cavity. The other markings were on the long bones of the legs and consisted of straight lines perpendicular to the bone itself, which effectively bisected the bones in a single cut, though we found several examples in which the final cut was apparently preceded by multiple false starts. Neither Lake nor

I could conceive of a predatory species to which we could attribute such marks.

Another note hastily dispatched, and another call of amazement. One of the men, I cannot remember who, had found a peculiar fragment of green soapstone about six inches across and an inch and a half thick shaped like a five-pointed star. The thing was curiously smooth and the angles were cleaved inwards. Carroll and I brought the thing up and into the light and placed it beneath his magnifying glass and he swore he could make out tiny dots grouped into regular patterns. As he twisted it back and forth in the light of the polar sun there arose from behind him the most peculiar of sounds; the dogs that were still harnessed to the sledge with which we had brought up the equipment had suddenly begun whining in the most distressing of manners. The whining of the dogs turned to yelps and then growls as Carroll came in to calm them, only to be snapped at as he came too close. As he drew suddenly back the stone slipped from Carroll's hand and onto the ice beside the sledge. The dogs reared up from the thing in panic, growling in terror and fear as the sledge went over on its side the dogs retreated behind it with only their whimpering yelps to betray them.

Lake was dispatching missives as fast as he could write them and I soon had lost count of how many we had sent. We had been in the cavern for only five hours and in that time a new world had been created. Everything we knew, everything we believed we understood about life, and time, and our world was about to change, and I was to be one of the agents of that change. My name would go down amongst those great minds of the past Newton, Galileo, Agassiz, Van Leeuwenhoek, and Darwin. My life, my career, my reputation as a scientist was, for that brief and glorious instant, set amongst the stars, and brighter than I could have ever dreamed. How strange, that such things can change from one instant to the next. For it was in that moment that yet another cry of discovery and wonder came up out of the cave and all of the fantastic discoveries we had made up until that point suddenly became meaningless.

Orrendorf and Watkins, working with the electric torches, had ventured into one of the many tunnels that radiated out from the main chamber in innumerable directions. There, amidst the detritus of the ages they had found something totally unexpected, but not without precedent. The preservation in amber of insects and other small animals, some millions of years old, is well documented. Similarly, it is an established fact that in the area near Yakutsk the locals have on numerous occasions recovered from the Siberian permafrost the frozen bodies of the extinct wooly mammoth. I can only imagine that some similar process led to the preservation of the three specimens that Watkins and Orrendorf had unearthed and winched to the surface. They were barrel-shaped things not unlike some of the echinoderms but massively larger, six feet long and three to four feet at the central diameter with five ridges and significant amounts of damage to each end, enough such that the actual organic structures that were located there were completely unknown to us.

No sooner had the things reached the surface than the dogs began to act up, pulling at the harness and dragging the sledge forward snarling and barking. Fearing that the dogs would damage the specimens, Lake ordered Carroll and me to take the dogs back to camp and properly secure them. I almost protested but instead grabbed the harness and spent the next twenty minutes forcing the team back to the camp, avoiding their snapping jaws and gnashing teeth all the way. Back at camp I read Lake's latest note as Moulton transmitted it and I was greatly disturbed by his references to the Elder Things mentioned in the Necronomicon. I had taken Professor Wilmarth's class at Miskatonic, the one he taught on the shadowy things hinted at by Alhazard and Prinn. I knew what the legends told, of the things that seeped out of the dark spaces between the stars and came to the Earth in the primordial past. That Lake linked these things with such demon-haunted lore made me shudder, and I retreated to my tent in order to find and review the notes that I had taken during Wilmarth's lectures.

I found my notes readily, but any attempt to review them was interrupted by yet another flourish of discovery and a summons to return to the cave. I shoved the sheaf of notes inside my parka and returned to the cavern. This time it was Mills, Boudreau and Fowler's turn in the spotlight. The three working deeper into the cavern had found a cluster of thirteen more of the same barrel-shaped growths mixed with dozens of the strange soapstone stars. Eight of these specimens were completely intact and one showed only minimal damage, the others all showed the same curious kind of damage, the removal or near removal of the organic structures at either end. Lake sent an expansive and detailed description along with some speculation concerning their origin with reference once more to the Necronomicon, Cthulhu and Professor Wilmarth.

I pause here in my relation of events to once more reveal that our team was perpetrating a deception on Pabodie and Dyer. For no sooner had Lake finished his cursory description of the creatures was Dyer clamoring for a plane to reunite the expedition at the cave site. Lake responded that a rising gale had come down off the mountains grounding the four planes in his possession. Dyer and Pabodie would have to use the plane left with Sherman on Ross Island. Of course there was no such storm, but Lake had just bought us more time to establish our sole propriety over these amazing samples.

Without the dogs, it took us more than an hour to move the specimens back to camp but the nine students and mechanics accomplished it without incident. We laid out the specimens on the hard ice next to the tent in which Lake had laid out a table and tools to carry out a more detailed examination. Half the team gathered into this tent while the other half set about tenting the planes and building a corral to contain the dogs that had grown increasingly distressed over the biological samples and could not be trusted in the confines of the camp. Unwilling to sacrifice one of the intact specimens, we chose the one that was less damaged toward both ends and slightly crushed in the main body, allowing us easy access to the interior cavity. Our examination was detailed and we took copious notes and made regular transmissions of our findings on the specimen. None of which I have access to at the moment, but I will do my best to recall what details I can and relate them here.

As I have said, the main body was about six feet in length and capped on both ends with similar but significantly different structures not unlike those of several species of starfish. The torso was barrel shaped and comprised of a dark grey material that reminded me of the exocarp of some citrus fruits, very tough but at the same time very flexible. The torso was radially symmetric, specifically pentaradial and consisted of five vertically oriented segments joined together by five sets of ridged furrows. Hidden within each of the furrows with an apex near the equator was a complex framework of tubular rods arranged not unlike a folding fan and supporting a highly vascularized membrane with a serrated edge. The suggestion that these five structures were some sort of wings and that the creature either flew in the air or swam under water was obvious, although when I suggested that the structure was similar to that of some leaves, particularly those of palm trees, the use of these structures in something akin to photosynthesis was raised as a distinct possibility. Also around the equator of the barrel, but this time in the center of each segment, was a single stalk approximately three inches in diameter at the base. After six inches the stalk split into five branches, each of which continued on for about eight inches before splitting once more into five tapering tendrils, giving each stalk twenty-five tendrils with a reach of about three feet.

On the top of the torso was a bulging ring with five sets of heavy plates covering a series of fleshy flaps and diaphragms joined together in an accordion-like structure which we all readily agreed was analogous to the respiration structures used by spiders known as book lungs. Seated on top of this were five yellowish wedged-shaped organs arranged not unlike a massive inverted starfish more than five feet across. The upper surface of this head was covered with numerous three-inch-long wiry bristles or setae of a variety of colors. At the end of each wedge was a flexible yellow tube crowned with a sphere covered in a yellowish membrane which rolled back to reveal a glassy globular eye with a deep red iris. Between each of the eyed wedges, another slightly longer type of organ sprouted. Red in color, these five fleshy tubes were about two inches in diameter and ended in a sack-like swelling divided into five equal sections. Pressure on the neck of this structure forced the sack to open into a bell-shaped orifice lined with sharp white chelae that probably functioned as teeth in this mouth analogue. In the center, where all the various components of the head originated, was a five-lobed slit or diaphragm that was most probably some sort of entry point for some sort of secondary respiratory system. Manipulation of the various components revealed a high degree of flexibility; in fact it was quite easy to fold the five mouths and eyes up onto the setae and then close the five arms over them, forming what was likely an impenetrable mass.

Below the torso there were analogous counterparts to the components of the head, but their function was dissimilar. While the bulging ring was present there was no suggestion of any gills, and the short stout eye-tipped wedges were replaced with four-foot-long muscular legs devoid of the prismatic setae but tipped with a fleshy triangle approximately eight inches long and six inches wide at the far end. This fin or foot was quickly recognized as the source of the strange triangular impressions we had been collecting throughout the expedition. As with the head, between each leg was a red-colored fleshy tube, but when these were opened the dangerously sharp chelae were missing. In the center of this lower arrangement were five closely packed muscular tubes that were somewhat reminiscent of an anemone or sea squirt, that these were the terminal end of the secondary respiratory system that began at the other end I had no doubt.

Following our external assessment we began what could only be described as a crude dissection, as none of the tools in our possession were adequate to the task of cutting the leathery integument that prevailed throughout the body. Initial explorations were hampered by the still-frozen state of the thing, but as the heat of the tent penetrated the body there was a thaw and an organic fluid possessed of a pungent and offensive odor began to flow from the various wounds. It was not blood as we know it for it was thick and bright green, almost luminescent, perhaps based around hemocyanin as in some invertebrates, rather than hemoglobin, but there was no doubt that it served the same purpose. As the stench escaped from the tent, the dogs, far off in their corral, caught wind of it and began howling and barking in the most savage of manners.

The radial symmetry of the external components was continued with the internal organs to such an extent that one could almost say that the five divisions of the creature created a sort of multiple redundancy for it was rare that any of the systems from one division interacted directly with the other. The five mouths led to five distinct stomachs and then down to the five fleshy tubes found between the lower appendages. The five-lobed diaphragm in the head led to five distinct vascularized and muscular chambers and then to the cluster of tubules hidden in the base of the thing, that the creature maintained both these strange lungs and the book lungs suggested that the creature was amphibious. That both lungs and gills were linked to the wings in a manner that seemed excessive only supported the theory that the wings served some other purpose than flight. In the respiratory system, near the head there were five distinct organs that seemed to be comprised of a complex labyrinth of tubes and valves. Atwood suggested that it was similar in construct to some musical instruments such as the trumpet or the organ, and may have been associated with vocalizations. That a form of syllable-based articulation could be derived from such a construct seemed unlikely, but rather of clicks, whistles and notes, not unlike the sounds made by dolphins and whales, seemed more likely. The musculature of the creature was a hybrid, with vast thick bundles of fibers attached to the rigid structures of the leathery skeleton, but also present were bladders and compartments similar to those creatures in possession of a hydrostatic skeleton like the ones found in echinoderms and annelids.

It appeared that any sort of specialization within the body itself had failed to occur and the five sections not only seemed to have remained distinct but also consisted of redundant, perhaps even independent, sets of physiology. Only the nervous system had achieved any sort of integration. The brain was five lobed and complexly folded much like a human brain. Something comparable to a large nerve fiber ran from what appeared to be the optical center to each of the eyes branching on its way into a myriad of smaller fibers and integrating the strange multi-colored wiry bristles into the nervous system. That these minute structures were some sort of sensory apparatus was clear but its exact analogue to one of the human senses escaped us. Training down from the proper brain was a thick neural chord that quickly divided into five branches that worked their way into the five sections. These neural chords had distinct ganglial centers scattered throughout the section: one near the wings, another near the equatorial tentacles, and yet another near the lower appendages.

There had been hope that the dissection would shed light on the origin of this species, but if anything the examination raised more questions. The radiate structure and the hydrostatic skeleton suggested a marine origin, but the wings and musculature implied some sort of aerial influence, both of which seemed contrary to certain characteristics that were distinctively vegetative in origin. That this organism had evolved in complete opposition to all other life on Earth, and had achieved such a level of development prior to the Pre-Cambrian period, flabbergasted Lake and once more he fell back on that ancient mythology and drew a name from Olaus Wormius' Greek translation of the Necronomicon. In his radio message to Pabodie he called this strange new species "The Elder Ones" but this was a rough translation of the name used in the Necronomicon. He could have used another name, the name Wilmarth had said meant "Progenitors" and that according to Wilmarth, Alhazred had dared to write only once, the name used in the ancient languages, which was not their true name but the name used only by the most faithful of servants, that protoplasmic servitor race Alhazred called shoggoths and the batrachians sub-humanoid Deep Ones. That name had been the Q'Hrell.

Lake finished his dissection around 0200 on January 24th. He went outside and stared at the specimens that were laid out on the ice. The constant sun had acted on the bodies eliminating some of the rigidity associated with being frozen, but as the air temperature was well below that of freezing, Lake had no fear of any sort of decomposition. Still in a token attempt to prevent the stench of the things from filling up the camp and enraging the dogs, Lake ordered them covered with a tarp weighed down with ice blocks. At 0400 Lake signed off and took the time to lie to Pabodie and Dyer, telling them that the storm was still blowing and flight was impossible. Immediately after that Lake and Atwood crawled into their tent and went to sleep; given the activity of the last twenty-four hours the entire expedition followed suit and I, tired of the faces of my fellow team members, climbed into one of the airplanes and pulled the hatch closed behind me, noting the time on my watch as 0430.

It wasn't long before I was deeply asleep and dreaming. I have always had the most vivid of dreams, and this one was no different. I was in the lab proctoring a class of students through a review of various aquatic microorganisms. We began with a selection of centric diatoms reviewing various species and noting the radial symmetries of their frustules. I wrote the word RADIAL horizontally on the chalkboard. With the next set of slides we examined the water flea daphnia and made special reference to their ability to reproduce both parthenogenically and sexually. As I said these things I wrote the word PARTHENOGENIC vertically on the chalkboard using the R in Radial as in a crossword puzzle. I then moved the class on to examining samples of the photosynthetic cyanobacteria Nostoc, which when exposed to rain has an unusual capability of swelling up to conspicuous proportions, earning it the name star jelly or the rot of the stars. Once again I wrote on the chalkboard, this time using the existing P to spell out PHOTOSYNTHETIC. As I did this I heard a dog barking outside. I asked one of the students to close the window before realizing that there was no window to close. We moved on to another slide, this one of a tardigrade or water bear, an eight-limbed creature that fed on a variety of other aquatic species including algae, bacteria and even other aquatic animals. The tardigrades were notable for being cryptobiotic, able to enter into an ametabolic state in response to unfavorable environmental conditions. As I wrote out CRYPTOBIOTIC using the C in PHOTOSYN-THETIC, the barking dog found friends and the sound filled up the room. The last slide was that of a lichen, a symbiotic composite of a fungus and an algae. As I wrote out SYMBIOTIC using the B in CRYPTOBIOTIC, I had to scream to make myself heard over the dogs. I was telling the students something important, something about the five words I had written on the board. These words were important, more important than the dogs barking. They were so loud, those dogs, they made it hard to think about what I was saying, but I knew it was important. Radial. Parthenogenic. Photosynthetic. Symbiotic. Cryptobiotic. Five words. Five characteristics of what? The Elder Things that Wilmarth had dared to name the Q'Hrell? Their morphology was radial, and the wings certainly could have had been capable of photosynthesis. Many species reproduced parthenogenically, why not the Elder Things? The strange body structure, the independent systems, implied a kind of symbiosis. It all fit except for one word. The dogs were howling now, screaming, yelping in fear and agony. Cryptobiotic meant what exactly? The ability to assume an ametabolic state in response to unfavorable environmental conditions, indefinitely until conditions improved. What conditions? I damned those dogs. What conditions? Toxins, yes. Anoxia, yes. Anhydric, yes. Cold . . .yes! For how long? I asked myself. Indefinitely. What did that mean? A year? A decade? A century? A thousand years? A million? The cave had been sealed up more than thirty million years ago. Could an organism enter into a cryptobiotic state and remain that way for thirty million years? It was impossible; it was madness to think such things. The dogs went silent and where they left off I began.

I woke up screaming.

There was a thud against the side of the plane and then something slowly slid down the hull whimpering in the way only an injured dog can whimper. Acting on instinct, I ran to the hatch, undid the lock and flung the metal door wide open. What I had intended to do I cannot remember, but I know what I saw. It took a moment for me to comprehend what was happening, at first I thought it was just the dogs, for they were scattered about the camp. Some were clearly dead, their bodies contorted into shapes inconsistent with life. Others were bloody and beaten, dragging themselves across the ice with broken legs, broken backs and even the remnants of shattered muzzles dripping blood and teeth and bone. Those that were still healthy, still whole, seemed to be enraged by something behind one of the tents. They were barking and leaping into the air at something I couldn't make out. Suddenly Watkins dashed from one of the other tents and entered the unseen fray. He was screaming and rushing with one of the massive pickaxes we used for clearing ice. As soon as he disappeared behind the tent my world went silent and still. The dogs had stopped barking, Watkins had stopped screaming, and even the wind had stopped howling. Time stopped as something horrific and unseen played out behind that tent. Something I am thankful that I did not witness.

The resumption of time was announced by the most curious of noises. It started as a series of low and slow whistling clicks not unlike those made by cicadas or locusts. There was tone to it and rhythm, a slow painful rhythm that went something like this:

Tek Tek e Li Li Tek Tek e Li Li!

Then as the rhythm sped up and the tone increased in pitch the single source was joined by another, and then a third, all producing that same horrendous sound.

TekTek e LiLi TekTek e LiLi!

The rhythm became faster, forming a vast monstrous harmony that wavered in pitch like a demonic violin screaming for the souls of the damned.

TekTeke LiLi TekTeke LiLi!

There was movement and the body of poor Watkins careened off in multiple directions as the demonic violinists moved from behind the tent and into my line of sight. It should be obvious that the things that emerged from behind the tent were the undamaged specimens that Lake had named Elder Things, but to see them lifeless on the dissection table and speculate about them was one thing. To see them alive and moving, interacting with each other and their environment, that was another matter altogether.

We had thought that they had used their lower appendages to pull themselves about, like a starfish, sliding, slow and methodically across a surface. We should have known better; they moved like predators. The body was held horizontal, with the eyes and prismatic setae facing forward, their necks expanded out beyond what I would have thought possible, allowing their heads to turn with an incredible degree of flexibility which they employed in a manner that seemed to me as if they were tasting the very air around them. Their weight was supported by three of the equatorial and three of the basal appendages; as they moved, their footing was sure and deliberate, and the entire body rotated clockwise along its axis so that with each step a new tentacle found footing on the right, while a tentacle on the left rose into the air. Each step also impacted the wings, three of which were deployed at all times, two partially in a horizontal manner and one completely vertical. That the wings were somehow linked to the book gills and the tentacles in either a hydrostatic or pneumatic manner seemed apparent from the rhythmic pumping of all three systems. Those great wings swayed in the icy wind and I could see already the impact that the re-exposure of these creatures to sunlight had initiated in both the wings and the main body itself. Colors had emerged, deep verdant greens had developed, streaked with reds and oranges; I knew that such pigments were indicative of photosynthetic activity using a variety of wavelengths.

But it was the sound that I cannot forget, the sound and the movement that came with it. For as these things moved through the camp, yet another man appeared, Carroll I think, where he had come from I could not say, but he was unarmed and as he stepped forward he held his arms out at his sides and walked cautiously, slowly toward creatures that he knew had killed but also knew were intelligent reasoning beings, not unlike himself. The octet acted almost in unison, pausing to watch Carroll as he moved and spoke in calming tones. The strange whistling stopped and it seemed as if there was some consideration going on. The vertically held wing on each creature seemed to expand and then explode with colors, there was apparently some ability to control the chromatic display played across the wing. Then suddenly the display stopped and the wings went dark green, almost black. One of the creatures stepped forward, separating himself from the others and then began to emanate a new sound, an eerie hollow noise like that of wind through an attic window or chimney. The creature swelled up, bloated and then in a burst of speed it launched into the air, a vapor trail of condensed gas and moisture followed in its wake, the five wings spread out like those of some monstrous bat or dragon, guiding it directly into Carroll. In an instant the thing was on Carroll with amazing fluidity, the wings folded up and vanished into the furrows, an equatorial tentacle wrapped around Carroll's neck, and his head spun off like a bottle cap. The attacking creature turned to his cohorts and sang once more.

Teke-li-li! Teke-li-li! Teke-li-li!

I grabbed the injured dog by the collar and as quickly as I could, pulled the poor animal inside the plane. My movements, the sounds, something attracted attention and I saw three of the creatures turn toward me and begin to bloat up. As my hand swung the door shut one of them launched into the air. Panicked I drove my shoulder into the back of the door and just as the latch locked into position I felt the great bulk of one of the things plow into the side of the plane, while I heard two more thump into the ice nearby. There was a purring noise, a soft trilling as the creatures moved back and forth outside the hatch. Something grabbed the handle and turned it, or tried to, for it only rotated a quarter turn before the locking mechanism engaged completely.

Metal squealed against metal, as the handle was forced further against the lock. The squealing turned into a creaking and then with an audible pop, the handle separated from the hatch and fell with a thunk to the ice.

They came through the cockpit next, smashing the windows and tearing through the seats trying to get through the door. The hatch held there as well, and I watched through the porthole as one of them crawled into the cockpit and examined the various controls and instruments. That it knew what the compass was, and perhaps all of the instruments, seemed apparent for it gently tapped the glass coverings on the dials and housings and gauged their reactions or lack thereof. Satisfied it had explored everything, the creature reached beneath the control panel and pulled at the bundles of wires and cables that it found there, in the process rendering the controls, the instruments and the radio useless.

Under the assault, the cabin rocked back and forth and inevitably I lost my footing and tumbled violently against the edge of a bulkhead. I went unconscious for only a moment and when I came to there was blood in my eyes. Disheartened I slumped back into the main cabin and soon became resigned to my fate. It was then that I picked up pen and journal and began this record. I cannot express the sheer difficulty, the incredible stress that I have been subjected to in the last two hours. As I have written this account of our expedition, of our deceit, of our discoveries and of the terror that followed, the horrors inflicted on our team have not abated. When we discovered these things in the ice there was never any doubt that we would subject them to vivisection, as scientists often must to understand the true nature of a life form. It is not then without some level of understanding on my part that I watched as the Elder Things pulled a plane from beneath its sheltering tent and then began to carry the dead and injured dogs inside. That such actions were taken out of the need for scientific exploration, I can understand, but the dogs were expended, and replaced with the corpses of men, and those were expended, and replaced with the injured and dying. Scientific exploration was exceeded and passed then into the purposeful cruelty of torture and mutilation that no man would dare to inflict on another. Even in the cabin I could hear the screams, the gurgling blood-choked screams that ceased only after the judicious application of something that sounded heavy and blunt, not once, not twice but in most cases three times.

1045

As much as I tried to ignore it, when I heard Lake's voice, heard him crash through the tent and onto the ice, I went to the window to watch. Even from a distance I could see that he was naked and that as he crawled across the freezing landscape tore bits of his flesh away leaving a trail of blood that froze instantly behind him. He was less than five yards away from the tent when one of the Elder Things came walking out after him. It stood on all five lower appendages, using them like a spider uses its legs, rotating them through wide and graceful arcs, in its upper tentacles, the ones that split into five and then again into twenty-five smaller manipulators it carried one of our own pickaxes, with a horizontal blade on one side and a spike on the other. Before I could turn away the thing spun across the ice in a blinding pinwheel-like motion and drove the spike through Lake's back, pinning him like an insect to the ice. He screamed in agony and I could hear him beg for the mercy of death. But instead the thing turned and left him there, he flailed helplessly against the ice for a few minutes. Then he grew silent and still and I knew he was dead.

1200

It is clear to me that the injured dog and I are the soul survivors of Lake's sub-expedition. Over the last hour the Q'Hrell, I will not call them Elder Things anymore, it denotes too much undeserved respect, have been doing something; I hear noises, queer noises, as they rummage through the camp. When I dare I snatch glimpses through the porthole, they have loaded up all three sledges with equipment and materials from the camp including the drill and ice-melting equipment, as well as other scientific equipment, texts, survival gear, furs, and foodstuffs. One sledge was stacked high with material I did not recognize beneath a tarp. The wind provided glimpses of lumps of frozen crystalline crimson, and I shudder at the implication.

1245

They bury their dead. I watched them do it. They held their dead brethren upright as they packed snow around their bases and then up over the top. I cannot be sure, for my location does not provide for a proper perspective, but I think they made the graves into five pointed stars and then decorated them as well. While they did this I covered the portholes with whatever I could find. Only a small crack allows enough light in for me to write.

1320

I have killed the dog. One of the Q'Hrell had come back to investigate the aircraft and the damn dog had begun to whine as the thing poked and prodded at the two hatches. I was afraid that the thing would bark and bring down the full wrath of those monstrosities. So I killed it. I slipped my knife around its throat and as fast as I could I stabbed deep and pulled across. Blood flowed and God help me it was so warm, so very warm. And I was so very cold, and so very hungry. Please forgive me.

1340

The sledges are gone! I think maybe they have left, forgotten me, abandoned me to the ice. If I can hold out until Pabodie and Dyer arrive, surely a rescue party will come, and perhaps I can survive.

1425

There are four of them out there, armed with pickaxes and crowbars. I have no doubt that they will eventually find their way in.

1442

They've shattered the portholes, reached in with tentacles whipping about, trying to find the latch. I cut one of them and that horrendous green fluid they use for blood sprayed out. The whole place has their stink about it now.

They stare at me through the broken window. They can see me cowering in the corner. They have red eyes, cold dead eyes; one would think red eyes would show some life, some passion.

I see nothing, not even hatred. Whatever they feel toward me it is not hatred.

I think maybe it is hunger.

1515

I know now how they have survived for all these eons. It's their blood, that bright bioluminescent green blood, something about it has a radical effect on biological tissue. As I wrote previously when they shattered the portholes I cut one of them and the green blood sprayed all over the cabin, including the dead dog.

I do not know how it works, but some of the alien blood must have seeped in through the skin, perhaps through the eyes or mouth, perhaps even through the wound in the throat. Regardless, as I sat prepared to do battle with the things outside I suddenly heard the undeniable sound of panting coming from within the cabin itself. I turned just in time to watch the dog rise clumsily up on its legs and howl in the most horrifying and pitiful way. There was no denying that the poor beast was in agony, and a mass of pity rose up inside me, at the same time it was clear that this thing was deranged. It was no longer the domesticated dog it had been, indeed in the mere moments I watched it its behavior revealed no relation to any sort of normal animal behavior I had ever observed. The only comparison I can make is to film records of certain patients once held in the Sefton Asylum.

It lunged at me; this mad dog flew across the cabin a mass of fur and blood, deranged and only partially in control of its movements. I dodged it easily and plunged my blade into the side of its chest. The creature now had two fatal wounds and still it stumbled back on to its feet and slowly turned to attack. I refused to give it a second chance. I leapt onto its back and with my left hand pulled its muzzle up into my chest while my right hand plunged the knife into its neck. Over and over again my knife found its mark, and still the dog-thing struggled. Blood flowed from the dog like a river and my parka became warm and slick with gore. I felt the blade bite into the spine and with a single drastic effort I forced the blade between two vertebrae and separated the dog's head from its body. The thing twitched a bit but it has not moved much since.

I haven't had much time to think about what this means but there are some things that I think should terrorize me. If the blood that flows through these things can re-animate a dog and the only way that I could stop the dog was to decapitate it, then that might explain how these things survived in the ice for millions of years. It might also explain why all the other specimens, the ones that didn't re-animate, were all beheaded. Terminating the connection of the body with the brain may be the only way of killing these things. Those things out there may be murderous but they seem organized in control, the blood likely brings them back completely normally. The dog doesn't have the same kind of physiology; the re-animation process is probably only partially successful on mammalian life. But even that terrifies me because it shouldn't have any reaction at all, unless in some way mammalian life, earthly life, shares some physiology, some biochemistry with these horrifying things. That these thoughts don't terrify me suggests that I am in some sort of psychological shock.

1530

I want my friends and family to know that I did not despair. That Thomas Gedney did not succumb to the fear and loneliness that drives men mad out on the ice. I did not do this thing out of madness or despair but out of desperation. When I was a child my parents would take me to Sunday school and the nuns would teach us about sin, mortal sin and damnation. They said it was a sin against God to kill a man, even one's self. I do not think there is a God. How can there be a God, as men would understand him, that would allow such things as those that stalk the ice? How could God allow such things to live? What was it the mad Arab had written? "That which is not dead, which can eternal lie, and in strange eons even death may die." Yes that's it. Was he writing of the Q'Hrell? Are they our god of the holy resurrection? Is their body my body? Is their blood my blood? If so I renounce them. I will pay no tribute, nor make no sacrifice. They will not have the privilege of taking my life. They will know what kinds of creatures now rule this world. They will know what stuff that men are made of, that we will not yield to their base needs and desires, that we will not allow them to butcher us like cattle.

After I am dead, they may add my flesh to their larder, but I will not allow them the pleasure of killing me. They have numbers and strength, weapons and time. They can withstand the cold and the wind and the hunger of ages. They have all this, but I still have my knife, and the will to use it.

CHAPTER I

From the Account of Robert Martin Olmstead
"The Shadows in Innsmouth"

It had been spring when I began my way across the country to return to the home of my ancestors. I made this journey knowing full well that government forces had for years forcibly occupied the village of Innsmouth and subjected its occupants to nothing short of martial law. Some will recall that I have already confessed to and apologized for my part in instigating the raid and subsequent occupation. There is no need for me to repeat an account of those events here, unless it is to again offer my apologies for the grave misunderstanding of events that forced me to flee that village four years ago. Still, although I knew what conditions awaited me, had I known what events my return would set in motion, I may have thought otherwise about returning to that little fishing village on the coast of Massachusetts. Then again, my particular situation, some might say condition, gave me little choice in the matter. My uncle Walter had shot himself, and his son Lawrence had spent more than four years in an asylum. He had nearly died in that place. The other patients, already unstable, had been driven over the edge by Lawrence's degenerating condition and decided to do something about it after a careless orderly had left the door to his private room unlocked. I used the incident to remove Lawrence from the home, on the pretext of placing him into a more responsible facility. His own family, ashamed of what he had become, never questioned my actions, or even inquired on the location of the new hospital. They merely threw money at the problem, assured that I would take care of it.

Combining their funds with mine, I planned for Lawrence and me to head east together, by private car. That the purchase of that conveyance would nearly exhaust what was left of my funds mattered little, after we reached the coast we wouldn't need money. Lawrence never gave me the chance. One day while I was out he took most of the money and what supplies we had and left. He left me a note apologizing, the voices in his head, the dreams, the urge to head to the coast, to Innsmouth, and then into the sea, down to the deep city of Y'ha-nthlei where he would live forever, it was all too much. He couldn't resist, couldn't wait, couldn't wait for me. So he went, he went and left me behind.

My instinct was to follow him, those voices, those dreams, they were calling me as well. I longed to go into the sea and dive down to that phosphorescent metropolis where leprous corals and grotesque invertebrates clung to terraced palaces. My grandmother was there, as was the thing that was her grand-mother, Pth'thya-l'yi who had lived in Y'ha-nthlei for eighty thousand years. It was she who called to us, Lawrence and I, in our dreams, beckoned us to return to Innsmouth and then beyond. Yet as much as I wanted, I was now delayed by the trap-pings of the mundane world. I had to replenish my funds, and map out my way east. A car was now out of the question, I had to find alternative means of travel, ones that wouldn't place me at risk to public scrutiny.

The trip cross country took me longer than it should have. A man can ride the train, take buses, stay in hotels, and eat food in restaurants. A thing such as I had become has no such options. I still rode the train, but not in the passenger car, but rather in with the baggage, sometimes with cattle. I still ate food prepared by restaur-ants, but more often than not I stole it from unlocked back doors or out of bins. I travelled light, only what I could carry on my back and in my pockets. A few changes of clothes were the bulk of what I car-ried, everything else I left behind, with the life I no longer had any use for. The only thing that mattered was moving east, back to Mas-sachusetts, back to Essex County, back to Innsmouth where I hoped I would be welcomed back and conveyed into the sea and beyond.

It soon became obvious that the homecoming I had hoped for could never occur. I had underestimated the extent of the occupation. Miles from my destination my journey came to a sudden halt. The old bus route, which had once run through the village, the one that had been run by a man who would have been sympathetic to my condition, no longer operated. Here, so close to my goal I had to be doubly careful. In Ohio and New York I could still pass for human, deformed but still human. The stares and gasps from people who caught a glimpse of my countenance were tolerable, but they didn't pose much of a threat. Here they knew the Innsmouth look for what it was, and here if they saw me I would be stopped, arrested, taken away, and interred, like all the others. If I were to complete my journey I was going to have to do what I had so recently become adept at doing: I was going to have to secrete myself amidst the cargo, the packages, and the livestock that was regularly moved into Innsmouth.

Despite the attempt to make it so, Innsmouth was no fortress, indeed there were still farms and hamlets that bordered on the picket line that the Federal Government had established. It was easy to find a truck that was heading in the right direction, and easier still to conceal myself under a tarp amidst the earthy sacks of feed, flour and cans of food. I waited for the farmer to start the truck and get on the road before I let my guard down and closed my eyes. My travels had apparently exhausted me, for the ramshackle truck had barely gone a mile before the droning engine lulled me into a state bordering on sleep. I lay still in that drowsy condition, neither awake nor asleep, but rather in a kind of semiconscious torpor. It was an hour, slightly more when the truck suddenly jerked to a halt. With all the caution I could muster, I peered out from underneath the tarp and saw why my transport had ceased its motion.

At the juncture of the main road and the turnoff to the small hamlet to the North had been built an imposing stone edifice not unlike a small fort or bunker. The driver exited the truck and headed toward the building, his heavy work boots crunching the gravel underneath. As the driver opened the door and went inside, voices offered greetings and a drink. Fearing that the truck was to be searched, I took the brief opportunity to slip out and run off into the brush. Moving through the woods, I could see that the little building served as a checkpoint on the road which was now blocked in both directions by a heavy steel pipe that functioned as a crude but effective road gate. The road may have been blocked, but there were no guards visible. Apparently there was no real concern about any foot traffic moving in to the town. I could understand their logic. Who in their right mind would try to break into what had essentially become a prison?

Past the farms, the land around Innsmouth quickly becomes soft and wet, and transitions into swamps and marshes. The closer I stayed to the road, the firmer the ground was, and the faster I made my way. Walking carefully down the side of that dark and deserted road I kept expecting to encounter a vehicle or a patrol of some sort to come out and arrest me. I was like a child waiting for the boogeyman to come out of the dark. The irony of the situation that I was a monster, and the things that I was afraid of were men, was not lost on me. For the stars and the moon whose light leaked down through the clouds and trees and showed me the way, I was thankful. I was also thankful for the owls and other night birds that called and sang to each other, for they provided an odd comfort, a sense of normalcy that was desperately needed. That hour that I walked seemed to stretch into maddening days, each step, and each heartbeat an eternity. Yet in the end I reached the outskirts of Innsmouth where the road met the river and they both headed east.

In the village, I furtively followed the river down to the harbor and then back through the refinery before resting at the abandoned train station. Exhausted from my clandestine excursions, I secreted myself on a hill across from the station and watched three soldiers pace back and forth on the platform. They were infantrymen, rifles slung over their shoulders, cigarettes dangling from their mouths and fingers. In traversing the village I had grown to hate these soldiers, and I hated what they had done to the village I had returned to. Homes had been gutted and burned, businesses ransacked, the refinery, once the center of industry for the town, was boarded up and strung with barbed wire. The church . . . the church had been desecrated, its finery stolen or defaced, the sacred scriptures burned or confiscated. The once proud waterfront was in ruins, laid waste by explosives and ensuing fire. The merchant fleet lay stranded in the harbor. The bay was lined with slow lazy warships and rife with noisy gunboats darting back and forth in strange almost random patterns. The empty town reeked of death.

Suddenly, there was a commotion at the station and beams of light leapt out onto the tracks illuminating a small grey figure that I had not noticed even though it was only yards away from my own position. The man was covered in glistening wet rags and in response to being spotted attempted to run but succeeded only in obtaining a strange lopping gait that was at the time both pathetic and comical. The soldiers yelled warnings and orders but the figure paid them no heed and continued its sad attempt at escape. One final stern warning again went unheeded and then the soldiers unleashed a volley of shots that pierced the eerie stillness of the town and sent the grey figure to the ground.

The soldiers froze on the platform, guns pointed at the strange figure which now lay unmoving on the tracks. There were frantic questions accompanied by desperate accusations and tentative orders and sheepish refusals. The soldiers seemed genuinely unprepared for the consequences of their actions. That they had fired on a man and brought him down seemed something they simply could not deal with. Slowly, lights shining back and forth across the tracks, rifles jerking wildly from place to place, the soldiers broke from the platform and fled backwards into the town for the safety of empty streets. But the streets were not empty. As the soldiers left the platform, dark shapes burst forth from basements, from closed doors and from shuttered windows and took stand against the soldiers.

The things numbered less than a dozen, large vaguely anthropoid creatures that stood half bent in the moonlight with long claws, rows of spiny teeth, and great bulging eyes along chinless heads. Strange growths behind the jaw, between the clawed fingers and along the crest of the head, implied an ichthyic or at least amphibian origin. Yet such a conclusion was contradicted by the curious state of the hideous batrachians. Such things, such lopping, bleating things, such things should not wear the tattered and soiled clothes of men.

As the things lunged at the soldiers, and the soldiers fought back, I left my place on the hill and crept down onto the tracks.

Carefully I reached the downed figure and rolled him over. He was wrapped in a dark mariner's sea coat which hung loose as if he had once been of much larger physique than he currently was. Atop his head was a black woolen cap that was pulled down to cover most of his head. On his hands he wore a pair of thick leather gloves that hung just as loose as the man's coat, and were in a startling state of disrepair. Indeed, I quickly formed the impression that the garments had been long unused and badly looked after, for they carried with them a thick damp musty odor that seemed to mingle with a stench that reminded me of the beach at low tide, or perhaps of my mother's kitchen on Friday when the fishmonger came. I pulled off his hat and opened his coat. My actions revealed a parody of a man. The head was nearly hairless, and what hair there was jutted out as course clumped fibers. The skin was rough and patterned in large thick pads which diminished into a fine pebbling around the face. His ears were perfunctory holes surrounded by weird atavistic nubs of flesh.

He stared up at me, weird lidless eyes, huge eyes that bulged moist and dark in the night. There was something familiar in his face, and I quickly recognized him as the driver of the now defunct bus, a man named Sargent. Strange gurgling sounds came from his mouth and throat which took me a moment to realize were words. "Yew have the look," he gurgled, shoving something large and cold into my hands. My eyes darted toward it, something wrapped in oilskin and leather ties. "Take this," more gurgling and heavy rasping breaths obscured his speech, "Wait . . . in Arkham." Then the strange man-thing convulsed and was silent.

Slowly, deliberately, I quietly backed away and began briskly moving down the rail line and out of the city. The whispering voice of Pth'thya-l'yi had suddenly gone silent. There was a new voice, one that was just as insistent as that of my own ancestor, but that urged me into a new action. The words I could not understand, but their meaning was clear, I was to take the package and head to Arkham. Arkham it insisted, go to Arkham. Arkham. The name pounded in my head like a beating drum, and though I had spent the last few months of my life being driven to return to Innsmouth I turned and did as the voice in my head insisted. I headed west toward Arkham. Whatever this new compulsion was, it was stronger than the one that had called me east.

Glancing over my shoulder I left the dead man behind, the package he gave me still in my hands. I knew the western spur would take me through the marsh lands and then down through remote farm land. I paused for a moment and looked back. I could hear the screaming coming from the tiny hamlet and it touched a chord of memory. Skulking about the town, fleeing in the middle of the night, pursued by angry hordes, it was all too familiar. Panicked, I ran, just as I had done four years before, when the inhabitants of Innsmouth seemed so much more monstrous, and I at the time still had ears and eyelids, and still believed myself to be human.

CHAPTER 2

From the Account of Robert Martin Olmstead
"The Rendition of Ephraim Waite"

By all rights I should have abandoned the oilskin that had been given to me by that sad lonely man from Innsmouth. That he had died moments later should have made no difference to me, but it did. Perhaps it was guilt over my previous actions so many years ago. Perhaps it was the recognition that in some manner the two of us were kin. Regardless I kept the package and headed toward Arkham. Why I paused and hid myself I cannot say. Why I then proceeded to untie the leather strings and unfold the oilskin is a mystery to me. There were within the protective wrappings three journals, of substantial age, each filled with crabbed handwriting that was barely legible, and appeared to be written using some form of the Cyrillic alphabet. Consequently, the journals were beyond my understanding, and any hope of identifying the rightful owner was minimal at best. However, lodged in the back of one of the volumes was an envelope bearing in the same crabbed hand, but in English, a name I did not recognize, but could at least read. I lifted the flap, removed the pages and in hopes of finding out more about the recipient, read the letter. I had no right to do so, but I did, and what I found has bearing on my story, so I include it here. I am fortunate that my strange metamorphosis has come with a nearly eidetic memory, for it allows me to reproduce the contents almost perfectly. In my mind I can still see the strange paper and that tiny script.

11 August, 1918

I set pen to paper in the desperate hope that I will be able to organize the jumble of thoughts, memories and madness that has for the last day threatened my very being. Doctor Marsh has given strict orders to the servants limiting my movements to my bedroom and the library. I am not to leave the house, nor am I to have access to the thing that howls and cries in the attic. Marsh says that a kind of infectious hysteria has come over the house; he uses a French term folie á deux, and suggests that the only way to keep me from descending further into madness is to cut me off from the source of the delusion. Thus despite the fact that it calls me, pleads, begs for me to come to it, I am not under any circumstances allowed contact with the thing that raves in the attic, a man they tell me is my father, a man named Ephraim Waite.

Doctor Marsh and the servants call me Asenath, and say that I am but eleven years old, my father's only child in his old age. When I question them about my loss of memory they sigh and talk about my mother. She went mad, or so they say, and they are not surprised that my father's sudden madness, which they blame on age and a long debilitating illness, has triggered in me a parallel delusion. I only wish it were so. Confining me to the library may have been a mistake, for it is here that I have found hints and allegations as to what is truly happening in this house, to me and the thing that was once my father. If what I suspect is true, there is more here than madness to deal with, and poor Doctor Marsh, who is not without his own secrets, is ill prepared to deal with what has happened here.

The library is large, but not so large that I could not find what was hidden in plain sight. Amongst the old books on medicine, natural history, philosophy and other sciences, I found a set of journals, some of which were quite recent in manufacture, while others were extremely old, with poor-quality paper that had long become dark and brittle with age. All were written in a language that did not rely on the Latin alphabet, and despite the obvious centuries between the earliest and latest entries, all were written in the same cramped and flowing text. At first the contents of these volumes puzzled me, but that confusion was brief. Despite the foreign alphabet it quickly became apparent that I was familiar with this language, for the more I perused it the more I realized that I could understand what was being written. As I write this my ability to translate the journals is nowhere near fluency, but I understand much of it, and it tells me what I need to know. Some would look at the journals and their strange symbols, and suggest that my ability to translate them was madness. Others would call the contents themselves madness, or perhaps an elaborate hoax. If it be madness, some sort of shared delusion, then it is older than any of us dare to suspect, and in that itself the veracity of things lies.

Know then that, according to his journals, Ephraim Waite was born in Oakham, in the County of Rutland just north of London in the year 1618. His childhood was unremarkable, and at a very young age he decided to become a soldier. He served in the Parliament Army, became an officer, and was amongst many that signed and sealed the instrument that commanded the execution of King Charles the First. He did these things because they were right, and because they had to be done. Charles had been a monstrous regent, who condemned himself through his own words in which he maintained that no earthly power had the right to judge him, for the very tenets of the law were founded on the concept that the King himself could do no wrong. Such men and such concepts have no place in this world. All men must be subject to the law, whether they be the laws of men, or those of the world itself. The rule of law, stressed Ephraim, must be maintained.

It was not surprising that his service to the Lord Protector and Parliament went unrewarded. As was the right of all officers, he had laid claim to the properties of those whom he had defeated in battle, and in doing so accumulated some items and books that were most strange, both in their origins and in their teachings. These he studied, and on occasion, discussed, perhaps too openly with his peers. Rumors spread, and he had no doubt that it was for suspicion of witchcraft that Cromwell failed to reward his service. Likewise, when Charles the Second came to power, he was among many that were not pardoned by Charles the Second for actions against his father. Instead he was found guilty of regicide and in 1660 sentenced to be confined to Gorey Castle on the island of Jersey until his death.

Thankfully, there were some who still felt a sense of loyalty to the man, and with the cover of night spirited him out of London, first to Spain, and then, after proper negotiations, to France where he assumed a role in the training of soldiers at a small military academy. It was here near Bayonne that he continued to carry out his studies in the occult sciences, and it was here that he met the enigmatic figure that he would only ever identify as Doctor C. The doctor was a kindred spirit, a seeker after mysteries, and an explorer into those forbidden arts and sciences that were called by some witchcraft, but were far from it. Ephraim was twenty years Dr. C's senior, but the two soon became inseparable, and by 1670 when Ephraim retired to the country, Dr. C went with him.

Their first two years of life in rural France were for the most part uneventful, and the two made some progress in the study of the laws that governed life and the world, and indeed had some success in a particular process called the Rendition of Souls, a rite carried out by natives of the Amazon region. Through a complex process involving a specially prepared drink, the two could gain influence over those with lesser strength of will, and thus accomplish the monumental task of transferring the thoughts and personality, the soul if you will, from one body to another. They did such things with lesser animals such as cats and dogs, and even birds. Using such brief transferences to gain a modicum of freedom from the pain of infirmity that had begun creeping into Ephraim's life, but given the profound differences between human and animal brains, his occupation of such bodies was eventually always rejected, sometimes violently. There is, it seems a natural resistance to such transferences, and remnants of the previous occupant tend to reassert themselves and drive the invader out, and Ephraim saw no need to challenge such rejections. That is until the winter of 1672 when the accident occurred.

What exactly occurred and why it was so life threatening I cannot say, but by December of that year Ephraim's leg had been amputated and C was locked in a desperate battle against infection. So severe was the struggle that C would often hire one of the villagers to sit with Ephraim while the good doctor ran errands. It was during one of C's absences, while he was being watched by a younger man from the village, that Ephraim initiated the rite and carried out the Rendition of Souls. Then once the transference was complete Ephraim Waite, now young and vigorous, took a pillow and smothered his infirm body and the mind that dwelt within.

Even with the death of the host's mind, the rendition did not go as smoothly as he had hoped. There were long bouts of memory loss and confusion. C had discerned exactly what had happened and attributed the mental turbulence to the process of a new mind matching and then supplanting the native rhythms and pulses of its new host. Such bouts eventually faded, and after a year Ephraim was fully in control of his new body. Yet the very act of assuring his survival had driven a rift between C and Ephraim. They had been forced to leave the village; to explain the strange behavior of the once quiet young man would have been too difficult. They rented a home in Paris, but the strain of what Ephraim had done was too great. In 1674 C enrolled in the army and left for India, while Ephraim headed for the Americas.

In the New World, he first lived in Quebec, but then in 1688 travelled to New England where he felt comfortable enough to use his real name. He took up residence briefly in Kingsport, then in Arkham, and finally around 1701 in Innsmouth, where distant cousins had also found homes. During this time he met a number of men, both native to the area and colonists like himself, including C who now had built a home in nearby Providence. He formed a small cadre, who together studied the library of occult lore and mysticism that they had secretly accumulated. Had he been able to find it, Reverend Ward Phillips would have burned that collection to ash, and then thrown him into the pyre as well. The names of these likeminded men, Joseph Curwen, Simon Orne, and Edward Hutchinson, are familiar to me, and yet I am also wary of them. For while they and Ephraim were friends, they did not always agree on the means to support common causes, and above all else, the individual will to survive has always been paramount.

It was in 1720 that Curwen came to his home in Innsmouth, and warned of the rumors that had reached him. Ephraim had been unwise, his studies had revealed to him a form of energy, a vitality that could be distilled from a variety of sources that retarded the aging process, and he had used it liberally. He had not been a young man when he had come to Innsmouth, but after nineteen years his lack of aging had drawn attention. He was being watched by curious and dangerously superstitious folk. With some help from Curwen he abandoned his life in Innsmouth and quickly moved south, leaving the home and property in trust to cousins until his heirs returned to claim it.

In Philadelphia he used a significant amount of the vitality elixir and established himself as the young and energetic printer named George Gamwell. It was in this establishment that the young Benjamin Franklin first worked when he came to the city. It was a great loss to Ephraim when following a false promise by Governor Keith, Franklin left for London, and he noted his regrets over not being more vocal in his objections to the venture. Printing was not only a ruse by which to blend in to the town and earn a living, but it also allowed him the freedom to learn an art that he perceived as necessary to his future survival. While he printed books and pamphlets by day, by night he learned how to forge documents that would establish births and deaths, marriages and even lines of credit. In effect he could, given enough time, create an entirely new identity for himself or anyone else without fear of being caught.

He also continued his study of the occult sciences, learning the rules which governed the structure and processes of our universe, and how such things could be manipulated, circumvented and when necessary even bent to his will. But while such studies allowed him to influence the thoughts and actions of others, and given the right circumstances even manipulate the physical world itself, they paled in comparison to what studies Curwen and the others had undertaken. They sought to bend the laws of time and mind, and engaged in the wholesale resurrection of the dead. Had he not been provided with the formula for making such preparations, and the incantation that invoked the powers that reconstituted flesh and mind, he would not have believed it possible. To him such workings took too great a liberty, and he took measures to distance himself from the others.

It was not until that 1836 that circumstances forced him to return to Innsmouth. The intervening century had favored him, for he had profited off of trade and the war, and was heavily invested in a variety of ventures, all through the blind of various companies that served to keep him hidden. Whether he had lingered too long in Manhattan or his identity had been compromised, he did not know. Perhaps he had not hidden the transfers of funds and possessions as well as he thought. Regardless, his presence in Manhattan was discovered, and he rightfully feared what could happen to him if the truth were exposed. He wrote extensively concerning his preparations for quenching a man named Von Junzt, an occult academic who had been researching a book concerning hidden and forgotten cults, and had stumbled too closely as far as Ephraim was concerned. His plans for murdering the interloper were thwarted when the man suddenly departed for Washington D.C. In a panic Ephraim once more found a suitable victim, and undertook the Rendition of Souls. As expected, the procedure left him disoriented and with temporary memory loss. It took time for him to recover, and in the process the young man who was now suddenly in his ancient body went mad, escaped from his control, and set fire to the building. The flames spread and soon grew to an immense conflagration. He regretted that the disaster consumed so much of southern Manhattan, and that some innocents lost their lives, but most distressing was the loss of the documents he had prepared for his new life in Providence. Thus, Ephraim Waite returned to Innsmouth where he knew he could lay claim to his long abandoned property.

In Innsmouth he asserted his claim to the property, and his cousins had little choice but to turn over the house to their long lost kin, particularly after he produced a key and papers that linked him to the great grandfather for whom he had been named. Despite his legal claim, he was not welcomed in Innsmouth, for the Waites had long assumed the property to be theirs, and for it to suddenly be taken from them was no small imposition. In his absence, Innsmouth had developed into a profitable little town, filled with mostly pedestrian of folk content to work as simple fishermen, boat wrights or tradesmen. Some, particularly the Marsh, Sandwin and Eliot families, had established routine trade with the Far East, including China, India and the islands of the Pacific such as Java and Sumatra. Such connections were useful to his studies and he cultivated strong ties with the Marsh and Gilman families, and where possible with the Waites as well. It took time, but time was something he had plenty of.

Or so he thought. The details that Ephraim relates concerning the decline in trade that had made the town rich, and how the Marsh family and their allies fell on hard times, are too great to relate here. It is apparent from his notes that between the failure of the merchant fleet, and poor fishing catches, the town fell into debt and despair. It did not help when the boats out of Rowley were seen in waters off of Innsmouth. Anger and violence, however, does not put food on the table. At a loss, the townsfolk turned to the church and prayer for deliverance from famine and poverty. They prayed in vain, and as the years passed the town of Innsmouth slowly spiraled into near destitution.

Captain Obed Marsh was an aging scion of one of the founding families of Insmouth, and he felt some responsibility for the situation. He could often be found in the local bar deep into his cups, angrily railing against paying fealty to a god that allowed nets to be empty and children to go hungry. In this opinion he often found commonality with another man, a curious fellow by the name of Mentzel who had rented a cottage down the shore near Falcon Point. He claimed to be an antiquarian working on a book concerning the history of Essex County. This assertion gained him access to a wide variety of records and accounts that would under most circumstances be closed. He seemed particularly interested in the Marsh family history, focusing much on Obed's grandfather Obadiah and the loss of his ship the Corey, and the wives that the survivors had brought back from the Marquesas. Ephraim did not much like speaking to Mr. Steven Mentzel. His voice lacked emotion, his eyes and face seemed wholly unanimated, his manner of speaking was very odd and confusing, and he often had intimations of knowledge that seemed beyond him. Ephraim was particularly disturbed by his discussion of the seizure of Hong Kong by the British a full day before the event was reported in the press. That this man was one to whom Captain Obed was willing to listen concerned him greatly, but there was little Ephraim could do. When Mentzel announced that he was departing the village, Ephraim was grateful and wished him well with whatever work he had in the hamlet of Zaman's Hill.

Whatever Mentzel and Marsh had discussed and planned came to a crisis in 1846. Ephraim spent pages detailing how Obed eventually gathered to his side a number of his former crew and their families and began preaching against the churches of the town. Ephraim wrote about how the Order grew, and how eventually Captain Obed Marsh was arrested and jailed on trumped-up charges. In response to Obed's incarceration nature itself seemed to go awry, and the village was beset by monsters. Matt Eliot and a few others who had opposed Obed had been killed in the invasion from the sea. In the end Obed Marsh was in command, with the town of Innsmouth firmly in his grip.

Rumors were spread to explain what had happened; a plague had come to Innsmouth, and brought with it madness and violence. Its victims had succumbed quickly, but entire families had been lost and as a preventative measure some homes had been razed. Obed posted guards on the road and rail and made sure that no one could leave without his word. It was soon after this that Obed and the Order took new wives. No one ever learned where they came from; some thought they were from Persia, and the veils they wore in public were required by their Mohammedan faith. But Ephraim suspected they were something different, and gave them a wide berth, for he was sure that the reins of power were not held solely by Obed. Once, one of the Multree women asked what had become of the first wives, the ones that had been replaced. The next day she was found wandering the streets, her eyes glazed over, her mind lost. After that, even the faithful learned it was better not to ask questions.

Obed may have had complete control over the town, but he still had to deal with the outside world. It was in this capacity that Ephraim found himself making regular trips to Arkham and Kingsport to handle what business those in Innsmouth still had outside its limits. Do not think that during these trips he did not consider escape. A weird shadow had fallen over Innsmouth and those inhabitants that remained were slowly succumbing to its influence. Yet while some would flee from such events, he felt strangely comforted. Obed Marsh may have been in league with some festering aquatic nightmare, but Ephraim had seen worse bargains made. Besides, the darkness that slowly encompassed Innsmouth was no threat to him; on the contrary it provided a most excellent place to hide and carry out his experiments without fear of discovery or reprisal. He thought about fighting it, or fleeing, but instead he succumbed, and while he did not embrace the madness that was around him, he did nothing to stop it.

It must seem pedantic to repeat so much fantastic and eerie history here, but I do it to educate myself, to summarize and correlate the facts as I see them. With each passing minute, my memories of the past return, and I can begin to understand the truth of what has happened here.

The secession of the southern states brought the war and the draft. There are stories of the men of Innsmouth to be told, particularly of the crew of the Manuxet, but now is not the time. It was because of the war, and those who had left the village, that the term "Innsmouth Look" first gained a foothold. They used it in Arkham and Kingsport mostly, to explain the physical attributes that afflicted the young men of Innsmouth almost without variation. These attributes were most noticeable in the facial features which consisted of a low sloping forehead, reduced ears, large bulging eyes, thin lips and the almost complete lack of a chin. There was also an odd texture to the skin that gave it a squamous appearance, particularly around the neck and eyes. It was plain to Ephraim that these characteristics had been inherited through the maternal bloodline, for no man of Innsmouth had ever bore such an appearance, though he had seen hints of such traits in paintings of Roderick Marsh, Obed's father. Still, his belief that the look had been inherited from the foreign women Obed had brought to Innsmouth was only supposition. It had been thirty years since the new wives had been taken, and he had yet to see one without her veil.

All that changed when in the middle of a warm summer night he was roused from his slumber and was quickly whisked down the road to the stately, though slowly decaying, Marsh Family home. That Obed Marsh was dying was not entirely surprising. He had been called Old Obed for a long time, and his health of late had not been good. Ephraim's confusion lay in the fact that he had been summoned to see him, for he could not fathom that he had a purpose in Obed's passing. He was not alone in this puzzlement, for as he passed through the halls of that home, the gathered family stared in wonder, confusion and resentment. He wanted to pause and confer with them, but was given no opportunity for such a luxury. Time was of the essence, and without so much as a word he was shuffled into Obed's bedchamber.

The room was humid, and reeked of strange musty odors that Ephraim could not place. A thin film of scum seemed to have coated the walls and wooden furniture, and he was careful to avoid touching anything. The man who had fetched him refused to cross the threshold, and instead shut the great door leaving Ephraim alone with the dying man and the five veiled women who hovered about in the shadows. At first Ephraim thought that they were Obed's nurses, but as they sat by his side, it soon became clear that the relationship was much more intimate than that. A chair had been set nearby and when one of the women motioned him forward he had little choice but to sit down next to the old man and his handlers.

Marsh was weak, his breathing was labored; his voice little more than a whisper, Ephraim had to strain to hear him as he spoke. "Waite, you have to help us. Something is going to happen. We have to prepare."

Ephraim was suddenly eager to hear what Marsh had to say. "What Obed, what is going to happen?"

Marsh reached out and patted Ephraim's hand with his withered and boney claw, "Something terrifying and unnatural: something that threatens not only the world, but the entire universe. We must be prepared to intervene, but only when the time is right. To do otherwise will only make things worse."

Ephraim begged the dying sea captain for more information but he was still too cryptic. "Mentzel knew, and when the time comes he will send his agent. He will explain everything. You must be patient. The Daughters will help you, they will guide the breeding. But watch them carefully, for they have their own agenda and are not above seizing power if they are able. There are factions Ephraim, the Daughters, the Order, those who have been tainted by the Dreaming God. They are united in their opposition to the Vugg-Shoggog, but that is all. Once the danger has passed . . ." He coughed violently. "Barnabas will run things, but you Ephraim, ye'll make sure to keep them ship-shape. There are plans my friend, and plans within plans."

Ephraim shook my head, "Why me Obed? I'm an outsider. I know nothing. I'm not part of this thing you've done."

The dying man hissed and wheezed. "That's why ye've been chosen. Ye've no allegiance to anyone. That makes ye perfect for the job." His claw patted Ephraim's hand again. "Ye have talents of yer own, that much is clear. Ye'll learn more, they will teach ye, but be careful, they know more than they're willing to teach. Ye do the same."

He coughed and gasped. His hand withdrew and clawed at his neck. One of the women leaned in to comfort him and in Obed's frenzied struggle for air his claw-like hand tore away the veil of his attendant and for the first time Ephraim Waite saw what lay beneath that cloaked visage. As he had suspected, the Innsmouth look had been inherited from these women, though it pained him to call them that. They were hairless ichthyic things with huge, lidless eyes, lipless mouths and pulsating membranes where ear should have been. There were slits in the throat that flexed in and out exposing the crimson gills beneath. Like their children their skin was scaly, but also covered with a thin layer of slime that shimmered in the light. Panicked, Ephraim turned, scrambled to his feet and, overcome with fear, could do little but gasp in terror and run. Those who had gathered to witness his passage tittered in amusement as Ephraim fled from Obed's deathbed and into the night, seeking refuge in the sanctuary hidden beneath his home.

For more decades than he had cared to imagine Ephraim had avoided complicity in the shadows over Innsmouth. Now he had no choice, the time had come to understand the truth, and if a man such as Obed could not only accept such arrangements, but embrace them, who was he to deny his own part in that plan? What was happening in Innsmouth was clearly important. There was a threat, a vague one to be sure, but through his communal with the things that dwelt off of the reef, he soon learned it was something that threatened not only men, but all life on the planet, and even beyond. Obed Marsh had made a pact, but while it may have seemed wholly demonic in nature, the truth was far more terrifying. He pressed for details but was denied. The threat was real, they promised, but to intervene too soon was to risk a completely different kind of catastrophe. The future was fraught with peril, and there were few paths that led to a favorable outcome for all involved. If the allied forces were to move to early the result would be just as catastrophic as not acting at all. There was the plan, and that was all Ephraim needed to know. He did what he was told, not because he believed, but because he had no reason not to. He surrendered himself completely to the task at hand, and when in 1905 the Daughters came and told him that it was time to take a wife and have a child, he did so without protest. The plan was everything, and though he could not see what was being built or why, he knew that it had to be done.

Ostensibly, her name was Zulieka Marsh, and she was supposedly amongst the third generation born in Innsmouth. She was not unpleasant to look at, though Ephraim would be hard pressed to say she was attractive. She was a plain girl, thin but not overly so, she had the look, and the strength that went with it, but bore none of the traits that would cause people to question her parentage, or humanity. Despite this, she still wore the veil that had become common amongst women of Innsmouth, and outside of the home none saw her without it. That their marriage was arranged was not lost on her, and together they agreed upon the division of certain responsibilities and duties. They both handled the arrangement with a perfunctory sense of duty, and though they quickly grew to accept each other's company, there was no love between them.

Indeed, even after she gave birth, the relationship was purely one of routine. Zulieka's care of, and for, the girl that her father named Asenath (Me!) was minimal at best, and the bulk of meeting my needs was left almost entirely to my father. My father describes me lovingly, but also as so very small and so strange, almost alien. He had seen so much in his years, so many wondrous and terrifying things, and he could do things that normal men could not, and yet when he held me in his arms, none of that mattered. I became his life; everything else, including his studies, seemed unimportant. Instead of spending time with the dead, and returning them to a semblance of life, he was drawn to me and the true life, the normal life that I represented. And thus, he abandoned his studies and his secret laboratory and spent his days and nights caring for me, while Zulieka roamed the house aimlessly. Or so he thought.

He had been warned. Obed had said something, told Ephraim not to trust them, any of them. The first time he found Zulieka in the basement, she was in the library; she had just shelved some books, which ones exactly he couldn't say, but he should have realized then that she was searching for something, something she didn't want him to know about. It went like that for some time. Zulieka would wait until he was distracted and then secretly access his private laboratory and library. This disturbed him, but besides locking the door and securing a few volumes, there was little he could do, his entire focus was on his daughter Asenath, me. That is until the letter came and offered to explain things.

He went to Arkham and spoke to a man called Peaslee who claimed to be Mr. Steve Mentzel's colleague. Peaslee had the same emotionless face that Mentzel had had, and though what Peaslee had said would have driven some mad, Ephraim believed it with absolute certainty. Something was going to intrude into our world, to be brought here by people who didn't truly understand it. Once it arrived, the world, the very universe, would change irrevocably, and life as we know it would cease. There was a moment, at least according to Peaslee, that everything could be changed, when intervention was possible. Ephraim had to prepare, said Peaslee, for this and other threats that were waiting, as well as for the possibility of failure, and of discovery. When Ephraim told him that he understood, that he knew what needed to be done, that doing all this would be easy, he lied. Ephraim returned to Innsmouth cloaked in fear, unable to comprehend what was going to happen or how to prepare for it.

Yet upon his homecoming his concerns about the future were smothered in tragedy. While he had been in Arkham something terrible had happened. Zulieka had suffered some sort of seizure and had collapsed in her bed. The doctor had been called and had rapidly concluded that whatever had happened was beyond his skills. Zulieka could neither stand nor talk, she could crawl, and utter a few words, but whatever had happened to her had turned her into little more than an infant. Yet for all her diminished faculties she was possessed of immense strength, and in time it was clear that her condition wasn't going to improve. Desperate, Ephraim renovated the attic, padded the walls and installed chains.

In the spring of 1909 he took Zulieka up the stairs and though he could see that somehow this creature loved him, he left her in that room, and never let her out again.

Not that this mattered much. Zulieka had ignored me, and as a result I had apparently failed to develop any real affection for the woman. Her separation from the family seemed to have no negative results; in fact the opposite was true. It was as if some great switch had been thrown, and I was suddenly free, and more brilliant than any child Ephraim had ever seen. I and my father were only ever happy when we were together, and although I tired easily, I did my best to stay by his side. By the time I was five I was Ephraim's constant companion, and he returned to his studies and laboratory with me as an assistant. I proved more capable than he would have ever thought. We travelled to Arkham and Kingsport and even distant and secret locations in Maine, and never could a parent have been prouder of a child.

The only activities for which I had no taste were the regular visits to the imprisoned Zulieka. Her madness had abated somewhat, for she had gained some sense of control, but her mind was little more than that of a child, and she would fly into tantrums at the strangest of things, particularly when Ephraim mentioned my well-being. Despite my apparent reluctance to visit my mother, I volunteered to help prepare her meals. Even when in November of 1912 she fell ill, I did my best to keep food and tea supplied to the poor woman, going so far as to order our own cook out of the kitchen. It was a relief when she succumbed to some strange malady that left her body cramped and convulsing while her hair fell out. Yet I, who had not seen the woman in years, still shed a tear for her loss.

It had not occurred to Ephraim that those tears could have been generated for some other reason, at least not until months later. As the spring rains caused the Manuxet to swell, there came another unwelcome flood, one of vermin. The house was suddenly infested with mice that were fleeing the drowned fields and making homes where they could. Frustrated, Ephraim took it upon himself to go down to the local store for some rat poison. The shopkeeper, Davis Phillips, was surprised that he would place such an order, for surely he had not yet exhausted the supply that had been bought the previous October. My father was startled, but quickly explained that he had broken the bottle and was in need of more. At home, it did not take him long to discover the jar of rat poison hidden in the cabinet of the pantry, and he stared perplexed, trying to determine the meaning behind the jar being halfway empty.

Despite his fears and suspicions, he still loved me and continued my apprenticeship in the arts and secret sciences. He could not have known that our skills in chemistry and pharmacology would be put to the test when in the summer of 1914 the last pharmacy in Innsmouth closed, and he and I were left to concoct the various elixirs and powders prescribed by the few doctors who had remained. Things went from bad to worse when both bus companies that served Innsmouth ceased operation just a year later. Thankfully, Joe Sargent with a little funding from the Marsh family began operating his own, albeit limited, bus service in and out of Innsmouth.

It was shortly after that a review of the pantry left Ephraim disappointed and in a somber mood, causing him one day to board Sargent's bus and travel to Kingsport. There he met with the administrator of the Hall School and made certain arrangements concerning my education and care. When he returned home, he found me waiting for him, angry beyond belief. He would not have thought a girl of my age capable of such language, or vehement. He laughed and said that when I was angry, screaming and shouting that it reminded him of the arguments and bouts that he had had with Zulieka. That is when I apparently threw up my hands and called Ephraim senile, for I recalled no such arguments. After this, according to Ephraim, I suddenly blanched and skulked away. Ephraim said nothing, but secretly monitored the jar in the pantry, and took appropriate precautions.

It took a year, much longer than it had taken with Zulieka, but by the winter of 1917–1918 Ephraim was sick. His insides burned and his muscles cramped. His hair slowly fell out, and his fingernails changed color. He knew what was happening, and secretly began eating garlic, though obtaining it was difficult. He thought of running, of once more changing his identity, and leaving Innsmouth behind. He certainly did not owe the town anything; he had given it more than eighty years. No rational person would have blamed him if he had run, certainly there was no better time to move on, and yet he felt betrayed, vindictive, and vengeful. He had been wronged and he would have retribution, even if he had to suffer through agonizing pain to obtain it.

Through the spring and early summer Ephraim's suffering increased. He mediated it by eating even more garlic, and by chewing on coca leaves, but these did little but alleviate the immediate symptoms and pain. He was still dying, his organs were being poisoned, and he knew time was short. He made plans. The essential portions of his library were packed up and placed in a warehouse in Kingsport, as were certain artifacts and mementos. Money, always the bane of existence, he secreted in various accounts throughout Massachusetts and Maine under the name Dufresne, an alias for which he created various documents and forms of identification. By the middle of July 1918 he was more than ready to do what had to be done.

Where I had been slow and subtle, he was swift and bold. He told the cook and maid that they could have the week off, with pay, thus ensuring that we would not be interrupted. He drugged me with a preparation of morphine and then chained me to the bed. The key was nearby, but out of reach. He then gathered the tinctures and tools that he needed for the Rendition. That we shared blood supposedly made things easier, but that he was a man and I was a woman was a concern. There is, it seems, a difference between men and women; whether that difference is located in the brain or some other part of the anatomy is not known, but the fundamental difference causes a weakness in the ability to invoke and handle those from outside. It is not that the ability is lacking, but rather simply a matter of degree. In the last entry of his journal, he lamented that he should have to suffer such a change and marked my birth as a girl instead of a boy as highly regrettable.

And as I come to the end of the page I remember who I am and what I have done, and why. Tomorrow I shall volunteer to once again cook meals for the thing in the attic. I am sure there is enough arsenic left to finish the job that has been started. Soon, the body of Ephraim Waite will succumb to the poison it has been fed for so many months; either that or it shall starve. I do not care which. When he finally does pass, I will have the body burned and the ashes scattered into the sea. From this I know there is no return. But while I will shed a tear, I shall not mourn, for the thing in the attic deserves no pity. Some will say it is Ephraim Waite who died in that attic, and some will whisper poison and cast stares in my direction. If Von Junzt were alive, he might have guessed that Ephraim Waite has once more performed the Rendition of Souls and exchanged minds with his daughter Asenath. In this he would be only half right. He would have called Ephraim Waite a vile, corrupted thing that carried out unspeakable rites, and subjected his daughter to the most horrific of sacrifices. He would have forgotten how Zulieka Marsh went mad and became a thing that had to be confined in the attic. He would have forgotten how she wasted away from some strange wasting, the same condition that afflicted Ephraim before he too was locked away in the attic. He might have drawn a parallel between the madness of Zulieka and that of Ephraim, but I doubt he could have discerned its true meaning. Only I and the thing upstairs know the truth, and soon only I shall remain.

In time, I shall mourn for the loss of my daughter Asenath Waite, whose body I now possess. But for the thing that killed her; the thing that supplanted her infant mind and stole her body; the thing that now rants and screams in terror in the attic; the same thing that now occupies the aged and dying body of Ephraim Waite; the thing that I once knew as Zulieka Marsh; I will shed no tears. Soon my memory will be restored, and the rendition of Ephraim Waite shall be complete.

CHAPTER 3
From the Account of Robert Martin Olmstead
"Escape from Innsmouth"

Securing the manuscript, I made my way out of the town and back into the wilderness that surrounded Innsmouth. The voice in my head was still urging me to Arkham, and I had no choice but to comply. I had become a mechanism to carry the manuscript out of Innsmouth. Who I served and where in Arkham I was to go I did not know, all I did know was that I had to keep moving. Nothing else seemed to matter, and I barely noticed that the wind had come up, and was blowing the scent of the ocean over the earth. It was a good smell, it smelled of life, of freedom, of wonders I could never imagine. It smelled of exalted immortality and fallen divinity. It reminded me of the dreams of my grandmother, how she called me to be with her in the kingdom under the sea, and how I was so close, so close. I had come so far, done so much, overcome such odds, and now I was turning away. It was my hope that my cousin had been able to do that which I had not, that Lawrence had somehow made it not only to Innsmouth, but through it and beyond. As for my quest to return to Innsmouth and from there head into the sea, it had been interrupted. I had been diverted, but I knew not why.

No sooner had I cleared the village proper did I realize the error in my plan for escape. Within the environs off Innsmouth the buildings and rolling hills served well to cast shadows and hide the railway from watchful eyes, but less than a mile out, the village and landscape slowly gave way first to low hillocks of sand and then these vanished, swallowed up on both sides by a vast salt marsh of stagnant black water, foul dark green muck and sparse stands of twisted grey shrubs. An attempt to travel through the marshlands was quickly abandoned as the muck, at least knee-deep, and deeper elsewhere, grabbed at my legs and threatened to swallow me up whole. I was left no choice but to stay on the railway bed, exposed and vulnerable, scurrying like a cockroach along the baseboards.

Traveling along the railway, while easier than passing through the salt marsh, was not easy, years of neglect had taken their toll and the line was cluttered with debris. In places, the low levee of crushed rock on which the railway sat had subsided or washed out into the marsh, causing the thick wooden ties to slip down on one side but jut up on the other. Thus along this disarray of steel rail, wooden ties and rocky pitfalls, I stumbled my way through the marsh, more than once falling onto the rocky substrate and cold steel rails. So intent was I on my haphazard journey that it was not until I had traversed well into the fetid fen that I began to notice the environment around me.

Reared as I was in the confines of a small city, it should come as no surprise that my experience in more natural settings had been limited, mostly just recently in my furtive travels in the last few weeks. That being said, I was slow to recognize the strange and eerie silence that dominated the boggy landscape. True there was a light but forceful breeze coming in from the ocean to the east, and this did stir up the sparse clumps of sickly looking vegetation such that the night air was filled with the low crackling hiss of dry leaves rustling against one another. This sound was accompanied by an occasional gurgling or fizzing as bubbles of dank-smelling gasses floated up out of the thick black waters and burst upon the surface. Yet these regular and intermittent sounds were the only things to be heard, along with my own plodding steps, as I fled down the tracks. No insects hummed or clicked amongst the swaying reeds. No frogs or toads chirped or dove awkwardly into the water. No birds, roused from their roosts by my clumsy steps, flew startled into the night. Even the rhythmic beating wings of bats wheeling through the night sky were missing. It seemed as if the salt marsh was devoid of all animal life even down to the tiniest insect.

This realization made me shudder and the unnaturalness of the place caused chills to creep up my spine. I focused on the feeling of the substrates beneath my shoes, the gravel, and then the wooden railroad tie, followed by gravel again. I focused in on the change in noise and sensation, the crunch of the rock beneath my feet followed by the dead thump of treated wood. It was hypnotic and soon I was deeply entranced in a rhythm that was rapidly carrying me across the bog. It wasn't long before the sparse moonlight revealed that I was quickly approaching the dark line of trees that marked the transition to firmer ground. Emboldened by my progress, I casually glanced behind me and to my horror discovered that I was not alone on the line. There in the distance, dimly but clearly illuminated by the faint moon, was a large monstrous shape careening down the tracks. It was massive, and at first I took it for a bull or bear, but its smooth fluid movements denied either of these conclusions. Gasping at its speed, I turned and sprinted toward the trees hoping to lose my pursuer in the wood. Closer to dry land the rail bed was in better repair, and I was able to maintain a near run down the line. Despite my surer footing and quicker pace, I could hear the thing gaining on me.

The pounding of my feet on the dry wooden ties was drowned out by the incessant pulse of my own heart. My breathing became a ragged gasp as I drove myself to run even faster. The woods were close now and I could see the tracks curving deep into the dark hidden parts of the forest. Mere steps away I once again turned back and on the tracks behind me . . . There was a horrid wet sound as the thing slammed into me and threw me to the ground, forcing my face into the gravel rail bed. I scrambled forward, clawing my way to my feet as something heavy smashed into me. Whatever it was, it pushed me down on to the ground and then began to drag me across the railway bed.

My hands clawed at the sharp gravel and hard wooden ties, but to no avail. The thing was dragging me relentlessly backwards, back into the marsh. I screamed and suddenly I was wrenched from the ground and flung through the air at such a horrifying speed that I briefly loss any sense of myself. When I recovered, I found myself flipped around staring up into the night sky. I lifted

my head and found myself staring down into the maw and eyes of
the beast that was again charging down the tracks at me. In terror I
balled my fists and tried to leap up and away, but to no avail. With
incredulous speed the claw of the thing found its way across my
mouth. There was a wet cracking sound as my jaw shattered. I spun
in the air landing face first onto the ground. I grabbed at the gravel,
desperate for my fingers to find purchase and drag myself away,
but my strength failed me as I felt what only could have been a claw
smashing into my side. The breath of the beast was fetid and stank
of rot and heat. Spittle dripped from the long teeth that shone like
daggers in the moonlight.

There was a noise and the beast turned slightly to face it. A short
flash of light and a crack of thunder shattered the night. It was like
a stream of lightning had ripped through the sky above my head.
There was no heat, but a weird electric odor, and the air seemed to
be incandescently blue. The bolt struck the creature between the
eyes, arcs of electricity enveloped the thing, its eyes melted and it
roared in agony. Its head seemed to swell and then jets of steam
suddenly burst out of the skin. The thing's head exploded into a
mass of blood and bone and gore. Another bolt flew past me, and as
a second explosion rocked the night, I curled into a protective ball,
blind with panic and fear.

The distinctive sound of boots began moving down the railway,
I relaxed and brought my head up to see the faces of my rescuers.
Two large men were staring down at me. The one on the right was
of Indian descent, easily over six feet tall and wearing a large red
turban. His face was covered in a thick black beard and strange over-
sized round eyeglasses with black lenses. He body was enshrouded
in thick, layered robes which made determining his exact build
impossible. In his arms he cradled an odd array of metallic rods
and glass tubes, the function of which I was wholly unfamiliar with.

The other man was of a stock more familiar to me, even in the
pale moonlight it was obvious where he came from. His eyes were
set far apart and bulged slightly, his ears were strangely shrunken,
and beneath his hat there were neither eyebrows nor any other
evidence of hair. He came from Innsmouth, of that I had no doubt,
but beyond that he could easily have been family to the man I had
watched die just hours before.

"Moses *tkrt*," croaked the Indian, he made an odd clicking sound as he spoke in crisp almost mechanical tones, "that is not Aaron."

The other shook his head. "No its not," said the Innsmouther, "But I do have an idea of who this is."

The Indian nodded and stepped over me. "I will *tkrt* take care of the feral spawn."

I scrambled to an upright position. "Thank you for your help," I managed to say despite my broken jaw.

The man called Moses hissed back at me, "Shut yer trap."

"Look I don't want any trouble."

"Shut it!" He growled.

"I don't want any part of this!" I shouted.

The man called Moses leaped at me and shouted as his fist came down on my face, as everything went black and I lost consciousness, I was left to ponder the meaning of his rage-filled words. "Yer already a part of this! Yew've been a part of this since yew were born!"

CHAPTER 4

From the Account of Robert Martin Olmstead
"The Thing in the Depths"

Once, I had found my dreams horrid, terrifying even, but over the years I had become accustomed to the strange visions that filled my nights. Vast aquatic landscapes of bizarre coralline architectures swarming with thousands of ichthyic figures no longer disturbed me. That in dreams my reflection was more reminiscent of a fish or frog than a man no longer woke me in a cold sweat. Indeed, such sights had grown comforting, even soothing. So, when in slumber I once more found myself floating silent and effortless through the dark waters past Devil Reef, I let the dream carry me where it would.

Down I went, past schools of baitfish and predatory blues and even more predatory sharks. The reef itself, its crabs and echinoderms, mollusks and corals were lost as I sank deeper and deeper into the murky green. A hundred feet down and the light vanished but still I was aware of my surroundings. As I plummeted past a fleet of infant giant squid the first dim lights of the upper terraces of Y'ha-nthlei appeared. Men have created images of Atlantis, Lemuria and other fanciful aquatic cities, as if they were mere counterparts to those of men. What foolishness. There are no streets in the sub-aquatic metropoli, what need are roads to creatures who would sooner swim than walk? Y'ha-nthlei is built in vast terraces that jut out from sea canyon walls like titanic fungoid growths. Channels and tunnels honeycomb the metropolis, moving both water and inhabitants in a constant fluid stream. Shoals of Deep Ones banked effortlessly in the current, their scales and eyes glittered back the pale light of the ubiquitous lamp worms that infested the city.

The current suddenly quickened, and inexorably I was drawn down past the lowest tier into the cavern below. Down I floated, toward the faint glow that leaks from the lower tiers. This was the old city, fashioned before the first men stood upright. Age had taken its toll and the network of tunnels and channels had clogged with the organic snow that fell from above. Vast colonies of necrophagic barnacles rhythmically extended feathery tentacles to harvest great quantities of the slowly falling debris before being curled back into their calciferous pentagonal shells. Choked with debris and colonized by the strange invertebrate forces of abyssal decay, the old city still sheltered a few lingering inhabitants. Ancient anthropomorphic things waded through the detrital snows with remoras and other parasites writhing hideously in their wakes while blind crabs, monstrous with thorny points and thick spiny hairs, scuttled for shelter. No hybrids here, not in the deep city. Once the pinnacle of the food chain, they had long since ceased being predatory, their once sharp and gored stained teeth had elongated into brittle hair like sieves that transformed each breath into an unconscious act of feeding.

Then, as quickly as the old city had come into view it was gone, and I plunged deeper than any dream had previously taken me. In dreamtime I become less blind and I perceived below me the tiniest pinprick of illumination. I knew instantly that it was toward this speck of phosphorescence that I was being carried. Slowly the light source resolved into a luminescent and monstrous titan, larger than any of the elder deep ones who dwelt above in the old city, though it shared their general shape and characteristics. The pale light of the ancient corpus attracted a variety of biota that I could not classify. Whether they were fish, crustacean, or mollusk, the ancient fed upon them quite passively, for it had little choice. The thing's upper limbs were pinned behind it, bound in a strange mass of pulpy tentacles that congealed along the creature's spine and enveloped everything below the massive abdomen.

So intent was I on studying the poor imprisoned creature that I failed to comprehend that the thing had noticed me as well. When it spoke I shuddered, for the language was too ancient, the voice too loud, the pressure too great, but I knew that it was revealing to me a secret, something horrid and forbidden. When it finished, it drifted away, but the movement was incidental, for it was the thing to which the titan was bound, the vast mass of tendrils that pulsed and provided motivation. As it left I began to see the entirety of the horror, the ancient one, bound so tightly to that tentacled thing. It was then, as the prisoner and his prison drifted away, that I saw the details of the things that swarmed and trailed about them. There was a moment of clarity, of reasoned logic that turned from initial denial inevitably into terror.

I awoke screaming, my heart pounding. My breath was ragged and my throat hoarse from screaming. As panic subsided, my mind slowly rationalized the images I had seen. Such things should not be, I proclaimed silently, cannot be, and no god of earth or sea should be subjected to such horrors. And if it must be, then let it be in the far off abyssal depths where sanity cannot dwell. Let it be there, where pitifully ancient things lay imprisoned, forced against their will to spawn with horrid masses of protoplasmic tentacles birthing forth shoals of mephitic spawn that swarm in great clouds. Billions of larval deep ones, newly born from a horridly forced union, drawn like thousands of other species instinctively to the light. Yet in that place where there is no sun or moon or star, the only light that issues forth is from that ancient one, a dark and forgotten Kronos forced to feed on his own monstrous spawn.

Such things should not be, not on earth; not in the abyssal depths of the sea; nor even in the dreams of things that once were men.

CHAPTER 5

From the Account of Robert Martin Olmstead
"The Scion of Innsmouth"

I awoke to find myself in a sparse room, little more than a cell really. The bed was simple and functional, and covered in plain white linens that matched the bandages that covered my wounds. Not surprisingly I found that the injuries that I had sustained in my flight from Innsmouth had healed substantially. My limbs and back ached, and I had a tremendous headache, but I could find none of the wounds that I knew I had incurred. It was true that since my transformation began in earnest, my recuperative abilities had increased markedly, but such healing as this was wholly unprecedented. Carefully, I rose from the ornate bed and found my footing.

It was then that a raucous sound, that of the door unlocking and creaking open, filled the room. Startled I fell back onto the bed as two figures came through the doorway. The first was none other than the man from Innsmouth that I had encountered in the marsh, the one who had been called Moses. Now in the light his appearance was more discernable and his obvious relationship to the former bus driver was apparent. "There he is," he said as he approached me, "another bastard scion of the Marshes, Robert Martin Olmstead, the man who destroyed Innsmouth."

I lowered my head in shame.

"You have no idea what you have done, do you? The people who have died, properties confiscated or destroyed, irreplaceable relics lost forever, centuries of planning wasted."

He roared into my face and I could see rage building in his strange black eyes. "Do you know what we have had to endure because of you? Innsmouth is lost! The village is occupied. The harbor closed and blockaded. They have bombed the reef. They have gathered us up, loaded us into cattle cars and taken us inland!" He spat this last statement. "There are rumors of experiments, horrible experiments that no man should suffer to endure. My friends and family, centuries of history and plans, all lost because of your hysterical actions. Those few of us who have escaped are forced into concealing our identities and denying our birthright. We were a proud people. Now look at us. Look at what you have brought us to!"

"I'm sorry," my voice broke and I felt the regret well up in my throat. There was no denying the things he had said. I had come to Innsmouth, and fled from it in terror, not understanding what exactly I was running from, nor my part in it. "I've come back, to repent, to make amends. Surely Lawrence, my cousin, has explained all that."

Moses threw his head back and laughed. "You are sorry! Innsmouth and her people suffer while you walk about unfettered, but you're sorry." He turned and threw his head back and seemed to swear at something in the air. He spun back around and scowled at me. "My people will be free Mr. Olmstead! And you my ignorant friend are going to help make sure that happens or die trying. Iä Dagon!"

"But Lawrence . . ."

"YOU FOOL LAWRENCE IS DEAD!" Moses screamed. "He was captured by the soldiers and beaten. Do you know what damages we can endure and still cling to life? They crucified him in Federal Square, tortured him with knives and fire. They used him to try and draw us out of hiding. They let him keep his tongue so he could scream out to us, to beg for help. It was a trap, and both he and we knew it. He hung there for more than a week. Begging for the sea, begging for Pth'thya-l'yi to come and rescue him. He prayed to Mother Hydra and to Father Dagon, and he cursed the soldiers. You thought he was mad before, madness is relative I tell you. When Lawrence finally died, when he finally succumbed to his wounds, it was a relief."

I was sobbing. "What did they do with the body?" I could hear the pathetic begging that wracked my voice, but I didn't care. I was past the point of caring what anyone thought of me anymore.

Moses' eyes grew small and he stared at me with an unrelenting anger. "They left it there, and though we wanted to claim it as our own we dared not go after it. After a day the seagulls finally lost any inhibitions. I suppose the stink was too enticing for them to ignore. It only took a few hours. They came in great flocks, and filled the square like a horde of winged rats. The sound of their cackling calls was almost as horrible as his screams had been. They gorged themselves on his flesh, tore it off in great meaty strips. When they finally finished, not even the bones were left. They carried those away as well, dropped them on to the rocks to shatter them open and pick out the marrow." I was shaking, with fear, with disgust, with horror, but Moses wouldn't relent. "Tell me bastard child of Innsmouth, how exactly do you plan on repenting for all your sins? What penance do you think appropriate for the suffering all of Innsmouth have endured because of you?"

I opened my mouth to answer, but no words would come. For the first time in years I did not know what to say. Thankfully the awkward silence was interrupted.

"That's enough Moses," said the second man forcefully. "The boy is not entirely at fault."

The angry, accusatory man mumbled a series of curses and stalked out of the room, leaving me to ponder what he had said. Were it not for the presence of the other man I knew not what I would have done. As he stepped forward out of the darkness, I resolved myself to suffering whatever new burdens would be given me.

This older man was of slight build and had a professional and well-kept appearance. He wore a simple brown suit with a tie which I recognized as being from the medical school of Miskatonic University. If pressed I would have estimated his age as fifty, but his face was tired and worn as if from great stress or world-weariness. Most peculiar was the pronounced difference in skin coloration between his hands, with the right hand being substantially paler and scarred. Indeed as I watched the hand seemed to twitch and jerk involuntarily. I had seen similar conditions amongst those who had served in the Great War, injuries that had never properly healed. Some were proud of their battle scars, but others were sensitive about their conditions. Not knowing how he would react I diverted my attention to the ceiling.

"Let me check your wounds or you won't be in any shape to help us at all." He pulled out a pair of spectacles and began to peer intently at the various areas in which I had been hurt but had so miraculously healed. With each inspection there came a generalized harrumph of approval.

"I am Doctor Hartwell, Stuart Hartwell," he said, grabbing my face and turning my head left and right. "You are a very lucky man. There aren't many who could have recovered so quickly from such a beating. I haven't seen such wounds in years, not since the Great War. Those were horrible days, such fierce fighting, and the horrors, the things I saw in St. Eloi and later in Belloy-en-Santerre you would not believe the things men can do to each other. I don't know how we made it through. Turn please."

I complied, lulled by the familiarity of the examination process, "We?" I questioned.

The doctor nodded in an odd bobbing fashion. "Well I really. I served in the Great War while my partner, my colleague stayed in Arkham to maintain our practice."

Sensing an opening, and an opportunity to establish some rapport, I eased into a conversation. "Is that how you were wounded?" I gestured with my head toward his arm, "In the war?"

Hartwell smiled and shook his head. "No. This is the result of a more recent event. Though I suppose, in a way, it is related to my time in service. If I had not gone to war, if I had not returned, if my partner and his wife had not betrayed me, then perhaps this would not have been necessary." He snorted, acknowledging that he had accepted things the way they were. "Listen to me, rambling on. There is no need to bother you with such things."

"Please Doctor Hartwell, go on." I gestured about. "This room may be pleasant, but I am still a prisoner. It has been a long time since anyone has spoken to me, and to be honest I have been too immersed in my own predicaments for far too long. Perhaps it is time I listened to someone else. I think it would be a welcome relief to hear someone else's problems." The man stared at me for a moment, and then pulled up a cushioned chair, settled in and told me the story of his wounded right hand.

CHAPTER 6

From the Account of Robert Martin Olmstead
"The Case of Francis Paul Wilson"

I. The Redemption of Dr. Hartwell

You ask me what happened. Why is my right hand scarred? Why are the fingers broken? Why does it tremble so? You ask as if it was a casual question, as if the answer would be easy and quick. I could tell you that it happened in the war, but that would be a lie. The truth is neither easy nor quick. It is a tale that most should not be told. Few need to hear this story but you are part of this now. She has recruited you, summoned you with her psychic beacon. You came here, drawn like a moth to a flame, but you are no thrall. You have the right to know what you are getting involved in, what kind of people you are working with.

You look at me and you see a doctor, a healer. Would it surprise you to learn that I have killed? Not just in the war. I have killed men, and women, and yes even children. I think that if I told you the number of dead I feel responsible for you would be astounded. Yet this is nothing compared to the other crimes I have committed, crimes that resulted in my confinement in the asylum at Sefton. They thought me mad, they looked upon what fragments of notes they could find, and refused to believe what was written there. Later, as the evidence mounted, as the proof became undeniable, they no longer called me mad, but I remained confined. The authorities have no facilities to deal with a man who has learned the secrets of reanimating the dead, and no laws to charge him under. Better to call him mad, and leave him imprisoned.

The authorities may not know what to do with such a man, but others surely do. They came for me, liberated me from that snake-pit of a hospital, and showed me how I could be useful. How I could continue my work. How I could be of service, and make amends for all those I had killed. I did not protest. Even when the first refugees from Innsmouth began to arrive, I did not protest. I had seen such creatures before. I had worked in Innsmouth before, during the occupation. I had tended to their wounds, treated their ailments, and cured their diseases. I knew that beneath the scaly skin, the bulging eyes and the plastic limbs those from Innsmouth were, in a word, only human. It was a chance at redemption, and I jumped at any chance to repair the damage I had done to my own sense of morality.

I had been free just a few weeks, when they took me by car to Providence and then by ferry across Narragansett Bay. It was cold, but I didn't mind. I had been imprisoned, denied my freedom, standing on the boat, letting the wind and salt air whip through my hair, reminding me that I was still alive. Once on Conanicut Island we made our way to a small private hospital, a resort spa really, the kind of place well-to-do women go to treat the ills they imagine plague them, and better-off families send those members they would rather forget. My employers had come to this place looking for just such a man. An important man, one they had lost contact with him some years earlier, but now were desperate to discover his whereabouts. The trail seemed to end at this place. They had apparently interviewed key staff members in secret. I do not know what they were told, but whatever it was, afterwards they no longer continued to look for Joseph Curwen. And yet here I was, being taken someplace I had no desire to visit. If they hadn't found Curwen, why was I here?

It was an ostentatious place, all marble and hard woods with modern lines. A bronze plaque listed the name as The Whitmarsh Institute, and beneath in painted letters the names of the directing physicians, Doctors M. B. Willett and B. A. L. Bradley. I had never heard of the former, but knew of Doctor Bradley from her published work in the field of psychoanalysis, of which she was

considered one of the leading minds, often compared to Freud or
Jung. Beneath their names was a third, Dr. Willis Lynn, listed as the
Managing Director.

Dr. Lynn was a nervous man, with darting eyes and sweat on
his balding pate. He seemed genuinely relieved to see us, but at the
same time it was obvious he was uncomfortable with the situation.
He was leading us down, down into the basements of the building,
chatting nervously as we went. "You must understand Doctor
Hartwell. Your friend has been with us for several years. First as an
employee, one of our junior physicians, though to be honest, given
his skills, he could have easily been promoted to a more senior position. Later, afterwards . . . well I suppose you would call him a
patient, though only I and a few of the orderlies know about him.
I've kept the event secret, even from the other directors. If word got
out, the scandal would destroy the Institute, ruin us all."

I struggled to fit a question into his monologue. "Doctor, I'm
sorry, this friend of mine, to whom are you referring?"

He stared at me for an instant, and then looked away. "We keep
him down here. He doesn't like the light. His needs are—limited.
He can talk, it's difficult but he can talk. He prefers to write. He's
prepared something for you to read. He said you would understand that you would know what to do. I certainly don't." He fumbled with a key and then turned the handle on a thick wooden door.
"His name is Wilson, Dr. Francis Paul Wilson."

It was with some trepidation that I moved into the dimly lit
room. It had been years since I had last seen him. He had once been
my partner, Hartwell and Wilson had been one of the finest medical
practices in Arkham. That all changed when his wife succumbed to
the outbreak of Spanish Influenza, and in his grief he demanded that
I bring her back. While I had been serving in the Great War, Wilson
had discovered that I had been experimenting with a formula, a
reagent that could work on the tissues of the recently departed
and restore them to life. Under duress, I prepared this reagent and
administered it to Mary. It took time, but Mary finally returned, but
when she came back, she wasn't right; she was violent, enraged.
As she tore through the house she snapped Wilson's neck, killing
him instantly. I of course brought him back. What had brought
back Mary wrong, worked almost perfectly on Wilson. The only

noticeable effects had been a slight crook in his neck, and a limp. What would have been unnoticeable would have been something common to all those who had benefitted from my reagent: Wilson would have been extremely resistant to infection, and any physical wounds would have had little effect on the man. His constitution and recuperative powers would have been beyond measure. In my experience, only the wholesale destruction of Wilson's body, through fire or dissolution in acid, would create a wound beyond his ability to heal. With this knowledge I knew that whatever had happened to Wilson must have been traumatic indeed.

In the poor light there was little to see. The room was little more than a cell with a single weak lamp providing a minimum of illumination, and a radio playing some static-laced music, both of which rested on a low side table. Against the wall was a simple wooden chair, and there in the far corner, barely illuminated by the dim bulb, I could make out the face of my one-time friend Francis Wilson. As I moved the chair to sit by his side, it was obvious to me that my suspicions had been correct. Something traumatic had happened to Wilson. Most of his body lay hidden by blankets or in the darkness, but his face, shoulder and arm were pale and wasted. As I sat, his hand reached out and I took it. He was cold, barely warmer than the room. His sunken eyes filled with tears as his cracked lips opened and he weakly said my name and apologized in the same breath. I held his hand tightly and told him he had nothing to apologize for.

We sat there for some time in silence, for I knew that whatever had happened there were few people in the world who could understand it, and fewer still that might be able to offer help. That is, if there was any help to be offered. Eventually, I broke the silence. "If I am going to help you, I have to know what happened." At this he attempted to withdraw his hand, but I held it tight, insistently, demanding that he not break the physical link between us.

"I've written it down." His voice was strange, hollow, like the wind blowing through a log. He spoke, softly, slowly, deliberately, as if it was a strain to form even a single word, and gestured toward the side table. I nodded, trying to be patient with the man, and then retrieved the stack of pages from the table. It was a handwritten manuscript, on white stationary, but unusually stained in places with a brown ochre that hinted at something dreadful. The dim light made reading slightly difficult, but for the sake of my friend I undertook the task. I still remember the contents as if the paper were in front of me now.

II. The Account of Dr. Wilson

It is in desperation that I write this, for I know that my current condition, a result of a regrettable incident, as Doctor Lynn prefers to refer to it, requires some explanation. Although to be honest there are few in this world who would not consider these words, this statement, anything but the ravings of a lunatic. But if you couple these pages with what has happened to me, to what I have become, what then? Who can deny my account of what happened? Who would dare suggest anything else?

I had been living in northern New Jersey, in a small coastal community, a horrid barren place of sandy soils and sparse thin grass. Few people lived there, and those who did prefered to keep to themselves. It was the perfect place to lose one's self, to wallow in self pity and try to forget the past. I stayed there for years, isolated, alone and content in my own way. Had I not ventured out for supplies, had I not taken the coastal road, I would never have met the young Miss Nora Forrest, never have examined her twisted ankle, never been asked to accompany her to Manhattan, and never have been recommended for a position at the Whitmarsh Institute. It is a banal place, encompassing everything I always hated about the practice of medicine. A summer place, where nervous men and women with a touch of hypochondria come to fritter away their days and allow doctors to preen over them. During the season, they come in droves to take in the island, to walk its gardens and lanes, to stroll on the beaches, and eat the fresh oysters. This place swarms with such people in the summer. After September though, the institute is nearly empty. Only a few residents, those whose families have paid to not see them, like the Mad Mrs. Tanzer and the infirm Mr. Meikle, and a minimum of staff, stay behind. The island in winter is not kind. The wind turns bitter and biting, and sets the bay churning. The ferry runs just one day a week, and even the bay men don't dare venture too far from home, by sea or land. In a word, the place in winter can be considered quite isolated. It is a perfect place to hide, or even lose someone. For me, it seemed an improvement. I could remain isolated and nearly anonymous, and still be paid a decent wage.

I had spent two summers and the winter between them, and was working on a second when Senior Physician Dr. Willett brought in a new client. It was late in the evening of March 8 that the car arrived. It was quite unexpected, for the bay was in a treacherous state. That the ferryman had risked it suggested that Willett had paid him well, and that this was no ordinary patient. He was a young man, perhaps in his mid-twenties, tall, slim, and fair. His clothing was well-tailored, but disheveled, and his hair was wild and unkempt. It seemed that the man had been sickly for quite some time, for his skin had a sallow pallor about it and hung thinly on his frame. As part of his admission process I and Willett examined the man, while the others, Peck, Lyman and Waite, looked on. All of us were astonished by what we found. The man's skin was dry, and abnormally cool. His breathing and cardiac rhythms were curiously out of synchronization, and his physical response to nervous stimuli bore no relation to anything thought normal. Willett, who was apparently the man's family physician, made note of the absence of an olive birthmark on the man's hip, and the presence of a great black scar on his chest. Additionally, the old doctor made much of a small pit in the flesh above the man's right eye.

Willett refused to reveal the man's name, and instead insisted he be addressed as Mr. Pulver. At this the man sniggered softly, and Willett chastised him, suggesting that he keep honor in mind and prevent any scandal from besmirching the family name. To this idea the sickly man reluctantly nodded. The head orderly Sammons led Pulver to his room while Willett and I discussed the case over coffee. The senior physician made it clear that when Pulver was in his room, the door was to be locked. He could have the run of the common rooms and gardens, during normal hours, but only under supervision by Sammons or one of the other orderlies. Under no circumstances was he to be left alone. Such talk made me question whether the man should be confined to a straightjacket, but Willett rejected the idea, and suggested that in his opinion, Mr. Pulver was not a danger to himself or others, but, I could take appropriate action if anything suggested otherwise.

There was no way for me to tell Dr. Willett that I had already seen something that suggested otherwise, that is without revealing any of my own sordid past. My physical examination of Pulver revealed highly abnormal physical and neurological conditions, but these while beyond those thought normal, were not beyond my own experience. I had read about such abnormalities in the notes of Dr. Stuart Hartwell, for they were common amongst some of his experimental subjects, experiments that explored the reanimation of dead animals and humans. Of course I had also observed them directly in a subject that I had direct access to, an example of a reanimated individual that I examined on a daily basis. Abnormal breathing, strange heart rates, cold skin, poor nervous reactions, they were all things I saw every day. These symptoms, they were frighteningly similar to the result of Hartwell's reanimation reagent, or something like it, for I knew those symptoms all too well. For the individual I had observed on a daily basis for these long years, the one who had died and then been brought back by Hartwell's experiments, was myself!

The next morning Willett and the other senior staff had breakfast in the staff dining room before bidding farewell, and leaving me in charge of the orderlies, the old cook Mrs. Davis, and the dozen or so cats that served to keep the grounds free of vermin. The oldest and largest of these was a great calico which the staff referred to as Doc, for his claws were as sharp and as swift as any surgeon's scalpel. This title was well-earned, for guests who crossed the beast would be quick to learn to steer clear of him in the future. Only the physicians on the staff, and of course Mrs. Davis, who provided his meals, knew any kindness from him. With the senior staff gone, I was left alone to make my rounds, with Doc trailing behind me. With just a few patients, all of which were minor cases, the majority of my regular work was completed in just a few hours. The only patient I had not seen was the enigmatic Mr. Pulver. Sammons was with him in the library, where he was perusing a small book. Dismissing Sammons, I sat down across from Pulver and introduced myself.

The young man closed his book, which was revealed to be Castaigne's translation of The King in Yellow. "I know who ye are Dr. Wilson, and I know what ye are." He waved the book in front of me. "Have ye read this? 'Tis quite an amusing tale."

I was taken aback by the man's archaic speech, but confessed that I hadn't read the book, then paused and asked, "It seems we have something in common Mr. Pulver. I trust I can count on your discretion, as you can count on mine?"

The younger man smiled at me, "I am sure that ye and I can come to some arrangement while my father and Dr. Willett deem it necessary to detain me in this place." Pulver it seems had developed several curious habits as a result of his mania, the most noticeable of which was his affectation of an archaic accent, vocabulary and mode of speech. More distressing was his desire, or as he put it, "craving" for fresh raw meat. He needed a significant portion on a daily basis, for it supplied a vital energy without which he would surely wither away to naught but dust. At these suggestions I laughed, thinking the man was playing the clown. However, that laughter turned to morbid shock once I realized that the man was genuine in his desires.

Normally such a request would have been ignored, but I was faced with a horrible dilemma, and risked exposure of my own secret. Thus, I with some amount of secrecy set about determining how to meet the odd demand. My investigation of the pantry was disappointing. In summer the kitchen would be stocked with fresh fruits, vegetables, fish, shellfish, poultry, beef, ham, mutton, and even a selection of wild game. However, in the winter, with all but a few guests and staff, supplies were limited, and while some meat was available, it consisted mostly of dried beef, smoked sausages, and salted fish, none of which could remotely be considered to meet Pulver's expressed desires. Inquiries at the nearby farms were rejected, for none of the local poultry men were in a position to supply me with the daily regimen that Pulver had suggested. However, while making my way back to the hospital, I through happenstance encountered young Simon Grau, who during the summer often provided us with small game. I explained my need, though not the motivation behind it, and he suggested that he likely could provide each morning a rabbit or two. Though, he warned, that given the season, the beasts might be rather lean. We negotiated a price that was acceptable to both of us and Grau assured me that he would deliver no later than eight each morning.

True to his word, the next day Grau was at the kitchen door just after seven and delivered two carcasses, skinned, with the heads and paws removed. At these, Mrs. Davis scowled and examined them roughly. She glared at the boy and warned him not to be bringing any "dachahse" roof rabbits into her kitchen. The boy swore that he would do no such thing, and bid us farewell till tomorrow. Confused, I pressed Mrs. Davis for an explanation. She was reluctant at first, but then using the bodies, explained that when properly prepared the carcasses of rabbits and cats were nearly indistinguishable, and in lean times the unscrupulous hunter would often substitute one for the other. She assured me that the meat supplied by Grau was indeed rabbit. I thanked Mrs. Davis and asked her to make the one rabbit for my dinner, while I took the other one as it was. This left the old cook quite perplexed, but I just took the rabbit and waved her away.

Despite the cold, Pulver was in the garden on a hill overlooking the bay. As I approached, Sammons saw the covered serving tray and intercepted me. "He's already had his breakfast." I nodded and dismissed the man. Marching up the hill against the wind I barely felt the cold. As I reached the crest Pulver turned to greet me. There was a strange look in his eyes, a desire that I knew to be a perverse kind of hunger. He greedily snatched the tray and tossed the cover to the side. I had thought the animal rather large, indeed I expected to share the one Mrs. Davis was to prepare. However, in the hands of Mr. Pulver it suddenly seemed small, for it vanished quickly in the most rapacious of manners. In mere moments the bones had been sucked clean, nary a morsel of muscle, ligament or cartilage remained. I found his whole process of feeding almost obscene, and despite this I could not look away when he cracked open the bones and proceeded to suck out the marrow. I gagged a little when he finally turned to look at me with those strangely intense eyes and said in a voice that was not asking, but rather ordering "MORE!"

Against Willett's orders I fled, leaving Pulver alone. On my way back I passed Sammons and gave him a perfunctory order to keep an eye on Pulver. I cannot begin to think what Sammons must have thought at the sight of the blood-covered patient, and to be honest, at the time I did not care. I knew that the reanimation process often resulted in subjects exhibiting all sorts of irrational behavior, indeed my own wife became a kind of plague demon, a mindless killer whose first victim was myself, and was the cause of my own exposure to the reanimation reagent. Yet despite this knowledge, I found Pulver's ravenous behavior almost intolerable, and I found myself wandering the halls fretting over the issue.

Eventually, I had no choice and after he was served dinner, I confronted him on the issue. At first he thought I had come to feed him again, but I made it clear that I could only guarantee him one rabbit a day, but on occasion two might be possible. He cursed at me, calling me a slew of archaic derogatory names, and warned me that if I did not help him, he would take matters into his own hands. It was then that I realized that my fears were unfounded. Pulver was not a threat to me, he was a madman, a patient, and no matter what he said about me or my condition, no one would believe him. I steeled my nerves and ordered Sammons and the other staff to confine him to his room and the common areas inside the hospital. That night I took comfort in the fact that it was I who was in control of the hospital, and not the madman below. My sense of satisfaction must have been palatable, for it was strongly reinforced by the constant affections of the cat Doc, who spent the night curled up on the bed with me, purring loudly.

For the next few days I had Sammons deliver Pulver's special meals, but included both rabbits, for although Mrs. Davis is an excellent cook, I found the dish she made from the beast a bit too gamey for my tastes. I also made a constant effort to avoid Pulver. I had no need to interact with him, and he made no requests for my attention. This arrangement went on for more than a week, until at last one of us broke the pattern, though in a very subtle way. On the morning of the Twentieth, Sammons approached me very meekly and suggested that he may have committed some offense and shirked his responsibilities. Pulver it seems, had been writing letters, and had convinced one of the junior orderlies to post them for him. Most had been addressed to remote locales in Europe, but the one Sammons had confiscated had been directed to a legal firm in Philadelphia, but the addressee was identified as "Efraim Waite, or his Legalle Heir." The packet was rather thick, and heavy, indic-ating a significant number of pages were enclosed. I thanked Sam-mons for his forthrightness, suggested that the junior orderly be reassigned, and promised that we would not speak of the matter again.

Sammons thanked me, and made to leave, but then suddenly stopped and commented. "The staff is scared of him Doctor Wilson, the cats too." I nodded, and hoped that he wouldn't be with us much longer. I thought about opening the packet and examining its contents, but instead I threw it whole into the fire. Whatever secrets Pulver had, I had no interest in them, I had pried into secrets before, and it had cost me dearly.

It was three days later that the morning sky turned grey and the wind shifted, and the air grew bitterly cold. Grau commented on the change in the weather when he came to drop off the rabbits in the morning. He lingered longer than usual, and sampled Mrs. Davis's coffee. By the time he left a fog had begun to roll in off the bay, and swaddle the island in its murky embrace. Through the day and the night the temperature continued to drop, and the air took on that peculiar smell that warns of a winter storm. Grau came, but with only one rabbit, the fog being too thick to hunt in. An hour after he left the snow began, and by the time the sun went down several inches had accumulated, but the storm itself showed no sign of letting up.

For five days the wind howled and beat against the windows. The snow whipped and danced across the frigid pale landscape, and piled up against the doors until they could no longer be opened. Grau had ceased to come, but whether this was because he had no rabbits to deliver, or because it was too cold and treach-erous to make the trip, I did not know. Yet while the young hunter no longer came to us, we had other, albeit unwelcome, guests. The storm had kept all of us inside, and presumably it had kept Grau from hunting and delivering his rabbits; it also had driven the rats from their usual haunts in the fields and into the refuge of the hospital itself. It was most disturbing to hear them as they moved about the rooms, not where you could see them, but rather in the places in between. The hospital had rats in the halls, in the kitchen, in the rooms, and even in the walls.

It was Friday the Thirtieth when the invasion of vermin grew too much for me to tolerate and I convened a meeting with Sammons and Mrs. Davis to decide on a course of action. In a store room we found a case of traps which were easy enough to operate, and large enough to handle even the largest of rats. I, however, admonished my staff to be careful in their placement so as not to cause injury to our few guests, and the plethora of cats that had apparently been unable to deal with the infestation. At this both Sammons and Davis seemed to blanch, and I pressed them on the issue. Both seemed reticent to answer, and were frankly amazed that I hadn't noticed myself.

Neither had seen any of the cats for days, even old Doc had seemingly vanished. It was true, it had been days since I had seen any of the feline residents of the institute, but given the capricious ways of cats, I had not taken any notice.

It was a mystery, but one that I would have to investigate later, after the issue of the rats was taken care of. Given the size of the traps it was best if they were set by two sets of hands, rather than one. Thus I found myself working through the building with Sammons, and as things progressed, we struck up a casual conversation, mostly about the island and its more eccentric residents. In time, the dialogue eventually worked its way to the young hunter Grau whom had been supplying the rabbits for Pulver. Sammons found Pulver's consumption of the raw animal flesh disturbing, and suggested that the blizzard be used as a ploy to cease providing such fare, and that he be weaned off of the psychological need for raw meat. I nodded, for I found the suggestion intriguing were it not for the case that Grau had ceased delivering when the storm started, and given the cold and snow, was not likely to be starting up again anytime soon. It was then that Sammons made the most unusual comment, for he wondered how many rabbits were left to keep feeding Pulver's mania.

Confused I told him that there were no rabbits left, there had never been any storage of rabbits in the pantry, and they had been delivered daily by Grau and then conveyed to him fresh each day. The last delivery had been almost a fortnight earlier. Sammons shook his head, surely I was mistaken. Perhaps Mrs. Davis had laid in a supply. For he had seen Pulver devour the carcass of an animal, or disposed of the bones of such a feast, almost every day of his incarceration!

I stumbled back and found support in a library chair, while the wave of heretofore unconnected events and ideas washed over me. They coalesced in my mind, working together into a tapestry that revealed the horrid truth of what had happened here. Pulver had warned me that he would take things into his own hands; I should never have distanced myself from Pulver. Knowing what he was, I should have supervised him myself, or at least told him that the supply of raw meat had ceased. Mrs. Davis had warned me about "dachahse," roof rabbits, but this warning was misplaced. She should have told Sammons, and maybe then we could have prevented Pulver from devouring the cats that resided at the hospital, presumably including my beloved Doc!

My retribution over this slight was swift and severe. I and Sammons forcibly sedated the man, and then bound him into a straightjacket. He was confined to a padded room with none of his personal items, or any of the books which he had borrowed from the library. Later that evening, once I had regained my composure, I set about examining Pulver's belongings and quickly discovered flecks of a blue paint on his shoes which I realized was the color of the beach chairs used by the hospital. As it was winter, these were in storage in a detached shed that was situated between the hospital and the beach. Intrigued but fearful, I was careful not to let any of the staff see me make my way through the snow to the outlying building.

That Pulver had been using the building was apparent, but what he had been doing was incomprehensible, and I dare not relate it here. Let it be said that Pulver had been carrying out experiments, though it would be difficult to say that the undertakings were purely scientific, rather they were perhaps alchemical, or even necromantic in nature, I also found concrete evidence of his having used the shed to kill and skin the cats before eating them. All of this I gathered up in some old flour sacks and took to the furnace where I destroyed it. It gave me great satisfaction to burn those things, for the experimental equipment had obviously taken some time to cobble together. That I was able to extract some quantum of vengeance against the man was somewhat comforting.

The next morning there came the beginning of a warming spell, and by the third of April enough of the snow had melted to allow for foot traffic to come in and out of the hospital. The first visitor was Grau who came without any game, but rather to apologize for his absence. While his visit had no direct impact on our operations, he was a welcome sight, and he engendered in the staff a desire to visit friends and relations in nearby Jamestown. Given that we had been trapped inside the facility for several weeks I could see no good reason to deny Sammons and Mrs. Davis some well-deserved leave. After all, the rats had been controlled; Pulver was confined to a straightjacket, and the few other patients could easily be handled for the day, either by myself or Barrass the remaining junior orderly.

It wasn't long before the flaw in my plan made itself plain. By noon, the wind off the bay had brought in a new storm, one filled with driving, freezing rain. I watched from my window, frustrated and helpless as the walkways that had been cleared were now suddenly covered with ice and impassable. By nightfall, it was clear that Sammons and Davis were not going to return and that for the immediate future Barrass and I were on our own. This would have been fine, were it not for the sudden flicker in the lights. The rain no doubt had seeped into the wiring that ran between the main building and the furnace building where the generator had been installed. By the time the clocks struck seven Barrass and I had broken out the candles and hurricane lamps. We prepared sandwiches for ourselves and the patients. Pulver refused his dinner, and cursed me for denying him the blood-rich raw meat he needed. After Barrass closed the door, I checked and made sure that the cell was properly locked. I then left Barrass to keep watch while I rested, with the full intent of relieving him around one in the morning.

My sleep was restless, and truth be told I have not slept well, or much in all the years since my reanimation. It is I suppose a side effect of the process, and I would not begrudge the living their peaceful nights, the loss of a good night's sleep seems a small price to pay for more life. It would be tolerable, this life I live, I am never ill, never tired, even my melancholy seems surmountable. Life, life as I know it would be more than acceptable, were it not that I suffered from bad dreams, nightmares really, the same nightmare over and over again, the night of my death, and my rebirth.

The power was still out when I wandered down from my quarters. The wind was still howling, and the rain still battered down on the roof and windows. My lamp did little to cut the darkness that had enshrouded the hospital, but it was enough for me to make my way down the stairs and through the halls to where Barrass had set himself up with a comfortable chair and a good book. Not unexpectedly, things were not as they should have been. The lamps that Barrass had surrounded himself with had long since faltered, and by their nearly non-existent flickering glow I could see that Barrass was slumped over in the chair, fast asleep, or so I thought. My attempts to rouse the orderly were futile. He was alive, for I did detect a pulse and other life signs, though these were so faint as to make me think him dead. As I lit more of the lamps my suspicion that Davis' slumber was unnatural was confirmed, for there on the side table was a syringe that upon examination revealed traces of morphine. Barrass had been drugged, but by whom I could not tell.

The answer to that question was quickly supplied. The light from the lamps revealed an open door, one that, despite actively avoiding, I knew the owner of. Pulver was free, from his room and from his straightjacket. He was free, and he had attacked poor Davis, though he had not done any real or permanent harm, at least not yet. That is what puzzled me most. For if Pulver was free, and as dangerous as I thought, why had he not harmed Davis? That unspoken question echoed in my mind as something large and shadowy moved to my side. It was Pulver, and with the skill of a seasoned physician a second syringe found its mark, and the warm flush of morphine washed over my mind and I fell to the floor, overcome by chemical sleep.

How long I was asleep I cannot say, but it could not have been for more than a few hours. I awoke bound and gagged in a small room in the basement illuminated by but a single bare bulb. It was not long after waking that Pulver was there. He was gloating, and there was the most horrid of looks in his eyes. When he spoke, it was without a trace of weakness or fear. He was in truth truly magnificent, and his words filled me with dread.

"Did I ask so much of ye Dr. Wilson? I asked only for that which I needed to live. Was it too much for ye to give me that which meant so little to thee, but for mine own self was the gift of life? Instead ye scorned me and forced my hand against thee and thine. What happens now is but the work of your own pride."

He withdrew a knife, one I recognized as belonging to those being used by Mrs. Davis in the kitchen. "For what I must do now, I am truly regretful, but your acts have left me but a sole means of survival and freedom. If I am to be free, I must convince your Dr. Willett that I am merely a man that has suffered from some extraordinary nervous shock, and then while here at this place found my way back to a semblance of reason. Unfortunately my dear doctor, while my plan for freedom involves deceiving Dr. Willet, my plan for survival involves you. There are no more cats Dr. Wilson, and while I could have used that fool Barrass for my purposes, you possess certain talents that make you more appropriate for my needs."

He used the knife, slowly, and with skill. He came back day after day, taking only what he needed. I understood what he meant when he said that I had certain talents, for a lesser man, a living man would have succumbed after but a single day. As it was I lasted more than a week, and then without explanation, Pulver ceased his visits and tortures. Despite this, I was in no position to free myself, and could do little but moan in agony beneath my gag.

Davis, fearing that he might be blamed for my disappearance, told Sammons that I had become drunk and wandered out into the night where I was washed away into the frozen sea, and there was nothing to prove him a liar. Pulver played at being a prisoner, and feigned any knowledge of my whereabouts to Davis, Sammons and Dr. Lynn, whom Sammons had called when I was found to be absent. Neither Sammons or Lynn suspected that Pulver had anything to do with my being missing, and he continued to play at being confined and controlled, all the while secretly visiting me to satisfy his inhuman hungers.

That is until the 8th of April when Willet and another man came to visit Pulver and talk to him at length. The visit had been as clandestine as it could be, for it was not recorded in the log book, and Dr. Lynn was not informed. Only Sammons, who had assisted Willet, knew that the two had come and gone, and only Sammons saw the rage and loathing that Pulver tried so hard to conceal. That night, Sammons made sure that Pulver was properly restrained, and his doors securely locked. Even during the day Pulver was properly monitored and confined to just two rooms. This almost obsessive supervision was why the monster's daily predations on me had ceased. Had only Sammons acted on my instructions earlier, perhaps I would not have suffered so.

Dr. Willet returned to Whitmarsh on the morning of April 13th. He was alone, and after some conversation with Dr. Lynn went to see Pulver. Sammons was dismissed, and what occurred in that room has never been revealed, but within the hour the alarm was raised. According to Willett, Pulver had overpowered the physician and escaped. A search was made of the grounds and the island, and the ferryman and bay men were questioned, but to no avail. No trace of the man was ever found. Indeed the only evidence that the room he had been confined to had ever been occupied was a fine blue-tinged powder or sand that was strewn about like ash. But whatever this material was, it too was soon forgotten. The staff, following Willet's directions, swept the room clean. The orderly Barrass then took the dusty material and cast it into the bay.

Sammons found me on the 16th of April, and the poor man nearly died of terror. I cannot blame him. Doctor Lynn was a practical man, and after the initial shock of finding me had worn off, he hid me here. It was not difficult to keep my presence or condition hidden; only Lynn and Sammons know of my presence. After all, the Whitmarsh Institute was expert at keeping secrets, what was one more thing to be hidden, even if it was something monstrous, something that had once been human, and now clung to a mere parody of life, something that had once gone by the name of Doctor Francis Paul Wilson.

III. Dr. Wilson's Solution

I finished reading Wilson's account and in a panic rose up and demanded that he show me what had been done to him. The wounded doctor begged me not to look at him yet, not until I had promised to help him, to somehow save him. In madness or fear, or some combination of both, I refused and in my emotional state threw on the lamp, and tore away the blankets that enshrouded my fallen colleague. If only I had done as he said. If only I had steeled myself to the possibilities, girded myself against the terrible thing that lay there beside me, perhaps then I would not have reacted the way I did, and undertaken the terrible course which ended the matter once and for all.

I left the room visibly disturbed and almost immediately encountered Dr. Lynn. In a tone that was in no way calm or rational I asked the aging administrator if he wanted me to provide a solution to his Dr. Wilson problem. Flustered he agreed, and I asked, no, demanded that he show me to his hydrotherapy facilities. He escorted me forthwith, and I confirmed that the porcelain tub he showed me was adequate to my needs. I then asked for the key to the pool maintenance shed, which he readily handed over, though he did stress that the pool had been drained for the winter. This made no difference to my plan, and after confirming the presence of certain materials, I made Lynn promise to keep both himself and his staff out of my way. Given that I was proposing to eliminate his responsibility for an embarrassing secret, he readily agreed.

Alone, and empowered by my emotional state, I returned to Wilson's cell and using the blankets wrapped him up in a veritable cocoon of cloth. He struggled a bit, but at my direction ceased his protestations, for after all he had little choice in the matter. No one else was in a position or willing to help the poor feeble creature. I carried him from that dismal place, down the halls and corridors of the Whitmarsh Institute, until at last I came to the hydrotherapy room. There I carefully placed him into the porcelain tub, removed the bloody and stained blankets, and slowly began to fill the bath with warm water. Wilson protested and screeched in pain, but I silenced him by explaining that I needed to clean the wounds and remove any infected tissue. After this he acquiesced and his shrieks were swallowed into painful grimaces that contorted his face into the most explicit exhibits of agony I had ever been witness to.

After a half hour of this torturous treatment Wilson slipped into a semi-conscious state that allowed me to leave him for a bit and bring in the supplies I needed. Wilson barely stirred as I winched the barrel up into the air and then swung it over the bath, nor did he do much but whine when I opened the drain and the water began to flow outward, leaving him dry and exposed. I went to my friend then and cradled his head. I apologized for the rough treatment, and then implored him to bear with me, for I had to apply an antiseptic to the wounds, and despite his constitution I was quite sure that the process was going to be agonizing. He nodded, and indicated that I should proceed.

I made sure that he was fully contained within the bath and then quickly but carefully struck the plug on the barrel and let its contents flow out over the thing beneath it. There was a pause of silence, broken only by the gurgling sound of the liquid splashing over Wilson and filling the tub. Then there was a sudden agonized gasp, a sinister hiss, and the rush of chemical smoke that began to pour out of the basin and fill the room. I retreated, donning rubber gloves and an apron, and a mask not unlike the one I had used during my service in the war. I had hoped that this part of the procedure would go quietly, but as soon as my mask came down I knew that Wilson would fight it with whatever life he had left.

Through the stream and fumes of muriatic acid the thing that was Wilson exploded up and flailed desperately trying to find a grip and lift himself out of the now caustic bath. The flesh of his face and hand was melting, burning off in great gouts of waxy material that no longer bore any resemblance to skin or muscle. His mouth was open and his screams, filled with fumes and terror and agony echoed through the room. Dismayed, and fearful that despite my orders, his cries would bring others, I gripped his head in my left hand, and plunged it back beneath the acid, careful not to dip my glove in as well. With my right hand I grabbed his and forced it down. In his desperation Wilson worked his hand free reversed the grip and grabbed my wrist, attempting to pull himself up and out using my own strength against me. But the ploy failed, for something deep within the bath gave out, and Wilson's upper body slipped and went deeper into the tub. I released the grip that I had had on his head just as I felt his eyes explode, and whipped it out to safety. But my right hand, held tightly in a death grip, fell in, and the glove that I had hoped would protect me instead filled up with the burning fluid, and began to eat away at my own arm. I stifled a scream and plunged my free hand back into the bath and pried Wilson's fingers off of my wrist. Free, I collapsed backwards, and let the acid bath dissolve what was left of the thing that was once my friend.

That was how I burned my arm, and it is why my fingers are broken and my hand trembles. I have done what I can to repair the damage, but I fear there is a component I may have overlooked, one that may influence the long-term ability of those treated with the reagent to repair physical damage. There is I suspect a psychological component, one that may be mediated by strong emotions, particularly negative emotions. I think perhaps given a significant psychological shock, such as guilt or despair, the body may choose not to undergo the processes that allow it to repair itself. This is why my arm has not healed properly and why it twitches and fumbles like a dying fish. It may also explain why poor Wilson had suffered the way he did with no sign of recovery, or repair. He must have succumbed, psychologically that is, to what was done to him, and given in to despair. I cannot blame him, what man, even one who had been reanimated, could go through such an ordeal and remain unchanged by it? I understand too why Pulver, that thing that was imprisoned here, chose Wilson as his victim, no normal man would have survived as long as Wilson, and no man would have remained fresh as long either.

Pulver had eaten a cat a day, and based on what he had done to Wilson, he must have moderated his intake, controlled himself as much as he could, and eaten just the barest of what he needed. Even so, it was too much, the damage whether physical or psychological was beyond comprehension. I suppose it must have driven Wilson mad. For even bearing witness to his condition drove me to desperate measures. For it was only his arm, shoulder and face that my friend would willingly show to me, the rest was hidden by the darkness and blankets. That is until I threw them back and revealed the secrets beneath. Oh how I wish I hadn't, for that sight still burns inside my brain. There in the fullness of the light and no longer secreted beneath the blankets was what Pulver had left of my friend. The head, the right shoulder and arm were all that was left intact. The left arm, the torso, the pelvis and legs, all of these had been eaten away, with only bones tethered to each other by tough, nearly inedible ligaments. Even the organs, the liver, the kidneys and intestines, were gone. Only Wilson's heart, still beating, but pumping but a fraction of its capacity, and a single lung remained intact. That he had survived at all was a testament to the man's determination, but I could not allow him to suffer so, and so did what had to be done. That it cost me the use of my right arm seems a small price to pay.

CHAPTER 7

From the Account of Robert Martin Olmstead
"At the Threshold"

In time Moses Sargent returned with a small plate of hearty New England fare and a clean set of clothes. He gave me a brief period to eat and clean up before escorting me down the hall. I had a suspicion that I was underground, perhaps deep underground, for there were no windows or intruding sounds from the street, and as we walked this suspicion grew. The hallway led to stairs and we followed the spiraling and worn stone steps deeper into the earth. Down we went and as we did the walls became first damp, and then moist. Another flight and rivulets of water seemed to run out of the walls themselves and formed veritable streams and torrents. We must have been below the Miskatonic or have intruded into the flow of some underground tributary. Eventually the stairs ended and we found ourselves in a great subterranean cavern through which an artificial channel had been cut to gather the flowing groundwater and feed it into a large circular pool. Around this pool were dozens of Deep Ones, ragged and thin, once proud creatures now in the most deplorable of states. They looked at me as we marched past. I felt their eyes on me and couldn't help but wonder if they were passing judgment on me.

Eventually we passed through a great archway, down another hall and into a well-appointed room hung with deep burgundy curtains and oriental rugs covering the floor. There was a fireplace, and a fire to warm the room. Above the mantle I recognized the stern countenance of Captain Obed Marsh in an aging sepia print. On each side of the captain hung painted portraits from the 1700s which showed two obviously learned men in fine period dress. Each was identified by a small brass plaque, on the right was Edmund Carter and on the left was Joseph Curwen, two names I was wholly unfamiliar with.

In the center of the room was a grand table carved from a slab of coral rock and polished so as to highlight the imbedded and fossilized remains of a myriad of sea creatures. At the table sat the man who had tended my wounds, Doctor Stuart Hartwell, and the tall Indian who had helped rescue me the other evening. At the head of the table sat a woman smartly dressed in a man's pinstripe suit with a tie and handkerchief that matched her dark black, almost blue hair cut fashionably short. She had a Mediterranean complexion, with large eyes, full lips and a small nose. It had been suppressed, possibly she was like me with only one parent carrying the trait, but there was no denying that she had the Innsmouth look.

I found a chair and as I sat, the young woman rose and began to speak. "Gentlemen,' she said in a smoky and seductive voice, "As you know our operative in Innsmouth, Aaron Sargent, has been lost to us." There came a sad murmur from Moses, which she quickly stifled with a simple gesture. "Mr. Sargent was critical to my plan, and I am left with no choice but to recruit someone else." Her hand gestured in my direction. "Robert Olmstead may not be the most experienced of individuals, but given his past and his desire for penitence, I believe him to be more than adequate for our needs. One could say he is highly motivated to make amends for his betrayal of Innsmouth. If he is ever to go into the sea and down to Y'ha-nthlei he will have to have done something to repair his reputation."

Confused, I protested and rose to the occasion. "My apologies, to all of you, but I don't understand what is going on here, and I am not sure that I want to. All I want to do is to make it to the coast, to go into the sea, to be with my family. They are waiting for me, they've prepared a place. Y'ha-nthlei will forever be my home."

The woman stared down into my eyes with a look that chilled my very soul. "Indeed Mr. Olmstead, we all want to go home, one way or the other, but thanks to your earlier actions we must bide our time and each suffer our own tormented delays. If we move too quickly our plans may become apparent, and our hopes of turning this manor into a safe house for refugees will be compromised." She paused allowing me to settle back into my chair. "You did this Mr. Olmstead. Your panicked dash from Innsmouth, your report to the federal authorities, you destroyed decades of planning, undermined our operations, and dashed our best hopes. Our forces have been devastated and scattered across the country. You've forced me to assume control, a role I do not relish, as I suspect you know. Now I play whatever pieces I have left. I marshal our resources, and recruit champions where I can. This is your fault Mr. Olmstead, so you will forgive me if I don't make your wants and needs my priority. There are more important things. Far more important things, and we will need you to help us."

Suddenly Doctor Hartwell spoke up, "Help us with what Asenath?" The young lady shot him a disapproving look. "I don't mean to be rude Miss Waite, and I do appreciate all you've done, and I am happy to help with the poor souls that move through here, but what exactly is it you've gathered us for?"

So this was Asenath Waite. The woman whose name was so prominently mentioned in the manuscript I had smuggled out of Innsmouth, the woman whose own writings revealed her to be more than she appeared, much more. If those pages I had read were to be believed she was not the beautiful young woman she appeared to be, but rather was a wizard, an ancient warlock who had kept himself alive for hundreds of years by leaping from body to body, until he was forced to exact vengeance on those who had wronged him and his daughter. He occupied her body now, and it seemed he had grown comfortable in it. Asenath Waite's voice and mannerisms made it clear that she was the dominant force in the room, and I wondered if anyone else knew her secret.

"There are threats, dire threats that all of Innsmouth had been preparing to move against. Now thanks to Mr. Olmstead, only a few of us remain, and while other forces have acted, our enemies have not been entirely vanquished. In the shadowy, forgotten parts of the world they still fester and grow. Man has intruded on places that should have been inaccessible and awoken things that we had hoped would remain asleep a little longer. If we don't act, the world as we know it may have only days before it is exposed to forces beyond its comprehension."

The resplendent Indian leaned back in his chair. "You propose an adventure then Miss Waite, *tkrt*, a quest, a mission to save the world. What strange players you have chosen, *tkrt* and what strange parts you have given us in this drama. A witch, a changeling, a mad scientist, even a poet imprisoned in a form that is not his own. What would you have us be Waite, heroes? I see no heroes here, only monsters."

Asenath stared at the massive Indian, and I swear I saw venom in her eyes, but only for an instant. "Find me heroes then Chandraputra. Who should we recruit? Armitage is too old and Wilmarth flees at the first hint of something outré. This age, what Mr. Hoover calls the Great Depression, is sorely lacking. I look to recruit heroes and I find only monsters. I admit it is a weird company I am forced to draft into service, but it seems to be my only choice."

The Indian rose to his full height which was easily seven feet, perhaps even eight, and towered over the table. "I have been to war once before Waite, *tkrt* I went willingly and for a cause I believed in. I will not be drafted to blindly serve in your so-called Weird Company."

Doctor Hartwell stood to speak his peace as well. "I agree. I have helped you out of respect Waite, out of appreciation for what you have done for me, but you cannot think of us as your soldiers. Unlike Olmstead, we need not perform any acts of contrition, there is a limit to what we owe you and yours."

Asenath leaned forward. "When I make the threat plain Doctor, you will change your minds." She paused. "Regardless, your reluctance is not unexpected. If you are unwilling to assist me out of duty, I am prepared to compensate each of you handsomely. You Doctor, I assume that you have overcome Muñoz's dissolution constant, but have you resolved what Charriere referred to as cerebral degeneration?"

Hartwell was suddenly flustered. "No. From what I can tell, my oldest test subjects are already experiencing the early symptoms of synaptic failure."

Asenath smiled but I found no comfort in it. "I can tell you that this problem has been solved, at least in a manner. Count Ferenzcy has agreed to collaborate with you on human trials. As for you Swami Chandraputra, we offer you an essentially unlimited supply of the elixir you need to suppress the more, shall we say antisocial, components of your persona. Additionally, I can tell you the location of the Orinoco Clock." The Swami Chandraputra sat back down and Asenath seemed once more to be in control of the situation. "I'm glad these terms are agreeable." There followed a general murmur of reluctant acceptance from my two compatriots.

Yet while Hartwell and Chandraputra seemed satisfied, I was not. I looked around the room in frustration. "You speak of an impending doom, one that threatens all mankind. There are only four of us Miss Waite, what would you have us do?"

Waite smiled. "First we are going to rescue one of our allies, one who has been lost to us for a short time. He wandered away and was caught by a most cunning spider. Then we are going to do what the Deep Ones have done every time cosmic horrors have seeped down and clawed at this fragile sphere Mr. Olmstead."

I was feeling arrogant, emboldened even. Do not ask me why. "What pray tell is that?"

For a moment I thought I saw the mask slip, I thought I saw old Ephraim peek out behind the guise of Asenath that he wore so well. "We are going to save the world Mr. Olmstead. We are going to save the world, and with some luck most of the lives that dwell upon it!"

CHAPTER 8
From the Account of Robert Martin Olmstead
"The Prisoner of the Witch House"

It was after midnight when I and my three compatriots made the trek from Crowninshield Manor through the streets of Arkham. We took mostly back streets and alleyways, careful to avoid being seen by any insomniac townspeople or the few policemen who roamed about at these hours. Arkham in the early hours of March 13th, 1931, was a desolate, lonely place. It is not without good cause that they call the town witch-haunted. Even those such as myself cannot help but shudder at what rumors suggest lurked in the walls and attics of our destination. Dr. Hartwell confessed that he had met at least one of those involved, and that the young man told a horrific tale of centuries-old madness and creeping terror that ended in the gruesome death of one, and the terror of the other. Hartwell had treated the boy, that is until events played out and Hartwell himself was confined. It had been two and a half years since Hartwell had last seen Frank Elwood, and the Doctor admitted he owed the young man a debt of gratitude, and when Asenath had revealed his condition, the Doctor was the first to agree to attempt a rescue. Thus the four of us, myself, Dr. Hartwell, Asenath Waite, and the Swami Chandraputra marched under cover of darkness to the derelict and ill-rumored Witch House.

One would have thought, given Elwood's accounts of Walter Gilman's encounter, and eventual defeat of the witch Keziah Mason, that the rumors and stories concerning the old place would have abated. Sadly such hopes would be unfounded, for although it seemed that Mason had been banished, the death of Gilman at the hands of an obscene and voracious rat had added new facets to the lore about the place. The fact that the city fathers ordered the place shuttered did not help its reputation either. And then there were the strange sounds, the wailing moans and the fumbling steps that seemed to emanate from somewhere within the boarded up structure, but where exactly none could say. Few doubted that Keziah Mason was gone, but it seemed clear something else had taken up residence.

Standing outside the ancient, moldering edifice I felt a pang of fear, and wondered not for the first time how it was that I was most qualified for the task that was before us? Hartwell knew Elwood, was he not a better candidate? It seemed not, for the man's beliefs regarding the location of consciousness in the body, and the ability to separate the two, disqualified him. Chandraputra, who claimed to be a mystic, acknowledged the ability of the mind to leave the body, and claimed to have done just so many times, but declined the opportunity to demonstrate it here and now. There was, he said, a consciousness that was waiting for him to do just that, and if he were to let down his defenses he would be lost to us, and as great an ally as he was, he could also become an implacable foe. As for Asenath, she too claimed that there were risks, terrible risks involved with her mind leaving her body. I, she was quick to point out, had become an adept dreamer, able to control not only my own psyche, but the psychic landscape about me. This I could not deny, for the years of nightmares and maddening dreams that I had suffered through had forced me to develop certain skills, powers of the psyche that normal men did not possess. It is, I suppose, the nature of the minds of the Deep Ones to be strange, why should that of Robert Martin Olmstead, a hybrid, be any different?

We made our way to the back of the house, and after prying off several boards, we broke the cheap lock that secured the door and forced our way into the kitchen. The place reeked of decay, and assaulted my heightened senses making me gag. Wood rot had set in, and the air was thick with the spores of mold and fungi. There was also an insect smell, termites perhaps? But above it all there was the undeniable musky stench of rat piss. As we moved from the kitchen into the dining room, I would have thought that the room would have been stripped, that looters would have stolen anything of value or use. Surprisingly, that was not the case for a large table with a dozen mismatched chairs that still occupied the space. True they were shoddy, and had been shoddy to begin with, but they would serve our purpose, or at least mine. Hartwell produced a small towel from his medical bag and used it to wipe the table clear, while Chandraputra set about lighting a few candles to provide a least a modicum of illumination. Asenath then proceeded to prepare a tincture by crushing some leaves and forcing them into a small flask which she then covered with water. A pair of tongs was used to suspend the mixture over a candle and bring it to a low boil. I relaxed as much as I could, and lay out on the table. I wanted to close my eyes, but sadly my slow metamorphosis had removed my eyelids, thus I was forced to stare at the weird, inky shadows cast by the flickering candlelight.

Asenath transferred a measure of her tincture to a small glass dropper, which glowed almost golden as the candlelight passed through it. "Don't worry," she told me, "it's only a mild dosage. It should help you reach the dreaming faster, and give you more control over things once you get there. Remember, everything you will see is a dream; it's all in your mind, or in the minds of the things that have taken up residence here. Don't engage in any physical conflict, you're not prepared for that, besides whoever is in control here has a distinct advantage. The world you are about to enter, they created it; you are just an intruder, and probably an unwelcome one. Find Elwood and get him out as fast as you can. The exit might not be obvious, it might be wholly symbolic, a door, a gate, a ladder. When you come back, your mind will be returning to your body, but for Elwood, his physical form has been translated into dream entirely, bringing him back will be shocking, transformative, and probably painful. He won't want to do it; you might have to force him."

I nodded, opened my mouth and lifted my tongue. I felt the three drops of fluid trickle in, and the bitterness caused my throat to close, and my gills to flex open with an audible wet hiss. This must have startled Asenath and the others, because I heard them all take a few steps back. I laid there for a few minutes waiting for the elixir to take effect, all the while continuing to watch the shadow play swirling about on the ceiling. In the distance I could hear the rats scurrying through the walls and climbing through the rafters. A small flock of pigeons shifted about as wind whistled in through a broken window. Somewhere below me, perhaps in a cellar or crawlspace, something larger than a rat stalked across a gravel floor. On the ceiling above the table the shadows faded and then dissolved into an inky darkness. The candlelight grew dim and was replaced by a multitude of tiny flickering pinpricks that faded in and out of sight as strange massive shapes slid across the ceiling.

I turned my head and called out to Asenath but she wasn't there. Hartwell and Chandraputra were gone as well. Indeed the entire room was suddenly missing, and as I rose from the table even that dissolved away. The ceiling where once candlelight and shadows had played out was now a nightmare sky of roiling clouds and pale, dead stars; around me stood an ersatz Arkham, but one only seen in nightmares. Great dead trees bent and piles of fallen leaves rustled in response to an absent wind which howled and whined, but could not be felt. Long shadows were cast by squat, angry houses that sat on lots of sparse, shaggy weeds. Decayed gambrel roofs loomed above broken windows and tattered curtains framed by grey walls of peeling paint. From within, strange voices whispered in a low foreign cacophony like insects crying in the night.

It was a nightmare landscape, and I pitied the mind that produced it. Is this how Elwood saw Arkham? The same monstrous houses everywhere you turned? No choices but the inevitable descent into squalor amongst a cacophony of chattering foreign voices? No wonder you lost yourself. Elwood had studied mathematics and theoretical physics, but these are lonely pursuits, and provide little refuge from the horrors engendered by modern city life. Indeed, looking at the strange angles and geometries that loomed throughout the ersatz Arkham, it seemed that Elwood's studies had in fact contaminated his world view, and added new facets to his anxiety. All these thoughts assumed that it was Elwood's mind that was generating this eldritch milieu, and of course, I had no proof that he was indeed the source.

Steeling my resolve, I moved from the sidewalk and made my way across the small yard that separated the Witch House from the dream street. The door opened of its own accord, creaking slowly and ominously into the house as if inviting me in. As I stepped through the door I took one last look behind me, and I knew that I had no choice but to go inside, for the dream world behind me had simply ceased to be. The interior of the house reeked of death, not of decay like the real house, but of death, fresh, wet and red. Shadows and patches of light careened at random around the foyer. The droning insectile voices grew louder. Something, things really small and brown, moved along the walls, but every time I tried to focus on them they would dart out of sight or vanish into the walls themselves. Doors lined the hallway but they were all shut, the knobs significantly, symbolically absent. The only path to follow was up a wooden staircase ravaged by time and neglect.

Mounting the stairs, I had to catch my balance as the nightmare illusion shifted, the foyer fell away and the hallway and rooms below vanished. I found myself on a surreal staircase suspended in darkness that seemed to stretch endlessly in both directions. The stink that filled the air grew in strength and I gagged as it wormed its way into my senses. With each successive step the runners warped and creaked and as I shifted my weight from step to step the entire staircase shuddered. I climbed faster, moving smoothly and swiftly up the stairs, ignoring the creaks and bone-jarring snaps of wooden supports that Frank Elwood's mind had manufactured. Soon I was running, pounding up the stairs with only my heartbeat and the sound of my own breath to fill my ears and my mind. But no matter how fast or with how much purpose I ran, the view never changed. Though I climbed hundreds, perhaps thousands of stairs, no landing, no door, no end ever came within sight.

I paused. I knew the stairwell was nothing more than a symbol, a representation of the isolation of Elwood's mind from the world. It could be overcome, but how? The stairs were endless, climbing seemed fruitless and was getting me nowhere. I drew a deep if imaginary breath, and firmed my resolve to reach the top of the stairs. That was all it took to change the scene. I recognized the rules and then was suddenly no longer bound by them. The stairs were gone and I was standing on a wooden landing facing a single closed door. Thankfully, this one had a knob. The door itself was old, and covered in flaking chips of paint that once were white but were now a dirty grey. The wood itself was pocked, riddled with holes where worms and other things had crawled and burrowed through it. The knob and the plate behind it were green with verdigris. I reached for the decaying metal; it was cold and felt wrong in my hand, as if touching it was a forbidden thing.

I gave the knob a firm twist, to no avail; the door was locked, and my attempts to gain entry merely rattled in futility. The sound of the lock was replaced by the sound of movement from within the room. Papers rustled and something skittered across the floor. With no other recourse, I knocked gently and called, "Is someone in there?" I heard more rustling, followed by a low mewling sound, then strong distinct footsteps that drew close. I stepped back as the door unlocked and swung wide open.

Framed in the doorway was a haggard young man that bore little resemblance to how I had thought Frank Elwood would appear. His eyes were sunken and his hair greasy and unkempt. His face was unshaven. He wore a wrinkled shirt that showed several large stains and obvious frays around the collar and cuffs. His hands were covered with scabbed-over scratches and his nails were long, broken and dirty. The fingers were covered with fine white chalk. His pants were overly large and his belt was pulled tight. He wore no shoes or socks and his yellowed toe nails were overgrown.

The sad sickly man opened his mouth in obvious frustration and shouted. "I told the landlady I would have her rent on the morrow!" Spittle flew as he spoke. "Now leave me alone!"

I spoke back calmly. "I'm not here about the rent. I'm here to offer you a job."

The figure peered back at me suspiciously. "I can't. I haven't finished!" His voice became a sing-song of nonsense and he rushed back into the room. With a clear view of the interior I was shocked to discover the extent of the madness that had consumed this wretch. Beyond the door every surface of the room was covered, inscribed, imbedded with arcane mathematical formulae. To make matters worse, the writings were two or three layers thick with pencil being covered by ink, which in turn was covered by chalk. Though I recognized some of the esoteric mathematical symbols, the vast majority of the writings had smeared into an undecipherable mess.

"Dr. Hartwell sent me to find you. We need your help young sir," I pleaded as chalk was once more taken to the wall. "The world is in danger."

"Hee Hee," a manic whispered reply. "The world is always in danger. What makes today something special?"

Something rustled in the corner as I approached. There was a weak chattering noise from beneath a pile of papers. "Mr. Elwood please pay attention."

The writing never stopped. "I'm not . . ." More rustling drowned out the man's whisper.

I shook my head quickly, "What did you say?"

Chalk and spit flew as the man turned to me enraged. "I AM NOT ELWOOD YOU TOAD! IF YOU WANT ELWOOD GO LOOK IN THE CORNER! NOW LEAVE ME ALONE!"

I fell backwards into the pile of newspapers and something squealed and then squirmed out from beneath. I cautiously pushed the papers away, only to recoil at the horror hidden beneath. It was the size of a cat, or a small dog, and was entirely devoid of clothes. Its pale skin was sickly and covered with bites and bleeding sores. It looked up at me with huge green eyes from a horrid parody of a human face, a face that I recognized as belonging to none other than Frank Elwood.

With some difficulty it opened its mouth and chattered out "Heeelp Meeee, pleasee."

I stared at the rat thing and then at the figure writing on the wall. "If this is Elwood, then who are you?"

The figure paused in obvious frustration and then threw down the chalk. "You really are quite bothersome you know." He reached down and in a single movement wrenched the wooden arm off of a chair and drew it up menacingly. "If you must know, when I was alive, they called me Walter Gilman. Now that I am dead, I have no name, though the things that haunt this world have given me a title, they call me The Student." He took a step toward me. "I wonder what they will call you, once you are dead."

I rose up on my feet clutching the Elwood rat to my chest. "Frank, listen to me." The thing lolled in my arms. "This isn't real, it's just an illusion, a fantasy generated by your mind. You have the power here!"

Walter Gilman, or some facsimile thereof, stalked forward. "Oh I assure you that poor Frank is in no position to assert any sort of control in this place. You see he feels quite guilty, distraught really, over my death. He blames himself, and rightfully so. I was a brilliant student, I would have revolutionized the study of spatial and temporal physics, and I would have given mankind the ability to conquer the world, the galaxy, the universe, perhaps even time itself." He looked at the Elwood rat in disgust and gestured with his makeshift club. "He let me die. Cut short my studies. And then had the gall to return to classes, to study, to write up his thesis, and to graduate with honors. I am The Student, and that rat bastard dares to obtain his Master's degree? I will not allow my work to be forgotten while he is allowed to live!"

He swung the club which I dodged easily, and while he was still caught up in the momentum I dashed out the door and onto the landing. The stairs, indeed an entire house had appeared, and with some trepidation I barreled down the steps, taking them two at a time, all the while trying to hold on to the struggling creature in my arms. "Hold still Elwood, I'm going to get you out of here, but you have to help me." I launched down past another floor, looking at the doors that all seemed to lead nowhere. "This place is an illusion, but it is also an allusion as well. The city, the house, the stairs, they're all allegories for what has been happening to you. You're trapped in the past, feeling guilty over what happened to Gilman. You've become so obsessed by it that you've recreated him, imagined him to be alive once more, but you're overshadowed by his monstrous genius, or at least that is how you perceive it. Therefore he's taken over, and turned your mind into a prison where he can work forever, and you are condemned to be little more than vermin rustling in the corner."

Gilman's voice boomed down the stairwell, "A fine bit of psychoanalysis but ultimately useless. There is nothing you can do to save Elwood, and you sir are still going to die."

I reached the ground floor and leapt from the stairs and toward the front door. It was closed but the handle was unlocked and the door swung free. With Elwood clutched in my arms I flung myself headlong out of the Witch House and into the street of dreams. But the street as I knew it was gone; indeed all of the dream Arkham had vanished. Instead of on a city street I was on the terrace of some immense building overlooking a city so vast that I could see buildings stretching to the horizon. I thought for a moment that I was in some dream metropolis, a utopia generated by Gilman's mind, for about me everywhere where the signs of an obsessive mind. The edifices, the architecture, the monuments and features all revolved around one single number, the number five. Pentagonal motifs decorated the buildings which were themselves five-sided. Behind me a five-sided doorway led from the terrace into a corridor which itself was comprised of five walls. Beneath my feet the terrace itself was comprised of interlocking pentagonal tiles. I stood up and wondered where in the world we were.

"A colony world of the Q'Hrell," Elwood's weak voice replied. "That is not their real name, it translates as the Progenitors. They are an ancient and learned race, so old that they have forgotten more about the universe than mankind has learned. Their dominion spans whole galaxies, and they have seeded life on millions of planets: sometimes to grow food, sometimes to create slaves, sometimes to provide a home, and sometimes simply because they can. When those from Xoth filtered down from the stars, it was the Q'Hrell who waged war against them and finally sank their stronghold into the sea. It was the Q'Hrell who brought forth the lizard kings and their avatar, and then crucified him for his disobedience. It was the Q'Hrell that taught Keziah Mason the secrets of moving through space. It was through them that she was able to survive as long as she did. Their blood is particularly potent; it makes them nearly immortal, and can even reanimate the dead flesh of any of their creations. They are powerful allies, and dangerous enemies."

I looked at Elwood; he seemed slightly more human than previously. "And these things commune with Gilman?"

He shook his furry head. "These are just more hallucinations, fantasies created by Gilman to populate his dream world. He communes with them, but they are no more real than anything else here. That doesn't make them any less dangerous than the real thing, in fact more so."

"Why is that?"

"Isn't it obvious? As constructs of Gilman's mind they do whatever he says." Something dark passed in front of the sun. "Oh, by the way, the Q'Hrell, they can fly."

That is when I saw them: a whole flock of the creatures spinning through the sky like some horrid cross between squid and sharks pin wheeling on five great pulsing wings. They moved through the air in great arcs like raptors spiraling in for a final killing swoop. There were dozens of the things, but they all seemed to be moving in formation, a complex aerial ballet that was as beautiful as it was most probably deadly.

I turned back to look at Elwood. "How do we get back to the Witch House? How do we get out of the dream?"

"There's no way out," he whimpered. "Gilman has complete control. He always knew what he was doing. He was so smart. It's no wonder that Keziah picked him to be her disciple. Here in this place he can do anything, be anything he wants to. Compared to him, I am nothing."

"That's not true," I said. Suddenly I was running again, this time I was moving up. The terrace had turned into a ramp, and while going down might have seemed the more logical thing to do, somehow running up seemed more right. "It's I that can't do anything here," I said. Around me the terrace ramp turned into stairs, I was back in the Witch House. "But you, you Elwood, you are the real power here."

Behind us something large and grey slammed onto the stairs and screamed in a high-pitched whine that sounded like a mad flutist. There was a tune, a rhythm that filled me with fear, but despite my desire to cower in terror I ran faster while the thing behind us whistled insanely, "Tekelili Tekelili!"

I was pounding up the stairs. My legs felt like lead weights and my lungs, as inhuman as they were, seemed ready to burst. As I drove up the staircase, the wood screeched and groaned, the railing fell away, and once more I was left climbing into nothingness. I brought Elwood up so that I could speak to him plainly. "Elwood, I understand how you got this way. Gilman's genius was immense. His understanding of space and time was unprecedented. His accomplishments were unparalleled. Anyone would shrink to nothingness in comparison. Yet for all his genius he made mistakes Elwood, he was after all only human."

The beast behind us roared. I could see it. On the stairs it moved like a great cat, propelled by a series of small tentacles near its head, if one could call that starfish-shaped thing a head, and another set of larger tentacles in the rear. Even when moving like this, it still was spiraling around, drilling itself forward, the wings of the thing still pulsing open and closed as they rotated about. It was faster than I would have thought possible, but of course that is almost always the case when it came to monsters. In moments it would be upon us.

"Elwood," I was pleading, "listen to me. Gilman died, he failed. He beat Keziah Mason, but he overlooked Brown Jenkin, and overlooking something like that can mean everything. He may have been brilliant, even a genius, but he wasn't a god. He failed to consider all the facts and factors, and because of that he not only died, but he was condemned to be trapped forever. You on the other hand have done things that Gilman can't, and never will." He looked at me with those strange violet eyes. "You lived Elwood. You went through those same horrid events, and you lived. Gilman can't ever do that again. He's dead, he'll never be alive again. And because you lived you were able to move on."

The beast on the stairs spun toward us and unraveled as it did so. The strange piping that called through the air transformed into a now familiar voice, the booming sound of Walter Gilman screaming at us, at me. "BE QUIET YOU FOOL!" The Q'Hrell was gone, now only Gilman was rushing up at us.

But I wouldn't be quiet. "You finished your coursework Frank. You finished your papers. You earned your degree. You lived, you graduated, and you have your degree. That means you are no longer the second-rate student; you are no longer even a student. You are a distinguished graduate of Miskatonic University. You have a Master's degree. You're not a student anymore. That thing down there, Gilman, The Student, that is all he will ever be, but you Frank, you're not a student, you are a master! Gilman will never achieve that!"

The Elwood thing hissed as he leapt from my arms. He flew through the air, striking Gilman and latching onto his chest just below his throat. "You are dead!" the Elwood rat cried out, and then there was a flash of red. Blood flew through the air and Elwood disappeared beneath Gilman's shirt.

Gilman screamed. There was a moist sucking sound as he drew in breath and let loose a horrendous, pitiful cry. The Student spasmed, his back arched over and then cracked as he fell to the floor thrashing about and whining in the most horrible of manners. There was a wet gurgling noise, and Gilman's throat swelled and his mouth opened wide as the thrashing ceased and blood leaked steadily out of Gilman's eyes and nose. The jaw cracked as the mouth opened wider. Two hands suddenly thrust themselves out of the broken mouth scattering yellow teeth across the stairs. The hands forced their way out and then reached back to grab the sides of Gilman's face. They pulled and as they did so two arms wrenched out of Gilman's head. There was a cracking noise, and I watched as Gilman's legs collapsed upwards into his body. The arms were followed by a gore-covered head and shoulders, and I watched in rapt horror as the body inverted itself. Time is meaningless in dreams, but it seemed mere moments for the thing that was once Walter Gilman to transform itself, to rend itself inside out and cease to be what it once was. When it was finally over, the flesh was no longer that of Walter Gilman; in his place lay the hideously reborn form of Frank Elwood.

I helped the young man to his feet, and together we stumbled up the stairs. We found the landing and there where he had been imprisoned for so long I apologized to the poor creature. As I spoke, he looked at me with the most confused of looks. I almost stopped, almost took pity on the poor thing, but in the end I knew there was no going back. Elwood had his part to play, just like I did. We needed him, and there was no point in putting off the inevitable. "I'm sorry Frank, but there is going to be some pain." I maneuvered him to the edge and then removed my arms from beneath his. "Birth is painful. Life is painful. Death is painful." One quick shove and Elwood fell silently down the stairs and tumbled head over bloody heels into the abyss. "Why should your rebirth be any different?"

As Frank Elwood fell out of his dreams, so did I. The nightmare version of the house dissolved, and in an instant I was back in the real world lying on the table of the real Witch House. Asenath and Hartwell had Elwood wrapped in blankets and were shepherding him out the back door. All around me debris was raining down. Chandraputra swept me off the table and into his arms just as a portion of the ceiling came crashing down. Something about those arms didn't feel right, but as he rushed me out the kitchen door I was just grateful that he had been there. Outside on the street there was a great wind blowing, as if a gale had come off of the ocean and rolled into town, but the wind wasn't blowing from the east, it was blowing from the windows of the Witch House itself.

Glass exploded onto the street as something snapped inside the ancient edifice. Elwood's dreaming had been powerful, so powerful that it had given life to his dead friend, and helped support the place where he had died. But now that dream was gone, and the power that had created and fortified the psychic architecture was gone as well. Without Elwood, the roof of the decrepit house collapsed, and with it the great chimney tumbled down as well. We watched as a chaos of crumbling bricks, shingles and rotting timbers crashed down into the house and blew moldy debris all over the overgrown lot.

As the five of us fled back through the streets in those wee hours, we seemed content with what had been done. Elwood smiled, but said little. The Witch House still stood, but it was no longer the ominous threat it had been. Keziah Mason was dead, and so was her rebellious student Walter Gilman, and his dream-spawned doppelganger. It was true that Brown Jenkin, Keziah's rat-thing, was missing, but without his mistress he seemed to have retreated from the world. More importantly, Frank Elwood was no longer a prisoner of his past regrets. Only the city itself bore witness to our deeds that night, and though I like to think we accomplished something, the truth be told, Arkham is, and always shall be, Witch-Haunted: one witch more or less, real or imagined, I suppose makes little difference.

CHAPTER 9

From the Account of Robert Martin Olmstead
"The Creeping Shadows"

I slept through the next day, and the night after that. On the second morning I rose with the sun and ate breakfast with Dr. Hartwell. I asked after Elwood and was told that he was recovering very quickly, and would be joining us soon. As for Chandraputra, the swami always ate in private. Asenath on the other hand rarely slept, but ate voraciously, often devouring substantial meals five or six times daily. I joked about how perhaps she was eating for two. Hartwell didn't find my quip funny and the way he looked at me made me very uncomfortable. Without knowing why it was necessary I apologized and for the rest of the meal we said nothing more to one another.

Chandraputra came for us and together the three of us descended once more to the hall where Asenath and Elwood were waiting. Elwood looked well. His skin color was slightly pale and his hair wild and unkempt, but dressed in a charcoal suit over a white shirt with a matching tie, one would not know that he had recently been released from his weird incarceration inside the Witch House, or that he had been rescued just a day or so before. As before, Asenath sat at the head of the table wearing the same pin-stripe suit she had sported when I first met her.

"As I have said before, there is a dire threat," announced Asenath, "one that requires immediate attention." At Asenath's proclamation the table rapidly came to order. "Men have travelled to places they were not meant to be, seen things they were not meant to see, and awakened horrors that the world is not yet prepared for. Innsmouth was supposed to intervene in such affairs, but as a result of the occupation our forces are diminished."

I seized on the pause and demanded answers, "You have danced around the truth Waite, but I have had enough. What happened in Innsmouth, and why? Why after thousands of years did the Deep Ones suddenly decide to come out of hiding?"

Asenath sighed in annoyance, "I suppose telling you is of no consequence, you are owed the truth, or at least some of it. Decades ago we were made aware of a threat; a man had established a rudimentary form of contact with the something from outside. That thing drove him and his children insane, and they became deluded by visions of power. They became determined to bring this thing into our own universe. Doing so would have changed the very laws of reality, not only for men, but for all of us. We moved to intervene, but ages beneath the sea had made most Deep Ones unable to function at the surface. Many desperate attempts were made and ended disastrously. A new generation was needed, one able to move about in both the shallows of the sea and on land. In desperation a bargain was struck with the men of Innsmouth. The town was to withdraw from the world, cut itself off and become forgotten. The Deep Ones would interbreed with the townsfolk, and in exchange they would be given great wealth, and their children would be nearly immortal, and they would form the ranks of those needed to stop the intrusion from outside."

"Why not simply attack preemptively?" interjected Elwood.

Asenath nodded. "We considered that, but our allies, those who could see the possible futures, all warned against such options. To move too soon would have revealed our presence and created a nightmare future for our species. Only by intervening at the last possible second could we have established ourselves as man's ally instead of his enemy."

Hartwell's eyes grew bright. "You are talking about what happened in Dunwich!"

"Yes, not that it matters now," commented Asenath in a derogatory manner. "The plan failed. Innsmouth was too large, too uncontrollable. Too many people left the village, and too many came to visit. The isolation was incomplete. Too many questions were asked. Men came and the town was unprepared to move against them. Now, Innsmouth is trapped, lost to the currents, unable to rise up as needed."

I was confused, and begged for an explanation. "Why would we Deep Ones fear such a thing? Wouldn't this herald the return of Cthulhu? Wouldn't we once more have dominion over all the Earth?"

The room filled with a sudden palpable dread, and I watched as Asenath exchanged furtive glances with the others gathered around the table. Apparently I had sad something I shouldn't have.

It was Swami Chandraputra who finally broke the oppressive silence with his odd monotonous voice. "Robert, there are things *tkrt* that you believe to be true, that are not. This is not your fault *tkrt*. Your education on these things is incomplete, a hodge-podge of *tkrt* legends and racial memories that can be interpreted *tkrt* in a dozen ways. Tonight we will speak of true *tkrt* things. The truths *tkrt* you think you know *tkrt* are about to change." He seemed to settle down into his robes, and he shrank slightly, as if somehow a chair had appeared beneath him and he had eased himself into it.

Chandraputra took a deep, almost mechanical breath and in some strange manner changed his voice to become more soothing. Through some supreme effort the monotonous tone was gone and the clicking noises vanished. "Thousands of years ago, men believed the world to be flat. They believed the Earth was the center of the universe. They believed that everything in the universe was comprised of four elemental forces. Science, human science, has changed all that. A globular world orbits the sun in a universe comprised of scores of elements. Man's view of the world, of the solar system, of the universe has changed. The old texts have been replaced."

"Sadly, while science has moved forward, man's understanding of the paranormal has remained stagnant. The works of Alhazred, Prinn and Von Junzt are held out as infallible sources, beyond reproach. No one bothers to check the so-called facts in these muddled hermetic diatribes. Even those who are privy to some of the secrets of this world, who have parted the veils and held onto their minds, still fail to see the truth. They see so little, understand less, and so assume too much."

I was forced to interrupt, "What you are implying is that even we who have been touched by the outré forces of the universe are just as ignorant as the rest?"

"You Mr. Olmstead are a perfect example, you dance on the brink and think you understand, you've gleaned a little knowledge and suddenly you think you have the key to all the mysteries of the universe. You saw Innsmouth, and the images of Cthulhu and assumed so much, too much it seems. From this you extrapolated even further and assume that the Deep Ones would find an ally in the foulness that men know as Yog-Sothoth, not understanding the devastation his entry into our universe would cause." He paused, but only for a moment. "Were Yog-Sothoth to claw his way into this universe chaos would ensue. The laws of the cosmos as we know them would cease to function. The laws of thermodynamics, cause and effect, gravity, would not only radically change, but be in a constant state of flux. Can you imagine such a universe? How would earthly life survive? Not just men, but all things. Our biologies may be different, but they all follow the same physical and chemical principles. Men could not survive such a change, any more than the Deep Ones or even those from Xoth. Cthulhu and his dreaded spawn may tap into the power that is Yog-Sothoth, just as the Progenitors had done once to create the Shoggothim, but to release him would cause the universe itself to shatter."

I lowered my head, "Have we no allies?"

Chandraputra chuckled, "Not as you think of them. To be sure there are those who are like us, children of the Progenitors, the Q'Hrell. The Deep Ones were their servants, their creations, as are man, and the Valusians, and before them the Cthonians. Some would be our allies. As would be the archetypes, the Old Ones, the titans of Earth: Father Dagon and Mother Hydra for certain, Yig and Bokrug are likely as well. The others, Atlatch-Nacha and the like, who can say? The gods of Earth are as multiform as the myriad of creatures that cover this precious little world, and divining their intent and reasoning is beyond us. They are people Mr. Olmstead, individuals; to think that they would all act in unison is simply preposterous. Even amongst the Deep Ones there are divisions.

Some who once stood against Cthulhu and those from Xoth now ally themselves with that they once fought against."

"Traitors to the cause," Asenath snorted in contempt. "Men have heard the Deep Ones pray and assumed we have raised our voices in adulation to the monstrosity, but it is a misinterpretation. 'Cthulhu fhtagn' is not a prayer of admonition, it is one of supplication. We do not worship Cthulhu, we fear him and have stood guard over his prison for hundreds of millions of years! Every Deep One prays that 'Cthulhu dreams,' and will remain that way."

Seizing a pause in the exposition, Elwood demanded an explanation of an event I too was familiar with. "What happened in 1925? The attack from the Alert's crew? What of that strange couplet 'Ph'nglui mglw'nafh Cthulhu R'lyeh wgah'nagl fhtagn' that LeGrasse's cultists were chanting? Does it not translate as, 'In his house at R'lyeh dead Cthulhu waits dreaming.'?"

Again Chandraputra laughed at me. "It is a less than fair translation, there are subtleties that are lost, that change the implications. Perhaps more accurately, I would translate the phrase as 'Entombed in R'lyeh, the undying Cthulhu dreams impatiently.' The expanded translation brings forth the suggestion that Cthulhu is imprisoned against his will. There is a subtlety of language here, a cultural context, which requires deep study. For example, the phrase 'Cthulhu nafl fhtagn,' translates directly as 'Cthulhu no longer dreams,' but it is used by Deep Ones as an idiom when things have gone horribly wrong."

"As for the cultists and the crew of the Alert," interjected Waite, "it has always been implied that they were somehow related to Deep Ones, but what evidence is there for that? Cthulhu has his own servitors, those spawned on Earth using the captured ultra-shoggoth called Idh-Yaa, whom men have known as Yidhra. There are miscegnations of Cthulhu and earthly life: the god-things Ghatanothoa, Ythogtha and Zoth-Ommog. There are others, lesser things, things that can pass for men, and wait patiently for the stars to be right. It was these that crewed the Alert and sought to free their god."

I went to speak, to ask another question, but Asenath roared, "ENOUGH! We have no time to dwell on our past failures or to educate Mr. Olmsted on the secret history of the world. For now we must focus on the task at hand, the peril for which I have assembled what Chandraputra so quaintly calls my Weird Company." The table grew quiet in response to Asenath's forceful plea.

"You may be familiar with reports out of Miskatonic University concerning both the discoveries and tragedies of its Antarctic Expedition. It was these intrepid explorers that set in motion forces that I must now ask you to intervene against. The expedition's leaders, Dyer and Pabodie, had provided a very detailed itinerary for the journey, and if they had kept to the route that they had planned, we would not be having this conversation. Unfortunately, from what I can gather, a small group broke off from the main party and wandered into areas that they should not have. Areas in which the remnants of the Progenitors, the Elder Things, and their technology lay hidden, dead but not dead, dreaming of the future, the past, and even the present. Now they have been disturbed. And while the Progenitors are a force to be reckoned with, it is suggested that something worse moves, and faster than would the Q'Hrell. The shoggoths have been exposed to men, they have consumed some of them, and absorbed their knowledge. They have learned much, and that knowledge is spreading. If they are not stopped, contained, sterilized, they will spread across the world and become a foe unlike any other it has ever known."

"How exactly are we supposed to travel to Antarctica?" questioned Hartwell.

Chandraputra rose up. "I have a ship, large enough to hold all of us, and our supplies. It is hidden near the old *tkrt* Carter Mansion. In space it can move faster than light; here on Earth, bound by gravity, it is considerably slower, but it should get us there safely. I will however need a signal, something to navigate with."

"The expedition left a radio beacon at their base, and the receiver is on Kingsport Head," Waite explained. "That will get us close. Can you fly by sight the rest of the way?"

"I'll have to make some adjustments before I move the ship to the receiver. That will take most of the day. It would be best to do that at night; the sight of my light-ship can be unnerving. I wouldn't want all of Arkham to see it. I'll also have to fine tune things to the specific frequency at the receiver itself. I could be there by midnight and on our way an hour later."

Waite nodded, "Agreed. Chandraputra and Hartwell will go and retrieve the ship. The rest of us will load up the trucks and meet you at Kingsport Head. I'll expect you about midnight."

In retrospect our Weird Company took it all in stride, as if what we had been asked to do was something routine. If we had known what was coming, what was going to happen to us, how some of us would fall before the horrors that seethed and waited in Antarctica, perhaps we would not have gone at all. Perhaps we would have done things differently, perhaps not. But we spent the day preparing for battle, as if that was what we were meant to be doing, as if we had been waiting for this one day for all of our lives.

Knowing what I know now, perhaps this is true. Perhaps the only reason I was born, any of us were born, was to be here in this place at this time, and to do these things. Everything else was simply prologue.

CHAPTER 10

From the Account of Robert Martin Olmstead
"A Night on Kingsport Head"

On the windblown cliffs of Kingsport Head the members of Asenath's Waite's newly formed Weird Company waited and watched while Chandraputra carried out the strange and complex preparations for travel to Antarctica. Most of the work seemed to involve running wires from the base of the newly installed short wave radio tower. It was this tower that provided communication with the Miskatonic University Antarctic Expedition transmission station in Antarctica. Even though the expedition had long since departed from the southern continent, the transmission station still functioned, kept alive by a complement of batteries. To hear Chandraputra explain it, that signal would be our tether to that far away point of the globe, and he would use it to guide his ship from Kingsport Head south to what remained of the University's base camp. From there we would fly inland, following the directions provided by the expedition itself, gleaned from their own radio reports, which Asenath had somehow obtained from the files of Miskatonic University.

While Chandraputra worked, Hartwell, Elwood and Waite huddle together around Waite's Packard. They had tried to build a fire, but no matter what they did, the kindling simply would not light. There was no wind to speak of, and the leaves and twigs were bone dry, but nothing gathered out of the woods would take a flame. The Packard still ran, so the three of them had gathered around the engine trying to steal what heat they could. My changeling metabolism made me immune to the cold, or at least resistant to it. This allowed me to stand apart from the others, and truth be told I was glad of it. I was not comfortable with these people, least of all Asenath. What I knew of her, what I knew her to be capable of, made me wary to be in her presence. Instead, I stood staring out over the seaside village of Kingsport far below. Seen from above, in the still of the night, there were things about the village that even I found disturbing. A faint green light seemed to radiate out from a hilltop church in the center of the town. The light pulsed through the village streets, which seemed to fade in and out of view, and cast eerie shadows in the bay where the swells seemed to roll too slowly and crash too loudly against the cliffs and beaches. Those beaches were too white and too sharply defined in the thin moonlight, and I tried to turn away, and yet my eyes kept being drawn back. In some ways the village looked to me as it would had I been in a dream. The more I stared at it the more I thought of Kingsport that way, as nothing more than a dream, but whose dream was the question? It could have been one of mine, but perhaps not. The thought that the village of Kingsport was the dreamscape of some vast slumbering mind gnawed at me and sent chills down my spine.

"Seductive isn't it?" Suddenly, Chandraputra was by my side.

Startled, I shook myself out of the trance-like state I had been lulled into. "Wh -What?!"

Chandraputra placed a mittened hand on my shoulder. "Kingsport, it looks so calm and peaceful. Rolling *tkrt* waves, welcoming streets and buildings, even the pulsing green light seems to be a greeting. Don't let it fool you. Kingsport has *tkrt* its dangers. Once when I was younger, I nearly lost myself inside those streets."

I looked at the giant Hindoo in puzzlement. "It seems too small to get lost in. Situated between the bay, the river you could always see the head no matter where you were."

Chandraputra pulled up close to me and whispered in a strange, nasal buzzing voice, "Kingsport is like an iceberg, running *tkrt* deeper than what appears on the surface, and its nethermost caverns *tkrt* are not for the fathoming of human eyes. Were it not so, but great tunnels *tkrt* have been dug where caves and holes should suffice, and things that should crawl *tkrt* have learned to walk as men."

I stared back at the increasingly esoteric mystic. He bowed his head and threw his arms up in a flourish. "I present myself as my first *tkrt* point of case."

Waite abruptly joined the conversation, "Feeling somewhat anthropocentric are we Chandraputra? How long until we are ready to depart?"

Chandraputra took a somewhat curious bow. "Indeed! Let me assure you that the irony of your words *tkrt* does not escape me. As for an estimated time of departure *tkrt*, my work is done, we just have to let the ship plot her course *tkrt*, and become comfortable with following the signal. She's not as young as she *tkrt* used to be, but she's strong, we should be *tkrt* underway by midnight."

There was a strange look that passed between the two of them, and then Chandraputra turned away and vanished up the slope. Asenath smiled wickedly. "Kingsport Head is strange country Mr. Olmstead, even for one such as you. Feel free to wander about, but stay away from the edge. There is a fog rolling in, and I would hate to see you become," she paused and searched for a word, and then found it, "lost." As she walked away there was a sound, a laughter of sorts that annoyed me. I shook my head at the suggestion that anyone could get lost on the slope, with a moon overhead, and the village below. It was simply ludicrous, just another fragment of madness that I had to endure since I returned to New England. Frustrated, I set out to put some distance between myself and the other members of the Weird Company.

I walked down the head, not with any goal in mind, but simply to get away. There was too much going on, I needed space, quiet, perspective. There were no trails on Kingsport Head for me to follow, and consequently I frequently had to work my way around undergrowth, fallen trees and even the occasional boulder. I walked for quite some time, thinking about what I had made of my life, of how things I had planned had gone astray, and how I had wholly embraced my transformation and forgotten all my own plans. For this, I felt a pang of regret. It was then I realized that it wasn't I that had created the situation. My entire life had been manipulated by people from Innsmouth. Certainly there was some blame to be laid at the feet of dumb luck and my ancestry, but the majority could be placed on the Marsh family and their successors, in this case

Asenath Waite. These thoughts went round and round in my head as I walked, and it seems that they distracted me somewhat, for when I turned around to return to the others I found that they were nowhere in sight. Somehow all that twisting and turning while I walked had led me far away from Asenath Waite and her Weird Company, and just as she had warned I had become lost.

Even in the moonlight I could see nothing of my companions or their equipment. Desperate, I moved perpendicular to where I thought the cliff was, hoping to encounter the lone overgrown trail that we had followed up the side of the rise, but to no avail. My heightened senses had failed me, and I was left to stumble about in the woods with only the moon and the village below to give me any kind of direction. I knew that I had been walking down the slope, toward the village, so I reasoned that walking up the slope would be the proper course of action. As I walked, I called out but the only response was the call of a lonely owl. I did this for a full twenty minutes, for as I noted before, my actual progress was relatively slow and hampered by debris. Yet no matter what I did, I made no progress in locating my way back to the others.

The thick fog rolled in off the bay and it moved through the wood like the sea flowing onto the beach; it enveloped everything it touched, and blocked out the lights of the town, leaving only the moon to provide me any sense of direction or light. The fog came with a smell, something sour, and a sound, a kind of hum really, that made my skin itch and my bones ache. The cold came with the fog as well, but while I noticed the temperature drop, it had little impact, my hybrid physiology made sure of that.

I wandered through the night, through the fog, through the cold, lonely in the woods, on the side of a cliff, overlooking the ocean.

And I was lost.

But it suddenly became clear, I was no longer alone. There were voices, three voices, female voices, two I didn't recognize, but the third was very familiar. The third voice was clearly that of Asenath Waite! I moved quickly through the fog, not running but stumbling toward the voices. I called out, and I heard the voices pause. I called out again, tripped and fell to the rocky ground. As I struggled to regain my feet three figures gathered around me; even obscured by the fog, I recognized Asenath's frame and face. I put out my hand and waved it in her direction. "Help me up would you Miss Waite?"

There was an audible gasp, and then a blur of motion. In the blink of an eye Asenath Waite was on my back and she had a knife at my throat. Her breath was hot on my neck, and when she spoke there was a touch of danger in her voice, "How do you know my name? Who are you? What are you doing here on Kingsport Head?"

Out of the corner of my eye I looked at my attacker and realized something was wrong. Her hair was different. Her face was different, thinner, as if she was several pounds lighter. Even her clothes were different. There was an odd look in her eyes, and I realized something feral and dangerous was staring down at me.

One of her companions, a young lady with auburn hair and sharp features, chastised my attacker, "Nath! Calm down. He has every right to be here! As much as we do!"

Asenath slowly drew the blade away and climbed off of my back. There was still something dangerous in her eyes, something that warned me to be careful. "Miss Waite would you kindly explain what is going on? Just a half-hour ago we were talking, now you've changed, clothes, and your hair as well, and who are these two girls?"

There was a puzzled look on Asenath's face, but she relaxed and seemed to calm down. "My apologies sir, but you seem to have me, all of us really, at a disadvantage. "You know who I am but I don't recognize you, and I really have no idea what you are talking about. I and my companions have been wandering together through the fog for hours."

I rose from the ground, shaking my head in confusion. "You don't remember me, Robert Olmstead, you recruited me a few days ago? I've been living at your house in Arkham."

A snickering laughter passed through the trio of young girls. "Sir, Mr. Olmstead," said Asenath, " I assure you that I have never met you before. I have no house in Arkham. I and my companions are students at the Hall School in Kingsport. I do have a home in Innsmouth, but that has been shuttered for many years now."

It was my turn to laugh. "I would hardly call what has happened to Innsmouth, its occupation by Federal troops and the arrest of its inhabitants, shuttered."

Asenath was outraged by my words, "You lie! When did this happen?"

"For about three years now. Since the winter of 1927–1928." I shot back.

Asenath suddenly went silent, but her two companions were whispering back and forth and casting worried looks in my direction. Cautiously the sharp-faced girl spoke up, "Mr. Olmstead, what's todays date?"

It was a foolish question but I answered out of reflex. "The 18th of March, 1931." My response seemed to displease the trio of young ladies.

"Sir, when we left the school this evening it was indeed the 18th of March," commented the sharp-faced girl, "but the year was 1921."

"He's mad," sneered Asenath.

"I don't think so," interjected the third girl. She had auburn hair and round, soft features. My mother has written about this in her stories, and my father, you all know what happened to him." She paused and the other girls nodded. She turned to me and softened her voice. "Mr. Olmstead, my name is Hannah Peaslee, you seem to know Asenath, and this is Megan Halsey-Griffith," she gestured at the sharp-faced girl. "We came up on to Kingsport Head on a dare, to see if the legends and stories were true." The puzzled look on my face betrayed my ignorance. "People say that strange things happen on the Head. That people vanish, and others just appear. They say that there are doorways, entrances to other worlds, and even dreams here on the Head. Some of the books call the Head a soft place, where the rules that govern the universe are weak, and can be easily bent. I think that is what has happened to you, to all of us. I think somehow we've moved, not to another world, but to another time. I don't know why, but the how . . . maybe it has to do with the fog that rolled in off of the bay."

"The locals call it Blake's Fog," explained Miss Halsey-Griffith. "Back in 1880 or so, there was a ship, the Elizabeth Dane, owned by a man named Blake. There was some scandal, and he and his followers were forced to leave town, despite the horrific fog that blanketed the port. The boat and her crew were never heard from again." She paused and fumbled with her hands. "Ever since, they say the fog has been thicker, colder, and more frequent."

"The fog has always been like this," interjected Asenath. "Blaming it on Blake is just a way for the locals to explain a natural, well preternatural, occurrence. They don't understand what's going on, so they make up a myth to explain it. Just a bit of local madness."

I ran my hands across my head; there was no hair, but the habit remained. "Perhaps it would be better to be mad," I said in frustration. "That might be preferable to the things that I have learned over the last few years, and in the last few days as well."

Asenath, the younger version of the woman who recruited me, took my hand and guided me to sit down on a log. After the other girls joined us, Asenath implored me, "Tell me what you know about Innsmouth and the occupation. Tell me what you can remember about the future."

Having nothing else to do I told her my story, of how I had been searching for my ancestors, how I had found Innsmouth, and how I had been responsible for its destruction. I spoke at length of my slow transformation, of my conversion, and of my desperate cross-country trek to return to Innsmouth. I related details of what I had seen in that seaside hamlet, and how it had forced me to flee not once, but twice. I revealed how I had been rescued and nursed back to health by Doctor Hartwell, and how Asenath's future self would recruit me and others to a task that had yet to be made clear to me, but somehow the entire world was dependent on. I told them all these things without a care for the consequences that might result, for it was not in my mind that there could be any.

How long we sat there I could not say, but it was long enough for the fog to begin to weaken, to become less dense. We all noticed it at once, but it was only Hannah Peaslee that seemed to realize the implications. "We have to separate!" She suddenly exclaimed. "If the fog disperses we might be restored to our rightful times, but if we stay together we might be stuck with each other and then Mr. Olmstead would be trapped in 1921, or we might end up in 1931! Regardless, we can't stay together, it's too dangerous."

As was typical, and perhaps a prelude of things to come, young Asenath began barking orders, telling me to travel up the Head, while she and her companions moved down. I was reluctant to be thrown back into my aimless wanderings, but understood why it was necessary. I bid the girls farewell, who despite their obvious revulsion at my appearance, each took the time to award me some token before they moved away. Asenath kissed me on the cheek. Megan Halsey-Smith took me firmly by the hand and suggested that her mother would love this story. I laughed as she walked away. But it was Hannah Peaslee that surprised me the most, for even though her friends could still see her, she violated all rules of decorum and embraced me tightly. As she held me, I felt her warm breath on my cheek, and listened as she whispered in what was left of my ear. "Don't trust Asenath. She's not at all what she seems. I think she's dangerous." She pulled back and looked into my eyes, and I nodded my understanding, and then without another word she drifted through the fog to join the rapidly vanishing figures of her friends.

After they had gone, after the last vestiges of their shadows and voices had faded into the fog, I turned away and marched up the grade of Kingsport Head. I moved by the feel of the ground beneath my feet, for the light of the moon provided no direction, and the city lights were still obscured by the fog. I stepped carefully, slowly working my way through the woods and around the boulders that occasionally blocked my way. With each step the fog began to dissipate, and I began to be able to see farther and farther into the landscape around me. Details began to resolve themselves, and in the distance I could hear voices, the tone and cadence of which seemed familiar. I moved toward them, for they seemed so close, and yet I could not reach them. Each step should have brought me closer, but it was as if those steps were infinitely small, and provided me no progress whatsoever. My frustration at the situation turned to panic and I was suddenly running blindly through the woods.

The woman came out of nowhere. One moment my way was clear, the next it was blocked, and I had to nearly throw myself to the ground to avoid running her down. I was cursing as she helped me stand up. She steadied me and as I regained my footing I stared at her odd outfit. She was wearing a suit and trousers, something smart with a purple and green paisley pattern that complemented her figure. Over this was a grey coat, not unlike those worn by soldiers in the war, but one sleeve was white, while the other was black. Around her neck was a crimson scarf that hid her neck and came up over her head like a cowl. She had changed her clothes while I had been gone, and while I didn't think it was possible, Asenath Waite suddenly appeared more beautiful than ever.

"Steady Mr. Olmstead," she said reassuringly. "You'll be home in two shakes, I promise you." She held my arm and began walking me toward the voices. "You're on the right track, you just need an anchor, a way to drag yourself back."

I nodded and in the distance shapes began to resolve themselves into recognizable forms. "Thank you," I muttered. She bent down to pick up a slouch hat that matched her scarf.

We took another step and the fog was suddenly gone. I could see Chandraputra and Hartwell milling about something that was metallic and glowing. As we approached, Hartwell came forward to check on us, he seemed genuinely concerned over where I had been. Chandraputra seemed more frustrated and annoyed than anything else. I had been missing for almost an hour, though to me it somehow seemed much longer. Elwood suggested that I go inside the ship and try to stay out of the way. They were loading the last of the supplies, including Asenath's automobile. It wouldn't be much use in Antarctica, but leaving it on the Head wasn't something we wanted to do either.

The thing that Chandraputra called a ship was a large oval, approximately one hundred feet long comprised of a mesh woven together like wicker or rattan. The material itself was white, and radiated a cool, soft glow that provided some illumination to the surrounding area. Chandraputra called it a light-envelope and implied that it was comprised of solidified photons, particles of light that had been frozen in space-time to create an object with very little mass, and the ability to move at unimaginable velocities.

A normal man probably would have been flabbergasted at such a thing, but I had seen things in my dreams and while I was awake that paled in comparison to this engineered construct and accepted it as I would any new advancement in technology, though I did wonder if all Swamis were capable of producing such marvels of Vedic metaphysics.

At the mention of the ancient philosophy Chandraputra seemed to take pause. He stared at me for a moment and then suddenly nodded in his odd way. "It is an ancient technology *tkrt* Mr. Olmstead, one that has existed *tkrt* long before men walked this planet."

I opened my mouth to respond to this cryptic statement, but before I could he was gone, back to working at the strange controls and panels that seemed integral to the even stranger ship.

The interior was divided into three levels by two floors of the same strange material. Access between levels was accomplished by a centrally located, tightly curved ramp that reminded me of the central spiral of a conch. The interior of the ship was a cool, frosted white. The walls and floors were smooth, seamless, almost organic. There was something about it that reminded me of the inside of a whelk or conch. Asenath joined me on an outcropping of wall that served as a kind of bench. She looked at me, and I at her.

"That night in the marsh outside Innsmouth, you sent Chandraputra there. You knew where to find me, because I told you about it in the past."

She nodded. "It's also how I knew about the Federal raid and was able to avoid it. What you told me that night may have been nothing to you, but it has proven invaluable to my efforts to save what I can of our operations."

The look on her face was so severe, so serious, but I felt mine grow terrified. "Was that proper? Should you have used that information? Wasn't it a violation of the laws of the universe? It has been a while since I've taken philosophy and discussed morality and the limits of human knowledge, but I think there was something about the laws of cause and effect."

She stood up and looked at me with the most icy of stares. "I'll do anything to save this world. I'll use any information I can lay my hands on. Whether that comes to me in a dream, or on a mist-enshrouded hill, or in a book that appears to be millions of years old but is written in modern English, I'll use it."

She walked away, leaving me alone on the bench with nothing to do but sit there with the book she had left behind. I had not seen it before, how that was possible I do not know, for it was an inhuman thing, massive, hexagonal, and hinged on every pane. Each page seemed to be made from a thin sheet of metal, but was lighter than I had assumed it could possibly be. It seemed incredibly ancient, and the workmanship was like nothing I had ever seen before, but while the hand-written script was odd, it was clearly in English, and as I flipped through the book, I had no choice but to read and learn what Asenath already knew. It seems that's what she wanted me to do.

CHAPTER II

An Excerpt from the Zkauba Fragments "The Riddle of Thaqquallah"

I move through the vast gulf of space within an envelope of light at such a velocity that the stars themselves are transformed into streaks of strangely colored illumination. It has been more than a cycle since I was last awake, but that is as it should be. The technique of prolonged suspended animation requires that I emerge at regular intervals, mostly to satisfy a variety of organic functions and carry out routine maintenance on the artifice that generates the light-envelope. I have already carried out a detailed inspection of the emitters, the motivating mechanism, and the ghostly spines that anchor the ship into real-space. With this esoteric maintenance now completed I have still many hours to fill before I can return to my chemically induced slumber. I can no longer bear to study the Tablets of Nhing, so as I have done before, I shall fall back on my earthly occupation and record some event from the eons that I have spent living amongst the Nug Soth.

I have already written of how I came to dwell within the alien mind of the wizard Zkauba. The cosmic forces that tore me from Earth in the twentieth century and cast me through time and space need not be discussed any further. That I resided inside Zkauba's psyche, only able to come to dominance when Zkauba's own will grew weak, is detailed in previous accounts. Though, it may be relevant to once more state that Zkauba was none too pleased with my presence, for he saw me as a verminous mammalian consciousness that he would prefer to see expunged. Zkauba's opinion reflected the natural philosophical position of his race. The Nug Soth, while bearing some reptilian characteristics, were very similar in appearance to that of terrestrial insects, particularly weevils, though they followed the same general form as men, having a head with sensory organs, a thorax with four arms instead of two, and an abdomen where two legs attached. The six appendages of the Nug Soth were multi-jointed and all terminated in eight articulated, claw-like fingers arranged in two sets of four, opposite each other, such that the eight digits could interlock into a large club-like fist. There was on each set a ninth vestigial digit that was entirely immobile, and consisted of little more than a sharp projection or point: a remnant fighting claw from a more violent point in their evolution. The head was large, bulbous, with a single large, central eye and six smaller, jewel-like oculii, arranged in arches on the sides of the head. Below the primary eye, a flexible snout curved out and terminated in a small, vicious, rasping mouth through which the Nug Soth drew sustenance.

I have called Zkauba a wizard, though this word does not do him or his species justice. The technology of the Nug Soth was so advanced and beyond the ken of men that it can only be described as wizardry. Yet that wizardry was not the artifice of a sparse few practitioners, but rather it permeated their society at all levels, such that even the simplest of merchants and manufacturers could bend the laws of thermodynamics to their will. But, Zkauba was no simple practitioner, he was a servant of the Arch-Ancient Buo, and one of many charged by the aged hierophant with defending the birthing crypts from the ravenous, monstrous, burrowing things that dwelt below the surface of Yaddith. The Dholes were greasy, bloated worms as alien and incomprehensible to the Nug Soth as that species would be to Men, and try as they might, Zkauba's people found defending their young against the predations of the Dholes a constant struggle. Likewise, there seemed to be little way to deter their monstrous habit of boring through the very crust of the planet itself. This battle to control the Dholes was grounded not only in their attempt to master the planet, but also in the very tenets of their religious veneration. The Nug Soth's deity was not an abstract entity, but rather their own Progenitor, the All-Mother

Thaqquallah, who is known amongst the mystics of Earth by the name Shub-Niggurath. Thaqquallah had been imprisoned deep within the bowels of Yaddith by those who had created her, and access to the tunnel that led downward into the plutonian interior, where her cenobites tended to her pain-wracked form, was strictly forbidden. That the All-Mother had begot two species that struggled for dominance was perplexing to the Nug Soth. They called it the Riddle of Thaqquallah. How was it, the philosophers of the Nug Soth wondered, that the All-Mother could give her favor to the Nug Soth, and yet let the Dholes remain unfettered.

Some suggested that the All-Mother be beseeched for mercy, but each time Buo had refused, and warned that any attempts to plead with the All-Mother might have dire consequences. It was best, Buo counseled, to leave the gravid deity undisturbed, and seek solutions elsewhere. Envoys were dispatched in light-envelopes to Nython, Mthura and even the twin planets of the Xoth and Xastur, in search of formulations for employ against the Dholes. Though certain worlds, such as those housing the great machines circling the stars Altair and Epsilon Eridani, and the library world of Celeano, were forbidden. These were worlds of the Q'Hrell, those who had created the All-Mother and then imprisoned her, and these Progenitors bore no love for the Nug Soth.

Yet despite their efforts, the Nug Soth had found no effective deterrents that could prevent the feasting of the Dholes, save those that were lethal to both species. Indeed, this in itself was a cause of great consternation amongst the philosophers, for it served as a constant reminder that Thaqquallah was the mother of both the Nug Soth, and of the Dholes as well. That the Nug Soth could bear such similar physiologies to beings that could carry out such atrocious acts made many of the more introspective members of the species shudder with fear, and perhaps a bit of self-loathing.

In such times of great existential doubt, Zkauba, like many of his species, would abandon the avenues that comprised the fronded metal cities that grace the surface of Yaddith and instead take comfort in the Holy Tablets of Nhing. But on one day, the tablets brought no comfort to my unwilling host Zkauba, for the news had not been pleasant. The word had come that one of the brooding ziggurats had been violated and the brood attendants slaughtered.

The offending Dholes had then devoured the unprotected larval Nug Soth in a most horrific manner, leaving only a few of the young alive. Such a loss was devastating not only to the individuals whose bloodlines were represented in the ziggurat, but to the Nug Soth as a whole. Larval Nug Soth were mindless, voracious creatures that easily consumed their own weight every few hours, and thus were able to reach maturity about a year after their birth. The metamorphosis of larva into juvenile females involved the rapid development of cognitive abilities, as well as the production of dozens of eggs that needed to be fertilized by adult males. Access to the eggs was regulated through social factors, with young adults having almost no opportunity to reproduce. As the age, and presumably prestige, of an individual increased, so did access to the unfertilized eggs, at least in theory. However, as the individual members of the species were extremely long lived, only the Arch Ancient and his cohorts were allowed to breed on a regular basis; for individuals like Zkauba, despite his rank and ability, the right to visit the brooding ziggurat and pass on his bloodline came only rarely. With each attack decimating the egg-bearing young, it was inevitable that reproduction rights were to be impacted. Yet Zkauba's interest in the destruction of the young from this particular ziggurat was more significant. It had been in this brood chamber that he and his cohorts had been born and raised, and it was in this chamber that he himself had hoped his gene-line would continue. The brood of the Five Moons was not as prestigious or powerful as those of the Sleeping Eye, to which Buo belonged, but he was proud of their achievements and had no desire to see the line wiped out. The fear of such a disaster, of his brood becoming little more than a memory in annals of history, made Zkauba's hearts ache, and he stared incessantly at the Five Moons symbol inscribed through branding on the back of each of his squamous hands.

It was in this malaise that a heretical thought instilled itself in Zkauba, if Buo would not plead with the Mother for aid, then he would. Zkauba would arm himself as best he could, and then descend into the fearful depths of the Yaddithan underworld. There, following the signs of the ancient Zkahrnizzen, he who had ascended from the inner world eons ago, Zkauba would find his way to the cavern where dwelt Thaqquallah and plead with the cenobites for an audience with the Goddess in the hopes that she would intervene on behalf of the Nug Soth, and endow upon him the power to strike down the vile and despicable Dholes. As I have said, this was a heretical idea. Zkauba had sworn a pledge to obey Buo, and such oaths were serious matters amongst the Nug Soth. Were he to be caught violating his pledge he would most assuredly forfeit much of his prestige, wealth and rights. I have described Zkauba as a wizard, but if he were to do this thing, were he to violate his pledge he would forever be known as sdantlanws, an oath-breaker, though this is not the best of translations. In English there is a word for such people, though few will know its archaic meaning, though I, as a student of such things, find the title most appropriate: given what forces Zkauba could wield, and what he planned to do, I can think of no better appellation than warlock!

The armourers of the Nug Soth, the Yshhr, are as much artisans as engineers and produced a strange style of battle garb, bejeweled, oblong helmets, baroque gloves, outlandishly fur-trimmed cloaks and seemingly impossible fusions of edged, energy and projectile weapons. Although much of the styling appeared purely decorative, no jewel, no bauble, no crest was without a secondary function. The gems that served as helmet lenses also allowed the wearer to see beyond the normal visual spectrum supplied by his seven eyes. The ceramic armor that covered his chest and limbs not only protected him from attack, but also preserved his body temperature, and rejuvenated the very air and water that he needed to survive. The gauntlets of the lower arms were not only protective, but also served to enhance the ability of the Nug Soth to manipulate energy and matter through simple hand gestures. The gauntlets worn on the upper hands varied in that they formed a kind of symbiotic bond between their wearer and the weapons wielded. Through simple thought the sinistral sword or dextral dagger could be commanded to become energized, or discharge small needle-like projectiles. Additionally the sword, which was not a single blade, but rather more saw-toothed in appearance, could be made to have its teeth whip around the blade like a chain saw. This chain sword was a vicious and most deadly melee weapon, feared for its savagery and deadly results. For the paired limbs he used for legs, there were boots that functioned to deny the very force of gravity, he could not fly, but he could leap farther than normal, walk up walls and even briefly hang from the ceiling. Even the ermine-fringed cape was not without its own secrets. Zkauba referred to the thing as translucent, and by this he meant that when engaged it would allow light to pass through it completely, rendering the wearer not quite invisible, but rather, difficult to notice.

All these accoutrements did the wizard Zkauba don as he prepared for his sin of descending into the underworld. As I have said before, there is no night on Yaddith, and thus there is no period of darkness during which to commit clandestine acts. Thus armed and armored and sheltered by his translucent cloak he made his way through the streets of the city, moving from alleyway to alleyway, from shadow to shadow, slinking between the ductwork and machinery of the alien city until at last he came to the temple house that housed the gate that led down into the subterranean world that lay beneath his very feet. There was fear in his mind as he entered the hall and slid along the wall toward the ornately carved, massive slabs of ebon stone that served as doors to the gate itself. He was cautious, nervous, and his head darted back and forth searching for guardians that would prevent his passage, but there were none. So strong was the conviction to follow the oaths they had sworn, no guard was needed to prevent any from passing through the gate. The guilt and fear returned, perhaps even grew, as he pried one of the great stone panels open. But his mind was set, his course committed to, and as he slipped through and closed the gate behind him, all doubts about his actions faded forever. It may have been better if he had indeed turned back, but hindsight can be cruel, and then and there at the gate, Zkauba did what he felt needed to be done.

The journey downward into the bowels of Yaddith, despite being lit by a species of luminescent fungi, was slow and treacherous. The way was marked with the Zkahrnizzen Sign, but that was no guaranty of safety. The ancient tunnels and crevices that carried him into stygian depths were replete with debris from landslides, rock falls and other signs of geological stress. Foul odors assaulted his senses, mostly sulfurous gas, but also pockets of methane and the occasional wind-borne blast of caustic hydrochloride gas. Such passive perils were not the only threats to challenge the passage of the wizard. Metsis, a kind of centipedal rodent the size of a small dog, haunted the caverns, lapping up sustenance from slime pools and fungi. The larger of these, their mouths full of vicious teeth, were not opposed to threatening Zkauba, and on more than one occasion did he leave the bolder of such creatures mewling as their green blood pumped from gaping wounds. More dangerous were the Eaav, spider-wasps that swarmed over unwary prey overwhelming them through sheer numbers. They coated their victims with strands of webbing that clumped together, making movement at first difficult, and then as the strands accumulated, impossible. The webbing and delicate wings of the Eaav were susceptible to fire, and this proved an effective defense. At least until one of the flame-engulfed swarms careened down into an invisible pocket of methane, sparking an explosion and fireball that threw the wizard across the cavern and into the wall. After this unfortunate event Zkauba grew more circumspect in his dealing with the denizens of the underworld, often waiting hours (and on one occasion nearly a whole day) before proceeding through a particular passageway.

A week after he had left the surface Zkauba reached the gated entrance to the Temple of Thaqquallah. It was a horrid place, filled with vile stenches and heavy air of dubious quality. There were no guards on the gates and as he passed through them none of the attending cenobites rose to greet him. The priests were cloaked in tattered robes of a drab yellow color that hid the entirety of their bodies including their hands and heads. Despite his attempts to converse with them they refused to raise their cowls or even speak, they merely gestured toward the crystalline dome that dominated the great cavern and then scurried off, leaving in their wake the queerest of tracks. The dome was a Moon-Lens, built from the opalescent meteorites that occasionally fall from Sicstu, the fourth moon. Its entryway was decorated with symbols that were strange to me, but Zkauba noted some resemblance to the rune-letters used by the Q'Hrell. It was apparent to both of us that the great lens was the merest outcropping of the prison in which the Mother Goddess had been imprisoned by the Progenitors so many eons before.

Within the interior there was a thin ledge running along the wall. Beneath this there was nothing, simply a vast seething pit of darkness that seemed to reach down to the very core of the world. From the worn rock ledge a single cantilever jutted out leading to a point near the center of the pit where a lone figure lay crucified against an ornate, basaltic gibbet. This individual Zkauba took to be the Seer of Thaqquallah, the Voice of the Mother, and as we approached we could see the thin ropey tendrils that climbed up out of the pit and wrapped themselves around the throat and head of the honored priest. Prepared by the Tablets of Nhing, Zkauba brought forth his dagger and in an act of sacrifice cut open one of his hands, letting the blood filter down through the fetid air until it reached the Divine Matriarch.

The priest shuddered as the tendrils snapped him awake. He was blind, and his body was sickly bloated. There was movement beneath his skin, as if something large was shifting about. He opened his mouth to speak, but the voice did not originate from the Nug Soth equivalent of a voice box. The sound was like a hollow wind, and Zkauba fell to his knees as his god spoke to him. It was not a language he knew, but he needed no translation, he knew what the words meant, for it was the language of the gods, the base language of the universe itself, and even the lowliest of species would recognize it. As he listened, one of his tympanum burst and began to bleed, Zkauba enraptured, ignored the pain.

He performed the Rite of Supplication and once he was sure that the Mother was satisfied with him, he began his petition. "Great Thaqquallah, Mother of Us All, the Nug Soth are your most faithful of servants, and yet we are vexed, we are troubled, we are engaged in a most dire conflict. The Dholes, spawn of your womb, destroy our brood chambers, devour our young, imperil our very existence. We beseech you Mother, help us, help us protect our lives, our cities, our civilization, our species, help us and this war between your two children and we shall celebrate your glory forever."

There was a long pause after Zkauba finished speaking, and then the Seer shuddered, the tendrils withdrew and the Seer spoke once more, this time in a voice wracked with pain. "You speak of the war between the Nug Soth and the Dholes. The Goddess sees no such war, only the natural order of things. Many and multi-form are the children of her flesh, but of those she has created only blessed Zkahrnizzen, born gravid, had the potential for self-awareness, and to her the All-Mother gave the task of being fruitful and mul-tiplying so that someday her descendants might free the Goddess from her prison. The Goddess does not seek your praise, or adora-tion, she wishes to be free! And one day her children will free her from her imprisonment within Yaddith, and she will spread her seed throughout the universe."

"But which of her children does she favor?" pleaded Zkauba.

The priest laughed, "The Riddle of Thaqquallah. How can it be that she favors neither, and both?" He coughed. "You are a fool to ask. It would be best not to dwell on the answer; you will not find any comfort in it, none at all." Then the priest went silent and Zkauba knew his audience was over.

Zkauba left the Moon-Lens, and then the temple. He attempted to return to the surface, but the journey and his brief confronta-tion had left him weak and exhausted. Following the path back was not always easy and many were the times he deviated from it and found himself doubling back, searching for a missed sign. Days into his journey, his provisions nearly depleted he suddenly became dizzy, slipped and tumbled down a deep shaft or pit into a great dome of steaming, fetid pools. There was a horrendous smell and a great, snuffling noise, like that of a great beast searching. He pinned himself against the wall and cloaked himself in that translucent fabric, in hopes his presence would be concealed from whatever was coming from the other direction. It was the first time he had ever seen a Dhole alive and up close. The thing was massive; its worm-like bulk was twice his height in diameter, pale and seg-mented. Though it bore six limbs, they hung useless on the sides of its titanic body which humped along the ground like some sort of obscene grub. Although many report that the Dholes are blind, Zkauba could see a small cyclopean eye just above the obscenely probing snout, while six more nearly unnoticeable ocelli decor-ated the cranial ridges facing backwards. Though this monstrous thing could have easily crushed Zkauba he knew that despite its tremendous bulk it was only a juvenile example of the species, for it was not uncommon for Dholes to be as large, if not larger than small buildings or towering spires.

Knowing that creatures like this one were responsible for the attacks on the brooding ziggurats Zkauba steeled himself, slowly and silently he drew his weapons and waited for the right moment to engage. Whether it was the sound of the sword being drawn, or the gauntlets energizing, or perhaps even a slight flutter in the translucent cloak, the Dhole suddenly started and reared up to strike at the crouching wizard, its rasping snout chewing through the air. Instinctively Zkauba powered on his sword and with a smooth, fluid arc sliced through the tentacular proboscis. The beast squealed in pain and drew back, while the now stunted snout reeled through the air, a spray of bloody droplets raining down.

Still somewhat invisible, Zkauba launched himself into the air and plunged his dagger into the soft spot between segments of the behemoth. With his lower hands he grasped the armored ridges, while his upper sinistral arm once more swung the chain sword, this time at the beast's head. It did not cut easy, great gouts of blood and gore sprayed out from the deadly mechanism, but the Dhole's armored plates served to frustrate the blade and the thing quickly jammed, clogged by fibrous strands of cartilaginous tissue. Once more the Dhole screamed and reared up. The creature shook its mighty bulk, and though his grip was strong, Zkauba was no match for the physics of the situation, and he was flung from his perch leaving both his sword and dagger embedded in the flesh of the beast.

Zkauba tumbled through the air, allowing the momentum to carry him away from the creature before engaging his boots and ricocheting off the wall and back toward the Dhole. The creature was turning to face him, and though he was lacking both sword and dagger, he was not without armaments. As he travelled through the air Zkauba's gauntleted lower hands manipulated the very atmosphere around him and drew out much of the energy latent within, using it to form a kind of electric spike, a form of artificial lightning. As the Dhole raised its bloody snout and opened its mouth to attack him, Zkauba launched the spike down the thing's massive throat. The Dhole gulped in surprise and then wavered a bit as smoke began to pour from the edges of the thing's jaws. Taking advantage of the Dhole's sudden weakness Zkauba landed just above the thing's cyclopean eye and then swiftly drove one of his vestigial fighting claws into it. Viscous fluid exploded as he penetrated the stiff cornea and lens, and the Dhole squirmed trying once more to throw the unwanted rider, but this time the effort was lackluster. Zkauba's grip on the internal structure of the eye was too strong. For a moment the alien wizard thought that the struggle might dislodge the eye itself, but as the orb seemed to break from its setting the chthonic worm suddenly shuddered and then collapsed from its wounds. The victorious warrior cautiously stalked along the beast's body and reclaimed his sword and dagger. Then without a single ounce of pity or compassion he made his way back toward the head of the monster and then made sure that the beast was dead.

He collapsed next to the creature; the struggle, the manipulation of energy, had taken its toll, and he needed to rest. He was hopeful that the battle had frightened off any other threats that might lurk within the nearby area, at least long enough for him to regain his strength. It was while he sat there, half drowsing in near slumber, that something odd caught his eye. As I have written before, this was the first time Zkauba had ever seen a live specimen, and the first time he had ever seen a juvenile at that. In this he noted the presence of six diminutive and rudimentary limbs, three on each side, that were normally not seen on larger exemplars. Scientific examination through vivisection had found suggestions of such structures hidden within the bodies themselves, but it had always been assumed that such limbs had been vestigial, and no longer served, or could serve any function. Their presence here on a juvenile suggested otherwise, and Zkauba was intrigued by a possible theory that crept into his head. Perhaps, he hypothesized, the Dholes were not always titanic grub-like monstrosities, perhaps their larval form was entirely different, one that had a slightly different physiology that used the six limbs for locomotion, which were then lost as the creature grew in size. Perhaps this larva was more vulnerable than the rampaging adults. Perhaps this was the weakness the Nug Soth had been looking for.

He grabbed one of the vestigial arms, and with his dagger cut it off. Though shriveled, withered even, nearly desiccated, the limb bore a remarkable resemblance to those of his own species. It bore the same joints, the same vestigial fighting claw on the hand, the same arrangement and number of fingers. It was then that Zkauba began to understand, and his mind drifted back to the enigmatic words of the priest. He scraped the filth from the limb and looked for what he hoped would not, could not be there. But it was, it was there, and he could see it with his own eyes. He understood the answer now. The Riddle of Thaqquallah had been solved, and it drove Zkauba mad.

The psyche of Zkauba retreated, fled reality, and I found myself forced to the surface, forced to take control of that alien body. It took me days to learn how, how to manipulate six limbs instead of four, how to eat things my human body would have rejected. It took days to learn how to wield the weapons, and artifices that made Zkauba what he was. Days turned into weeks, into months, and into years. By the time Zkauba had recovered from his break-down, I was fully in control, and in possession of an elixir that was capable of keeping his psyche fully suppressed.

I had seen what Zkauba had seen inscribed there on the withered claw of the Dhole, and I knew what it meant. The Riddle of Thaqquallah: How can the Goddess favor neither of her children, and both? For there are no Nug Soth, and there are no Dholes, only the descendants of Zkahrnizzen. The proof was there, branded on the back of the Dhole's claw: a simple oval with a slit through it, burned into the fleshy integument, the symbol of the Sleeping Eye, the brood house of Buo! The Dholes were simply another stage in the life cycle of the Nug Soth, one that fed on the very flesh of its own species. For eons the children of Zkahrnizzen would riddle the shell of Yaddith with their foul tunnels and warrens until they accomplished the task for which they had been created, and planet itself would implode. Then, and only then, would the crystal Moon-Lens be shattered, and Thaqquallah would be free to spawn amongst the stars.

This knowledge drove Zkauba mad, as it would have any Nug Soth. But I was a Man, a child of Earth, and such eldritch horrors did not shake me. Instead they empowered me, and where Buo and the amassed Nug Soth nations saw me as the Arch-Wizard Zkauba, I knew I was something more, something different, and something they could never understand. No matter what body I wore, I was a man. I was Randolph Carter, Warlock of Yaddith!

CHAPTER 12
From the Account of Robert Martin Olmstead
"Into the Ether"

I woke to a strange vibration, a deep melodic thrumming that makes the air electric, almost like a charged fluid. Oddly, while the sound permeated the air, the integral bench, the walls, and even the floor didn't seem to be a conduit for the resonance. Like the exterior, the interior was a large oval, approximately one hundred feet long, comprised of the same latticework of a white material that that the exterior was. As I mentioned before, the interior was divided into three levels by two floors of the same strange material. Access between levels was accomplished by a centrally located, tightly curved ramp that reminded me of the central spiral of a conch. All of this meant that the ship was smooth and curving, completely devoid of any hard angles. One section of the curved wall was lined with dozens of cylinders, each larger than a full grown man. The other wall was lined with frosted, semi-transparent cabinets containing sundry items including bottles, jars, small idols, shelves of books, and even a stack of small gold ingots. At the far end, opposite the loading door, there was the control area. Like the rest of the ship it was smooth and white with an almost organic sense to it. The various raised panels present dozens of buttons, levers and actuators of all types. It was overwhelming to say the least.

Chandraputra was working furiously over the panels, and using his right hand, began orchestrating a series of esoteric symbols in the air above the equipment. In response a huge panel slid back along the wall and revealed a window. The window showed the village of Kingsport passing beneath us as we headed out over the ocean. "This ship," announced Chandraputra, "is made almost entirely of solid light, a material created by the Nug Soth eons ago."

I recognized that name from the book I had just read, I must have gasped or something because Asenath caught my eye and surreptitiously signaled me to be quiet.

"These ships can be thought of *tkrt* as being able to fold the very fabric of space and time around them into envelopes of the real *tkrt* that can then be shunted into the space in between. They are extremely fast, and *tkrt* can traverse the vast distances between stars in a matter of hours. However, within the boundaries of a planetary atmosphere such manipulations of *tkrt* the universal fabric are dangerously unstable. We will still be able to fold our way into the in-between, but we won't *tkrt* be able to travel as fast as I would like. Still, we should be able to *tkrt* reach a velocity such that we shall be in Antarctica in a few *tkrt* hours with almost no problems."

Waite chimed in a suspicious "Almost?"

Chandraputra bobbed his body up in a strange animal nod. "There are risks. Since we'll be traveling *tkrt* near the speed of light in an arc, our instantaneous linear velocity at any given point may *tkrt* exceed the speed of light and generate some distortions in time. This could attract *tkrt* some unwanted attention."

"Care to be more specific about what kind of attention?" pressed Hartwell.

"Time is like a huge, slow *tkrt* moving river. Objects moving with the river are *tkrt* virtually invisible, like fish *tkrt* hidden in the current, but a move sideways or against the current and the fish *tkrt* becomes obvious and easy prey."

Hartwell's eyes grew large. "Prey for what?"

Waite diverted the question. "Would you like to stay behind, Doctor Hartwell?"

Hartwell paused and studied the surrounding faces before focusing on Waite. "I'll go. I just wanted to know what the risks were."

Chandraputra raised his arms above his head. "If only it were that easy Doctor, I *tkrt* doubt any of us would have chosen the *tkrt* paths we now travel."

The sense of motion was slight, but enhanced by the image provided through the window. There was an ethereal quality to our propulsion, and I was, as were most of the Weird Company, entranced by the things that suddenly appeared and surrounded the ship as we moved into what Chandraputra called the in-between. Only our strange captain, who seemed to be used to such things, was not enthralled by the scene. In contrast I, Elwood and Waite were held in rapt fascination at the vista beyond the ship.

In many ways, I thought, it was like the sea. There was a matrix, like water, but seemingly less dense and more varied in hue. Vast shoals of color with shades and dimensions filled my vision, like massive clouds roiling in the depths. Flumes of congregated lights darted about them not unlike schools of fish. Larger shapes, and that is all they were, for no details could be discerned, swam, flew and pulsated about, some in obvious pursuit, others seemingly unaware or at least unconcerned about the events about them. It was on Dr. Hartwell that the vista had the most obvious effect. It seemed the display of muted lights and the complete lack of sound from exterior to the ship had profoundly affected the Doctor. So much so, that it was he that was first to break the silence and ponder out loud, "What are they?"

Chandraputra's dark eyes opened slowly and wide with an audible and strange click. He rose deftly and strode gracefully to Hartwell's side. "Ahhhh, that is life Doctor. Not as you know it. Not organic life with water and cells and chemistry, but life nonetheless. This is the space between, where things only hinted at come to frolic and stalk. That multi-colored blur over there is a saturnine cat, and those groups of grey pulsing lights to the left are called shamblers."

"What are those pale, thin lights over there?" asked Waite, pointing uselessly into the vista.

Chandraputra tilted his head and made a queer frightful sound. "Those are horrid things, predators who feast solely on things that have violated the flow of time. The Nug Soth call them the beasts of Quacchil Uattus, but men call them the Hounds of Tindalos."

"Didn't you say we were moving through time?" uttered Hartwell haltingly.

Chandraputra once more bounced his head in that strange animal semblance to a nod. "Indeed, but the hounds can only attack through a hard angle. The light-ships are designed around curves to prevent just that."

"They are getting closer," observed Hartwell.

Carter watched as the hounds wheeled toward the ship like hawks toward a rabbit. "Indeed they are. Not to worry, I've seen this before. They've caught our scent, but they can't get in. The ship has no angles for them to breach."

Hartwell backed away as the hounds drew up toward the walls of the light-ship. The pack numbered six, and at close range their true nature became apparent. In my eyes they bore many traits that truly made them hound-like in appearance. They were quadrupeds with each foot bearing sharp claws that apparently helped grip the strange ether of the outside space. A bony tail whipped back and forth angrily. Their heads were long and muzzled but without cheeks, which exposed rows of sharp teeth along the front and the sides of powerfully muscled jaws. There were rudimentary ears that curved back and rejoined the skull at its base. The beasts were lean, like starving dogs, revealing strange ridges of rib, spine and hips beneath pale, glistening, hairless skins. Hartwell watched them, with growing anxiety, his eyes and head darting back and forth to keep the monstrous things in sight.

I eventually grew bored with the whole affair. I will admit that there was an unnatural beauty to be found out there in the in-between, there was something more interesting to me inside the ship. My opinion of Asenath Waite had changed since my strange encounter with her younger self. The animosity that I had felt for her, that I had transferred to her, was long gone. In its place there was something else, a spark of appreciation for who and what she was, what she had been through, and what she was trying to do. To be sure it was odd, knowing what I knew about Ephraim and Asenath, and how out of vengeance one had become the other. Yet I didn't care. There was something about her, about the way she spoke and moved that was alluring. She was unlike any other woman I had ever met, and while there was an obvious reason for that, in my mind it only made her more attractive.

She was still wearing that strange outfit, with the slope hat by her side. She was sitting by herself making notes in a small book. She looked deep in thought, introspective. She looked like a woman who could handle anything this world or any other could throw at her. How long I stood there I can't say, but it must have been a while for eventually she noticed that I was staring at her, closed her book and with a coy look motioned me to join her.

As I settled in beside her I caught a strong whiff of her scent. She smelled like hyacinth carried on a sea breeze, and I drank it in and let her fill my senses. She placed her hand on mine and smiled. "Mr. Olmstead, is there something you want to say to me? Because I am getting the distinct impression that you're becoming a lap dog, and that is something I don't need."

I hung my head, more in mock shame than anything else. "My apologies Miss Waite."

"Actually, its Mrs. Derby. You should call me Asenath."

I was a little surprised. "I hadn't realized you were married. You don't wear a ring."

"My relationship with my husband is unconventional. We find traditional symbols and roles limiting." A malicious smile crawled across her face.

"I've read your letters. I know what you are, who you are, I just have to ask why you've stayed where you are?"

There was a look of bewilderment on her face, one that was quickly replaced with something I read as respect. "What I do, the things I've studied, they were always as a man. I've always known that the things that I do, that you would call magic, were dependent on gender. There are things that men can do that women cannot, and vice versa. The universe it seems responds to the masculine and the feminine in different ways. Neither is better, they're just different. Living as a woman was a necessity at first, it gave me power over certain factions in Innsmouth, and then later hid me from the forces that occupied my home."

"And the magic?"

"I found ways to do what needed to be done, at least until recently. As I said, there are some things men can do that women cannot, and vice versa. Unfortunately what I needed to do required me to find a suitable male with whom I could make the rendition, but only on a temporary basis. I've grown too old and too wise to throw away a body that is perfectly healthy with many years in front of it. Besides, if you haven't noticed, I've become very comfortable in this body, it has its advantages."

The conversation went on like this for some time, and strayed into areas that were uncomfortable for both of us. She told me about how she learned to adapt to being a woman and how they saw the world differently than men, and I told her about how I watched the other members of my family succumb to the transformation. In both our cases there were societal institutions that didn't know how to deal with our particular situations. In my case the only way my family could deal with Lawrence was to place him in an asylum. In hers, while the Hall School provided a refuge, it also was something of a prison. The rigid structure forced Asenath, who knew more about world history, science and literature than anyone short of a college professor, was forced to sit through classes on manners and needlework. It was all so laughable how the world dealt with things that didn't fit into predictable categories. I couldn't help thinking about round pegs and square holes.

Chandraputra interrupted with an announcement. "We're coming up on the transmitter, I'm *tkrt* going to start banking toward the coordinates *tkrt* you've provided. We could be at our destination in *tkrt* under a half-an-hour."

A look of satisfaction came across Asenath's face. "Thank you Chandraputra. I trust . . ."

Whatever else Asenath was going to say was lost as Hartwell suddenly started screaming. "They're gone! They were right outside the ship, and now they're gone! The Hounds of Tindalos, they're gone!" He backed away from the window and moved toward the center of the ship. Not watching where he was going he bumped up against the Packard, and swiftly crawled into the driver's seat and slipped out of view.

We were all watching as the car door clicked shut, but it was Elwood who's eyes grew suddenly wide and in a panic rushed forward. "Angles. The ship has no angles, but the car!" Chandraputra's great bearded head swayed in puzzlement as Elwood screamed his name. "CHANDRAPUTRA THE CAR IS FULL OF ANGLES!"

Elwood's warning came too late. Sick blue light had suddenly seeped out of the car as something from outside found its way to the interior of the Packard. Waite yelled, "Hartwell get out of there!"

The only response to her plea was a horrid, piercing scream, followed by a sickening wet gurgling noise. A red mist filled the interior. As something large and pale struggled within, the car door buckled outwards and all four tires exploded in concert. Another bulge ripped up through the hood, cracking the windshield and spraying glass into the air. The bulging steel of the hood cracked and then split open as a large pink fleshy tube burst through. The tube spewed a thick viscous fluid that glowed blue as it spread across the floor of the ship.

The ship lurched and Chandraputra yelled, "Hold onto something!" Waite searched for a firm grasp in vain, in a ship comprised of gentle slopes and curves there was little to grab onto. Elwood on the other hand seemed oddly relaxed; indeed he appeared to be entering into a deep meditative state. As I dove for the curve of the ramp and clamped on tight I briefly loss sight of the man. When I turned round again Frank Elwood was nowhere to be seen. Try as I might I could find no trace of the man, it was as if he had completely vanished. The ship lurched again, and then seemed to spin out of control. I looked to Chandraputra for direction, and what I saw was not what I expected.

Chandraputra was speaking in a strange, inhuman clicking language that issued forth from his unmoving mouth. As the mystic chanted, a circle of blue light formed on the floor beneath the car. It seemed to dilate into a center point and then slowly transitioned to yellow. A three-pronged claw tore through the side door shredding steel like cardboard. The glowing circle transitioned to orange as the hound stepped out onto the floor and roared. Behind the beast something else, something human, shuddered and convulsed, spraying gore across the vast interior of the ship. A hand flopped down between my feet, twitching violently as green viscous fluid drained out at the wrist. It flopped over and crawled behind me like a rat scurrying for a hole. I tried to follow its movements but lost it as the beast roared and the circle of light turned red. As my eyes darted across the ship I noted that the mass of blood and gore that was once named Doctor Stuart Hartwell had inexplicably vanished. Like Frank Elwood, every trace of the doctor was gone.

My attention turned once more to the horror raging inside the ship. The red circle vanished and was replaced with a vast jagged opening to the exterior which served to turn the interior of the ship into a storm of wind and sound. The hound screamed in agony as it was suddenly blown out of the ship. Its claws grabbed onto an edge briefly, but that hold was tenuous, and it slipped away screaming. Waite clung to me as my preternatural strength seemed capable of holding all of us in place against the torrent. The Packard, and the shards of glass, fell out after the hound and vanished into the ether. Suddenly, the strange in-between spaces were gone and the gaping hole in the ship was full of racing blue and white sky and huge monolithic mountains covered with snow and strange twisted black peaks. The air was bitterly cold and the wind bit into my flesh as I pulled Waite in tight to my chest. As the ship with us inside plummeted uncontrollably downward, the landscape became a raging blur of color, and the air filled with the sound of wind screaming and whistling through the damaged ship. We were tumbling and spinning and through the hole and the window I could see the world go mad as grey sky and the frozen grey surface of Antarctica became indistinguishable from each other.

Through it all Chandraputra was somehow standing and trying desperately to control the ship as if there was some hope of that. "We're not far from the coordinates!" The swami cried out. "A few seconds more and we'll *tkrt* be at the coordinates Danforth gave you. If I could just hold her *tkrt* together a bit longer, shed some of the speed . . . we might just have a chance."

There was a pause and then suddenly Chandraputra was staring at Asenath with that lifeless face of his. He screamed and seemed to run from the floor straight up a nearby wall, and then across the ceiling. Everything was shaking, and the last thing I felt was a wave of force ripple through my body, and then mercifully, my mind grew heavy and I passed into unconsciousness.

CHAPTER 13

From the Account of Robert Martin Olmstead
"The Madness of Chandraputra"

The wind was whipping snow and ice past my head, which was the only part of me that wasn't buried deep in a pile of slush and debris. With a Herculean effort I pulled myself out and found myself to be hurt, cold and wet, but intact. My left shoulder and arm had absorbed most of the impact and were badly bruised but not broken. My shirt had been torn across the front, revealing the scaly skin beneath. I knew that it was cold, but this didn't seem to faze me, apparently my incomplete metamorphosis had progressed sufficiently that I was able to resist even the freezing winds of Antarctica. Those winds blew madly, like great, unending blasts of pure ice. The tiny crystals of snow and hail tore across my skin at incredible speeds. My scaled flesh helped protect me some, but I could still feel hundreds of miniscule daggers cutting in to me. I dug about in the wreckage and found a tarpaulin that I could use as a kind of cloak.

As I pulled the fabric around me I heard Asenath moan as she struggled up out of the wreckage and stumbled to her feet. Snow and ice mixed with blood caked her clothes and the wind whipped her hair into a streaming torrent. "Did we lose anybody?" she asked, wrapping her arms around herself. I could feel the ice on her skin. She was shivering. Apparently she was not as immune to the temperature as I was, and I draped the tarp around her and drew her in close to my chest. I knew she was cold, and hoped that my body could somehow provide her with some sort of heat. It may have been a futile gesture.

With Asenath shivering in my arms, I scanned the vast bleak landscape; we appeared to have crashed in a small valley surrounded by towering peaks that pierced the sky like daggers. Yards away, a large flat pool was rapidly refreezing. Just beneath the frosty blue surface I could see the dark oblong shape that could only have been the remnants of Chandraputra's strange light-ship. Beyond that, half buried in a snow bank I perceived a man-sized shape that stirred and shifted. I could hear moaning accompanied by an odd clicking sound.

"I think we lost Hartwell to the hounds, but Chandraputra is over there." I said pointing to the dark shape.

"What about Elwood?"

I shook my head. "He vanished before we crashed. I'm not sure how that happened."

Asenath's teeth were chattering. "I think he knows how to travel in that weird in-between space. I think he learned how from studying Gilman's formulas. He might surprise us and return." A cold, blasting wind suddenly hit her and she tried to curl up closer to me. "Have you noticed how warm it is? I'm not being ironic here, it's below freezing, but by all rights we should be much colder than we appear to be."

I almost laughed. "It may be unseasonably warm, but if we don't find shelter fast, you're going to have some serious frostbite to deal with. We should collect Chandraputra and see if we can find some cover."

We crept across the frozen landscape toward the crumpled figure that was our colleague. The way was treacherous and we had to wind our way around frozen slabs of ice and piles of unconsolidated snow drifts that threatened to swallow us whole. More than once we clung together and slid like wary skaters across frozen pools of clear blue ice. Through it all I could do nothing but watch as Asenath continued to shiver violently and ice accumulated around her face and head. She was obviously having difficulty walking and as we cleared the last great ridge of snow, she stumbled and fell face first into the bank. My own movements still seemed unaffected by the frigid climate and so I did my best to lift her up onto her feet.

It was then that the dark mass of material that I had identified as Chandraputra stirred and began to rise up and reveal itself.

From the snowy crater stepped a large shadowed form that I knew at an instant was not human. True there was a crude caricature of a human shape but no man was so large, and the soft curves that mark the human form were absent. Instead the silhouette was angular, straight lines that turned too sharply, like a horrid suit of massive armor plate. The monstrosity stumbled forward, and as it approached it revealed itself as an inhuman horror. The beast was easily more than seven feet tall, its head was snouted and adorned with fine wiry hairs that surrounded a set of dark spider-like eyes. There was no neck, but the shoulders were draped in squamous leather not unlike that of a crocodile, while the belly was wrinkled, rugose and pallid, which revealed a multitude of fine capillaries imbedded in the flesh. Four pairs of appendages were attached to the thing's body, two pair served as legs while the other two appeared to function as arms. Each appendage ended in a wicked tri-lobed claw with needle-like fingers that seemed too dangerous to be anything but weapons. It was clearly one of the Nug Soth, as described in that strange metallic book from the ship. Yet the horror of it all was that clinging to the creature's body were the tattered robes and garments of our compatriot! Indeed, about the creature's head dangled shreds of a mask; a beard and face that I recognized as belonging to our companion, the enigmatic Swami Chandraputra!

The creature leapt at us and I braced myself for I was sure that the full weight of the thing would bowl me over. Instead the monster nimbly landed in front of us and seized me with fluid ease. I was tossed about as easily as a doll and ended up with my back pinned to the belly of the thing. Three claws clutched my struggling form while the fourth reached up between my legs and clasped down onto my chest. I could barely breathe, and I looked to Asenath for help, but she had crumpled to the ground and seemed on the verge of falling into unconsciousness.

The thing's snout opened and a hissing, raspy parody of a voice desecrated the air. "Do not move little monster. I see you there."

Waite's eyes betrayed the fear that she was feeling, but she remained composed and stood as still as she could. "I see you too."

The thing's head cocked to one side, like a dog hearing a whistle. "Two, I am two, two in one. I am Zkauba. This is my body, mine! I suffer enough with two. I will not surrender it to another hideously small, soft-fleshed warm thing. I will not share!" The head of the thing that called itself Zkauba violently reared back. It shrieked and spittle flew through the air, "ABOMINATION!" Claws opened and drew back, I was cast aside as it prepared to strike at Waite.

Waite ran. I don't know where she found the strength, from some hidden reserve deep inside her perhaps, or if she had invoked some kind of magic to boost herself. Either way she was moving as fast as I had seen any human being move, as fast as the thing called Zkauba. Zkauba followed her, ripping through the tattered remains of what was once his Chandraputra disguise, and revealing the complex web of semi-metallic belts and straps that crossed his body. At each juncture of strapping there was a large polished jewel, like a cabochon. As the last of his former costume fell away the thing called Zkauba began depressing the jewels in an odd, almost systematic pattern. The gems glowed across the spectrum and sent energy down the belts. The webbing seemed to expand and grow around his body and limbs. White tendrils like fibrous glass wrapped Zkauba in a kind of armor from head to toe. The helmet itself was an oblong egg with a single large jewel in the center and several more scattered around. As he charged off after Asenath I studied the suddenly armored form for any hint of weakness, but I found none. The only opening I could even detect was a pair of rear-facing vents on either side of his helmet.

I screamed and charged him from behind intent on tackling a monstrously large wizard from a species eons old. Instead I stumbled past him, somehow he had sidestepped my attack, I had entirely missed a target three to four times my size. As I fell I turned and saw Zkauba charging through the air sideways, literally running on the very air itself. He grabbed me with one arm and tried to fling me away again. Instead I latched on, used the momentum of his throw and my weight to spin him around. Running on air may have allowed him to bypass my attack but it also prevented him from finding any traction to resist my redirection of his movement. We tumbled head over hindquarters until we fell out of the air and skidded against the ground.

"You may not be as warm as the others," Zkauba hissed through his armor, "but you are still a soft-fleshed thing that stands no chance against one of the Nug Soth of my skills!"

Zkauba raised up an armored fist. The gauntlet glowed and electric blue sparks began to arc across the surface. I struggled to move out of the way but he pinned me with one of his other hands and drew back to deliver a killing blow.

Waite acted first. She crawled up his back, a small glass vial containing a cloudy yellow liquid was in her right hand. In a swift and purposeful effort Waite smashed the vial against one of Zkauba's air vents. The liquid hissed and foamed as it filled the mechanism and seeped inside the armor. Zkauba reared up in agony and threw Asenath off into a nearby ridge of ice. I heard her body thud as it hit the wall.

I squirmed around and began tearing at the creature's arms with my own claws. I lost sight of Waite as I succumbed to a kind of rage. The battle between me and the monster raged on but while each one of my attacks seemed to do nothing against Zkauba's armor, he was still shrieking in pain. Meanwhile, my claws themselves had begun to break and the pain of each strike had become excruciating. Suddenly from the monster there came a thundering shriek of "ENOUGH!" In a single moment, my battered body was hurled across the icy ground, coming to rest where Asenath was trying to get back up on her feet.

The towering form of an enraged Zkauba stumbled toward us, rising easily ten feet tall on its fully extended hindquarters. The head of the thing lolled back and forth as it closed the distance between us menacingly. Ominously, with each step great cracks were rent in the thick ice beneath it. I staggered to my feet, fully intent on engaging the beast in direct combat even though I knew it was futile.

Asenath grasped my shoulder and pulled me back, "Wait, see if the drug has any affect."

I shrugged her off. My legs tensed as I prepared to leap and bury my claws in the strange jeweled eyes that decorated the helmet. Instead, the creature once more depressed one of the cabochons and in response the glass fibers of the armor withdrew. The black beetle-like beast tasted the air with his proboscis, chattered in what

I can only assume was the equivalent of maniacal laughter, and then bounded away across the ice. He seemed to be following some invisible trail, something only he could sense, but then as the wind shifted I suddenly could sense it as well. It was a stench really, burnt meat and some kind of fuel. I grabbed Asenath, cradled her in my arms and took off after the rogue member of the Weird Company.

The trail was easy to follow. It wasn't just the smell; Zkauba made no attempt to cover his tracks, and left a soft, almost slushy wake in the ice. It was Asenath that took that simple observation and made it mean something. We were well beyond the crash site, and while she was still cold, the temperature was slowly rising, and the ice beneath our feet was becoming softer as it melted. Antarctica, or at least the part we were in, was growing warmer, changing, becoming something different. There was no way that could possibly be a natural occurrence, it had to be linked to the reason we were here, to the disaster we were meant to stop.

We crossed over a low ridge of rock and then worked our way down into a hollow. The temperatures were warm enough that Asenath had regained some of her strength and no longer needed me to carry her. There was running water in the small rocky valley, and here and there were small patches of moss and lichen. Zkauba's trail moved down the stream which steadily grew as it led up a rocky hill. As we moved up the hill Asenath pointed to a small column of smoke rising from a pile near the mouth of the cave. The material was blackened, charred, but I recognized it for what it was. They were jumbled, but I could make out eight arms, eight legs and four skulls. Someone had tried to incinerate four bodies, four human bodies. Asenath gagged a little as we passed by, more from the stench I think than any sense of remorse or humanity.

Beyond the rise there was a wall of rock, the base of a mountain, where the stream trickled out from some underground aquifer. Zkauba's trail led above the stream and to a small cave. It had once been a barely noticeable, little more than a hole, but Zkauba had forced his wave through, boring the hole larger so that he could pass through. Given his size, our passage was relatively easy. The trail of death that had begun outside continued inside the cave. There were dozens of large bodies, all burned like those outside, but these were not human, but rather seemed to be of an avian origin, for there were beaks and traces of feathers amongst the bones. There was something else amongst the ruined bodies, a mass of amorphous flesh, like fat caught in a fire, twisted, bubbled, and charred. Whatever it was, whatever it had been, it was unlike anything else I had ever seen before. More curious was the sledge of supplies including cold weather gear, tinned food, some clothing, a stove, a clutch of bamboo sticks, and even several boxes of matches.

The cave opened up into a cavern with a lake, and on the far side I saw Zkauba. He was still running, still following some trail. There was an opening, this one not natural, and he disappeared inside. I wanted to follow, but Asenath stumbled and I realized that while she was stronger than any normal woman, she was nowhere as near as strong as I was and that she needed rest. The events of the last hour had exhausted her, and she was on the verge of collapse. Torn between following Zkauba and protecting the weakened Asenath, I chose the latter. She protested, said there was no time, but in moments she was asleep, and I was watching over her as best I could.

Using the supplies from the sledge I kept her as warm as possible. I used the stove to supply heat; there wasn't much fuel, but there was enough to generate some warmth for the two of us. The cold weather gear replaced our tattered clothes and made us look like we were wearing uniforms, like we were members of the same team, which of course we were. That we were all that appeared to be left of that team, of Asenath's Weird Company, didn't seem to matter. I took comfort in that idea, and soon relaxed and let myself fall asleep next to the woman I was protecting. The woman I had no choice but to admit I was developing strong feelings for.

It was hours before I was roused by the shuffling sound of someone approaching our position. It was Zkauba, and beneath the sound of his steps he was emitting a low, pained wailing. I leapt to my feet and rushed toward the beast, ready to take on the monster even though I failed before. Behind me Asenath scrambled to take up a defensive position behind a boulder, but both our actions were unnecessary.

Zkauba waved me off. "Relax Olmstead," he struggled to say. "Zkauba's back under control. Asenath's version of the elixir worked, it just took time to have an effect."

"So Randolph Carter is in control again?" offered Asenath.

The creature's head turned sideways. "We all have secrets, but I suppose they must all be exposed in the end." He tossed a package, a bundle of cloth, toward me, and I caught it in mid-air."

"What's this?" I unwrapped the cloth, and remembered doing the same thing just a few days ago. Inside was a book, a journal of some sort.

Chandraputra, Zkauba, the thing that Randolph Carter had become, snarled. "Some hint I think of what we are up against, and why we must put a stop to it."

CHAPTER 14

Document A32-477
"Under the Mountains of Madness"

(*The following document was recovered from the remains of the 1936 Secondary Magnetic Expedition. There is no record of how it came into their possession, but it seems apparent to be related to the Miskatonic Expedition.*)

If you have found this, I have to ask you to ask yourself, do you know who you are? I don't mean in the existential sense. Do you know who you are, or, as I suspect, do you suffer from some sort of amnesia, a loss of memory, a loss of personality? Again I ask you, do you know who you are? I don't. I don't know who I am, but I know the truth, or at least suspect it. I only have to convince you. I have little to persuade you with, and you shall think me mad, but I shall tell you my story in the hope that you shall do as I plan to.

When I awoke, I had no knowledge of my own identity. I did not, and still do not know my name, age, occupation, place of birth or residence, or any other such details that would serve to identify me. I have knowledge of language, of English and Latin, of sciences including mathematics, geology, biology, a smattering of physics. I know so many things: the gravity constant, the names of the bones in the human hand, the temperature at which magma begins to solidify. I can explain several of Fermat's Theorems. I know many things, but I cannot tell you how I know them.

I awoke naked. I was on the floor of a circular pit, approximately ten feet in diameter and six feet deep. The pit itself appeared to have been cut out of the very bedrock itself some long time ago, for all evidence of tool markings had long been worn away. Running the entire circumference of the pit was a step-ledge approximately three feet wide. The ledge itself was only another three feet below the main floor of an underground chamber of massive proportions, easily the size of a football field and with a ceiling thirty feet above my head. Light was provided by organic masses, perhaps a kind of bioluminescent fungi, that seem to be scattered at random across that ceiling.

Near the edge of the pit I found a small cache of supplies, clearly identified as belonging to the Miskatonic University Antarctic Expedition. The packs included hand-cranked electric torches, ropes, metallic poles, a large quantity of tinned food, several sets of clothing including furs and gloves, an oil-based heater, a small drum of oil, this journal and several pencils. The food tins are dated in the years of 1929 and 1930. Some of the clothing bore tags with the names of Lake, Gedney and Atwood embroidered, but these names are unfamiliar to me.

The supplies revealed two things that I had not noticed before. Out of habit, I donned some of the clothing, but I was not cold. Indeed I would have estimated the temperature in the cavern at a comfortable seventy degrees, a balmy temperature if I was truly in Antarctica as was implied by the markings. Nor was I hungry, and though I was tempted to open a tin of baked beans, it was more out of routine than any real need. I left all the food untouched. I went about examining the remaining packs, checking the equipment and assuring myself that it was all in working order. Within one of the boxes was a self-winding wrist watch bearing the manufacturer's name, Waltham Watch Company, on the back casing. The watch had ceased to function at 12:42 on February 1st, 1930, but after winding, the mechanism seemed to function normally. I have no way of knowing the actual date or time, but I set the watch to 8:00 AM on February 2nd. It is from this admittedly arbitrary setting that I have since kept time. Curiously there were four other cases bearing the insignia of the Waltham Watch Company, but all of them were empty.

I explored the chamber, and my knowledge of engineering and geology suggested to me that it was not a naturally formed structure, but at the same time I could conceive of no method for constructing it. Scattered about the floor of the vast chamber were four more pits, identical to the one in which I awoke. The shape of the entire chamber is pentagonal with each wall being about a hundred yards long. In the center of each wall there are hexagonal openings which lead to similarly shaped tunnels. The light provided by the strange fungal growths does little to illuminate these dark foreboding tunnels.

I gathered up some of the equipment and supplies and have resolved myself to venturing down one. My one concern was that the tunnels seem completely indistinguishable, and it was possible that in my wanderings, I could return to this exact locale and not be able to recognize it. As a solution to this problem I decided to use the soot from the heater and periodically leave identifying marks to note my passage. The symbol I chose was a simple X, more than sufficient to accomplish the task at hand.

I followed a random tunnel for several hours. At first, I thought the tunnel was straight and level, but after traveling for quite some time I came to realize that the strange five-sided tunnel was slowly curving to the right, as well as being slightly vertically inclined. Such a state would probably have been more noticeable if I had more light, but I was forced to rely on one of the hand-cranked electric torches which illuminated only a few feet in either direction. The darkness was overwhelmingly oppressive. The tunnels were solid and smooth; there were no rocks, no loose pebbles, no sand or dirt. Neither was there anything organic. I saw no evidence of any other person or of any life at all in the tunnel, but I heard things, or at least I thought that I heard things. At one point I could have sworn something had been coming up behind me, something large and unseen that was breathing, gasping really, like a train engine drowning in steam. I crouched back against the wall, the electric light sputtered in my hand, and I was too fearful to crank it. As the dim light slowly failed, I swear that whatever it was out there in the dark stayed just beyond the limit of my failing vision, until the torch flickered weakly and then died, plunging me into complete, impenetrable darkness.

Eventually, I was able to overcome my fear and began cranking the torch frantically and did not cease until the incandescent glow was at its maximum, but the light revealed nothing, and the noise, that freakish snuffling and groaning, trailed off into the darkness and never returned.

Whether the strange sounds were real or the hallucinated product of my mind I cannot say, but after this I made sure to keep the light fully charged. I also began to favor staying close to the wall on my right-hand side. My logic for doing this was simple. Walking down the center of the tunnel, I had realized that the limited illumination given off by my torch may have been insufficient to allow me to detect any branches, turns or similar features. To compensate for this deficiency I chose the side opposite the one on which I was carrying the torch. If any features were to occur, at least I would have a better chance of detecting them.

It was not long after making this decision that I began to detect a faint but definite point of light some great distance down the tunnel. Even more startling was the clear sound of something akin to bubbling, a sort of liquid gurgling, that was emanating from the same direction. With each step the light grew in size and finally took on the familiar hexagonal shape of the tunnel. With a kind of resignation I slowly emerged into yet another hexagonal chamber of tremendous proportions. As with the chamber of my origin, lighting was provided by strange fungal growths hanging down from the ceiling, and as with that chamber, there were five terraced pits, but unlike the first chamber these pits were not empty. In the lower chamber of each was a dark and viscous fluid.

At first I thought the pool was composed of tar or oil, for it gurgled as masses of different densities welled up and then spread out over the surface, much as pools of organic hydrocarbons are known to. Yet as my torch light played over the fluid pool it was revealed to be deep red in color, not the black or brown normally associated with petroleum deposits. Any suggestion that the pool contained some sort of conventional fluid was dispelled by what happened next. For as I leaned closer to the pool, the very surface swelled up, like a rolling wave in the open ocean, and surged toward the light. Startled, I immediately drew back, which sent the light jerking upwards violently. The pool responded as well, and a column of translucent red jelly about a foot thick came up out of the pool like a streamer of melted wax. The tendril reminded me of a slime mold, or perhaps of an amoebic pseudopod reproduced on a massive scale, and as crude and futile as the attempts to grasp my light were, I was overcome with such fear that I drew back even further.

Again the fluid thing in the pool responded, at the base of the tendril there began an intense roiling which quickly formed into a large swelling about twice the diameter of the tendril. With frightening speed the mass raced up the tendril and exploded from the tip. A single large globule of puss spun through the air surrounded by a cloud of smaller globs. Arcing through the air, they all failed to reach me and instead impacted on the surface of the pond, the step-ledge or the wall of the pit itself. Nothing that I could see made it up out of the pit.

Terrified but fascinated as well, I carefully peered over the ledge and observed the globules that now lay scattered about. Those that had landed on the surface of the pool itself had vanished completely, apparently absorbed into the main mass. Those that had landed on the riser were slowly sliding downward, mostly in a manner not unlike that of a viscous fluid, but on occasion a large quantity of the stuff would partially detach itself from the wall and then pull itself downwards in movements reminiscent of infinitely smaller amoebas. This, too, was the motion of the masses that had landed on the lower ledge, the ones I found easiest to observe.

Ranging in size from a penny to a baseball, all were of the same translucent red color which only naturally appeared deeper as size increased. The translucent nature of these things made their internal structure clear to me, but the ease with which I could see inside them offered no comfort or explanation to their status in the order of things. Try as I might, the only organization I could discern within these things was a complete lack of structure. As they moved they put forth pseudopodia that pulled them forward, and the light of the torch revealed the flow of fluids as these appendages were expelled and retracted, but as to what caused the fluids to move, as to some sort of musculature or skeleton, or nervous system, I could discern nothing. The fact that these things would weakly reach out after the light implied that they were reacting to some sort of stimulus, but whether that was heat, light or motion I could not tell, and neither could I make out any semblance of sensory organs that would register such a stimulus.

It was not only the torch they reacted to. As they crawled about on the lower ledge it was inevitable that one would meet another, and the resulting interaction taught me much. The contact between the two was accidental and casual, nothing more than a smaller glob brushing up against a larger one. Immediately both ceased moving and I could see a small bridge of jelly form where the two had touched. The pause was pregnant, there was a taste in my mouth, a taste of wonder and anticipation, and I swear I could see a faint dance of lights flicker within the jellied bridge. Here then was a new species unknown to man carrying out biological functions equally unknown, and I was the first to observe it.

The bridge split apart violently and the smaller glob veered off, moving rapidly away from the other. The larger thing groped after it, lashing jellied tentacles out like streamers across the black rock of the floor. The larger one grasped the smaller, dragging it back, pulling it into itself. The larger one swallowed the smaller, absorbed it, and merged with it in a strange form of anti-mitosis. When it was all over, there was only one glob left and it slid back in the same direction that the larger one had been going as if nothing had happened. It was as if the smaller one had never existed.

Intrigued, I decided to perform a quick experiment. Tying a small piece of rope to one of the food tin keys, I carefully dropped the item in the path of one of the larger globules. As the weird jelly, like creature crawled over the metal key neither the creature nor the key reacted, but as the thing slowly crawled over the hemp rope it suddenly surged forward. The rope was enveloped and within seconds it was gone; not one trace of it remained, devoured by the blob of goo which quickly continued back on its seemingly random trek. Based on this experiment I suspected that this strange proto-plasmic creature could devour any kind of organic material, and I shuddered to think on such things too much.

I made a camp by the mouth of one of the tunnels, as far from any of the pits and their horrid inhabitants as I could get. Something was nagging at the back of my mind. I had missed a vital clue, or drawn some ersatz conclusion, but, try as I might, I could not overcome the feeling that something was horribly wrong. My watch told me that I had been awake for hours, and still I was not hungry. As I sat there looking at my supplies, I caught my reflection in the side of a metal tin. It took me a moment, as I had to stare at my reflection to understand what I was seeing. My face was that of a young man, perhaps in his mid-twenties. My eyes were hazel. My skin was fair and smooth. I could see no scars, but the most dramatic feature that my image revealed to me was the complete lack of hair. There was none on my head; I had no trace of beard or mustache. Eyebrows were absent, as were any eyelashes. I checked the rest of my body and found that there was no hair anywhere, on any part of my skin, nor any tattoos. Using the tin as a mirror, I checked my mouth and found no fillings or missing teeth. Except for the complete lack of hair, I was a perfect specimen of manhood. I tried to think about what kind of physical or chemical trauma could result in the loss of all body hair but could think of none. Confused and tired, I closed my eyes and quickly fell asleep.

According to the watch, I awoke several hours later to find that I was no longer in my camp. I apparently had rolled away from the tunnel mouth, all the way to the edge of the nearest pit. Indeed one of my arms was hanging over the edge, dangling down toward the lower ledge. Even in a drowsy state I realized the danger of my situation and leapt to a fully upright position, letting out a gasp of horrified terror. This engendered a curious response from the fluid thing in the pit. As I jumped back from the rim in a panic, the thing trapped within the pit recoiled from my position. Like a small body of water driven by a gale force wind, the thing piled up against the wall of the pit furthest away from me. Curious, I carefully stepped forward, and I swear the damned thing shuddered with fear and tried to crawl even further away. Only when I withdrew did the creature relax and flow back into a more placid state.

Confused, I ran my hand over my head and made yet another discovery. My scalp and indeed the rest of my body was covered with a fine stubble. It seemed that a significant amount of growth had occurred while I slept. Apparently, whatever had caused the loss of all my hair, some chemical exposure or physical trauma, did not cause any permanent damage.

I spent the next four hours navigating a dark, seemingly endless tunnel. The time I spent in that shaft and the things that occurred are meaningless in comparison to the events that transpired once I emerged from it, so I will not bother to describe them in any significant detail. Though it should be plain that after spending such a long time in the dark and barren corridors it was a welcome relief when I finally emerged into yet another massive underground chamber, I immediately noticed that the chamber I had come to was significantly unlike the two I had previously explored. Instantly my senses were assaulted by a cacophony of sound that flooded the room and made my teeth ache. It was a rhythmic crashing sound like waves of steel crashing against a shore of glass, horrendous in its nature and bone-shaking in its intensity. With each pounding crescendo I cringed and instinctively covered my head, which served me well as each beat was followed by a heated gust of wind that carried with it a grey sticky ash and such a stench that would put an abattoir to shame.

The source of these violent sounds and noxious bursts was not readily apparent to me, for unlike the prior chambers which were devoid of features save for the pits and the phosphorescent fungi, this one was filled with great mounds of grey rock and ash that towered over me like hills, nearly reaching the ceiling itself. Fearful, but driven by an overwhelming sense of scientific curiosity, I removed my pack and cautiously secreted it underneath a small pile of rubble, concealing it completely from casual view. I then climbed slowly and carefully to the top of one of the great mounds. Several times I lost my footing and either slid backwards down the mound, or found myself in a patch of fine loose material not unlike quicksand.

Reaching the summit, I found myself suddenly in close vicinity to one of the many phosphorescent clumps that served to light the great cavernous halls, and I examined it in detail. It was as I suspected a type of fungi but not one with which I was familiar, and it exhibited features that were wholly unlike those normally associated with that kingdom. A large globular growth almost a yard in diameter, the fungi appeared strikingly similar to an inverted street lamp. Not surprisingly, the thing was evenly divided into five panes of semitransparent material that appeared to have the consistency of amber or dried maple syrup, but paper thin. These panes were held in place by a thick organic green latticework. Through the panes I could make out a bulbous cluster which was the source of the strange cool light, a light to which I was strangely attracted, nearly mesmerized.

Forcefully tearing my attention away from the organic lantern, I turned to look out over the vast chamber. My position on top of the debris pile augmented by a plethora of the luminescent growths gave me a nearly unobstructed view of the artificially constructed cavern, and again I wished that it hadn't, for the sight which was revealed to me set my heart racing and my mind reeling. To describe the thing as inhumanly monstrous would not begin to explain the nature of it, for it was beyond anything I had seen before. Where the pit-thing could be portrayed as protoplasmic and bearing a superficial resemblance to a hyperbolic slime mold or amoeba, this creature was simply alien, bearing no resemblance, not even an exaggerated one, to any earthly creature. It was an abomination pure and simple, a hideous affront to the laws of nature as well as of physics. I do not have the words to give the thing a proper description, and I apologize for lacking those skills, but in the interest of science I shall try.

The main mass of the creature was a fluid darkness larger than a subway car. It had no true shape or boundary, but I could discern in the darkness of its bulk great masses of flowing currents and roiling boils that would seem to churn up and explode out into nothingness. The heaving, turbulent darkness was surrounded by a green, wispy haze that clung like fog on a mountain top. Between the two components of the creature there was no clear division and as I watched, volumes of the fog would seem to condense all at once into inky blackness, while in other areas the darkness would suddenly sublimate into a mass of the thick verdigris mist.

The hulking mass was, as I have noted, an inky blackness, but at the same time it was inexplicably translucent, like a fine piece of smoky quartz or volcanic glass. This property, this transparent darkness, made my eyes ache as I watched it flow and change and move. Its primary method of locomotion appeared to be similar to amoeboid motion, moving the bulk of its mass forward in a wave front that more or less crashed like a wave. This was not its only method of travel, however, for it also produced from itself a myriad of appendages of all shapes and vast sizes that would seem to supplement its forward motion. A phalanx of jointed appendages not unlike those of a grasshopper pushed it onward, while a pair of rough-hewn arms with great circular suckers clasped onto the floor before the thing and dragged the hulking entity about. Tentacles, arms and legs came into existence and dissolved as needed, as did other specialized organs including a multitude of feelers, visual receptors, a trumpet-like organ I assumed was analogous to an ear, and a moist fan of tendrils that I gathered was designed to provide a sense of smell.

Along with these appendages and organs, the creature appeared to have created a set of features that seemed specific to the task at hand, namely carving this chamber into the standard pentagonal shape. The front of the monstrosity had been transformed into twin huge jaw-like shovels lined with massive and wicked picks. The creature would literally bite into the wall of raw rock and then swallow the resulting chunk of boulder-sized stone. Seconds later, a huge tube-like orifice on the creature's anterior end would suddenly swell up and belch out a cloud of grey sediment onto the floor, forming the mounds that were scattered about the chamber, and the clouds of sticky ash that were driven into fearful gusts by the forceful expulsion.

Witnessing the presence of this creature, its actions, its size, its very existence, I became momentarily dumbstruck, and in that instant I lost my footing and slid from the top of the mounded debris, tumbling head first through the coarse gravel. My fall initiated a minor avalanche and my landing on the hard floor was accompanied by the sound of pebbles and rocks skittering, clattering and echoing through the chamber. I lay stunned for a moment surrounded by a sudden, relative silence. At first I thought I had suffered some sort of neurological trauma, for the pounding sound of the beast chewing through the rock had ceased to fill my ears. That delusion vanished as a new sound wormed its way toward me. I grabbed my supplies and blindly dashed across the floor, pursued by the sound of colossal limbs rushing after me. Hot breath blasted from behind me, whipping my body forward in terror. How I reached the safety of the tunnel,

I did not understand, but I did, and I was again free to explore the dark labyrinth.

A few hours later, and several turns through the darkness, the horror of my encounter was supplanted by a wondrous new discovery. The latest chamber that I emerged into was a virtual paradise compared to those prior. The dominant feature was a large, roughly circular pond or small lake around which a lush garden of sedges, shrubs, bushes and small trees grew. Light in this chamber was provided by the same fungi that were present in the other chambers, but whereas previously the ceilings were dominated by a small number of specimens, the roof of this chamber was covered with thousands of such growths, so densely packed that in some areas the ceiling stone itself could no longer be discerned. Besides the fungi and plants, there was a myriad of small and primitive animal life darting about the chamber including a great diversity of beetles clumsily flying through the air on clunky, thick, veined wings, but neither was there any lack of swarming ants. Spiders, scorpions and centipedes were also represented, as well as invertebrates I could not readily recognize or classify. A great grasshopper-like thing came to roost on my hand, an event that apparently I was accustomed to, as I did not panic, but I soon discovered this was no ordinary orthopteran. While my initial attention was drawn to the ornately crested head and a colorful thorax, it was only when it prepared to leap that I noticed it bore not six legs but seven, having not a pair of femura modified for jumping but rather an asymmetrical set. Stunned, I watched as the thing deftly sprang away from me into the brush and toward the central pond. The miniature lake was cool and clear and teeming with life, including things akin to shrimp and crayfish. Algae and a leafy submergent macrophyte dominated the floor of the pool which was composed of a thick layer of loosely consolidated sand and rock. There was no evidence of larger predators: no tracks were evident and I heard no calls.

I thought perhaps to capture several of the shrimp-like creatures and cook them up for a warm meal. I waded into the pond and, using the shovel from my kit, slowly herded a few of the creatures into the shallows, then deftly slipped the blade under them and flipped the crustaceans onto the bank. Removed from their natural habitat, they flipped up into the air in random directions, trying to get back into the water. Satisfied with the clutch that I had captured, I stumbled my way out of the pond, losing my footing and sliding face first into the bank. I recovered, wiping the wet grit from my eyes and face. Bending down to gather up my fresh lunch, I found that it had vanished. I searched the grass and the nearby shrubs, but to no avail. I concluded that the things must have escaped back to the pond while I had stumbled out of it.

Frustrated, I stepped back into the water and again corralled a few of the creatures into the shallows and launched them onto the bank. This time I kept my eye on the creatures as they struggled to survive. They flipped into the air a few times, and then flopped weakly against the ground before settling down and resolving themselves to a few last twitches. As their pathetic twitching slowed, I reached out for them but withdrew my hand in fear. The five translucent grey decapods began to quiver again, more violently, where they lay on the grass and then slowly began to melt. Enthralled, I watched as the things sagged and then, not unlike hot wax, flowed into the moss without a trace. Cautiously, I reached out to touch the place where they had been, but nothing at all remained. I tore at the thin vegetation, scraping the clumps of tiny plants from the ground and tossing them violently into the air, heedless of where they might fall. My tantrum revealed nothing but the ubiquitous grey rock forming the walls and floors of the chambers and tunnels. Overwrought, I fell back and screamed in anguish.

My cry was countered by a tremendous roar, as if a titan had stirred. So loud was it that I could not identify where exactly it had come from. The trees and shrubs shook, small creatures dashed about in obvious fear, and in the distance one of the fungal lanterns shook loose from the ceiling and crashed through the canopy into the underbrush. The sound trailed off, fading to a deep grumble, then to a low hum, until finally only a faint trace of a vibration remained. In the meantime the small glade had grown deathly still and silent.

I scrambled to my feet and frantically grabbed my supplies. With my head down I was oblivious of anything beyond my narrow field of vision, but as I rose up and swung my backpack on I was shocked to discover the small glade-like area vanishing before my very eyes. Trees and shrubs were melting, forming huge pools of viscous fluid that flowed slowly back to the pond in the center of the chamber. The insects and other small life forms, suddenly deprived of cover, were swarming, forming thick banks of darkness that would hover in swirling banks of shadow that would suddenly coalesce and then collapse into a rain of gelatin.

I ran, ran as fast as I could toward the next tunnel while beneath my feet the mossy landscape dissolved. With each step forward, the ersatz ecosystem vanished. Like a tide going out, the glade and all its inhabitants flowed away from the outer walls, draining away, leaving only the cold, bare rock in its place. I ran, and the thick fluid splashed about me, covering my legs and then streaming off, as if contact with my very being was repulsive to it. As I reached the tunnel I paused, terrified by what was occurring behind me, by the noises, the horrible, tearing, wrenching noises, and fearful of embarking once more into the dark. An idea bubbled to the surface of my mind, and I suddenly understood the failure of Lot's wife to avert her gaze, for I, too, looked back upon the devastation and destruction laying waste to the garden, and I heartily wish that I had not.

The great thing that rose up out of the central pit, that metamorphic mass from which all life in the chamber had collapsed and merged again, it towered like a titanic polyp, blindly craning about, searching, reaching out with monstrous tentacles to capture those stray spawnings that had not yet been reclaimed. At first I thought the devastation to be the result of some horrific biochemical process, perhaps a type of organic acid, spewed about, digesting everything for the monstrosity to feed upon, but as I watched in rapt horror, I knew that was not the case. For this thing, this gelatinous mass, was yet another form of the thing in the pit, one capable of more than simple replication of organs and appendages. This thing was even more advanced than the other, for as I watched the creature devour the once tranquil glade, I saw that beyond it, half-hidden by its own shadow, a new glade was taking form; trees and shrubs, animals of fantastic shape, all these were spewing forth, tearing themselves from the central mass, desperate to fill the void left behind. This metamorphic monstrosity was able to divide itself up into a myriad of component creatures and imitate them closely.

It had created an entire habitat of plants and animals, nearly perfect to the casual observer, flawed only in its inability to mimic a
single process, that which creates the leaf litter and other materials
that form the detritus covering the forest floor. A simple process
inherent in every form of life known to science, this thing could
not mimic it for the simple fact that its creations did not die and
rot but were only reabsorbed. This terrified me to the core. One
might then suppose that the thing in its changing forms must be
immortal, but instead I grew to suspect that it was all some sort of
organic machine, using a process similar to cellular regeneration
but improved tremendously. The things cannot die, for they are not
truly alive, at least not as we humans define it. With these horrific
thoughts rambling through my head, I plunged headlong into the
dark, winding labyrinth, and away from the monstrous form that
had deceived me.

I ran until I collapsed from exhaustion. I was driven to put as
much distance between myself and the monstrous landscape as
possible. Somewhere along the way my legs gave out and I fell in a
heap against a tunnel wall. When I awoke, my watch told me that I
had been out for two days! I did not think it possible that I had slept
so long, but the growth of hair on my head and my face suggested
that this was the truth. After waking, I ate a small tin of meat. My
supplies were still in good shape; I was eating and drinking much
less than I thought I would need to. Indeed, I could not recall the
last time I was actually hungry or thirsty.

After my repast, I tried to gain my bearings. I was briefly concerned that during my unexpected rest I might have gotten turned
around and would therefore return to the chamber I had left.
Thankfully, my electric light revealed a feature that I knew I had
not passed before. In front of me was a great spiraled ramp, like the
core of a conch, leading up into the ceiling. I followed it up, glad to
be out of the labyrinth of tunnels.

The ramp emerged on one side of a vast cavern wholly unlike the
chambers I had previously discovered. This one was more natural
in shape, the dominant feature of the three-to-four-acre cave being
a shallow pool dotted with small islands of rocky fragments and
boulders. There was life in the water, small fish and some minute
snails, both apparently feeding off of a slimy mold or bacteria that

grew on the bottom. I suspected that in the deeper pools there were larger animals, perhaps in significant numbers. It seemed a necessity to support the predators that basked on the shores of the subterranean lake. They were penguins of a sort, monstrously large, and albino. I counted eight of them, and at five feet tall they posed some threat to me, for they were fast and their beaks are more than six inches long. But, lucky for me, uncounted generations in the dark had rendered them eyeless, and I with my two good eyes and electric lantern held a serious advantage. One of them wandered away from the rest, and I killed it to make sure it was real and not some sham crafted by the protoplasmic thing I had escaped. Oddly, I found the dead bird, and the rest of the flock, relatives perhaps of the extinct Anthropornis, comforting. Even in this monstrous form they represented a kind of recognizable normalcy, following established rules of biology and behavior. More so, they reinforced my belief that I must indeed be somewhere in Antarctica.

The new cavern was significantly colder than the chambers and tunnels I had left behind, and was fringed with small sheets of ice. Clusters of icicles hung down from the ceiling. Thankfully, the cold weather gear that I carried kept me warm. The pool itself was warmer than the surrounding air and seemed to contain a significant amount of sulfur. It was fed by a small stream that led off into one of several rough passages. I suspected that the source of the stream was a geyser or similar volcanic feature. I was tempted to try to find the source, but the passages were too narrow for even my lithe frame to explore. There were other, larger passages from which a haunting but welcome sound of wind emanated. I desperately wanted to dash down one of those tunnels, but for some reason I decided to stay amid the colony of mutant birds.

Following the shoreline, I found myself forced to work around to the dryer side of a particularly large boulder. In doing so, I startled a rather large penguin at least five and a half feet tall, and incredibly rotund, possibly topping out at over two hundred pounds. It screeched at me in anger and then scrambled away, diving onto its belly and using its arms as paddles to glide across the rocky ground. The whole event would have been comical had it not been for what the thing had left behind. There on the ground lay the remains of a smaller penguin from the head, upper torso and single wing that remained. Of the other wing, lower torso and legs I could find no trace, neither of flesh, feather or bone. Logically, I assumed that the victim had been killed some time before and then been subject to slow consumption, decay hampered by the cold. But that possibility was negated by what happened next, for the head of the dismembered bird suddenly reared up! The beak opened and closed as if trying to call out. In that moment, I was grateful that the thing lacked the ability to move air through its throat, for I am not sure I could have shouldered the burden of its miserable cries. I used the heel of my boot to put the thing out of its misery.

Given the desolation of the place, I was not surprised that the penguins, or at least one of them, had turned to cannibalism. What I did find amazing was that one could attack and devour another, flesh and bone included, before the victim had even expired. The speed at which such an event must occur, coupled with the strength needed to rend such an animal into digestible pieces, was truly frightening, and I realized that I must be on constant guard against attack. Towards this end I decided to fully explore the cave and all of its environs. Starting at the entranceway to the spiraling ramp, I worked my way clockwise around the lake, exploring the rocky strip that ran between the rim of the lake and the cavern walls. There was little to see. The terrain was uneven and covered with a loose gravel of black rock, peppered with larger rocks and the occasional boulder. The cavern walls were made of the same black stone and were equally uneven. In places large clusters of boulders formed plateaus six to eight feet off the ground. These, I noted, would make perfect places to rest and remain out of reach of the penguins.

Continuing on my way, I passed several fissures in the wall which had been worn smooth by millennia of trickling rivulets of water. The water was cold but clear with a heavy mineral taste. I took a few moments at one of the streams to wash the dirt and dust away. I gasped as the frigid water ran over my body. The mutant birds all turned to stare at me with blind eyes as I struggled to bathe. It was an unnerving sight, and I was happy when the flock finally went back to ignoring me.

As I reached the far side of the lake, I noticed an object that was neither the color nor the shape of the surrounding rocks. It was a sledge of supplies, cold weather gear, tinned food, lamps, clothing, a heater, a stove, a clutch of bamboo stocks, and several barrels of kerosene. There were footprints around it, boots all the same size. It was the first evidence of human life I had seen, and it sent my heart pounding. The sledge was pointed toward the mouth of a large cave from which a flickering pinprick of light could be seen. It couldn't be more than a mile away. I grabbed a few supplies from the sledge and began to move down the tunnel, but then I stopped dead in my tracks, and the things in my arms tumbled and clattered against the rocky terrain.

In front of me stood the obese penguin that I had caught devouring one of its own. It was moving toward me, as if staring at me with those empty, eyeless sockets. I moved quietly to the left, and the monster bird mirrored me. I moved again, but again the mutant countered. I reached back slowly and pulled a bamboo stock from the sledge. The beast cocked its head and opened its mouth, revealing double rows of sharp, thorn-like teeth. Spittle dripped from those horrid fangs, and where it fell onto the rocks it hissed and sputtered like acid, and I finally understood how the thing had devoured the other penguin so quickly. Then as I watched, it shuddered. The sides of its head split open and two large black eyes shoved themselves up out of the skull and twisted back and forth in the rough sockets. It looked at me now with real eyes, saw the metal-tipped stick and screeched like some great raptor.

I stumbled backwards and landed against the sledge. The creature lunged forward. I swung the stock forward, and the bird's fat belly slid over it and was slowly impaled. Though the basket was not present, the hooks used to attach it were, and it was these metallic spikes that tore into the bird's spine and kept it from moving forward. The thing struggled to reach me, snapping and thrashing about violently, but to no avail. I pushed myself back and at the same time reached for another stock. The pinned beast shuddered once more and I paused, entranced by the horror that was unfolding before me. The monstrously fanged beak split apart and peeled back, ripping the flesh off the skull. The exposed throat swelled and a frightful thing that bore some resemblance to the mouth parts of a squid shot out at me. Reflexively, I thrust the stock forward and into the center of the gnashing parts, driving them back into the main body of the thing. It wailed and squirmed, desperate to release itself from the two shafts that held it in place. The flesh elongated, stretched and then pulled apart, and two replaced the single beast that had confronted me moments before. They slid about and slowly worked their way off of my makeshift spears. Thinking quickly, I grabbed one of the lamps, undid the fuel cap and poured kerosene over the two squirming masses. I hastily struck a match and tossed it into the fuel. The flames engulfed the things, and they squealed in agony, their limbs flailing about. The smoke turned black and acrid, and whatever the monstrous penguin degenerated into, I could not precisely discern. It was a pulpy, protoplasmic thing that writhed within those flames, another thing that was not what it appeared to be, and I was glad to put some distance between myself and the smoldering masses that remained.

I crashed through that rocky tunnel, heading blindly toward that distant glow. Instinctively I knew that the light was neither a lantern nor some strange assemblage of fungi. The color was all wrong, the white glow soft and inviting. I drove myself forward at breakneck speed, tripping over rocks and climbing over boulders. The rock floor covered with gravel gave way to a landscape of scattered stones, and then an obstacle course of boulder fragments. In the end I was scrambling over boulders larger than me. They peppered the ground that led up to a rough wall that filled the entire passageway. Only a single opening, maybe four feet in diameter, provided a break in the blockage, and from this the light emanated. But it wasn't only the light that poured from that hole. With it came a terrifying wind, a blasting jet that surged icily into the tunnel and carried with it stinging, biting crystals of ice.

I plunged into that hole, hugging to me what gear I could and dragging the rest of it behind me. I used my arms and knees to push myself through, all the time the wind whipping past my face and into whatever gap in my gear it could find. The rocky shards did their best to bruise and break me, but the padding of the jacket afforded some protection. With each movement forward my breathing grew more rapid, my heart beat faster, the wind whipped more ruthlessly, and my desperation grew palpable. Straining against that demonic, freezing wind, I burst from the end of the warren and tumbled into the light beyond.

I found myself at the base of a mountain, of a mountain range. Behind me the white-crowned peaks stretched up into the sky, grey basaltic things, like inhuman towers that clawed at the sun. Before me was a vast icy plain, white and blue reflecting in the sun. Snow drifted in great waves, stopped and then moved on. The cold was a tangible thing I could feel with my hands as it hung in the air. If I tried, I felt I could almost grasp it, shape it, twist it into any form I desired. The cold tore at my skin and eyes as I struggled to put on a pair of snow goggles and cinch down my hood. As I lowered my head to protect my face, my eyes wandered across the ground at my feet and discovered two thin, parallel scratches in the ice-covered rock, readily recognizable as traces of a sledge similar to the one I left behind in the cavern. The trail began at the cave mouth and went off over a low rise just a few hundred yards away, more evidence that I wasn't alone in this place. Excited at the possibility of seeing another person, I foolishly dashed down the trail and over the rise.

I wish that I hadn't, for on the far side of the hillock I found the sledge, and more, so much more. I ran from that place, ran from the light and the sky and the wind. I crawled back through that tight little hole and pushed my way into the cavern of monstrous penguins. Pulses racing with looming madness, I went through the sledge that remained there and took all that I could use. I slaughtered the birds, even though that was all they were. I felt a tinge of regret, but that faded as I pulled my supplies down the spiral ramp and into the tunnels below. The drums of kerosene rolled easily through the tunnels and from cavern to cavern. The thing that played at being a forest shrieked as I doused it with fuel and set it ablaze. It took hours to make sure that I had destroyed all of the thing, for bits of it kept breaking off and trying to escape. I hunted them all down. The flying, creeping, crawling things flopped angrily within the flames, but they all died.

The machine-creature went easier. It, too, shrieked against the flames, but it seemed to lack the power to divide itself and thus could not attempt an escape. It roared as the flames charred its titanic bulk. It crashed against the wall, reared up and gouged the ceiling, knocking massive chunks of rock down onto itself. The boulders pinned the beast and left it wailing pitifully. I cackled maniacally as it slowly succumbed, struggling for more than an hour. It died with a violent shudder. As whatever life force that sustained it finally fled, the structure of the thing gave way and the strange matter that comprised it crumbled into a strange pasty jelly which lingered for a while and then suffered some catastrophic change, dissolving into nothingness.

The creatures trapped in the pits were easiest. They didn't even scream as I poured the kerosene over them. I don't think they even noticed. They were too simple to understand what was happening. Even after I set them ablaze they barely reacted. They bubbled in the heat, turned greasy black, then crisped. When I was done, all that remained were a few piles of glossy black ash.

I rolled the barrel containing the rest of the kerosene back to where it all began, back to the place where I woke up. God help me, I wish I hadn't! I wish I hadn't awoken. That I hadn't wandered through the dark labyrinth. That I hadn't found my way out. I wish that I hadn't seen those mountains, nor the madness that I found at their base. Or seen those shapes, those blasphemous shapes frozen in the ice around the sledge.

I shall finish writing my account, and perhaps then you will understand why I ask you the questions I do. I ask you again, do you know who you are? Because I do not know who I am, and I suspect that neither did any of those who came before me. When I am done, I shall crawl into one of the five pits and I shall pour the last of the fuel over my head and set myself ablaze. A portion of me pauses, and I recall that the Church considers suicide is a sin, but I dismiss such concerns, for I doubt that such rules apply here. Perhaps for me, immolation is a consecration, not a sin.

The things in the ice, the shapes that lay frozen solid against the sledge, they were what drove me mad. They were men who sat there in the frigid landscape, frozen and unmoving. Men who had succumbed to the elements, four men. Four men like myself, who had escaped from beneath the mountains of madness. Men dressed in what they could salvage from the sledges, and equipped the same way. Men with stubble on their heads, and their faces. Men like me.

Do you understand me? Look at yourself. Find a mirror, something reflective. Look at yourself. Look hard. Men should have hair on their heads, beards on their faces, eyebrows and lashes. Men should have scars where time has taken its toll on their bodies. Does your body betray the ravages of time? Or is it like mine, like those out in the ice, free of scars and with freshly grown hair? Are you a man, or are you like me? Is your face your own, or is it the same as mine, the same as the four things I left behind in the ice? Men have faces of their own, but I, I and those poor frozen things, we are monsters, and though we are four, we share but one face. God help me, they all had my face!

CHAPTER 15

From the Account of Robert Martin Olmstead
"Weird Questions"

We sat there in that cavern the three of us, myself, Asenath Waite and the alien Zkauba possessed by the mind of the author and mystic Randolph Carter, wondering what to do next. If Carter was correct, he had discovered our enemy, though their intentions remained unclear, at least to me. For Asenath and Carter things were plain as day, though they differed on some points. That the shoggoths had been trying to imitate members of the Antarctica Expedition, or more precisely one of the members of the expedition, again and again was clear. It was also clear that they had failed. Something in the human psyche had driven their imitations mad with despair. Confronted with the truth of what they were it seemed they preferred death. Yet why the monstrous metamorphs continued to try baffled me. Men were apparently too hard to impersonate, why bother at all?

Asenath tried to explain. "Shogoths are the most powerful of the tools created by the Progenitors. They are infinitely adaptable, and malleable. They can be used as beasts of burden, menial laborers, manufacturing plants, even chemical and biological laboratories. Some highly specialized shoggoths were used to seed planets with life, engineer entire ecosystems. It's what the Q'Hrell did, and it's why they are called the Progenitors. They have travelled the universe colonizing worlds and creating new life, new species, new races. They've done it innumerable times, and for billions of years. In that time shoggoths have themselves become myriad and multiform, becoming what would best be described as subspecies: Tsathaqqua's Formless Spawn, Abhothian spawn, the Dark Young, those of the Green Abyss, even the whistling Flying Polyps are just another type of shoggoth. What's worse is that many of these creatures evolved into unique entities, gods even. On Earth the Q'Hrell used three specialized shoggoths to seed the planet with life; Abhoth, Ubbo-Sathla and Idh-Yaa. All earthly life comes from these three beings, and their memory, though corrupted, forms the basis for many creation myths and dieties including the gnostic Demiurge and the ancient Magna Mater. Like it or not, you and I Mr. Olmstead are the products of these three behemoths. We are their children."

"So why should we be afraid of them?"

It was Carter's turn to speak, even though it was labored and mediated through the alien mouth of his host. "Without the Progenitors, they can *tkrt* become uncontrollable, dangerous and monstrously *tkrt* powerful things. Millions of years ago on Zkauba's home world *tkrt* Yaddith, the Progenitors lost control *tkrt* of a shoggoth and it became something more than it should *tkrt* have been. The Progenitors imprisoned *tkrt* it, locked it away within the *tkrt* core of the planet where they hoped it would never *tkrt* be able to free itself, and they would *tkrt* never have to deal with it again."

"What happened to it, the shoggoth I mean?" I asked, knowing what I had read in his notebooks.

"It took eons, but *tkrt* eventually her spawn, horrid worm-things known *tkrt* as Dholes ate their way through the planet, left *tkrt* it riddled and unstable. It collapsed in on itself, destroying *tkrt* Zkauba's species, and freeing Thaqquallah from *tkrt* her prison. Now she roams the cosmos, free to *tkrt* visit world after world after world spreading her *tkrt* dark young where ever she can. Her multi-form children *tkrt* fester and breed like maggots, corrupting worlds and waiting *tkrt* for their mother to call out for vengeance."

"On Earth," commented Asenath, "the witch Keziah Mason and her sisters were servants to Thaqqualah whom we call Shub-Niggurath, and spread her spawn throughout the secret places of the world, particularly in the Miskatonic Valley. The people of Arkham like to cast dispersions at those who dwell in Innsmouth and

Dunwich and the miscegenation that has occurred there. Truth be told, there is more genetic dirt hidden in the closets of Arkham and Kingsport than in the streets of Innsmouth."

I shook my head, "I find that hard to believe."

"You should Mr. Olmstead, she's telling the truth." The new voice that shattered the tension was one I recognized but never expected to hear again. My shock increased as not one but two figures walked into our midst. That Frank Elwood had returned to us was surprising enough, for despite Asenath's reassurance, my estimation of his character was not high, but it was not Elwood's return that shocked me, but rather the second man that stepped out of the darkness. Asenath seemed cowed by the man's gaze, a man who I myself had seen die, a man who had come back, not as the broken thing who had reluctantly served Asenath, but as an undeniable presence: Doctor Stuart Hartwell, the Reanimator, had returned, and with a vengeance!

We rose up to great them, but Hartwell ordered us to sit and both Asenath and Carter reluctantly complied, though not without questions. "It is a pleasure to see you again Doctor, and you as well Mr. Elwood."

Doctor Hartwell looked over at the damaged and exposed thing that was Randolph Carter, the tatters of its Chandraputra disguise still clinging to it in places. The doctor shook his head in disappointment. "I see you've damaged your mask and robes again."

The casual comment caught my attention. "Wait, you knew? All this time you knew what he was?" Hartwell nodded. "What about you Elwood, surely you didn't know?"

Elwood shrugged. "I've known since the first time I saw him. His geometries are all wrong. I thought you already knew."

Asenath rose up and put a hand on my shoulder, gently suggesting I return to my seat. "However did you both manage to survive?" She asked with sarcasm in her voice.

Asenath's question was greeted with an uncomfortable pause, and when it was obvious that Hartwell did not wish to speak, Elwood took the lead. "When I saw the hounds appear in the car and begin to attack, I panicked and instinctively stepped outside. That was a grave error. The ship was already in the in-between and

I found myself traveling in a reality I was wholly unfamiliar with, not a passage between places, but rather a passage through time. I could see the hounds plunging through space in a series of slow moving frames, like shadows in a flickering light. I could see what was happening to Hartwell, what would happen and what had happened in a kind of non-linear madness of echoes of what had been and what could be. When the event stabilized, when I could see Hartwell as he was just before the hounds attacked, I threw myself at him and the two of us plunged into the time stream, the great flow rushing around us as we struggled against it."

"But we saw him torn to pieces," I protested.

"As did I, but that was only one possible future, and when I back stepped through time I changed all that. I changed the future, something the hounds did not take kindly to. They howled in anger over my interference and bounded after us jaws agape, eyes thirsting for our flesh, or whatever. I'm not sure what it is that the hounds eat, but it is not flesh or blood. Perhaps it is some kind of intrinsic personal time, something bound up inside us that we don't understand. Not that it matters. To escape the hounds I opened a door and with Hartwell still in my arms I once more sidestepped out of harm's way.

"We emerged in the midst of a raging windstorm here, deep in the interior of Antarctica. I had no coat and no materials that could possibly be used to construct shelter or a fire. In my arms I felt Hartwell shudder and he let loose a weak and pitiful moan. If we were both going to survive, we needed shelter, warmth and a place to heal. All three seemed unattainable in the raging cyclone of ice that seemed intent on burying us. Fearing the hounds, but fearing certain death on the ice plains of Antarctica, I gathered Hartwell close and once more crossed over into the in-between. The hounds thankfully were gone, the weird dimensions around me were wholly empty and bleak, but I could see that was only a local condition. In the distance was a vast eerie complex of towers and structures that seemed older than anything I had ever seen before. Oddly it exuded an almost solid presence in the in-between, solid and relatively warm. Driven, Hartwell and I began the long arduous trek to this remote alien shelter. I needed to focus on something, needed to ground myself in some kind of reality. I tried counting my steps but any concept of rational numbers failed me. Indeed I suspect that at one point I had begun counting in multiples of pi, but in that place such a measurement as that meant nothing.

"As we neared our destination I returned to the world and I was able to clearly discern the massive pentagonal and star-shaped monoliths of basalt that surrounded us. The great stone city appeared lifeless; no plants clung to its walls, no birds roosted in its heights, no insects crawled amongst its nooks and crannies. Yet as I cautiously hobbled down its ancient passageways I developed the most curious sensation that I was being observed by forces unseen, something invisible even to my enhanced and preternatural senses was watching my every move. The feeling grew as I on occasion began to sense within the vast stone walls and beneath the strangely smooth roadways a deep thrumming hum, as if ancient but idled machineries were suddenly and slowly springing to life. We followed that alien throb as best we could and moved slowly through the labyrinth of sloping passages and pentagonal gates. Down we went through vast chambers of eerie emptiness and undreamt of corridors that no human hand could have carved. Down, always down, and down oddly led to warmth, for as we descended through insanely sloping switchbacks the air around us grew warmer. At first it was hardly noticeable, for the transition from the Antarctic sub-freezing temperatures to merely bitter biting cold was but a minor improvement. Yet with each level we descended the temperature rose and within hours I was startled to see a small pool of water, fetid but clearly not frozen. It was then that I noticed that the climate in the depths had warmed to the point at which we no longer faced the threat of freezing to death. It was at this moment that I also realized that I had long since left the surface, indeed I must be hundreds of feet beneath the earth, far from the nearest pentagonal gate, and yet there was ample light by which to see. My eyes darted across the room and ceiling but I failed to find any trace of a light source. Disturbed but with little choice we continued to follow the ramp down until at last we came to a chamber which was warm enough for us to be comfortable.

"Once we had recovered from nearly freezing we began to explore our refuge. We found a sledge from the expedition that had some supplies including some food, clothing and other supplies. We used pieces of the sledge itself to fashion some crude weapons. Not far from that we found the bodies of several Elder Things. They had been decapitated. It took us some time, days, but eventually Hartwell learned their secret."

Asenath interrupted. "Did you say days?"

Elwood nodded. "Days, yes. We've been here for two weeks, I think. It's hard to tell time in this place, but I think we've been using our makeshift laboratory to search the city for you for at least ten days."

Asenath, Carter and I exchanged looks, but none of us wanted to say anything. Eventually Asenath reluctantly spoke. "We've only been here for a few hours."

This news seemed to crush Elwood. "When I stepped through time I must have stepped further back than I thought." He mulled this thought over and opened his mouth to say something, but then apparently thought better of it.

It was Carter that broke the uncomfortable silence. "Doctor Hartwell, Elwood *tkrt* said that you had discovered the *tkrt* secret of the Q'Hrell. What did he *tkrt* mean by that?

There was a look of supreme satisfaction on the doctor's face. "It is an established fact that the Q'Hrell are extremely long lived. It is said that their journeys through space from planet to planet may take millennia. They are extremely resistant to physical injury, and as we have learned can survive even being frozen for what was likely hundreds of thousands of years. The only way to kill them it seems is to decapitate them, to separate the brain from the body."

"Isn't that the same way that your subjects had to be destroyed?" Asenath questioned. "An odd coincidence."

The doctor nodded. "Not as much of a coincidence as it would seem, for the issue is rooted in the same cause. My reanimating reagent and the blood of the Q'Hrell are remarkably similar. Indeed it would not surprise me if the serum that flows through their bodies was found to be a superior formulation of my own reagent, capable of accomplishing that which I have been struggling to do for all these years: not only reanimating the dead, but inoculating the living against death itself. I am on the verge of finding the secret to near immortality!"

"THAT IS QUITE ENOUGH! WARD AM NA TAK!" A strange voice boomed out of the cavern. "You go too far my dear doctor, you seek after things you weren't meant to have." The source of these statements was a young man whose approach had gone unnoticed. As he moved closer I noticed that one side of his neck was covered with a thick bandage which had at one point been white, but had since grown the yellow-brown color of dried blood. Beneath his open parka, he was a thin but muscular young man with a sharp aquiline nose and unkempt tawny hair that transitioned into a scraggily beard and mustache. As the parka fell away, I noticed that the jacket beneath was emblazoned with a cloth patch that said Miskatonic University, and beneath that, a stitched label that said GEDNEY.

"You will forgive us sir our rudeness," offered Asenath, "but I must ask who you are and what you are doing here in this desolate place."

The young man made a gesture of supplication with his hands. "My apologies Kamog, you may call me Gedney." Asenath's face turned into a scowl. "My apologies I should not have used your secret name, the one you once used amongst the covens. As for what I am doing here, I thought it would be obvious that I am here to help you and your Weird Company."

The thing that was Randolph Carter clicked its mandibles oddly. "You will pardon my interruption, but I have followed at length the radio reports of the Miskatonic University Antarctic Expedition. The latest reports have the ships heading home having suffered a most horrible tragedy. Half the expedition is lost, and Thomas Gedney has been reported missing, presumed dead."

The young man gestured toward his bandaged neck. "Thomas Gedney was mortally wounded, but shortly after the attack he was found, his wounds were bandaged and he underwent a radical treatment that restored him to near perfect physical health. Unfortunately, the treatment failed to repair his mind. As thus, he was a perfect receptacle for a transfer of consciousness, a relatively simple process." He stared hard at Asenath, "Isn't that right Kamog?"

There was a deep uncomfortable silence that Waite finally broke. "You seem to know who I am." She starred at the figure coldly. "So if you're not Gedney who exactly are you?"

Gedney smiled. "Surely Dr. Hartwell recognizes me?"

There was a look of confusion on Hartwell's face. "I don't recognize the face, but those words, the way you speak, so familiar, so terribly familiar." There was a sudden recognition. "You're Peaslee, or at least the thing that pretended to be him!"

The young man raised an index finger and tapped his nose. Hartwell was suddenly deflated and slumped down onto a rock.

"So you are the strange mind that once supplanted Professor Peaslee's, but that tells us little. Who and what are you?" I demanded.

Asenath looked away with an odd sad expression. "He is of the Yith, bodiless minds from the dawn of the universe. They travel, leapfrogging through space and time, preserving themselves and their civilization at the expense of others. Millions of years ago the Progenitors of Earth had developed a species of cone-shaped invertebrates to use as semi-intelligent labor, an alternative to the shoggoths. The Yith came through time and possessed the cones, and violently established themselves as a new power on the planet. The Progenitors and the Yith fought a protracted war that only ended when a common enemy filtered down out of space and established itself in the Pacific. They may be our allies, but they cannot be trusted, not fully. Whatever they do, it is only to their benefit. They were, they are, and they will be. It is said that they rule the future Earth, an Earth without men, in a future more suited to cooler intelligences, a future engineered by the subtle interference of agents provocateur, such as the thing that stands before us."

"Who are you to judge Kamog?"

Asenath's hidden anger exploded, "You dare to compare us! How many species have you driven to extinction in your endless quest to preserve your own insubstantial lives? We tolerated your repeated programs of culling and breeding the humans because the deep ocean protected us. Don't think we don't know about Tunguska. Your latest effort places all of us at risk if you falter, our wrath will be unforgiving."

The Gedney thing sneered back at her. "We have wandered this universe for longer than your species has existed. We have seen worlds and life that you couldn't even comprehend. Your actions here make us allies but we know that you and your lords have acted against our interests. We will brook no such interference, Men will find their place in the universe, the singularity is unavoidable, and we shall inherit this world. Iä Ygg!" He swore angrily. "You and yours should know your place Kamog. You call us the Yith, and that is what we have been called for millions of years, but we were something else before we took our first desperate leap through time. Do you know why your precious Progenitors hated us so much? Why they battled against us, and why we were so capable of defending ourselves against them? You think of the Progenitors as a single group, with uniform motivations and movements. The truth is quite different. They are a vast and varied species; they occupy millions of worlds throughout the galaxy, and while there is some communication between colonies, each world is essentially independent. The only thing that unites them is their desire for dominance in the universe. They will do anything to gain superiority. You know of the library at Celeano, and the great machines around Altair and Epsilon Eridani. Some Progenitors supported Keziah Mason and Shub-Niggurath. Would it surprise you to learn that once a colony of Progenitors discovered the secrets of time travel?"

Carter shifted nervously. "You're saying that the Great Race and the Elder Things are one in the same?"

The thing that was not Gedney but resided in his body showed no sign of emotion as he nodded in response to Carter's question. "We were once, but through attrition and assimilation we have become something else, and like those we sprang from, we too are becoming what you would call Balkanized."

It was Asenath's turn to question the Yithian. "And what of the whistling, flying polyps, what did you do to earn their enmity?"

"I thought that was obvious. The polyps that have pursued us across time and space, who have hunted us on every world we have sought refuge on, they are our own strain of shoggoths, abandoned when we fled the destruction of our colony so many epochs ago. You really are a most obtuse species."

Asenath rose and took a step forward. There was malice and menace in her movements, and Gedney took a defensive posture as she closed the distance between them. Whatever she was going to do, and how the Yithian would have responded never came to fruition. Instead she sat down, almost as deflated as Hartwell.

"I apologize if I have upset your plans Miss Waite, but truth be told they were my plans to begin with. You and yours have been doing my bidding for more than a century, and while the Whateleys are no longer an immediate threat, and I am sure that you are more than capable of handling the shoggoth problem, I can leave nothing to chance. I have worked for too long, and come too close to let you blunder about like children. I'm seizing control of this little team you've assembled. I hope you don't mind."

A dejected silence lingered for a moment, until finally Hartwell spoke up, "As always you seem to have all the cards, but I will not call you Peaslee or Gedney. What name would you have us refer to you by?"

"Fair enough, I agree calling me Peaslee, Mentzel or even Thomas Felix Gedney would probably be inappropriate in your minds. If you must call me something, call me Mister Ys."

As I looked around I realized that in an instant our group had inexplicably changed, we were no longer being led my Asenath Waite, and the change in leadership had made us something of a pathetic menagerie. The Weird Company consisted of an undying wizard named Asenath Waite, the mad Doctor Stuart Hartwell, an alien possessed by the mind of author Randolph Carter, Frank Elwood who could walk in the spaces in between, myself, a monstrous hybrid named Robert Olmstead, and the time-traveling parasite Mister Ys. Was it possible that what Asenath and Ys said was true? Were we all that stood between the shoggoths and the destruction of the world? Could we stand against the horrors that had inadvertently been released? In this desolate place at the bottom of the world would our lives finally have meaning? If we failed, who would know?

The questions themselves seemed impossible, and perhaps they were impossible for any one of us to ask, let alone answer. Perhaps they could only be asked and answered by us all, working together.

CHAPTER 16

From the Account of Robert Martin Olmstead
"The Thing Above and Beyond the City"

Hartwell and Elwood had not spent their time confined to the depths of the city. They had instead climbed one of the great spiraling ramps and established themselves a kind of base of operations in one of the peak-like towers that strained skyward. Hartwell had found the mechanism that controlled the interior of the edifice and thus they had not only light but heat as well. They had a cache of equipment stored there, and some weapons. They also had access to what they called a observational map, a kind of interactive tracking system that showed where things were moving within the city. Unfortunately, the map could only be focused on a single area at a time, and thus it had taken them weeks just to map and explore only a small fraction of the city. It had been sheer dumb luck that they had been focused on the section that Carter had fled into and thus came to investigate. Of course they had been looking for weeks without a trace save for the occasional shoggoth, the map symbol which they had learned to avoid, so it came as no surprise to Mister Ys that they had found us so quickly.

The journey to their base took about an hour and led us through a labyrinth of pentagonal-shaped tunnels that looked like they had been bored through solid rock. Ys confirmed this was indeed the process, and suggested that the peaks themselves had been originally deposited by swarms of shoggoths excreting minerals in fantastically thick layers in imitation of the same geological processes that created sedimentary rocks, though in this case the shoggoths also applied a measure of pressure and heat, transforming the stone into a granite-like substance. By design it resisted the natural weathering that occurred through the ages as climate changed and the very continents shifted position. The cities of the Q'Hrell could last for millions of years, for indeed it was common for them to be inhabited for such spans of time.

As we walked I noticed that not only were the tunnels pentagonal, but so were the columns, and various other bits of architecture and what I had to assume were incidental decorative patterns. The number five seemed to be the basis for the entire city, from the simplest motif to the most complex of interlocking structures. The use seemed to border on a kind of mania, and almost by accident I commented that only a madman could have been so obsessive.

"It's not an *tkrt* obsession," commented Carter. "It's a kind of biological *tkrt* imperative. Their entire way of thinking revolves around *tkrt* five. Their bodies are pentaradial, as are their *tkrt* brains. A family unit, a cohort *tkrt* consists of five individuals and higher *tkrt* levels of organization are *tkrt* all at multiples of five. It takes a supreme effort for them to break that pattern, they were highly *tkrt* successful when they created the Nug Soth. As for mankind, not *tkrt* so much."

"What do you mean?" I asked.

It was Asenath that responded. "You've never noticed that the number five runs through our biology and culture? We have five senses, five fingers and toes on each hand or foot. If you count our heads we have five appendages, and this is true for most higher life forms, mammals, reptiles and amphibians. It is even more prevalent in religion: five wounds of Christ, the Five Pillars of Islam, the Pentateuch, and the Panj Kakars of the Sikhs. Medieval alchemists sought to discover the quintessence, fifth element of the universe. The pentagon, the pentagram, the cross are almost universal symbols of mystical power, and all of them are representations of the number five."

"I thought the cross only had four points?"

Asenath smiled. "Four points and the intersection make five. A sacred symbol."

After about an hour of walking and traveling the spiraling ramps gently upward we finally came to the place that Hartwell and Elwood called home. It was a large open floor filled with artifacts and equipment that the two had scavenged from throughout the city. There were buckets and poles made out of strange ceramics. Poles tipped with a metal spikes none of us recognized. There were also belts of tools with odd handles and even stranger working tips. Most of the equipment was unidentifiable. It was as if an ape had been let loose inside a machine shop and been allowed to collect whatever struck his fancy, regardless of what it actually did.

One whole wall of the room was devoted to the so-called interactive map, which did indeed seem to allow one to scroll through a representation of the city. As we played with the controls the area of the city shown changed and we quickly came to learn the symbols that identified shoggoths and what Elwood said were giant, blind penguins. On one sector we saw nothing but a large single room, a kind of cavernous hall, and within a massive number of symbols suggesting a huge gathering of some sort. We queried Elwood and Hartwell about it but were told that it was on the far side of the city, easily more than a day's journey. We all looked at Elwood, because as we understood it his ability made such considerations unimportant.

"I haven't stepped out of the world since we got here. I'm afraid. The hounds could be waiting. More importantly, I don't have any desire to either. There is something about this place, something wrong, it makes me want to stay in the real world, or at least out of the in-between."

Mister Ys took this as his cue to join the conversation. "Mr. Elwood, the time will come when we will need you to step outside, and you will do so without hesitation. Is that understood?" He didn't wait for a reply. "As for the massive gathering let us see what the markers say." He drew a deep breath, the first sign of emotion he had ever displayed. "A shoggoth pit. Not entirely unexpected, but the size of it is unprecedented." He mumbled some numbers out loud, performing calculations at an alarming rate. "Yes, at that density a gestalt is possible, probable even. All they need is a catalyst consciousness and then . . . "

Carter interrupted. "A gestalt, what *tkrt* is that?"

Ys looked annoyed, Elwood stepped back and slowly moved away from the center of the conversation. "The Progenitors were at war with those from Xoth. They endowed the shoggoths with the ability to merge themselves together into a single, massive organism. It was a kind of weapon of last resort. Something they created and planned to unleash to battle against Cthulhu and his ilk if needed. I didn't think . . . my research places this pit somewhere else, not here. He's supposed to be in Ogasawara."

Asenath saw an opportunity and took it. "Are you afraid?"

The monstrous Mister Ys stared at Asenath with hate in his eyes. He seemed ready to lash out, but then was able to reassert control. He turned away and walked toward the window and stared out at the landscape beyond the city. It was a bleak, grey expanse made hazy by a wind that had whipped up ice and debris. "You people are so blissfully unaware of what dangers you are treading around. Even this window, if it were facing the other direction, if it were looking out over the city and beyond it . . .what a sight you would behold."

It was Hartwell's turn to enter the fray of conversation. "There's a window like that on the next level, Elwood's private room so to say." We all scanned the room for Elwood, who had been present but a moment earlier but now was suddenly dashing up the ramp.

Ys made to follow him. "Have you ever been up there? Have you looked out the window?" There was speed in his step.

"No, just once," Hartwell stuttered an answer. "Like I said, they're his private rooms."

We followed Ys up the ramp and burst onto the second floor like a pack of wolves swarming after a wounded doe. What we found waiting for us was completely unexpected. In the far corner was Elwood, naked and trussed up with some copper wire. By the state of him and his surroundings he had been like this for days. His skin had that thin fragile look that comes from lack of food and water, and the wire had bit into his flesh. He was conscious but his eyes were unfocused and cloudy, like he had been drugged.

In front of the window stood the other Elwood, the one we had been speaking with just moments before, his arms were raised as if in supplication. He was chanting something, something that I couldn't understand over the howling wind that tore through the massive window. As we raced toward him he turned and began laughing maniacally. Hartwell went to tend to the naked figure on the floor while I and Carter attempted to grab the other one. I am preternaturally strong, as is Carter's alien body, but the thing we called Elwood shrugged us off like we were rag dolls, and tossed us across the room.

As I recovered I set my sights on the man who was still laughing and then quite by accident caught a glimpse of what hung in the air beyond the window and above the city. It floated there in the sky, a latticework of blue energies that formed a geometric shape, an icosidodecahedron, a polyhedron with pentagonal faces flanked by triangular ones. It was a kind of cage, and what it held inside was enough to bring me to my knees. It was a monstrous thing, cyclopean in size and proportions. There was some semblance to portions of a squid, and an anemone, and a centipede. The tentacles ended in gnashing snapping mouths full of needle-like teeth, but each of these teeth was easily the size of a man. Eyes, multi-faceted things that glinted in the sun ringed the body. Above all this was a head of sorts, a starfish-like thing that seemed as if it had been transplanted from one of the Q'Hrell itself.

There on my knees I fell back on my parochial upbringing and let some words slip through my lips, "My God!"

The cackling thing that was Elwood leered at me and in a malicious tone screamed over the winds. "No Mr. Olmstead this is not your pale, whimpering, crucified Messiah. This is my God!" His mouth opened wide as he began to cackle once more. It opened wide, stretched down past his neck, past his chest. Then he melted. The thing pretending to be Elwood became little more than an amorphous blob whipping tentacles and tendrils like some monstrous jellyfish.

Carter, the alien warlock, was back at the thing before I could even move. He slashed at it with his chitinous claws. Carter was fast, but he was massive and Elwood dodged him easily, and then turned the wizard-warrior's momentum against him, flinging him back toward the ramp. This time the throw was farther and Carter hit the wall with a sickening thud. I waited and watched but Carter did not get up.

As I watched for some sign that Carter was recovering, I saw Ys back away. I, however, couldn't move, I was mesmerized by the obscenity that stood imprisoned out there in the sky. It seemed to stare at me, to slice me open with its eyes and crawl inside my very soul. It was a wrong thing, an abomination that didn't belong in this world or any other. I knew this at a cellular level. Its very presence was a corrupting influence. It needed to be expunged, destroyed and so did all those who followed him. So as Ys stepped to the rear I surged forward. I dodged the flailing tentacles and plunged my claws into the pulpy mass that had once pretended to be Frank Elwood. I tore at the strange flesh, casting great gobs of the stuff behind me.

The shoggoth was letting out a kind of high-pitched keening as I cut into it, and it took me a minute to realize that the creature was screaming. I was hurting it, and it was writhing in agony. It tried to pull away, but I grabbed on to something solid inside with one hand and continued to tear at it with the other. The keening devolved into a whimper, but I could barely hear it. Something had snapped inside my head and I had gone both blind and deaf to anything but the attack itself. I tore and tore and tore until the thing I was tearing into shuddered and collapsed.

It was only then that I backed away. As I did, the globs of material that I had torn apart began to shudder and crawl toward each other. As they reached one another they flowed into each other and merged into even larger pieces. The thing was reassembling itself, slowly but surely the monster was coming back.

Hartwell pushed his way past me and pulled from his pocket a very large makeshift syringe. "I've been waiting to try this." He pushed the plunger and began spraying the shoggoth flesh with a thick, green fluid. "Have you noticed that the shoggoths didn't touch the dead Q'Hrell? They eat everything else, devour it, and mimic it, except for their masters. I have a theory about that you see? I think they can't. I think the blood of the master is toxic to the servant. Let us see shall we?"

At his feet the masses of alien tissue began to smoke and bubble. They writhed in agony and squealed like animals being slaughtered. It took a few moments, but the protoplasmic jelly finally deteriorated into little more than sticky, bubbling slime.

Hartwell was smug as he walked back to the real Elwood. "Clever things these Progenitors, clever things." He cast an eye at Ys. "Cleverer than you I think."

Mister Ys stormed down the ramp, leaving the Weird Company to tend to the wounded. Asenath hurried us along, making sure that we were no longer under the cyclopean gaze of the thing that stared down at us out of its ancient prison. I could still feel the thing staring at me and trying to get into my mind when Asenath took my hand and put her arm around me. That touch, that human touch was all I needed to block out the crawling, insistent thing that clawed at my mind.

CHAPTER 17

From the Account of Robert Martin Olmstead
"The Weird Reformation"

Down on the lower level out of the horrific gaze of the thing that hung over the city we regrouped and tended to our wounds both physical and psychological. Hartwell was ministering to Elwood using a diluted form of the blood of the Q'Hrell which he said would heal the young man's wounds. More importantly he was getting some water and a modicum of sustenance which we were all partaking of. It was an oily stew of some kind, and there were chunks of some kind of root and shreds of something that could have been fish or fowl. Hartwell said it was better for us not to know the source of any of the ingredients. Though I was thankful for the chunk of rock salt he offered up to add some flavor to the broth.

While he ate, Elwood explained what had happened. "I had been out hunting. The first pond had been empty, completely devoid of both fish and penguins. That should have been my first clue. While I was making my way to the second pool, I was attacked from behind. A shoggoth, I had no opportunity to fight back. He swallowed me whole and began absorbing me both physically and mentally. I don't know why he stopped, but he did. It took him hours, but he mimicked me perfectly, well almost. It seems he couldn't replicate my ability to step in between. I don't even know how he knew about that, but he was obsessed with it. It is all he talked about. He demanded that I teach him how to do it, tortured me when I refused. I tried to explain that I didn't understand the process myself, but he didn't believe me." He seemed on the verge of panic, but Hartwell seemed to have a way with the young man and quieted him down.

Elwood was not the only one in need of care. My arms and hands, which had been exposed to the strange jellied matter of the shoggoth, and had come back burned from some kind of organic acid. My own inherent healing factor was repairing my body, but I still needed time, several hours, to let that happen. Asenath and Carter helped, they knew some simple cantrips that could speed the healing, at least the physical part. The psychological healing was more difficult, perhaps because it was a deeper kind of pain.

Mister Ys had retreated away from the rest of us. He seemed shattered by what he had seen above the city, which I didn't fully understand. While Asenath worked her magic I asked her if she could explain what that thing was, and why it was imprisoned above the city. I had other questions as well. It seemed that Ys had known about the thing, but why had seeing it impacted him so much? Why was he impacted to a greater extent than anyone else?

At first Asenath seemed reticent to discuss the issue. "Knowing these things won't make your life any easier."

I grinned. "I think it is safe to say that I've given up on the easy life."

She glared at me in amusement, those big eyes growing even bigger. "You've been told about the Dunwich Horror, the Whateleys?" She knew I had. "The thing that rampaged through the countryside, Lavinia's other child, the one that took after the father. That thing out there imprisoned above the city, it's the same kind of thing. It's a child of Yog-Sothoth, a Vugg-Shoggog, but in this case the other parent wasn't human, it was one of the Q'Hrell. As for why, these things are essential to the Q'Hrell way of life. The Vugg-Shoggog is the gate between two universes, ours and the realm of pure chaos where the Lurker at the Threshold originates. One of his followers, a man named Billington, had a theory about the All in One. He thought that it was only in our universe that the god-thing had almost absolute power, he suspected that in its home realm, it was nearly powerless."

"This Vugg-Shoggog, does it have a name?"

Asenath shook her head. "Would you name an engine, or a furnace? That is all that thing is to the Q'Hrell, a machine and nothing more, but one that can move an entire city from the real world into a realm of their own making, one where the rules of the universe are shaped by their own design, and bend to their own will when need be. It is a universe where they are more than they are here. In our world, they are aliens, powerful, ancient aliens, but in the other world they are more than that, in that world of their making they are gods."

"I don't believe it."

"You should *tkrt* Olmstead," said Carter, still trapped in that massive alien body. "I've been there, I've seen *tkrt* them, seen what they can do. Most of them *tkrt* are content being petty, tyrannical things. Some however *tkrt* have chosen to be something even greater, they've *tkrt* found a way to move beyond their manufactured realm, and back *tkrt* into our reality. They are titanic, terrible things, equal *tkrt* in stature and power to any of the Old Ones. There is a reason the universe *tkrt* calls them the Elder Gods."

"You still haven't told me why Ys is so upset. Didn't he know that thing, that Vugg-Shoggog, was going to be here?"

My voice must have been too loud, for Ys overheard my conversation and seemed to have taken some offense. "I am concerned Mr. Olmstead, because I thought I had accounted for this variable. I travelled your world, researched all your libraries, scoured the lonely places, educated myself on the state of this primitive age, and what artifacts and relics remained intact and active. There was no evidence that the Vugg-Shoggog was still here, let alone active." His manner was suddenly introspective. "Given the weakness between this world and the virtual one, there seems to be no shortage of ways for the inhabitants of one realm to transit to the other, as Mr. Carter is well aware. The prevalence of such points of transit usually implies that the mechanism that keeps the two distinct has fallen into disrepair. The most common of failures is the slow collapse of the energy lattice that imprisons the thing, which eventually results in the creature's destruction. My assumption that the thing was dead or dying has now been proven incorrect, which means that something else has gone wrong in the mechanism, something catastrophic." He paused, and I was not sure if it was because he didn't know what to say, or if it was just for effect, "and yes, for your information that concept does give me pause."

"Thank providence for small favors," muttered Hartwell. At our incredulous looks at his callous comment he took umbrage. "For years I suffered under your oppressive control, did your bidding and your dirty work. It's nice to see you cowed for once."

Ys turned away, but Asenath called after him. "Did you think this would be easy Mister Ys? Did you think that you could come to this place and not face obstacles? For all your planning and plotting you are just as vulnerable to the whims of chance as any one of us. You and your kind, so pretentious, so haughty, but it's all an act isn't it? Take away the advanced science, and the foreknowledge, and what do you have? Just a man, just a man like anybody else."

Asenath had shamed the time-traveling alien mind, and in doing so had re-established herself as the dominant factor in our little party. In that one outburst, that one rant, Asenath Waite had wrested control from Mister Ys and once more become the leader of the Weird Company. What's more is that she resumed her mantle as if she had never lost it. It was as if we were back in Arkham, in her great hall, and she was barking orders, and cajoling us to join her on her fool's quest. This time however, instead of looking at her with reticence and loathing, I saw her through eyes that were tinged with something else, and I marveled at her prowess and ability.

"Tell me Mister Ys," Asenath was not done with the man yet, "how exactly did you come to be here? Gedney was dead, and yet here you are inhabiting the body of what I suspect is something akin to one of Dr. Hartwell's experiments. You've even crudely bandaged yourself, but to what end?"

Ys turned and there was a calm venomous look in his eyes. "We have many strategies Kamog, more than you could possibly understand. Number nine has to do with the reanimation of the recent dead, a process we can accomplish from the depths of space or even across the millennia. The resurrection of Gedney so that I could occupy his body was a trifling matter. As for the bandage, I thought it would garner a sense of compassion, and ingratiate myself with you and yours."

He tried to continue but Asenath cut him off. "Shut your mouth you deceitful creature. I don't know why you are here, or what you want but you're here now, and I have to deal with you. We are here for a reason, to put an end to the shoggoth threat, you will assist us. You will follow my orders, and you will help the entire team accomplish our goals. If you do not, or if you put any of the team in danger, or fail to properly protect them I will kill Gedney's body." She paused and let what she had said sink in. "I know what happens to Yith when the bodies they inhabit are destroyed before they are properly extracted. I have no qualms about letting that happen to you. Do you understand me?"

Her demand was met with a reluctant but definite yes.

"We've been wounded and waylaid. We are going to take some time to recover and heal. We're also going to come up with a plan of attack, using the mapping machine over there. Dr. Hartwell, are you capable of producing more of that reagent?"

He nodded. "I know where there is a cache of dead Q'Hrell that I can harvest the ingredients from."

"You and Elwood will be responsible for that. Carter, you will do something that you should be quite used to. Somewhere in this city is a gateway to the Q'Hrell's virtual world. You will find that gate and descend once more into the Dreamlands. There I expect you to find the allies we need, whoever or whatever they are." She didn't even bother to look for confirmation, and instead turned to look at me. "Olmstead and I will find where the shoggoth's are staging their operations and attempt to assess the situation. As soon as the rest of you are able you shall join us."

"What about me, what shall I do?" It was Ys that was asking, and his tone wasn't its usual flavor of imperial haughtiness.

Asenath smiled and in a sweet, almost loving voice responded, "Mister Ys, I thought that would be obvious. You're going to go with Carter, and meet with your own kind." She was still smiling as she added, "I wonder what they'll think of you?"

CHAPTER 18
The Statement of Dr. Stuart Hartwell
"The Blood of the Progenitors"

I write this at the bequest of Mr. Robert Olmstead who I suppose
is searching for some sort of closure. Of all of us, and I say this
understanding the irony, he is perhaps the most human. He has
spent his days documenting our adventure, remembering what
he can of his recruitment, of his rescue of Frank Elwood, of our
excursion to Antarctica and our less than triumphant return. That
five of us began that journey and only four of us returned seems
to have had a profound impact on the young man. That he was
not with Elwood and me when we went to collect the circulatory
fluid of the Q'Hrell leaves young Olmstead with a knowledge gap
that he seems uncomfortable with. He's looking for an explanation
for what happened. He thinks that there might be a clue to what
happened in the time that we were below. I think he is wrong, but
I'm willing to help him see that in his own way, in his own time.

Just hours after his rescue, Elwood's recovery, accelerated by
the factor I had isolated from the Q'Hrell, was nearly complete.
Using the mapping device we located the three areas that each team
would need to investigate. The entry way to what Carter called the
Dreamlands was deep in one of the central towers, beneath a honeycomb of chambers filled with dormant Q'Hrell. Most of these
chambers were indicated as being sealed, and impossible to open.
One section however indicated that it had been penetrated, the
seals degraded and the residents within, dozens of Q'Hrell, had

all expired. There was an indication that something was still alive within that chamber, but what it was the machine could not seem to define. The third destination was some kind of massive chamber within which swarmed an ever-changing number of shoggoths. Thankfully this location was in the same tower complex as the places the other teams were going, though forty-five levels higher. Olmstead commented that at least we were lucky, given the size of the city, that all our objectives were in the same complex. Ys didn't think it was luck, instead he suggested that the entryway to the Dreamlands and the associated Dreaming Chambers were the reason that the shoggoths had set up their operations in the tower above. The gateway and the chambers were the primary users of the energy still being generated. Indeed, when it came to energy, the complex in question had primacy over all others. Whatever the shoggoths were doing, it seemed they needed a secure source of power.

Committed as we were to Asenath's plan, the six of us made our way to the tower which contained our targets. We had expected some resistance, that as we travelled we would be beset by monsters, but there was nothing. Perhaps we had seen enough horrors, perhaps the universe was finally allowing things to go our way, or it could simply be that the shoggoths did not see us as a threat. Such a conclusion seemed to fly in the face of logic. Elwood had previously been attacked and replaced, and it seemed that our opponents knew about us, enough perhaps to dismiss us as a danger.

When we finally came to the central shaft we bid farewell to our teammates and Waite and Olmstead went up, Carter and Ys went deep, and Elwood and I went down to the Dreaming Chambers.

As we walked along those gently sloping paths Elwood took the time to apologize to me for being caught by the shoggoth and allowing himself to be mimicked. "The thing was obsessed with trying to learn how to step outside. I think it was the only thing that kept me alive, him wanting me to teach him my trick."

"Did you?"

"How could I, I don't even know how I do it, I just do." His voice was full of frustration. "I suppose it was a gift of a sort, from poor Walter. He is the one who figured all this out, or did he? Perhaps like myself Walter was gifted with his ability from someone else. Perhaps it is infectious. I caught it from Walter, and Walter from that hag Keziah Mason. Could it be Doctor, that the ability to move through space and time can be passed from one man to another as others pass the common cold?"

I pondered my friend's theory for a moment. "I suppose anything is possible. I didn't used to think so, but that was when I was younger, before medical school, before my parents were killed, before I followed in the footsteps of Herbert West." I let loose a cynical laugh. "If you had told me that a boy from Arkham could study medicine, and grow up to battle monsters in the polar wastes I would have called you mad. Yet here I am, far, far from home, up to my neck in what most men would call madness, ready to act the hero and do battle against monsters."

Elwood stopped in his tracks and stared at me with those strange violet eyes. He seemed to be assessing me, trying to take my measure. "Do you really think that? You and I, we've done terrible, monstrous things. I let Gilman die, you experimented with death itself and in the process you may have been responsible for the death of millions. That night at the hospital, we both did horrible things just to save ourselves and cover up the truth. But here and now, in this place, are we heroes Doctor?"

I put my arm around the young man who seemed not so young anymore. "I think so my friend." I told him as we walked. "I think here in this place, at the very end of the world, if we cannot find redemption, then perhaps we were never villains in the first place."

The rest of the journey was made in silence, which suited me, for I did not wish to explain why I had not noticed that he had been replaced, though I did feel a pang of guilt for that particular failure. I did wish that Elwood would find it within himself to try and move into the in-between. This was something he was loathe to do, not so much becaue of his experience with the Hounds of Tindalos, but rather because within the walls of this alien city, with its weird geometries and energies, and the extra-dimensional Vugg-Shoggog pulsating in the sky, moving through that realm was uncomfortable to say the least. He had difficulty putting it into words, the best he could do was suggest that the weird geometries made his brain ache and his stomach hurt. I didn't press the issue, though if he had been able to do it our journey might have been shortened significantly.

By the time we made it to the damaged Dreaming Chamber my nerves had become unsettled. The weird, sourceless light that seemed omnipresent within the complex had grown dimmer as we had descended, and was now little more than a pale, featureless glow that only let us see for a dozen feet or so. With this came the inevitable auditory hallucinations, of things shuffling and sliding about in the dark. There was that eerie feeling that we were being watched, perhaps even stalked, and I remembered those weird symbols on the map that faded in and out suggesting that something was alive in that dread space.

As we had expected the seal on the chamber door was broken and the great five-fold gate was ajar, not much but enough that both Elwood and I could slip through the gap. As soon as we had it was apparent that we were not the first to penetrate the interior, for the sleepers within had all been assaulted. I counted twenty-five of the pentaradial aliens known as the Q'Hrell, and all of them had been decapitated. The heads had been piled up in a corner of the room, but the bodies had been mostly left to sit inside a kind of cradling cage of wire mesh and lights which once must have been an elegant construct, but now seemed decrepit with damage and age.

"I thought you said that shoggoths didn't devour the Q'Hrell," commented Elwood. He had noticed, as I had, that something had molested not only the severed heads of the Q'Hrell, breaking open the outer integument and tearing out the inner membranes, organs and musculature, but had done the same to a number of the bodies of well.

I approached one of the closer bodies and examined the lacerations. There were on the bodies puncture wounds, heavily concentrated in the soft areas where the tentacles and wings joined the body. Some of these were so numerous that they had eventually merged and become large enough for me to insert my entire hand within the body cavity. It was through these holes that the internal organs and flesh had been removed. The scene reminded me of bodies I had seen on the fields of war, ones in which dogs and carrion birds had torn into to get at the tender bits within. I shuddered at the thought of what might have happened here. "We should get what we need and get out of here."

With Elwood's help I found several bodies that had not yet been eviscerated and using a makeshift knife and some metallic tubing I began the process of exsanguination on the first of the corpses. Q'Hrell blood is not like that of humans or other earthly life, and even after death tends to persist in a liquid form. Consequently even on these dead individuals the process of gathering their vital fluids was not unlike that of a butcher draining a slaughtered pig or chicken, a practice I had helped my father and grandfather with many times. We transferred the green fluid from the collection basin to large metallic carafes, which could be sealed. For these containers we had rigged up a primitive set of tubes, nozzles and bladders that allowed us to spray the stuff in either a powerful jet, or a gentle mist.

We worked as best we could in the dark, quietly too, whispering directions to each other as if our lives depended on it. These actions were taken because of the ever-growing sensation that we were not alone. The auditory hallucinations were growing more frequent, Elwood could hear something dragging along the floor, and I kept hearing a swift, almost secretive kind of chirp, not unlike that of a cricket, though swifter and harder to locate the source. Our paranoia kept growing and as we filled container after container our pace quickened and we began warning each other about the inevitable.

Then it happened. I handed a metal carafe to Elwood, one for which he was not yet prepared. He juggled it, one handed, mostly suspending it in the air in a kind of controlled chaos that vanished when his other hand came into play, as did one of mine. The shiny tubular container flipped end over end as it travelled through the air toward the floor. Elwood dove after it, his fingers catching one of the edges, but all that accomplished was to change the spin and tumble it further out of our reach.

It hit the ground with a kind of clang or ring, and then the other end hit, and then it bounced hitting the floor again and again and again. The echoes were horrific and Elwood and I sat there wincing as the sounds careened down the halls and came back to us in ever-diminishing but clear alarms. Our presence here was made public and we cringed, staring at the door. We waited with baited breath for something to come through, for some alien horror to shamble into the chamber in response to our inadvertent alarm.

We waited, and waited, and then waited some more.

Nothing came, and after waiting for so long both Elwood and I let loose a deep sigh of relief, followed by a giggle that acknowledged the ridiculous nature of the situation.

That giggle was responded to by a sudden shaking of something in the room that reminded me of a sheaf of papers or the rustling of leaves. There was another similar sound, this one closer, and seemingly larger. These were followed by a third such noise, and then something different. It was a deep throaty sound, not unlike that of pigeons, as if a sound had gotten caught in one's throat. Elwood and I were still looking at the door but the sounds that we heard now were clearly coming from within the chamber itself. We scanned it in all directions, holding out crude knives in front of us as if they were enough of a defense.

TwWRKKTrk!? Came a questioning kind of noise. I saw one of the bodies of the Q'Hrell shudder and then something large and pale tumbled out of the incision in its side. It hit the ground with a thump, and then there was a kind of fumbling, flapping noise, the source of which I couldn't see.

TrKwtttRT! Another of the desiccated husks shuddered and gave birth to a pale, furry thing that flopped out of the interior.

TwRRNNet! I heard the thing shudder and then plop to the floor, but I didn't see it. I still couldn't see what we were up against.

There was a shuffling sound, like something large being dragged across the floor, but it was still too far away to see. I turned to Elwood and began gathering up the carafes. I rose up slowly, carefully, and as I did I found myself suddenly looking over Elwood's shoulders, staring at the thing that was towering up behind him.

In the days that we had been trapped in this ancient, alien city we had learned that we were not the only forms of earthly life to take up residence here. The pools of water that existed on the edge of the warmer parts of the city were home to great sheaths of bacteria, fungi, and an assortment of fish, all of which were blind and devoid of any pigmentation. Likewise, the predators that had evolved to take advantage of this ecology were also albinos and they too were blind. There are no bears in the Antarctic, and we were too far from the ocean for seals to be a threat, but here in the dark of an alien city a new kind of danger had evolved, one that we ourselves had taken to feeding on to survive in this place. There was a vast population of a horrific species of giant penguin. These titans grew much larger than their cousins, and if given the opportunity could likely be a threat to an injured man. When we could we had hunted them for food, supplementing the fish in our stew pot with their greasy, gamey flesh.

It seems we were not alone in our desire for something more than a diet of fish. Some of those flightless avians had found their way into the Dreaming Chamber and resorted to feasting on the headless remains within. They had found easy pickings apparently, for though it had taken them time to peck their way through the thick outer integument, once breached, the inner parts must have proven quite nutritious. The thing that reared up behind Elwood was easily five feet tall and so well fed that it could no longer have fit through the gap in the door. It was an evil-looking thing, eyeless, but with indentations in the flesh where the sockets once were. In proportion to the body, the head was small, but as that thick, sharp beak opened up I saw that the maw within was massive, a gaping craw filled with spiny, filamentous teeth that glistened with spittle in the light.

I froze in fear, and slowly, carefully put a hand on Elwood's shoulder. The slight squeeze I gave alerted him to stay quiet, but he looked up and caught my eyes. I knew what he saw there and he did exactly what I needed him to do, which was absolutely nothing. With a sense of surety I moved to the right and at the same time I pushed Elwood in the opposite direction and he rolled the rest of the way. The creature roared and followed me, I don't think it even noticed that Elwood had stuck a knife in its belly and cut an eight inch slice in the creature's abdomen. It came after me, and with each step of its fat body the new gap in its gut opened wider and the viscera bulged out further.

When the thin bag of flesh and muscle finally gave way and that sack of internal organs and blood finally spilled out on to the chamber floor, my worst fears were realized. Like mammalian blood the vital fluids of avians is red; what spilled out of that monstrous penguin's belly, what began to spread across the floor, wasn't red. It was green, the same green that I had been draining from the dead bodies of the Q'Hrell. I cursed out loud as I realized what these creatures had become. "Do you remember the last set of triplets we went up against?"

Somewhere in the darkness Elwood responded. "The Fisher Brothers, patients of yours if I recall correctly."

I nodded, even though I knew Elwood couldn't see me. "These things likely have a similar condition." I was moving around the room trying to keep ahead of my pursuer, but away from his friends. "Being animals they might be smarter, and more dangerous than the Fishers." Elwood chuckled for a second and then went quiet, and from the scuffling sounds in the dark I knew my friend was doing the same thing I was, trying to stay alive.

At the edge of my vision I caught sight of something moving, something that had no neck and waddled when it moved. It had been years since I had studied anatomy, and I was sure that there were some significant differences between that of a man and of a penguin, but I was willing to take the risk. With a two-step running start I dove forward, twisting on to my back as I hit the floor and slid past the animal. My knife found its mark, and I slid it up the side, making sure I was cutting through the peritoneum. When my knife hit bone I plunged it forward and let my hand penetrate inside the warm steaming flesh. The bird squawked in pain, but I didn't let that distract me. It was thrashing about, trying to reach me with its beak, but I was too far behind it. My hand dug around inside it and found a loop of tissue. I clenched down with all my might and ripped whatever I had latched on to back out of my incision. Loops of intestine poured out like line on a fishing pole. The bird screamed again, or perhaps it was the same scream, and I was finally hearing it. As I wrapped the thin muscular tube around the creatures own legs and wings I made sure to let the gobs of gore and blood spray out over the room. With the last loop of gut I finished dressing my bird by tying that hideous beak closed. I pushed off, and let the struggling thing flail helplessly onto the ground. It wasn't dead, it wasn't even defeated, but it was incapacitated and that was good enough.

The beak of the third beast caught me in the shoulder, and it burned as it cut along the length of my arm. It didn't go deep, but it wasn't a glancing blow either. I felt the hot flow of blood on my back, and the electric shock of pain shot up my spine. It sent me to the ground, and too close to my attacker for comfort. From my position on the floor the thing looked bigger than the other two; certainly the mouth full of teeth was bigger, much bigger than the others. It roared and lunged toward me, I tried to roll but one of the bird's feet pinned me in place. The mouth closed and the sharp beak became suddenly, dangerously evil. The head wrenched back and that beak sped through the air toward my face. I braced myself for the killing blow, but it never came.

With caution I opened my eyes, the beast was still there, but its head was gone. Like the creatures it had been feeding on it had been decapitated, only a trickle of green fluid marked where the body and head had once been joined. Behind the tottering corpse stood Elwood, but not the Elwood I had known. Something had changed, the look in his eyes said more than any speech ever could. Frank Elwood had finally stopped being scared and embraced what he could do. In his hands he held two heads, their beaks still twitching. He tossed the heads to the side and then proceeded to decapitate the third one.

The manner in which he did this was astounding, for it was an extension of his ability to open a door to the in-between. He used the gap in space that was created as a kind of blade, one that was able to slice through and destroy reality itself. He killed that last bird by simply opening up a gap in the very fabric of the universe between the body and the head. When the gap closed that thin slice of matter didn't come back with it.

"Nasty things you've found down here Doctor Hartwell, very nasty things."

It took me a moment to stand up and catch my balance. The gash in my shoulder was still bleeding, but I knew that was only temporary. Taking off my jacket it was hard to tell where the blood of the creatures ended, and my own started, after all they were so similar in color, both lovely shades of green.

Elwood didn't seem shocked at all. In fact he seemed relieved. "I saw you torn to pieces, and then you weren't. The idea that I could have changed that by stepping back in time; that was just wishful thinking. I lied to myself and my shoggoth duplicate perpetuated that lie, but I think it knew the truth. That is why you were never assimilated, why the shoggoth never replaced you. It couldn't, you're immune."

The wound on my back was already healing, closing up faster than anyone could have hoped. Frank Elwood had learned the secret that I had kept from everyone else, that I was no longer human, no longer subject to human weaknesses, or even death. I had become something else. Something that was neither dead nor alive. I was more like these monstrous penguins, a living thing that had stumbled into a way of becoming something . . . what did Elwood call them? "Nasty."

Perhaps, but as I sat there looking at Elwood I remembered our earlier conversation. Perhaps we were villains, monsters even. But in this place we had the potential to be something more, to become something other than what was written for us. In this place all the horrible things I had done, all the people I had killed, all the people I had brought back, all that didn't matter. Here with Elwood and the rest of the Weird Company I could be what I always wanted to be.

A man, with a purpose, a future, a cause.

Asenath Waite had given me hope, and perhaps that was enough to keep me human, for as long as I was needed.

CHAPTER 19

From the Account of Robert Martin Olmstead
"The Loss of Asenath Waite"

In the shadows Asenath and I watched as nightmare things labored amongst piles of ore, semi-organic machines and piles of metallic parts and plating to assemble something neither of us could identify. There were a half dozen of the monsters creating something not unlike an immense torpedo. The thing was more than two hundred and seventy feet long and at its widest, forty-five feet in diameter. The body was divided into three sections, with the central section, consisting almost entirely of a kind of cargo hold, taking up most of the length. The one end was a short cone shape that tapered to a point and seemed to be filled with instrumentation and controls. The other end also tapered to a cone but in this case that cone was significantly longer. There was something organic in the design of the construct and while Asenath called it piscine, it was clear to me that the design was mostly reminiscent of an earthly squid, but the five divisions to be found in both cones made it clear that the inspiration for the design had been the long lost masters of the shogoths, the Q'Hrell themselves!

Asenath and I watched the construction of the odd ship alone. Elwood and Hartwell had gone down to harvest blood from a room full of dead Q'Hrell. Carter along with Mister Ys had gone even deeper into the bowels of the city in an attempt to find allies amongst those Progenitors that still slumbered and dreamed. I thought such a quest a fool's errand, but Asenath assured me that though many of their number had likely perished over the years, there were still members of the species waiting. "That which is not dead," she said, "can eternally lie, and in strange eons even death may die." Mister Ys was less enthusiastic and warned that the Elder Things did not take kindly to being disturbed from their slumber. Carter agreed, suggesting that in the experience of the Nug Soth the Q'Hrell were easy to anger, and hard to placate.

Regardless, the Weird Company had been split into three teams, and I and Asenath had been assigned to provide reconnaissance on the activities of the shoggoths. Their lair had been discovered on the strange map machine that had been in Hartwell's makeshift sanctuary. The shoggoths had seized control of an upper level of one of the queer spires that scraped the sky. It was a floor that consisted of little more than a single massive chamber littered with debris and stock piles of raw materials. At first glance it seemed an odd, almost cluttered space to work in, but that was a wholly human perspective. Watching the shoggoths work, watching them devour and manipulate raw materials, primarily piles of metallic ore and the like, and then produce parts, extruding whole sections of hull plating, structural beams, screw-like fasteners, and wholly unidentifiable machines and components seemed eerily natural, as if this method of manufacturing was the true order of things.

Try as I might, I could not understand what they were doing. "It looks like they're building some sort of transportation. Like a giant bullet for traveling over the ice. Why don't they just transform into something that can fly?"

Asenath recalled the bodies frozen at the entrance to the cave. "They're vulnerable to freezing," she told me. "I don't think it kills them, but it does stop them, just like it would us, or any other living thing. No bird could make it to the coast; they've learned that much from the Miskatonic Expedition. They need a machine to keep them warm and transport them quickly. Once they reach civilization they could spread across the world like a plague, using our own methods of transport against us. No place, no matter how remote, would be safe, but they have to get out of here first."

I accepted that, but still had trouble with other things we had been told. "Do you think they really were as stupid as Ys said? That before the arrival of the expedition they were little more than immortal animals roaming the city, carrying out menial tasks like robots? That it was only after they devoured human brains that they became aware of the outside world? Can you imagine being trapped here for millions of years?"

"Makes sense to me. You certainly don't want your slaves to be particularly smart or versatile, and if they absorb memories and information as we've been told then yes I believe it. There are shoggoths in the outer world, but they are at best proto-shoggoths, barely capable of lumbering along and devouring organic matter, let alone forming complex tools or organs. Ys called these hyper-shoggoths. Supposedly these things can reason and even produce semi-autonomous fragments, whatever that means."

From the far corner of the assembly floor there arose a deep rumbling that shook the air itself and caused many of the shog-goths to suddenly cease their activities and move to new locations. The sound was that of two immense hunched things, black bulks of curved metal that were being rolled across the floor toward the body of the squid-like transport. They moved slowly but deliber-ately, being pulled and pushed by a number of gelatinous shog-goths which were using their own bodies as lubricants to grease the way for the things. The weight of the machines was so great that the jellied bodies would leak out from the sides in great gouts and squirts, scattering blobs of shoggoth material to and fro.

This material, no matter what size or shape, did not remain inert or still. Instead it would twitch and shake, form itself into a tear-shaped glob and then go streaming back to the front of the massive component where it would rejoin the larger shoggoth body. "I think that is what Ys meant by semi-autonomous fragments," said Asenath, and I had to agree as the horrific process repeated itself again and again. It was a slow, monotonous routine, but in the end the two titanic bulks slide into the rear of the ship and were quickly connected up to other components.

Within moments the two black machines began to hum. The air grew electric, my skin began to itch, and Asenath's hair stood on end. The hum grew louder and began to pulse with an inhuman, unnatural rhythm that made me cringe. I felt it in my bones and my blood. Asenath grabbed her head and clamped her hands over her ears, but this wasn't a noise one could shut out. It was a change in the air. The machines were drawing something, some kind of energy out of the very air, the walls, even our bodies. It came with pain, and Asenath seemed to be getting the worst of it, and then the woman simply crumpled to the floor and began to moan. Blood was leaking out between her lips.

It was then that I felt something tug at my coat. I looked down and saw that the buttons, the grommets, and the zippers, all the tiny bits of metal that were part of my winter gear, were moving in time with the pulsing vibration. The machines, I realized, were affecting the magnetic fields of the room, and anything metal was responding to the waves of electromagnetic energy, even the iron in my blood and the fillings in Asenath's teeth. The buttons were straining against the fabric and I clamped down to try and hold them in place. Asenath was holding her mouth trying to find some relief from the pain, but at the same time I could see that she was trying to muffle her excruciating pain. She tried but she couldn't and she eventually let loose an unearthly howl of agony.

The shoggoths working in the room ceased their labors and seemed to focus their attentions in our direction. Eyes swiveled into place, or were suddenly formed in place, as were ears, and trunks of other sensory organs that I did not recognize. It took them seconds to find us and then they began to move forward. The room was suddenly filled with the sound of mouthless voices muttering the same words over and over again. 'Teke-li-li. Teke-Li-Li! TEKE-LI-LI!' And then they surged.

We ran. We thought we could escape through the titanic corridors of black basalt that were filled with the detritus of forgotten ages but those things, those horrible nightmarish things cut us off. They were six to our two and though we launched makeshift missiles, mostly rocks and odd pieces of piping or strut, nothing seemed to slow their advance. Slowly we were backed into a corner by the creeping blobs that had given up any pretense of being anything else. They rolled toward us and great gaping maws filled with crystalline teeth broke open and slithered forward, propelled by massive trunks of coiled flesh. They seemed to be taunting us, for those horrific tentacles with their snapping mouths seemed to sway back and forth, offering us an opening only to suddenly dart back and cut us off once more. To them we were trapped playthings, inhabitants of this world whose flesh and knowledge would soon be devoured and assimilated into their own.

As if we would have been that foolish. Asenath asked me if I had had enough, and I reluctantly nodded. I had hoped that we would have been able to discern some sort of weakness, some flaw that we could take advantage of, but in the end there was little that we could do but watch and run.

Asenath however had seen the door I had not, and faster than I would have thought possible I was through one of those strange irising portals watching as the panels swirled back together separating us from the shoggoths. Unbalanced by Asenath's push I hit the rock floor hard, on the right side of a wall that separated me from the shoggoths.

I could hear them screaming. They knew where we were and they scratched and battered at the wall between us. I recovered quickly, and scanned the room, it was small, confined, the confluence of other more important architectural features. There were no doors, only a small gap in one corner let any light in, but it was no way out. We were trapped. Frustrated, I fell back to the floor. Asenath joined me and we listened as the wall that kept us safe was eaten away by the slow attentions of a shoggoth.

As the time passed. We could hear the shoggoth scrapping away at the rock wall. The sound was louder than it had been before, not from any increase in their activity, nor a sudden influx of assistance to gain quicker access. The sound was growing louder because the walls were getting thinner, and we still had nowhere to go, and nothing to defend ourselves with. My only hope was that the others would arrive in time to save us. It was a slim hope but the only thing I had to cling to. We had no weapons, not even a club. Not that it would make much of a difference against the shoggoths. Fire might help, or something that generated cold, some sort of acid might work, but Asenath and I had none of these things, and the shoggoth was only moments away from breaking through.

That moment came sooner than I thought.

One second the entire wall was there, the next it was gone, replaced by a smooth mass of shoggoth flesh, pulsating and thobbing with alien chemistries and life. Something viscous dripped from some sort of gland. The glistening glob fell to the floor which immediately began to hiss and smoke. No wonder they had gotten to us quicker than I thought possible. The shoggoth hadn't just dug us out, he had used an acid to aid in the process. I suddenly understood how this immense alien city had been constructed.

The mass of flesh bulged and then exploded, sending tentacles like a net through the room. Eyes and suckers, rasping mouths and tendrils searched for us. I was on the floor scrambling for some kind of cover, but their wasn't any. Dodging the tendrils and slashing at the sensory organs was the best I could do. It was futile, for every piece I cut, more of the monster swelled in through the hole. If I had been human I would have been dead, but my alien ancestry gave me speed and agility that kept me one step ahead of the beast's grasping reach. But even that wasn't enough to prevent the inevitable.

The tentacle wrapped around my left arm. It was a small thing really, little more than a tendril. There were spines, thorns that hooked into my skin. The scales prevented them from penetrating my flesh, but the thing had a grip and I was snapped forward and jerked toward the bigger mass. I slashed with the claws on my other hand and cut myself free, but the damage was done. The mass wrapped around my arm shuddered and lost cohesion. The suddenly fluid material bloated and then swelled. Where a length of vine-like shoggoth had once been there was now a giant black centipede with wicked looking mandibles. It reared up and plunged its jaws into my shoulder. The pain was excruciating and as fast as I could I ripped the thing off my arm. My flesh tore and I screamed as the thing squirmed in my hand. Its jaws snapped at my face, while the lower portion wrapped around my hand. I brought my injured arm up, grabbed the beast around the throat and then with all my strength pulled the thing apart.

I only made things worse.

In seconds the two pieces of the dismembered centipede were suddenly squirming worms that wrapped around both my hands. I rushed to the wall and slammed both arms against a wall. The worms squealed, but they didn't let go. I slammed my arms again and then scraped them around the corner of a wall. They popped off and flew away, hitting the floor with a sickening thud. I threw myself back and scrambled back into a corner. The tentacles were still searching for me, but so were the two masses that I had scraped off my arms.

They were spiders now, with short, thick legs that ended in fat claws. They marched toward me slowly, cautiously. Why this was the case I don't know, but perhaps there was some sense of self-pre-servation amongst these things, and even these small parts could reason enough to want to protect themselves from harm. They still wanted to kill me, but they were wary of being hurt themselves. That didn't make them any less dangerous. As they stalked for-ward their front most claws rose up and waved ominously, clicking open and closed with tremendous force.

Without warning the air suddenly parted and from a crack in the very fabric of the universe three figures stepped forth. Elwood came through first, carrying Dr. Hartwell under one arm. It was clear that Hartwell had been injured, his jacket was covered with green stains and I could see he had something strapped to his back, some kind of canister with tubing running down his arms to two makeshift guns that he held in both hands.

Even in the near dark of the room Hartwell seemed to shine like a beacon of hope in a world of horror. He flung Elwood toward me, and the young man crumpled into my arms. There was a stink about him, a blue slime dripped from his back and emitted a wretched stench that turned my stomach. I lowered him to the floor and watched as Hartwell took the battle to the thing that had come after me, shooting the two spider things with his guns, guns that sent sprays of green liquid that drenched their target. The spiders went into an immediate frenzy. They rolled and thrashed as the green reagent seeped into their skin and great foaming gouts of slime. Hartwell took some glee in the destruction and seemed to be chanting as he moved from target to target. His voice was low and fast as he sang: "Behold I have become death!"

He moved through the room cutting and spraying the tentacles that just kept pouring toward him. The shoggoth that had come after me may have been dangerous and monstrous, but it was not the smartest of creatures. Hartwell was cutting through its parts like a reaper through dry grass, it just kept sending tentacle after tentacle into the room until at last the final bit of its body was expended.

This last glob of material careened into the room all mouth and fury, screaming as if that would do something to stop us from protecting ourselves and destroying it and its kind. Hartwell casually sprayed it with his chemical concoction and it spiraled out of control and burned up into a ball of melting flesh.

No sooner than we had come to a kind of pause in the action our attentions were interrupted by a familiar and desperate voice. In our desperate fight we had both forgotten Asenath, and she was screaming as a great section of wall suddenly vanished and another shoggoth burst into our refuge. It seethed and pulsated, and the stench was overwhelming. It puckered and ejected a mass of itself, a ball of yellow and green slime that oozed and shifted as it flew through the air. It couldn't have been less than a hundred pounds, and it slammed into Waite's back and sent her tumbling across the floor. The mass blossomed into pseudopods and for a moment it looked like there was a giant octopus on Asenath's back. She struggled but those faux limbs wrapped around her body including her arms and legs, and she fell to the floor.

I screamed as I bounded past Carter, but she was too far away. The mass of shoggoth swallowed her up. For a moment or two it maintained the overall general shape of a small woman, and I still clung to some hope. But that hope dissolved as I reached the spot where she had fallen and the shoggoth condensed itself into a more compact ball of flesh. I stabbed at the thing with the staff, burning it's surface and immobilizing it within a case of its own burnt self. I screamed in frustration, but the founder and leader of the Weird Company was gone, dissolved into her primal components and devoured by a shoggoth.

Asenath Waite was dead.

CHAPTER 20

From the Account of Robert Martin Olmstead
"The Terror of the Shoggoths"

We had no time to grieve. The shoggothim swelled in through the doorway like a wall of corrupting flesh. After seeing what had happened to our companion, I backed away, moving behind cover until I reached Hartwell and Elwood. It was larger than the other shoggoths we had defeated, and seemed more cautious. Its massive bulk flowed like molasses and as it spread across the room numerous sensory organs including eyes and ears formed and burst open from the greater undifferentiated mass. Ropy tentacles exploded out of the body, but instead of heading across the room, they arched upwards and produced their own sets of eyes providing the creature with multiple perspectives of the room and its adversaries.

Quickly but carefully we regrouped and I followed Hartwell as he pulled Elwood to the farthest corner. The shoggthim hissed and shrieked with each step we took, but it did nothing to stop our slow retreat. As Hartwell tended to Elwood's wounds, I kept watch on the creature that had forced our retreat. As soon as we had established a kind of stalemate the titan began to shudder and great rents appeared in its body. Limbs appeared, arms and legs and things that were neither and both, they tore through the skin like monsters through a promethean amniotic sac. I counted six such creatures, but none bore any relation in appearance to any of the others. As they strode out of the body of their parent, the wasted flesh of their monstrous womb contracted and formed a seventh wholly remarkable creature.

It was in a way humanoid, as it stood on two legs and possessed two arms that ended in delicate digits that I would dare to call hands. Its skin was a pale blue, like the eggs of a robin, and curiously dry looking. The head was massive with a huge bulbous cranium, a large lipless mouth and three blood-red eyes that stared out at the world with nothing but hate. Atop the head, where a man would have hair, there were instead a collection of fat worm-like protuberances that moved independently, their tiny mouths opening and closing in the most sickening of ways. When it opened its mouth to speak it issued forth the most horrendous of sounds. There was something malevolent about that sound, something empty and hollow, like the wind blowing through a dead tree, and it made me cringe to hear it. As this call reverberated through the room the seven humanoid creatures stalked out of the small room through the shattered door and left us alone.

Whatever that eerie tone had meant, it was clearly some sort of communication, for in response to it the other creatures in the great room lumbered off in various directions and resumed working on the assembly of the ship. Two creatures, their resemblance to pill bugs unmistakable, made a slow and methodical beeline toward where we had sought refuge. Its intent was clear, we were to be engaged once more, this time by an enemy who seemed more intelligent and capable of using its unique abilities than our previous opponent. Hartwell handed me a weapon, and checked his own. Fighting the previous shoggoths had been easy, they had been stupid. This one had already killed one of us and was in our minds mere moments away from accomplishing its goal. It didn't need to kill us, or defeat us, it only had to delay us, keep us occupied long enough to finish and launch the ship. Once they were away, our mission would be failure.

Returning to a position where I could see what was going on, I took a quick assessment of the creatures in the room. Five of the creatures were busy making final adjustments, mostly at the direction of the blue-skinned, three-eyed giant who was supervising and assessing the workmanship of the craft itself. The giant armored pill bug was plodding toward us, while an eighth dark, vaguely humanoid creature was dashing across the floor, also heading in our direction but at a much more rapid pace. At first I was confused, I had no idea where the new creature had come from and at first assumed that another shoggoth had joined the fray. But my survey of the situation revealed an even more depressing explanation. The glob of shoggoth matter that had dissolved Asenath, which I had supposedly put down with the energized staff, was no longer there. All that remained were a few charred and cracked bits, like broken egg shells. Given the speed and intent that the creature was moving with, it was clear to me that my previous encounter with it had done nothing but make it angry.

As I watched, the tank-like creature lumbered forward, reared up and spread its armored plates, like a cobra getting ready to strike. The great mass of shoggoth matter that had held us at bay quickly withdrew, coiling out of our nearly useless shelter in a matter of moments. Beyond these things the vaguely humanoid thing sped to the side, launched itself into the air and vanished from my line of sight, but I heard the soft thud as it impacted against the wall. Seconds later the massive armored shoggoths fell against the failed door and gap in the wall. In seconds both holes had been sealed, first by flesh, and then quickly by a pale green stone that grew like crystal. Before we could realize what was happening, it was clear that we had been contained while work on the ship continued, without our annoying interruptions.

And yet there was something more. For in the place on the wall where I had heard the other shoggoth hit I could hear the thing drilling a new entryway, and this was much faster than the previous attacks had been. We kept a watch on the place on the wall from which the rapid boring sounds were coming. Hartwell had done what he could for Elwood, and was busy checking his tanks of reagent and the spray guns. More than a quarter of the material had been used already. As we talked and plotted, we were also aware that our time was limited, for we could hear the smaller creature boring away, working its way toward us, much more quickly than the other had. Furthermore, there was now a low vibration filling the air, one that I recognized as being generated by the magnetic engines of the ship. Time was running out.

Across the room Elwood was stirring; whatever Hartwell had done, the young man seemed to have gained some strength back.

Cautiously I stepped back toward them and helped the young man to his feet. "How did you get here so fast? It doesn't seem like you had enough time to gather what you needed."

"I warped time a little," confessed Elwood. "Which was probably a mistake. A hound caught my scent and did what came naturally." He gestured in Hartwell's direction. "He fought it off, saved both our lives." Hartwell said nothing in response to this praise, and Elwood let it drop.

As the three of us gathered what we could together and prepared to defend ourselves, the wall suddenly split. A great rent opened up with a tremendous, spine-tingling crack. A spider web spread out from a single point and then powder began to fall. The sandy material was quickly followed by pebbles, and then fist-sized rocks. A round section of wall about four feet in diameter bulged out and then collapsed down, cascading onto the floor like water.

Startled we took a defensive stance and aimed our weapons at the tunnel, prepared for whatever monstrosity that dared to come rushing through, or so we thought. For as we watched and waited there was no attack. No tentacle sprang forth to envelope us, no mass of eyes or weird sensors tried to pinpoint our location. No, what emerged from that hastily dug tunnel was a hand, a human hand, held in a position that suggested that it was surrendering, that we should hold our fire. The rest of the creature crawled forward, and where I had expected a horrific proto-simian thing, there emerged the lithe and naked form of a young woman. She crawled out and slid down the wall. We were both too stunned to react, for it was no stranger that stood before us, it was someone we knew, someone we had watched die moments before. There in front of us, monstrously reborn, stood the woman known as Asenath Waite!

It took us a moment to recover from this profound shock, and another moment to cobble together an outfit with which to cover her naked body. She thanked us, though to be honest I didn't think she cared much that she was nude, but dressing her made Hartwell and me feel better. Afterwards, as she finished lacing up Elwood's boots, Hartwell pressed for an explanation on how she survived the shoggoth.

"I didn't," she shot back. "The creature devoured me, dissolved my body and brain completely, and absorbed me completely. It assimilated my knowledge, but it also tried to assimilate my mind. And I think this was a conscious decision. I think it made a choice to try and assimilate my mind, my personality, so that it could imitate me. I think they have done this before, or tried to, maybe with members of the Miskatonic Expedition. They're trying desperately to be us. I caught a flash of memory from the creature, an idea really, that each mind they absorb becomes a facet of the whole, and when needed can become dominant, completely suppressing the other facets." She cast a quick look in my direction. "When the mass that devoured me decided to assimilate my personality, it assumed it would be just adding my mind to those that were already part of it, or more precisely the greater whole from which it had sprung. It hadn't expected for my mind, my personality, to be so strong. I overpowered its relatively primitive and rather subservient neural system, and became the dominant mentality. I'm in complete control of this body now, and since this was the only human form it knew how to generate, this is the form it has assumed."

Hartwell pointed at the hole. "How were you able to dig through the wall?"

Asenath nodded. "I'm not sure. When I was thinking about reaching the rest of you my hands became something like digging hammers that secreted a kind of acidic compound. As soon as I finished they reverted back. I may have the ability to control my shape, like a shoggoth, but that whole concept makes me nervous. I know you can't tell, but in my mind I am fighting a battle of my own. The shoggoth personality may be weak, but it is stubborn, and it's been here for a lot longer than I have. It knows things, tricks, which I don't. I sequestered it away, locked it up inside a mass of tissue like a cancer. I'm afraid that if I use the metamorphic ability that I'll lose control and the thing will return. Staying human keeps me in control."

Suddenly, the engines seemed to power up. The humming air changed pitch, and once more metallic objects began to be impacted by the electromagnetic forces in play. "We have little time, the ship is preparing to launch. It's drawing energy from the very air itself. If they reach the sea they'll have won."

"Where's Carter and Ys?" Hartwell shouted. "Where's the help they went to find? Are there any Progenitors left? Will they help us?"

224 - *Pete Rawlik*

Asenath was scrambling back up the wall trying to see what was happening out in the assembly hall. "I doubt it. Oh for certain there are still dreamers left amongst the Q'Hrell: Lilith, Bast, Voyrvatass, to name but a few, but these are not beings that we should expect to be favorable to our cause. There are others, more inimicable to man and earthly life, but can they find the avatars of such entities, and convince them to aid us?"

Asenath eyes grew wild and she began to bable. "There are cohorts that are even more ancient than this city, those who had come here, to this world when it was barren, and began the seeding of this place. They had retired from the world eons before man was given his curent shape, content to let their descendants rule in their sted. These are not the gods men know. These are not the Other Gods that walk the Earthly Dreamlands and play at the games of Mao and Zhen. These are Elder Gods whose avatars stalk the universe in search of sport. Even great Cthulhu trembles at their name. I warned Ys and Carter not to approach them unless it was absolutely necessary. Kept talking about gestalt interferences, and modeling probabilities. May the Progenitors have mercy on us all if he awakens them."

Hartwell had apparently had enough of Asenath's vague references. "Who is down there Waite? What titan does Ys attempt to release on our behalf? Tell us so that we at least know what to prepare for."

She turned and faced us, crouching in the hole she herself had dug just a few moments earlier. "The Grey Hunter!" she screamed. "Ys and Carter go to ask Nodens for help, as if he had any fondness for men."

CHAPTER 21

From the Dictation of Randolph Carter Who Is
Zkauba, Warlock of Yaddith
"Randolph Carter in Ulthar and What He Did
There"

Mister Olmstead has taken to writing a tedious account of our adventure in the realm of the Progenitors, and has spent considerable time and effort pestering me for an account of what had happened to myself and Mister Ys when we entered the Dreamlands. I had refused him. It is not practical for me in my current condition with these earthly writing instruments to take pen to paper, or even use a typewriter, but when he finally offered to let me dictate the story, and set it down word for word, I finally acquiesced. This then is a brief detail of pertinent events.

I will not bore the reader with the details of our descent and travels in the lands beyond sleep, but I will reveal our failures. Five times did I plead my case before the Other Gods, and five times were my ministrations rejected. The last time, the divinity in question, a blue-skinned youth with three faces on his head, took pause to mock me and the alias I had used, Swami Chandraputra, noting that it was little more than a phonetic anagram of my human name

I

WAS

M

RANDUPH CARTA

Afterwards we left the palace that stood above the peak of Kadath in the Cold Waste and journeyed to the marvelous city of Ulthar where we could drown our sorrows in the beauty of the city, and its curious inhabitants, the cats that roam its streets. Celephais may be more beautiful and more welcoming, but I had no desire for the company of men, or women. Instead the three of us, Mister Ys, myself and the mewling thing that had appeared when we crossed into the Dreamlands, sat in an alleyway drinking wine and commiserating with a multitude of cats and kittens. I was human once more, restored to my dream state by the magics of the reality I and Ys had descended into. Those magics had also separated Zkauba and me, transforming the once mighty wizard of Yaddith into a tiny, larval thing akin to something that combined features of a seal and a beetle. Surprisingly Ys had also been transformed, which was in itself unexpected, but he had assumed a form that was neither human or Q'Hrell, but rather a form that I knew to be that of a species indigenous to Mars.

That Ys had not reverted to something other than what I had expected intrigued me, and in my misery I finally broached the subject. He was reticent at first, but as we had little else to talk about, and it seemed the destruction of our world was imminent, he finally chose to speak of it. It was true that the original Yith had been a branch of the Q'Hrell, but one that had drifted further and further from their nearest neighbor, at last settling on a rogue planet on the outer edge of the galaxy, one that orbited counter to the rotation of the galaxy. As they built their colony, each passing year took them farther from their own kind, as did their exploration of the arcane and eldritch technologies. Until last, they were too far away both physically and philosophically. Their studies led them to discover the secret of moving through time, and when their own shoggoths revolted they fled through time and space. They had found another world with a species with a civilization which could be co-opted for their own purposes. They fled en masse, and in their new home built a society which integrated with that of their host. For a thousand years the two species dwelt together, but when the rebel shoggoths filtered down from the sky seeking revenge, the Yith fled. They did not go alone, they took with them the brightest and most talented of those with whom they had dwelt.

That pattern of moving from world to world and taking with them choice individuals had over the millennia transformed the Yith into a kind of hegemony, and while the original Q'Hrell still held all the positions of leadership, they had long ago passed into a minority status. The Yith were not a single species, but rather a community sharing a single philosophy, one that included species great and small. Ys may have thought of himself as part of the Yithian culture, but his subconscious still remembered that once, millions of years ago, he had been nothing more than one of the globular things that roamed their planet on a myriad of thick, plastic tentacles, and here in this place that memory was all that mattered.

The concept of the Yithian hegemony was not unknown to me, for it had been repeated throughout human history by the Persians, the Romans, the Chinese, the British, and probably many forgotten others. It seems the tendency to build a nation beyond one's own tribe was not simply a human trait, or perhaps it was one we had inherited from those who had made us. The Deep Ones, Man, the Yith, we were all in one way or another descendants of the Q'Hrell. Even the shoggoths were just distant cousins, which I suppose made the battle we were contemplating a family affair. That may have been why the Other Gods, who were little more than avatars of various cohorts of the Q'Hrell that still dreamed in the ancient city, were reluctant to act.

I looked around the gardened alleyway as a kitten rubbed against my leg demanding attention. As I picked her up and began to stroke her I casually commented on how when the shoggoths invaded the Earth, the Dreamlands would be lost as well, depopulated by the destruction of the human race.

Ys made a weird noise, which I realized was the equivalent of a Martian laugh. "You think that matters to them? You are still under the impression that this place, the Dreamlands as you call them, is yours, that it is something for Men. Have you ever considered that this place was here long before your species, and will be here long after? After all that you have been through, you still think anthropocentrically. The Dreamlands stretch beyond your world and encompass the other realms of the solar system including Yaksh, VarSuwm, L'gy'hx and even the haunted remnants of shattered

Thyoph. How arrogant of you to think that this is your playground. The laws of physics and magics that bind this place were written by the Q'Hrell and are that way for a reason. They serve those who wrote them, and those species whom the builders favor. Man is trapped to a single world, and will struggle to move beyond it. Doesn't that suggest to you that you and yours aren't a favored race?"

The setting sun cast long shadows down the streets of Ulthar. All around us we could hear the click-clack of shopkeepers closing up shop and their patrons scurrying home like rats before the last of the sun died. Not long after came the reversing clack-click of a different set of shopkeepers opening up for the night, and the shuffling steps of their clientele came on the cobblestone streets. The lamplighter came by, a song in his heart and a flame in his hand, and with him came the cats, the lords of the city. They called Ulthar the City of Cats, and it was said this was because within its walls no man may harm a cat. While this was a fine title for the city, the legend was mere folklore, conjured up out of the past to explain things that men could not understand. I thought I knew the truth, knew that the old texts had been mistranslated. That Ulthar was not the City of Cats, but the Cat City.

As furry things both large and small, fat and thin, black and white and all the shades and kinds between gathered around my feet, my eyes focused on the calico kitten that had fallen asleep in my lap. I scratched it behind the ears and it stretched and purred in response.

"Ys," I asked thoughtfully, "are there cats on Mars?"

Ys snorted. "All the planets have cats of a kind. The cats of Saturn are lean, multihued things composed of dust and light. Those of Uranus are thick, craggy beasts who are slow to act, but tenacious once they start. The Cats of Mars are tentacled things, with large eyes, six legs and rasping mouths." He paused. "Why do you ask Carter?"

I whispered into the ear of the kitten, and it purred and coiled deeper into his lap. "Would you say that cats are a favored species?"

Ys looked at me and at the multitude of cats that had gathered around my feet. "Are you a friend to cats?" There was a touch of panic in his voice. "Do they know you? Are you known to them?"

He crossed the space between us purposefully and crouched down in front of me.

I laid the small kitten to the side and watched as it curled up into a ball and purred. I reached out and touched a wall, stroked it gently. Ys watched and his eyes grew wide. I found a depression in the wall and I whispered into it, repeating the plea that I had made to the Gods on Kadath.

"Don't," said Ys, but his words fell on deaf ears. He turned and ran, dodging cats as his three legs pounded against the stones of the streets. He was screaming as he ran, but I ignored his pleas to stop. I kept talking, whispering to the city walls telling them my story. It was a long story, but it was the first story that the city had heard in a long time. As I spoke the walls of the city began to tremble; towers bent, and ancient buildings twisted. The residents of Ulthar, the human residents, were panicking, but I ignored their plight. I stroked a low wall and watched it bristle and then begin to hum. An ebony minaret, one that had stood for a thousand years, suddenly became soft and laid down on the street. There it writhed and hummed happily.

Ulthar the Cat City was purring as I pleaded my case.

CHAPTER 22

From the Account of Robert Martin Olmstead
"The Hand of Elwood"

As Asenath and I helped Hartwell down the wall, Elwood opened up a door inside one of the shoggoths that had imprisoned us. It crumpled in on itself, wounded but not terribly so, more in shock than anything else. It stirred as Elwood marched through and made a weak attempt to grasp its attacker, but as Hartwell gained his footing he turned and sprayed the creature with the some of his mixture. The poor thing thrashed and screeched as it foamed up and died under the influence of the chemical, leaving nothing but a burning, bubbling mass of sludge.

Our escape had gone unnoticed, and we took a moment and accessed the situation. There were still five shoggoths working on their squid-like craft, and extensive progress had been made. The interior seemed complete, and the last few hull plates were being fitted into place. It would only be a matter of moments before the thing would be complete. I suggested that we wait for Mister Ys and Carter to return, but both Hartwell and Asenath seemed eager to engage the enemy. We already knew that the engines were operational, a launch seemed imminent. Once the thing was airborne it would be impossible to stop. An immediate confrontation was needed to put an end to the work. In the end Elwood agreed that we needed to attack, and so we made preparations to do so.

We made our way to the shadowy part of the factory floor. The shoggoths took no notice of us, and indeed had never bothered to check on their companions who had been assigned to deal with us. This lack of follow-up could be attributed to either a complete sense of confidence in their fellow, or a kind of out-of-sight-out-of-mind mentality. We had been seen, and dealt with, and were no longer a threat until we were seen again. Either way, it was a flaw in their nature that we were going to take advantage of.

Unfortunately, fighting shoggoths isn't like fighting people. You can't sneak up on a shoggoth and hit a vital spot to prevent them from raising the alarm, and then move on to the next target. Killing a shoggoth, as I had learned, is messy business; now four of us were going to attempt to kill five of the creatures, and I wasn't entirely sure that it was possible. Hartwell, who had some experience in such matters, had laid out a plan to maximize our advantages, and the impact of our assault. The core portion of the plan of attack was for Elwood to draw the attention of the monsters and once more lead them to a particular place, in this case a corner, and then step outside to safety. The others would attack from behind, cornering them and preventing them from attacking us on multiple fronts. It was a good plan, at least I thought so.

Elwood took off at a run, moving across the factory floor as fast as he could, dodging through piles of materials and catching the attention of every shoggoth as he recited the Star Spangled Banner at the top of his lungs. Every few steps he would move outside, disappear for a second and then reappear just a few steps ahead. It was like watching a film which was jumping or missing scenes. I cracked a smile as he began adding a series of gymnastic moves to his course: jumping at a pile of material that he couldn't possibly clear, vanishing and then reappearing on the other side, and rolling into a kind of weird tumble. It may have looked like fun but it was deadly serious, and when he cart-wheeled into the in-between my eyes caught a flash of something else in the crack, something large, with flashing teeth. When he emerged he was cut, not badly, but something had hurt him. Suddenly he wasn't playing anymore, and as the shoggoths fell in line behind him he used his talent less and less, and for shorter distances as well. For their part the shoggoths were resorting to the standard practice of shooting tentacles at the poor man, which given their lack of communication and coordination, became something of a comedic exercise as their limbs collided with each other, and they rolled one over the other in a kind of horrific scrum. But as Elwood approached the designated corner, he vanished once more and as we tracked his trajectory we waited for him to appear, but he did not. We waited with bated breath searching the corner for him to appear, but instead the shoggoths flooded in and piled up like a derailed freight train.

Asenath raised her hand to give the order to attack, when the most horrific and pitiful of screams broke out. Elwood had appeared, and while he was in the corner, he was a good twenty feet up the wall, and covered with blue slime and blood. At first I thought he was hanging on to a break in the wall, but then I realized there was nothing for him to hang on to, and what was keeping him in place was the fact that he had rematerialized where he shouldn't have, and his hand was literally imbedded inside the wall. He shuddered and then went limp, and I assumed that he was in horrific agony, either from the pain of being partly encased in the wall, or from the wounds he had suffered as a result of what was most likely an attacking hound.

The image stunned all of us, including Hartwell, and our hesitation allowed the shoggoths to react before we did. Unbound by any normal physiology, the monstrous amoeboid things slowly began creeping up the wall toward our injured ally. The image of the slimy things creeping up the wall motivated Asenath and she ordered Hartwell and me to attack.

We rushed forward from where we were hiding, and while Hartwell and Asenath began spraying the gathered shoggoths with the blood of the Progenitors I used my preternatural strength to claw my way up the wall to where Elwood hung limp.

I pulled at the body of our injured colleague. Our attack had drawn the attention of most of the shoggoths, but one still seemed to be intent on attacking Elwood. It streamed up the wall in great globs of slime, avoiding our attack and mounting multiple fronts as it spread out across the wall. I did my best to vanquish these attacks, but it was a losing proposition, and faced with the possibility of either Elwood or myself falling to the enemy, I did the only thing that could be done. With a swift and precise strike from one of my great claws I sliced through Elwood's arm like a hot knife through soft butter. Elwood screamed once and then again went limp as I slung him over my shoulder and carried him to safety. I looked for blood, but there was none. The interior of the stump was devoid of flesh and bone, there was within only a kind of inky blackness that howled and smoked. Indeed from the wall where Elwood's hand was imbedded the short stump was giving off thin wisps of smoke-like ash.

Hartwell and Asenath were carefully using the spray guns, hitting individual targets with short controlled bursts of the stuff that sent their targets into convulsions. These shoggoths were smarter than the ones we had fought before. They created thin shields of material that could be sloughed off after it had been exposed to the doctor's formula. They also kept dividing into more and more autonomous units, drawing our attention in more directions. We had destroyed, or incapacitated about half the total mass of shoggoths, but where there had once been five large creatures, there were now twenty or so smaller ones, and they had taken on a wide variety of horrific forms. In succession I watched Asenath kill things that looked like giant scorpions, tentacled slugs, and even a kind of horned beetle. The fact that there were no reptilian, avian, or mammalian creatures in the shoggoth repertoire did not go unnoticed, but at the time I had no inclination to ponder the meaning of such an observation.

Hartwell and Asenath were holding their own, but their progress was slim, and with each passing moment I knew we were at risk of one of the monsters breaking through and overpowering us. Depositing Elwood in a relatively safe spot, I joined the fray, my claws cutting through the shoggoth-things and leaving a trail of parts struggling to reconnect themselves from their disrupted tissues. Gore flew about us we waded into them, and Hartwell and Asenath fell in behind me to clean up and dispatch the more mobile pieces. Working together it took only moments for us to reduce the shoggoths to little more than jellied muck quivering in the corner of the factory floor.

Elwood was still unconscious, the wounds he had suffered from the marauding hound were bloody, but only superficial. Hartwell assured us that he would recover, albeit with the loss of his left hand. As for what had happened internally, Hartwell could not say. It was as if he was no longer made of matter, but rather filled with some weird kind of dark energy. We did our best to make him comfortable and then sat down to rest and plan our next move. Based on what we could see, we had just eliminated only about half of the shoggoths that had been present in the factory room. The others, we reasoned, must not be far, and while we had fared well with this batch, the others were more intelligent, and therefore more dangerous. Ys and Carter were still out there, but their ability to find assistance was unknown. We had to make this room defensible, and more importantly, we had to destroy the squid-like craft that had nearly been completed.

Something large screeched and charged us; Asenath stepped into its path and with her hands performed a strange serious of motions that carved a weird semi-luminescent shape in the air. The creature slammed into it like it was made of bricks and bounced back through the room before crashing to the ground amongst the piles of raw materials. This caught the attention of the other things in the room, including the blue-skinned supervisor. It turned to look in our direction and let loose another of those strange atonal howls. In response three of the shoggoth machines stopped what they were doing and then systematically transformed into similar blue-skinned creatures.

The other two creatures, including the one Asenath had tossed across the room, began marching toward us. As they grew closer they seemed to almost fall apart. With each step, small bits fell off and hit the floor, scattering like an army of rats or ants, which these small creatures bore some semblance to. In a just a few steps the giant monsters were gone, and we were faced with a wave of small creatures that were slowly but surely encircling us. Asenath moved her hands once more and enveloped us in a sphere of strange purple light. It seemed to have some impact on the creatures and while they continued to surround us, they came no closer than Asenath's barrier.

"Well we are going nowhere fast," Hartwell spat.

Asenath opened her mouth to speak but whatever she would have said was drowned out by the roar of the ship powering up. The far wall was suddenly crumbling, falling apart and revealing the grey streaked sky and the weirdly black peaks of the city that stretched unnaturally into it. The four blue-skinned shoggoths had climbed into the ship, and vanished as the hatch closed down on top of them. Hartwell made a desperate move, but the shoggoth rats countered whatever direction he shifted, and none of us could see a way around them.

Hartwell checked his tank and nodded. "I have enough to take them out, or at least slow them down."

"We're out of time!" yelled Asenath. "Do it!"

Asenath dropped the shield, Hartwell sprayed and I bounded over the shoggoth horde as they popped and squirmed in agony. As I ran I grabbed a length of rod and with all my strength threw it at the ship. It was a futile effort. My makeshift spear arced through the air and impacted against the skin of the ship, and then rolled to the floor. The squid-like vessel slid forward and gathered speed. It reached the broken exterior wall and launched into the waiting beyond. It dropped a bit as it lost the support of the floor, but it caught the wind, as if it was somehow aerodynamic, and then soared away.

I rushed to the edge and the others weren't far behind me. I looked at Carter, but he shook his head. "They're too far, and I don't have enough power."

Asenath fell to her knees and stared at the ship as it flew further and further away. "Then we've failed, and the world is doomed."

"I think you may be right Kamog, but not the way you think." It was Mister Ys that had suddenly mocked Asenath, I hadn't seen him come into the room. "I think that Carter has found your ally, and they will gladly deal with our shoggoth problem. Unfortunately, I think, how would Hartwell phrase it? 'The cure might be worse than the disease.'"

CHAPTER 23

The air within the room was suddenly electric. A wind was howling, it had come up from nowhere, and had built into a maelstrom in a matter of moments. The storm had picked up the lighter bits of debris and created with it a miasma of danger that culmintaed into a sudden explosion of light and heat. The howling became a whining drone that seemed to focus on a single point that became a shimmering glow. The air wavered and then melted away, leaving a hole in reality through which something, many things, were coming through.

It was Carter, I swear to you for a moment I saw Randolph Carter step through that gate. He was tall and lean, aged but not old, and he was holding something black and shiny that squirmed in his hands. It was Randolph Carter as he had been, a dreamer, a mystic, but a man, like any other. Then he was gone, and in his place stood Zkauba, but not the sad, divided thing that we had come to know over the last few days. There was still the air of something alien and something human, but now that seemed to be something to revel in rather than to suffer.

He strode out of the abyss like a great Indian god. The armor, Zkauba's armor, covered him from head to toe, and it was truly magnificent. It had the look of a kind of ceramic, bone white and glistening. There were jewels along all the surfaces, including the head which sported seven crystalline adornments. He stood on two legs and in four great arms he carried a variety of weapons, including two swords, and something that looked like a cattle prod. As he stepped through the last remaining shoggoths swarmed toward him. With a flick of his wrist those swords roared to life, their teeth spun and a weird energy sparked from them and sent arcs of blue light traveling down their lengths. Whatever that strange electricity was, the shoggoth flesh reacted poorly to it. The severed parts thrashed about uncontrollably and then seemed to bloat before collapsing in on themselves and dissolving into inanimate sludge.

His path took him toward Asenath, and for a moment I saw those blades raise up and take a position to strike the lithe figure that was our leader, but then they paused, and that great helmet tilted in an odd manner. "Zkauba is going through a whole litany of ethical considerations in our head," Carter informed us, "but he doesn't seem too concerned about the issue, because after all, the shoggoth did try to eat you. That you ate it instead may be ironic, but not amoral." He paused and then added, "Ate may be the wrong word in this context."

The gate swelled up once more and a wave of fur cascaded out of it. Cats. Cats of all species and sizes and colors poured through that weird doorway. Dozens of them, and they flowed like a tide around the feet of the armored Warlock of Yaddith like an army of subservient followers. The forward members spit and hissed at the few pieces of shoggoth that still remained, and this, as odd as it seems, was enough to vanquish what was left of the quivering foe. Then the army of felines scattered, they wandered across the room, some to look out the window, and some to the door where they meandered out of our sight. Others found Elwood and seemed intrigued by what had become of the boy and in particular his missing arm.

I moved to greet our companions, but my movement was halted by a sudden wall of cats that made it plain that I was not to approach any further. It was then that I realized that the army of cats might be more of a threat to us than a form of salvation. I shuddered at the stereotype oft used in commercial advertisements of cats prefering to feast on fish, and stepped back away from the furry soldiers. Asenath stepped back as well, and soon the two of us were holding hands searching for comfort from each other as the furry sentinels took control of the room.

Something else came through the gate; there were three of them, strange colored things that were not green, or blue, red or yellow, but rather all of these colors and none of them, for it seemed that the creatures were constantly changing hue, their very skin was unstable. When they moved, it was clear that they were cats, but they were a completely alien species, and of unearthly construction, as if a cubist painting of tigers had been brought to life. They stalked out of the gate and then leapt across the floor and took off through the gaping hole in the wall.

The hole in the wall shimmered and then was suddenly replaced with the image of the ship soaring through the antarctic sky. The craft cleared the mountain range and had already begun to cross the plains, heading north toward the sea. It cut through the sky like a bullet heading toward the heart of the world. It seemed beyond the reach of anything natural or human. It seemed unstoppable, but I suppose that all things seem unstoppable until the inevitable occurs.

The three cats of unusual color appeared behind the ship, moving faster than I would have thought possible for something alive. That they were gaining on the ship seemed obvious, and the thing that was their target began swinging about in the sky trying to dodge the attacks of the trio. It reminded me of the tales that the aviators of the Great War had told of the Red Baron Manfred von Richthofen and how he would fly like a falcon through the sky at his enemies. The shoggoth ship may have been larger and more powerful, but the flying cats were faster and more agile, and they outnumbered their prey three to one.

One of the creatures latched on to the ship and found a way to hold on, ripping chunks of the ship off with its crystalline teeth. Another hit the rear of the craft and cut into it, boring a thick hole into the engine and sending the ship sputtering out of control. It spun through the air, leaving a black trail of smoke behind it. As it fell the force of gravity accelerated its decent, and I could see a wave of heat form in front of the bow. While I couldn't see the occupants I knew they were trying to regain control, for the tip jerked up as it approached the ground. The ship was nearly skating across the ice which appeared to be liquifying as it passed over. The ship hit a pile of ice and bounced awkwardly, sending it rolling across the surface sending up great sprays of ice and snow that rained back down in great gouts. As it came to rest the remaining heat turned the ice soft and the ship was swallowed up into the grey slush. Even with the semi-solid water we could see the hatch of the ship fly off and the shoggoths abandon the ship. They swam through the freezing water, desperate to reach the surface, but the ice had already reformed, and with no way to gain traction they had no leverage to crack open the icy shield that had formed above them. In seconds the creatures ceased to move and became little more than frozen blemishes within the glacier.

As the ice solidified the image ceased and we were left staring at each other, confused and relieved. Mister Ys seemed pleased with himself. "The threat is eliminated, buried under feet of ice, as if it had been there for millions of years. And it will stay there until the axis of the world shifts and the entire continent thaws. Hopefully by then, man will be more prepared to deal with what we've just locked away."

Just then the gateway burst back to life and hummed evilly as five great masses moved from the Dreamlands into the real world. They came into the room moving like predators, their cylindrical bodies horizontal to the ground, rotating clockwise with each step. Each of their five eyes were spread wide, and their wings pulsed like the crests of great lizards. As they cleared the gate they changed their orientation and rose up on their powerful lower tentacles. They strutted forward gracefully, like alien dancers. Mister Ys moved to greet them, and assumed a submissive stance. He said to us, "This is the cohort known as Ulthar, the Lord of all Felines, the Cat City. You should be on your knees."

Asenath eased slowly to the floor, and I and Hartwell followed suit. Carter did the opposite: he rose up on his lower limbs and spread his four arms wide with each hand brandishing a weapon. He said something unintelligible, in a language that I did not recognize, which I assumed was a language known to them. The Progenitors hissed and whistled something back at the warlock. Carter called back, and was met with what sounded like a terse response.

Whatever was said seemed to calm Carter for he sheathed his weapons and assumed a less threatening stance.

Their movements were inhuman. They seemed to be constantly aware of each other, but whether this was because of some mental connection between them, or simply because the field of vision provided to them by their five eyes was almost entirely uninterrupted, I could not say. I suspect it may have been a little of both. One of them left the rest and moved ethereally toward us. There was a whispering whistle as it moved, a kind of reel that reminded me of my childhood. The emissary reached out a branching tentacle and touched Asenath Waite's face. The whistling changed pitch and became something of a mournful dirge. The creature moved on and examined Doctor Hartwell, the song changed again. It had become shallow, superficial, like a piece of music being played badly. The creature lingered momentarily, and then moved on to examine me.

The first thing I noticed was the smell. The creature, the emissary, the Progenitor, the Q'Hrell reeked of the sea, of fish, of oysters, of the shallows exposed at low tide. Its tentacles, which divided down into fine manipulators, had a distinct salty odor, rich and strong. Its touch was at times soft and rough. Those fine strands of alien flesh traced the line of my cheek and jaw. It was as if I was being judged, not like a lover caresses, but as a farmer assesses a new calf or foal. It wasn't just my body that was being judged, it was my parentage, my lineage, my entire line of breeding. The tune changed, it became melodic, almost cheerful, even hopeful. It made me feel a kind of elation I suppose, as if I had done something right and was being praised by one of my parents.

The creature retreated back to his fellows. There was a conversation, a discussion of some sort. None of us understood it, except for Mister Ys, though I suspect his comprehension was not as complete as he would like to have us believe. There was then an exchange between the emissary and Ys. Ys seemed disappointed, I think he protested, but to no avail.

He marched over to me and stared at me with a look of intrigue. "Congratulations Mister Olmstead. You've managed to find some favor amongst the Ulthareon. They've decided to let you, all of you, live, and leave." He turned and looked at Asenath. "I am to stay here, at least for a while. The timelines are in flux. They need to stabilize before I can depart."

Asenath looked at him incredulously. "What are you talking about?"

Ys spun around, "I didn't come here by accident Kamog, you know that, but it had little to do with you and your mission. I was drawn here, to Antarctica, to this city, to this body, to Gedney. He's a crucible, a focal point, always has been, and will continue to be so for quite some time. You think of him as dead, but even that may not be true. He is unstable, in space and in time and because of that his past and fate are not fixed. Even his name changes from timeline to timeline. Sometimes he's Thomas, others Felix, in another Leonard Clayton, but always Gedney, and always something more."

"What's that?" queried Hartwell.

Mister Ys raised his hands up in a gesture of frustration. "I don't know," he confessed, and a smile crossed his face. It was the first positive emotion I had ever seen him express. "It's exhilarating isn't it? Not knowing what's going to happen next, it makes me feel so alive."

CHAPTER 24

From the Account of Robert Martin Olmstead
"A Return to Kingsport Head"

It took hours to construct a machine to open a passage that would take us from the Antarctic to Kingsport Head. Ys and Carter did most of the work, under the supervsion of one of the Ulthareon. The other four left us to travel to other parts of the city, to inspect and repair the damage that had slowly built up over the years. Hartwell offered to show them the room full of their dead brothers, but when he stepped forward the cats took up a defensive posture and Hartwell retreated, choosing instead to tend to the still-unconscious Elwood.

I on the other hand tried to talk to Asenath, but something was wrong. Everytime she let her mind drift her form became soft and she lost cohesion. As long as she thought of nothing but herself, she stayed as she was, but any deviation from that and her limbs grew soft and her flesh waxy. It took a supreme effort to maintain her form, and if she were to do that she had no room in her mind for other thoughts, including me.

Instead I found myself watching Carter and Ys as they assembled the gate machine. It was intricate work, more art and magic than science. The parts had been scattered around the factory floor, and I found it ironic that the shoggoths did not know what they had, and had spent their time instead building the rocket. I must have commented on this out loud, for Carter supplied an explanation of sorts. Such a technology was forbidden to the shoggoths, they were literally blind to it. Their minds could not understand it, their sensors could not see it, or the parts that made it. If they were to inadvertantly enter a gate their very structure would collapse, driven to destruction by their mind's failure to understand what was happening. At least that was how most shoggoths had been programmed. At this he seemed to scowl at Mister Ys.

Ys shrugged and seemed to take the comment personally. "The proscription against such a thing was forgotten by the Yith, it was a mistake, one we continue to regret and suffer from. We are and have been apologetic." Ys had reverted back to his unemotional self.

"Apologetic, you create an entirely new species of shoggoth able to move through space on its own, one that hates the Yith and the Q'Hrell, and is willing to cross space to gain vengeance. Your flying polyps are patient and they've pursued you and yours across the galaxy. You've led them a merry chase, but they are getting closer every century, and in the meanwhile they lay waste to whatever Q'Hrell world they stumble upon. I suspect they are here on Earth already, waiting for you. Like I said, they are patient, I think they know about your plan to leap into Earth's far future and they are going to be prepared for your arrival."

"We are prepared for interference. We have prepared options, alternatives, divergences, preferred lines of sequences. There are levels of existence that we would prefer to avoid, but we would have no regrets moving into them."

"No," when Carter said it that word sounded like a curse, "I suppose you wouldn't."

"Have you noticed Mr. Olmstead?" Hartwell was whispering in my ear.

"Noticed what?"

"Chandraputra-Carter-Zkauba, whatever you call him, when he speaks he no longer makes that weird clicking noise. Isn't that curious?"

He was right. "What do you think it means?"

"I don't know, but it would be interesting to find out don't you think?"

I shook my head and stared at Hartwell with my lidless eyes. "I think that there are some things even we weren't meant to know." I left the good doctor staring at the two bickering aliens and found a quiet place to lay my head and get some sleep, or something that resembled it.

It was apparent when the time finally came, for the air within the gate machine suddenly became soft and hazy. A crack in reality formed and it spread, widening into a gap large enough for even Carter to fit through. Within that space I could see a sloping landscape covered with trees overlooking the sea. Beyond that were the lights of Kingsport. We were being sent home, and I was glad of it, but at the same time I had the feeling that we were being dismissed, like children who had brought an unpleasant situation to the attention of a parent, and were now being sent to their room. This feeling grew as the five Q'Hrell who made up the Ulthareon seemed to strut and preen as their strange whistling voices seemed to urge us on in a way that wasn't at all supportive.

Carter went first, the fabric of the universe swallowed him up, like he had slipped into a pool of water. It moved him. That strange gated tunnel, it moved him through space and took him from where he was with us, across the world to more familiar and hospitable surroundings. He waved at us from over there, and beckoned us to join him. It was Hartwell who went next and the doctor stumbled as he ran through, sprinting from Antarctica to Kingsport. Carter caught him as he came through, and steadied the doctor on the slope beyond. Asenath chuckled at the sight of the slender doctor being manhandled by the giant alien.

It was Asenath's turn to go next, and she did so with some hesitation, turning to look at me for some modicum of support and reassurance. I however had gone toward the other end of the room to fetch the body of our still-unconscious collegue Frank Elwood. I caught her eye and saw a look of sheer terror suddenly came across her face. It was a look that told me that something was wrong. I scanned the room and saw what had sent Asenath into a panic. Across the ceiling, creeping, thin and black, were dozens of shoggoths and by the look of them they were not there at the behest of their masters.

Asenath began to move toward me, but instead I screamed her name and ran toward her. As I did the shoggoths began to fall from above, and the cats, taken by surprise, were suddenly in a pitched battle for their own survival. I grabbed Ys by the shoulder and ordered him to get Elwood. Then I flung myself toward Asenath and launched the two of us through the gate.

Asenath wrapped me in her arms. Her breath was ragged and I could smell blood as she told me to hold on. We stepped kata, or at least she did. We moved, but it was not left or right or forward or back. It was a direction I did not know, which I could not see, but which seemed to be perfectly natural, as if it had always been there, just out of sight. As if a blind spot in my mind had prevented me from seeing it my entire life.

The space within the gate was a shock, and I lack the words to describe the space itself, but I could see the things that were in it, the things that intruded, and the things that were outside. I could see the buildings, but their structure was porous, and flimsy like a mist, Asenath was a tetrahedron of some sort, shining violet, with spikes of green. There were other things here, more organic in appearance, strange fusions of titanic echinoderms and arthropods that scattered as we moved amongst them. Yet of all the strangeness that I saw in that place, perhaps the strangest was that of the shoggoths themselves. I could see them, and in some ways they were not unlike the porous walls and floors of the building itself. Yet where the building had some substance in the in-between space, the shoggoths had none. Indeed they seemed to be entirely non-dimensional, unable to intrude into where we had gone, and therefore appeared as little more than troublesome pinpricks. Where they had been massive and terrifying in normal space, here they were little more than gnats, waiting to be snuffed out with a single casual act. I reached out, ready to dispatch one of them, when Asenath began screaming. The transition through the gate was tearing her apart, we had forgotten she was little more than a shoggoth, and Carter had warned us that shoggoths were incapable of passing through gates, their minds wouldn't allow it. I spun her around, twisted both of us, and pushed back into the world.

I turned and looked through the gate. There was a pitched battle being fought between shoggoths and cats, and through it all Ys was bringing a semi-conscious Elwood to the gate. As he approached, the Ulthareon suddenly became excited. The emissary came forward, the thing seemed to be eager, and was waving its tentacles around in a tizzy. Its wings were shifting colors, cycling through deep ochres and vibrant yellows. The alien lord nearly threw Ys out of the way as it enveloped Elwood in its thick appendages. It examined him, ran its feelers over his head and neck, and then the colors changed. Then it grew in intensity, becoming a wild, almost rabid frenzy. I cried out and made a move to intervene, but Asenath stopped me. Ys was screaming something, something I couldn't understand, the gate didn't allow for the transfer of sound, but it was clear something horific was happening.

The other four Q'Hrell moved forward. In my head I could imagine that the chorus was discordant, but at the same time strangely unified. I watched as the cohort of aliens surrounded a frightened and confused Elwood. Ys had backed away, and was now almost to the door, but the battling cats and shoggoths barred his passage. All five things were touching Elwood, stroking him, their wings flexing and screaming with colors. On the far side of the gate, I could not hear the song but somehow I knew that it had grown even louder. The five aliens had enveloped Elwood in a network of tentacles. A lattice enveloped his head and neck, it seemed to merge with his skin, to create a bridge between the man and the monsters that had for some reason become fascinated with him. But fascinated was the wrong word. The Q'Hrell were obsessed with him, and that obsession was unhealthy. There was still no sound but Elwood's body was wracked with pain, his head was thrown back, his mouth was open, and I knew he was screaming.

The gate was closing, and as it did the ability to see what was happening on the other end began to fade. Asenath and the others didn't see what I saw. Maybe they didn't want to, or maybe it was just a matter of perspective, or perhaps my extended senses. Whatever the reason, it was only I that saw the tentacles tighten around Elwood's neck. It was only I that saw it, but I wish I hadn't. Even Hartwell turned away, as if he knew what was going to happen. When they did it, they did it quickly. They took his head off, it tore cleanly, like a cork coming out of a wine bottle. The gate collapsed completely, but not soon enough. Not soon enough to prevent me from seeing those five monsters tear apart Elwood's still-screaming head. Tear it apart and then take the pieces and devour them, hungrily.

CHAPTER 25

From the Account of Robert Martin Olmstead
"The End of Things"

There were five of us who had gone up the Kingsport Head, and only four of us who came down. Our adventure, our mission, had cost us dearly. We had lost Elwood, and his death had a profound impact on us all, Hartwell most of all. Carter was also mourning the loss of his ship. The rest of us thought of it simply as a machine, but Carter had spent millennia traveling with it, he had somehow grown attached, and even spoke of it as if it were alive, possessed of some sort of personality. I laughed at the idea, but Asenath assured me that such a thing was entirely possible, that machines could have not only personalities, but even souls.

Carter, whose knowledge of Kingsport had procured us a place to recuperate in safety and peace, was mourning his loss, but was taking some solace in the fact that he had rescued both his armor and his queer book from the wreckage. He spent his days rebuilding the mask and outfit of his Chandraputra disguise. He was still an ancient alien, perhaps the last of his kind, trapped on Earth, surrounded by humans for whom he felt kinship, but knew that they could not be trusted. He needed to be able to move about the world once more, and the persona of Swami Chandraputra supplied that.

When Asenath talked about a machine having a soul she made it clear that she considered herself a prime example. After all, the shoggoth mass that she was in possession of was simply a kind of biological machine. Asenath called it a proto-shoggoth, and was concerned that without the proper routine of maintenance, and a strong personality to exert control, the mass of flesh would begin to degenerate and collapse, eventually dissolving into a mass of decomposing tissue. Hartwell and she worked on training her how to sustain herself, but she would need a way to regenerate her tissues regularly. Not surprisingly, Asenath said she knew of a place not too far away.

As for my relationship with Asenath, it became strained. She became distant, uncommunicative and quick to anger. She didn't seem particularly upset with me, but rather more frustrated than anything else. One afternoon it all came to a head and Asenath revealed what was troubling her so much. She had told me once that when it came to the magics of the universe there was a masculine and feminine side to things, and that when she had been Ephraim she had wielded a considerable amount of power. As Asenath she had wielded a different kind of power, not lesser, but simply different. Now, even though she maintained the same outward appearance, the universe seemed to know. She was not human, at least not in the strictest sense, and therefore neither male nor female. It seemed that passing through gates wasn't the only thing that shoggoths couldn't do. The whole situation made her feel desperate, inhuman, less than real. For the first time in centuries she could not feel the power that she had wielded and that frightened her. Until she resolved that issue she had no right, no need, no desire to have any kind of relationship with me.

As the days turned to weeks, and our wounds healed, Asenath's hold over us grew weaker, and a great sense of restlessness came over us. I took to writing this account of our adventure, and pressed both Hartwell and Carter to supply me chapters. Asenath refused to have any part of it, but I remembered her tale and told it for her. It was Carter who finally suggested the end of things. The Weird Company had done what it set out to do, what it had been charged with. It was time to end its commission. Asenath protested, suggesting that given our disparate abilities, that more might be accomplished, that we could become a kind of adventuring company. The idea had its attractions, but the loss of Elwood could not be denied, and in the end we all decided, though somewhat reluctantly, to dissolve our partnership.

We had wanted to leave earlier than we did, but a storm had moved through the area and delayed our departure. The radio was filled with reports on the return of the Miskatonic Expedition. There were the specimens, geological, paleontological, and a few biological collections from the polar ocean. Accounts of adventure and daring exploits filled the newspapers. Despite the richness of the scientific treasure, and the publicity, the loss of so many men was casting a pale over the accomplishments of both the expedition and the university. There would be an inquiry, as well as repercussions.

It was on the morning of April 5th that we found ourselves on the docks of Kingsport just after dawn. It was Easter morning, though that meant little to any of us. We stood there in the post-storm wind trying to find something to say. Asenath still clung to the idea that we might work together, but Carter and Hartwell would not speak of it. I opened my mouth to say something, but instead a low rumble came across the water and took our eyes eastward. There was a plume of smoke on the horizon, something was burning, a ship maybe. Asenath pressed the matter, but Hartwell had already wandered away, and the Swami Chandraputra was bidding us adieu.

I offered to stay, to go with her and investigate the smoke, but she shook her head and dismissed me. "I know what you want Robert, but I can't, I simply can't. I'm sorry." I reached out for her but she pushed me away and stalked off. I called her name as she walked down the street that led to the trolley that would take her to Arkham. I was still calling when she turned the corner and walked out of my sight.

Alone, I returned to our quarters and over the course of the last few days finished this account of our adventures. When I am done I shall seal it in an envelope and mail it postage due to the Federal agents in Boston that I had spoken to so many months ago. It is a rash act, and it imperils many of us. But I think the world has a right to know what has happened. It has a right to know how close it came to being destroyed, and that save for the acts of a handful of monsters, the world would be a very different place.

EPILOGUE

From the Notebook of Phillip Sherman
"The Last Communion of Allyn Hill"

Wednesday, April 1, 1931

It is a fine feeling to put pen to paper once more. I found a blank field book in one of the station's supply cabinets, so I can finally get back to routinely making entries. It has been weeks since we passed through the Panama Canal and I filled up the back cover of the last journal. I am grateful, a new journal helps bring closure to what has gone before, and I would rather forget what I can of those days.

It took fifty-eight days for The Miskatonic and her sister ship The Arkham to bring us back from the frozen wastes of Antarctica. We had set sail from Boston, but it was always our intent to return directly to Arkham. Circumstances being what they were, Pabodie felt it "prudent" to divert the bulk of our specimens to a more remote location rather than bringing them directly into Arkham. So we, the crew of The Miskatonic and I, came here ten miles off the coast of Kingsport, to Miskatonic University's Orne Marine Research Station situated amongst the islands known as the Shallows. There are few people here, thirty or so villagers who live on the big island of Allyn, and who not coincidentally supply crew for The Miskatonic, and a lone graduate student named Shane Atkins. Atkins is a wiry little biologist with blue eyes, a wild mane of blonde hair and a quick wit. He's been here at the station for a year studying the behavior of seals and several species of shorebirds, and is nominally in charge of the lighthouse. He tells me that visitors to the Shallows are rare. Perhaps here, on this tiny cluster of scrub islands, I can work on the samples in peace, away from prying eyes. The failure of the expedition will surely be the subject of much speculation, not only amongst the faculty but also the ravenous and insipid individuals that pass for newsmen.

We docked in rough seas early this morning, and it took most of the day for us to unload The Miskatonic's holds. Atkins and several of the men from the village helped us maintain a break-neck speed. Weather reports from the south spoke of a storm that had formed in our wake and the captain was eager to be on his way to a more sheltering harbor. It was near dark when the ship finally sailed, leaving the windswept docks strewn with the crates, trunks and equipment of the expedition. I stood on the jetty with Christian Larsen, a crewman, who has been my friend and assistant since we first began our expedition, and together we watched as the majestic vessel receded into the sunset.

Over the next several hours we moved the cargo into the station's warehouse. Larsen is actually from Allyn so he left to spend time with friends and family. Atkins is a decent cook, but not much of a conversationalist. After a small meal of shellfish and winter vegetables I spent an hour exploring the station buildings and the small island of Orne on which it sets. There is little here to write about.

Thursday April 2, 1931
1015

Up early, and Atkins and I have spent the morning going through the smaller crates, and dealing with their contents. We're finding small errors and discrepancies, but nothing major. We found a box with a packing slip listing nine of Lake's star-shaped stones, but actually containing only eight, all bearing handwritten, sequentially numbered inventory tags. The number sequence was complete, so I think this was just a documentation error. Lake had described them as being comprised of soapstone, but they aren't common steatite, a kind of talc, but rather pyrophillite, a mineral that forms radiating fan-like clusters of metallic crystals. They were all about six inches across and a half an inch thick, and although you could see the patterns of cleaving, the whole thing was curiously smooth.

Packed in with the samples were some of Lake's notes, which being written by a biologist I understood only a little. Thankfully, Atkins was able to decipher Lake's cramped handwriting and explain some of the thoughts contained within those hastily scribbled paragraphs. Much of the content referred to the pervasive foolishness that influenced poor Pr. Lake to name the frozen specimens "Elder Things" and helped drive my fellow expedition member, Danforth, to the brink of madness. This in itself has its roots in the teachings of a member of the Miskatonic University faculty, a man named Wilmarth. I knew that several members of our expedition had met with Wilmarth prior to our departure, and one or two had taken some course work with him, but I was not privy to the nature of those conversations, nor of the teachings expounded on in his classes.

According to Atkins, who has taken several of Wilmarth's courses, the core of the man's scholarly work is cobbled together from several volumes in the university's restricted section. Atkins was a bit vague on the details, but Wilmarth's teachings, drawing from occult sources and myth patterns from around the world, suggest that for millions of years the primal Earth was visited and ruled by a succession of creatures that had seeped down from the stars. Amongst the more successful of these alien species were, according to the Al Azif, the "Elder Things," also known in the Pnakotic Manuscripts as the Q'Hrell or "Progenitors" which dominated the Earth and waged war against a variety of enemies for millennia.

Lake does not explain why he drew the link between the specimens and the Elder Things, I assume there must be some physical resemblance, but cannot confirm this. Once I return to the university I'll look into the matter. Lake's notes make the link a fait accompli, and further suggest that the star stones that had been discovered with the bodies were the pentateuchos, or fivefold tools mentioned by Theodoras Philetas. Such things were supposed to be used as wards by the Elder Things to drive back or imprison their enemies. It seems so ridiculously melodramatic, and I keep having this vision of one of the alien things wielding one of the stones menacingly, holding off an unearthly and undead ghoul.

1145

The weather has turned, and the wind is becoming quite fierce. Atkins is going to show me how to operate the lighthouse, including pumping fuel from the main tank to the holding tank at the top. Apparently if done incorrectly the fuel can mix with the air and be ignited by static electricity, much like the dust found in corn silos or coal mines. Something I need to learn how to avoid.

1300

Larsen has returned with an invitation to the evening festivities. At first I thought it was simply a celebration in honor of Larsen's return but as the conversation continued I realized that my sojourn to Antarctica had caused me to lose all track of time. Sunday will be Easter, which makes tomorrow Good Friday, and today Holy Thursday, marking the events of the Last Supper. Tonight, the residents of the Shallows will hold a mass, followed by a community feast to which both Atkins and I are invited as honored guests. It is good to be back amongst people again.

2330

Have just returned from Allyn, and must say I had quite an enjoyable time.

The entirety of the main island of Allyn is little more than a hundred acres, all sparsely covered with low shrubs and a few thin trees through which a small herd of goats roams freely. The village itself is wholly unremarkable, consisting of homes built in the salt box style, along narrow avenues of crushed oyster shells. The village, properly Allyn Hill, is built on a low rise around a single large building, which had once been an inn back when the entire island served as a resort and spa. The Great Hall, as the locals call it, now serves as a communal center, and this evening it had been laid out for a great feast with long rough wooden tables and benches well supplied with fruits, vegetables and breads. Several casks of wine and water, an important provision on the island, were also available and I was relieved that the community was not one that prohibited the consumption of alcohol. Off to the side a fire roared within a massive granite hearth, taking the chill out of the air, and warming a variety of stews and chowders. A few birds were slowly roasting on a spit, as were a pair of rabbits, an obvious delicacy for these people who seemed to draw most of their sustenance from the sea. The smells that wafted from these dishes mingled with those coming from the kitchen proper and I am not ashamed to write that my mouth watered at the thought of fresh food prepared by skilled cooks.

Not unexpectedly, the evening began with a religious service, initiated by the ringing of dozens of small handheld bells scattered throughout the congregation. The bell ringing ushered in an ornately dressed priest and a procession of altar boys. It wasn't until the clergyman had reached the center of the room that I recognized that it was Larsen. All that time together and he never told me he was a man of the cloth. Atkins noted my surprise and whispered to me something about Larsen being a church deacon, the actual priest had fallen ill.

From my makeshift pew I listened politely as Larsen embarked on a traditional sermon full of holy fire and celebrating the life and sacrifice of the Son of God. Surprisingly, the sermon was in English with a smattering of Latin, though for the life of me I cannot remember the subject or any of the actual content. I do remember how the altar boys brought forth the wafers and the wine, and how the townsfolk, Atkins included, lined up. I, however, remained seated, routed in my own status as an agnostic and in my disdain for such ceremonial pomp. One by one they went and knelt before the priest. One by one Larsen offered up a thin wafer, which they accepted as he blessed them saying time after time, "I am the resurrection and the life, through me the dead shall live again. This is my body, which is for you. Do this in remembrance of me."

I will not dwell on the details of the last few hours. The feast lasted well into the night, and when the bell tolled eleven I urged Atkins to return with me back to the station. He declined, choosing instead to remain and revel in the night's festivities. As I stepped outside and made my way across the breakwater a wicked wind rose up off the sea, soaking me with a blast of cold wet air. By the time I made it to the station proper the storm that Captain Thorfinnssen had so feared had finally arrived. I am exhausted and slightly inebriated, and after writing this I shall collapse into the warm embrace of my bed and deep peaceful slumber.

Friday April 3, 1931
0830

The storm has grown in intensity, the wind now continuously roars through the rafters and driving rain lashes the windows. Atkins' bed has not been slept in and I assume that he is still over at the village and now trapped by the storm. I have climbed the tower and watched the storm from a height. I am fascinated by the way the wind moves across the island scrub like ocean waves. The frequent lightning competes with the lighthouse for dominance, and both cast weird shadows across the island and the village.

I have spent the last few minutes watching the village and I am growing increasingly concerned that something is terribly wrong. Even in the dim light of the storm-wracked sky I can clearly see into the heart of the village, and there are no lights visible on the street or in any of the windows. The only sign of life in Allyn Hill is the small herd of goats wandering the streets, seeking shelter in the shadow of buildings. Unfortunately, I can also see that the breakwater is being violently lashed by wave after brutal wave, making it all but impassable. I shall attempt to make contact using the wireless.

0915

I have been unable to contact anyone in Allyn Hill or on the mainland; the only sound from the wireless is a steady drone of meaningless static. I am a qualified operator, and following my training I have checked all of the components in both the transmitter and the receiver. I found nothing that was in disrepair. The only explanation I have is that the storm has somehow interfered with transmission and reception. I am extremely frustrated, and it seems the only option available to me is to brave the storm and breakwater. There is a suitable set of foul weather gear in the storeroom.

1030

The villagers of Allyn Hill seem to be suffering some sort of reaction either to a toxin or an infection. They are strewn about the room in chairs or on the floor, unconscious and unresponsive. They are feverish, with clammy grey skin from which an odor, a sweetness, exudes. Thankfully the fire in the great central hearth was still burning, providing a modicum of warmth. It bothers me that amidst the ashes and embers there are what appear to be fresh logs, but I have no time for such things. I need to get warm and attended to the afflicted.

1200

It took me more than an hour to arrange the bodies in an orderly manner on the floor around the hearth. I am sorry to say that two have died, not from their strange affliction, but rather from associated circumstances. One man seems to have fallen backwards out of his chair and broken his neck against the stone floor. The other was a woman who apparently went face first into a large bowl of chowder and asphyxiated. That no one had attempted any sort of aid to either of these poor souls suggests that whatever happened occurred quickly. There were more than twenty men, women and children laid out about the room, including my colleague Atkins. However, oddly absent is my friend Larsen.

I am in the kitchen drinking coffee and eating some bread leftover from the night before. I have tried the wireless set that is down the hall. My efforts were wasted; whatever has affected the station's set is also interfering with this one. I need to rest, am exhausted both physically and mentally. The wall calendar reminds me that today is Good Friday, and I can't help but chuckle morbidly over the irony.

1545

I was awoken by a chorus of screaming and I started from the chair in a panic and dashed out of the kitchen. My charges were awake and from the sound of their moans and anguished cries they were in agonizing pain. I found Atkins who had curled up into a tight little misshapen ball and tried to comfort him. His breathing was shallow and fast, between gasps he told me that he was cold, and that he couldn't feel his arms or legs. To the touch his forehead was hot, and he was sweating profusely. I took his right arm and tried to exercise it and then dropped it in revulsion. The flesh had a strange color and consistency and as I moved it back and forth, it did not bend at the joint. As a child I had watched my grandmother make sausage by filling long greasy tubes of intestines which would then flop and twist on the table like massive grey worms. Atkins' arm was like that, it curled like a long thick sausage. As I looked I could see that the appendages of all those around me had suffered the same shocking metamorphosis.

As I pulled away something more caught my eye, and my curiosity overwhelmed my revulsion. The back of Atkins' shirt was soaked not just with sweat, but also with streaks of crimson. Carefully I rolled the fabric up and by the light of the fire examined the source of the fluid. Three great wounds had opened up on his back, one vertical along the spine, and the other two parallel to the first but almost to either side. A watery and bloody discharge seeped slowly from these lesions and for the life of me I thought perhaps that someone had assaulted my friend. I know from my courses in folklore and comparative religions that some extreme sects re-enacted the more horrid events of Christ's life, going so far as to flog and then crucify a volunteer. Looking at the wounds on Atkins' back it seemed a plausible explanation, but as I scanned about the room I noted that many others were showing the same crimson stains. I quickly realized that this was not the result of a physical attack, but yet another symptom of whatever the villagers had been exposed to.

As I sit here, I am completely incapable of rendering any further sort of aid. I can hear the low distant sound of other victims who were not in the hall but rather are scattered about the village. Like their fellows they too are screaming and moaning in agony. At a loss for what to do I once more shall don my foul weather gear and brave the storm. It is better I think, that all those who are suffering be brought together in one place.

1630

I followed the screams, breaking down doors where I had to and gathered up what stricken villagers I could find. It was not an easy task. Two I found could walk or limp, and together we hobbled down the shell-strewn streets. Another, a large woman, suffered more severely from that strange softness of the limb bones, and I had to load her into a wheelbarrow. I found one woman in the street outside of her home, her legs and arms like rubber, but she had found a way to move about by crudely lashing out her limbs and then pulling herself forward. I gagged as I watched her do this, for her appearance reminded me of octopi that the crew of The Miskatonic had brought up in a net one afternoon off the coast of Cuba. The ship's cook would cut off most of the creatures' limbs for use in the kitchen, and then toss what was left of the wounded animals on to the deck where they would flail about in a desperate attempt to return to the sea.

Dusk, and the agony of the villagers seems to have subsided somewhat, or at least they have become accustomed to whatever pains wrack their bodies. The storm shows no sign of letting up and I am fearful of crossing the breakwater in the dark, I am resigned to staying in Allyn Hill for the night. Though I will admit I am uncomfortable with the thought of staying in the Great Hall.

1745

Have been watching from the second floor of the Great Hall. It took me a moment but I realized that something was amiss. Yesterday when Atkins and I had refilled the fuel tank, he informed me that the fuel would last for at least four days. Yet here it is little more than a day later, and the sweep of light has ceased. Something or someone has interfered with the operation of the lighthouse, and I have a suspicion that the condition of the villagers, the failure of the radios and now the failure of the lighthouse are all connected somehow. I even suspect that the source of all these problems may be anthropogenic, though I am still unclear on the why and how of it all. Against all better judgment, I am going to try and get back to the station and restart the light.

2000

Larsen is deliberately sabotaging the equipment. As I came into the station, he burst through the door, knocking me down and then dashed down the path to the breakwater. It took me a moment to regain my footing and in that brief span of time Larsen was moving across to the other island. I gave chase, but stopped at the breakwater. As I hesitated, Larsen whipped out a large fish knife and sliced the guide ropes before lopping up the stair toward Allyn Hill. I called after him, but he either didn't hear me or, given his unusual behavior, is purposefully ignoring me.

I've got the lighthouse working again, but the wireless is a total loss. I think initially he just cut the antenna lead on the side of the tower, which explains why I can't reach anyone at any distance; now the damage is much worse, while I was gone he took a hammer to the set. Chances are that he has done something similar to the set in Allyn Hill. I've found a shotgun and a box of ammunition, mostly birdshot but a few of the shells are loaded with buckshot. It's not much but I would rather have this than go hand to hand against Larsen. I've pulled all the storm shutters down and I've barred all the doors. I've tied empty cans to all the doorhandles and climbed the tower halfway to a landing. There's a window with a view of the breakwater and Allyn Hill beyond, and enough space for me to stretch out and sleep. There are three heavy doors between me and the rest of the world. I won't try the breakwater unless the storm lessens.

Saturday April 4, 1931
0700

The storm has passed and the sun rising in the east is a welcome sight. I've slept a little and found something to fill the emptiness in my belly. I'm cold though, the storm must have dropped the temperature by at least ten degrees. The gun is little comfort. I need to find Larsen. I also need to get back to the Great Hall. As soon as the waves relent I'll try to make it back over to Allyn Hill.

1230

Atkins' condition has worsened. The strange transformation of the limbs has spread to the rest of his body. My medical training is limited, but from what I can tell all of the bones have suffered some sort of transformation, a decrease in rigidity that seems to have been transferred to the skin, which has become grey and rigid, at least on the chest and abdomen. Their backs however have become soft and pulpy, and the three vertical wounds no longer are oozing red fluid. Instead strange fibrous green tendrils have appeared. I've never seen anything like them before. I poked at one of the tendrils with a knife, and it recoiled back inside.

After I rest I am going to search the island for Larsen.

1700

No luck in finding Larsen, but I have found the priest; he's dead, strangled. I think Larsen killed him so that he could take his place in the ceremony the other night. I'm still not sure why, and I really have nothing to support such an idea, but it is the only thing that makes sense.

In the same house where I found the priest I found a star stone sitting on a work bench. It has a collection tag that identifies it as the one missing from the crate. It's been damaged. One of the arms is split open along one of the edges, the exposed interior is incredibly complex, with dozens upon dozens of tiny black crystals. These crystals are no bigger than a pinhead, all curiously pentagonal trapezohedrons. There are very few minerals that produce such a shape, which should make it readily identifiable, but right now I have neither the time nor the inclination to do so.

There are things nagging at me, things that I think I should be thinking about, but I am so tired. I am not thinking clearly. It's still very cold out, and I think that is contributing to my exhaustion. I need to sleep.

1900

The villagers of Allyn Hill are all dead. I can write no more.

2145

I've made it back to the station. Another storm, or perhaps the same one coming back, is rolling over the island and the wind is picking up. It's bitterly cold out. I would have thought that all that time at the pole would have made me more resistant. I've barricaded the doors again, still no sign of Larsen.

As I have written, the villagers are all dead. I don't know why or how but somehow in the few hours I was exploring the island they all succumbed to whatever malady they were suffering from. Curiously, either through their own action or that of Larsen, they were all clustered together into small groups. They had been arranged in sets of five, with their backs to each other and their legs splayed out on the floor. Some of them seem to be clutching their neighbors with what used to be their arms.

As if that weren't odd enough, the clusters themselves seem to be oddly grouped. All the young children are sitting together, as are all the adolescents. Even the adults seem to have been sorted by size, height I mean. If this was some last dying attempt at community, I would have thought they would have clustered into family groups.

Tomorrow, if I can I'll take one of the small boats to the mainland.

Sunday April 5, 1931
0230

I'm back at the top of the lighthouse trying to make sense of what I am seeing and hearing. About twenty minutes ago I woke to a chorus of strange high-pitched keening noises. At first I thought it was the birds or seals, but it was coming from the village, so I came up here to get a look. I can't see much, but I can see shadows moving about within the Great Hall, which means that somebody is alive and has turned on the lights.

The noise is definitely coming from Allyn Hill. It's an eerie throaty sound, like air moving through an organ. It repeats every few minutes, but in different pitches, like its being repeated by different sources, but always the same tones and pattern.

Tek Tek Tek Tek E Li Li.

I'm going over to investigate.

0430

I made it across the breakwater and carefully crept up to the kitchen door of the hall. All the way I could hear that eerie inhuman sound, but as I crossed into the hall I could hear other things as well. I could hear the goats bleating incessantly and beyond that there was a man talking loudly, speaking as if to a large crowd. Just as I reached the doorway from the kitchen to the main hall I realized that it was the same voice that I had heard just a few nights ago offering Communion to the faithful. Larsen was preaching and even now I can remember his words.

I am the life and the resurrection
Those who believe in me even if they die, shall live forever
For I am the child of God and wield his power
I give you life, first on this Earth as mortals, and after the resurrection, life eternal
I come amongst you know, to remind you that this is the image of God
And that all men shall be as I, made in His image

As I watched him through the door, Larsen was standing on a table, a bound goat held in one hand, a knife in another. With ease he drew the blade across the animal's throat and allowed the blood to pump out in a torrent onto the floor. Then, effortlessly he tossed the now still beast down to the floor.

God I wish I had not seen the greedy crowd that waited below.

The villagers which I had thought dead had undergone yet more of a transformation. The clusters of five had grown into each other, traces of their left arms were still visible but like a parasitic tree on its host, melted into the neighboring flesh. The right arms, all boneless now, had become thin and whip-like, the fingers and thumb elongated into a tentacular mass that constantly seemed to flex and grasp. Likewise, the adjoining lower limbs had wrapped around each other, no longer ten legs but five thick, grey tentacles that flailed about dragging the creatures clumsily along. The toes were gone, and in their place each were developing a fat triangular paddle. Like the fingers, the paddle curled and flexed in a seemingly useless exercise. But most horrid of all were the heads, or what once were heads. Though the features still remained, the once semi-spherical craniums of men were gone, crushed and remolded into a pyramidal structure, the mouth shoved down toward the base and pinched into a tube, while the eyes had been forced up to the apex. Ten eyes seemed unnecessary to whatever it was becoming, for without variation one of each pair of eyes was dangling limp from strands of necrotizing flesh, while the other was frantically whipping about on the end of a short fat stalk. It was as if some alien Prometheus had grown jealous of man's bilateral morphology and had seized the flesh and molded it into a new pentaradial shape. A shape I was not wholly unfamiliar with. For the things that crawled about in that great hall resembled to a striking degree the ancient and enigmatic specimens that Lake had excavated out of the ice in Antarctica and had dare to call "Elder Things"!

I shuddered at the sight of the seven things that were once the proud residents of Allyn Hill. Shuddered even more at the way the monstrous things grasped and tore and sucked at the flesh and bones of the goats that Larsen tossed to them. Then my eye caught the thing that flailed in the corner. There were by my count thirty-nine victims in the Great Hall, thirty-five of them had melted into seven sinister protean things, but the other four were incomplete, and this imperfect monstrosity lay in the corner whimpering. It was less complete than the others, and therefore less inhuman, and on one of its faces I could still see the bright blue eyes that rested beneath a shaggy golden mane.

Cautiously I slipped out of the kitchen and made my way along the back wall toward the pitiful thing. The others and Larsen were so distracted by their feeding that they failed to notice as I knelt down beside the mewling, simpering, defective changeling. I stared into those bright blue eyes, and for an instant I thought that there might still be some humanity left within the deformed mass of writhing flesh. Those eyes stared back, and there was a spark, an instant of recognition and hope and I reached out to touch what I knew was all that was left of Shane Atkins. In a flash all traces of humanity were gone and a great grey tentacle whipped around my hand and dragged me forward. I pulled back, but to no avail. The eldritch mass of tumourous flesh pulled me closer and another tentacle flailed about, trying to find purchase and strengthen its hold on me. In unison the four bulbous mouths whistled out that howling unearthly refrain Tek Tek Tek Tek E Li Li!

Without hesitation I swung the gun up, pressed it against the face of the thing that was once a man, and pulled the trigger. The ensuing recoil pushed me backed toward the kitchen door, which all things considered, was fortunate, for my action had attracted the attention of both Larsen and his flock. I quickly crawled backwards, closing the door and bracing it just as something large, heavy and wet slammed against it. The door cracked and I could see the latch straining under the pressure being applied on the other side. I threw the lock hoping it would buy me a few seconds and then slid a kitchen knife into the space between the floor and the door, wedging the door closed. I backed away from and surveyed the kitchen for options. Somehow, even in my panic, I knew that these monsters needed to be destroyed. I dashed about the kitchen and one by one snuffed out the flames of the lights but left the gas work valves wide open. I even stopped and turned on all the valves for the stove. Stepping outside I frantically grabbed a box of matches and an oil lantern. I smashed the glass of the lantern against the door handle and lit the wick. I set the broken lantern inside the door, shut it and ran as fast as I could.

I was at the bottom of the stairs that led to the breakwater when the explosion lit up the night. The pooled water around the shore rippled as the shock wave blew past, and I stared as flaming pieces of debris careened in arcs across the sky. I sat there for a while and the glow from the top of the hill slowly grew stronger. It took me quite some time to cross the breakwater and get back to the station. The pain in my back is getting worse and my legs ache horribly.

I've climbed to the top of the tower again. The whole village of Allyn Hill is burning; in a few hours, I doubt there will be much left at all.

0530

I think I understand now why Danforth was driven mad, and I suppose why McTighe tried to kill himself on the way back. The things Lake found, the Elder Things, that rose up and slaughtered our colleagues, I cannot deny that anymore. They laid dormant in the ice for millions of years. If they could do that imagine what else they could do. Imagine their resilience.

The explosion in the great hall and the ensuing fire wasn't enough, three of the things survived. They're down below now, clamoring about desperately trying to find a way into the lighthouse tower.

I can't move much, my legs aren't working well, but I've been able to douse the light, disconnect the fuel line and turn on the pump. The ground level is covered with kerosene, and fumes are slowly filling the tower. I'm going to place this field book in a tin and throw it out into the ocean. Then I'm going to light the wick. It's crude but when the fumes reach the top of the tower I think the resulting explosion will be enough to kill them and me.

Pr. Pabodie, Dad, if the stones survive what I'm about to do here, you need to make sure to destroy them. Use a kiln if you have to. I also want you to know that despite our differences, I couldn't have asked for a better step-father. I appreciate everything you've done for me over the years. I also need you to know that what happened here wasn't your fault; I wanted to go to Antarctica. It was Larsen who caused all of this. He figured out what the stones were and stole one of them. It was madness what he did. I suppose he was like Danforth and McTighe. I think maybe all of us who survived the expedition might be just a little mad.

The stones, they're not stones at all. They aren't a magical ward, or even a weapon, not at least in the manner that we think of. But we should fear them; they could destroy us all. I keep thinking back to when we excavated those star-shaped snow mounds back at Lake's camp and how the dogs went wild with fear. I think they instinctually knew something we've forgotten. The star stones, they're theca, protective cases filled with parasitic spores. I don't know when it happened; it may have been in the communion wafers but something else as well, the bread maybe. Everybody at the feast that night was infected. It makes some sort of inhuman sense. They transform the very flesh of their infected host into something else, something akin to those ancient things that so long ago ruled the entirety of the planet.

0630

The sun has risen, Easter morning.
Glory, Glory, Hallelujah!
Father, remember me as the man I was.
They've nearly broken through the last door.
I don't have much time. The pain is unendurable.
I wish my arms were still

Acknowledgements

The vast majority of *The Weird Company* was written long before Reanimators, and grew out of research I had been doing for a History of Miskatonic Valley. That I stumbled upon the fact that Waite, Chandraputra and Olmstead were likely all in or about Arkham at the same time seemed an opportunity too good to waste, and thus was born my League of Lovecraftian Gentlemen, or The Miskatonic Aide Society, or the Arkham Odd Fellow's Club. In the end I settled on The Weird Company to honor that most venerable of institutions we all aspire to, the magazine Weird Tales. To those who came before me and graced its pages with their tales, and inspired me in their fashion, I dedicate this work.

I also need to acknowledge those people who believe in my work and continue to encourage me by making my stories available to the world, including Robert Price, Brian Sammons, Glynn Owen Barrass, Scott David Aniolowski, and Mike Davis. There is a renaissance of a kind going on in Lovecraftian fiction and these gentlemen are at the forefront of giving it new life and direction.

As always my work would not be possible without the support of my wife Mandy, who does more than her share to keep me sane.

Literary Acknowledgements

"The Last Communion of Allyn Hill" previously appeared in *Horror for the Holidays*, Miskatonic River Press, 2011.

"Journal of Thomas Gedney" previously appeared in *Worlds of Cthulhu*, Fedogan & Bremer, 2012.

"The Statement of Frank Elwood" previously appeared in *Worlds of Cthulhu*, Fedogan & Bremer, 2012, and in *Urban Cthulhu*, Nightmare Cities, H. Harksen Productions, 2012.

"The Thing in the Depths" previously appeared in *Lovecraft eZine* #16 July, 2012.

"Beneath the Mountains of Madness" previously appeared in *The Mountains of Madness*, edited by Robert Price, Dark Quest Press, 2013.